GW00455932

THE SARATOV DOSSIER

Martin O'Brien

"A week is a long time in politics,"

Harold Wilson

1

Oslo, Norway
Sunday November 13 - 20:17 Central European Time (CET)

Yusuf's eyes lifted away from his knife towards the television. Yells emanated from two teenage lads who were watching the football action on the box and ignoring their food. Fenerbahçe were still trailing Beşiktaş by a goal and time was running out for them to equalise.

He returned to dicing up meat when another cry went up, this time from the gaunt old man sitting at the table next to the youths. Yusuf's knife slipped and it sliced into his hand between his thumb and index finger causing blood to spill out over the thumb. Regular cuts were one of the downsides to the job. He could never get used to seeing his own blood, no matter how insignificant the cut.

Yusuf placed his tingling hand under the cold tap, using his good hand to turn it on to an acceptably icy level and surveyed his café. Most of the clientele were watching the Istanbul derby on the television, except for two middle-aged men who were sitting in front of the window next to the entrance. They were talking quietly yet with an unmistakable air of intensity.

He dried his hand and placed a blue plaster over the wound before he left the kitchen to collect some empty plates and mugs. The teenage boys were sitting with their backs to the wall next to the entrance to the kitchen area. They were still nursing their Cokes and hurling a steady stream of abuse at the Beşiktaş players on the television.

Yusuf took away the plate of half-eaten kebab remnants from the haggard old chap who didn't take his eyes off the football playing on the flat-screen television which was awkwardly situated in the corner of the café, diagonally opposite the kitchen and till. Yusuf proceeded in the direction of two regulars wearing overalls who were also watching the football but they indicated they hadn't finished with their food.

He glided between tables and edged around a young, short-haired woman who was drinking a coffee and absorbed by her mobile phone. Before Yusuf could start inwardly bemoaning the youth of today obsessing over technology, a man entered the café. The opening of the door triggered a blast of ice-cold air throughout the café. The old man sitting alone muttered something derogatory about the newcomer's mother in Turkish but the recent arrival ignored him.

The man was young but had a remarkably bushy beard. Yusuf had grown something similar when he was his age. The man casually tossed his backpack onto the floor and he almost crumpled into his seat with a look of shock on his face.

"Coffee, please," the man said, with an accent that clearly wasn't local. That also probably explained the concern etched in his face. You need to be prepared for the conditions in Oslo as winter approaches. The shock to the system of such extreme cold can be brutal.

Yusuf only lasted eighteen months the first time he moved to Norway nearly twenty years ago. By the time of his second winter in Oslo, Yusuf believed that you had to be insane to live in Norway and he headed back to Turkey.

However, after a year back home in Istanbul, he found himself missing the long summer nights and even the winters. The vast change in seasons gave a rhythm to life that he hadn't experienced back home where eight months of sticky warmth would be followed by four months of unpleasantly cold and wet conditions.

Yusuf decided to move back to Norway and he began

working at a distant cousin's takeaway for nearly ten years before he saved up the money that enabled him to open up his own café. The café was the one thing in life that he was proud of. He was content working twelve hour days when he knew that it was his own place and the fruits of his labour were his to keep.

He walked to the door to check it was fully closed and he saw snow beginning to fall. The sky was lighting up despite the time and he knew a big snowstorm was on the way. It was always terrifying but also thrilling and irresistable.

"Of course, let me know if you need any food," Yusuf said, returning to his position behind the counter. The man shook his head and started watching the game. It's funny how a television draws your eyes to it, no matter how disinterested you might be in what is being shown on screen.

Yusuf stirred a big mug of coffee to warm up the new customer and he certainly had the look of a man who would greatly benefit from it. Yusuf noticed that the two men in the window were still chatting rapidly at each other. He couldn't work out what language they were speaking, but it wasn't Norwegian or Turkish.

The one sat to the left was a tank of a man, with a rich tan body with tattoos creeping out of his smart navy shirt across his hands and neck. He had the appearance of someone who could quite easily punch you senseless with one hand while talking to his mortgage lender on the phone about a new rate with his other hand. The other man was balding, with an angular, serious face. He was dressed in a suit but it was grubby and too small on him as though he had dug it up and stolen it from a corpse after passing by a cemetery earlier in the afternoon.

The young guy had wandered up to the counter and handed Yusuf the thirty kroner without being asked and took the drink. He sat down and immediately started drinking it. Yusuf watched him with admiration, the bloke must have an asbestos mouth.

Yusuf turned around and began washing the plates in the sink. With the weather turning bad, he contemplated closing the café after the football finished and taking an early night. More howls rang out and he popped his head over the counter and asked the youngsters what had happened.

"Penalty for the Beşiktaş *hıyar*," said one annoyed boy. Yusuf didn't have the heart to tell them he used to be a Beşiktaş season ticket holder. Yusuf stared at the screen as a Fenerbahçe player attempted to exact vengeance upon the referee by grabbing him by the scruff of his jersey. The referee sent off the player from the field of play who refused to comply and was now being dragged away by his team-mates and pushed off the pitch.

The skinny old man was so pissed off, he appeared ready to lob his glass at the telly. Yusuf knew he would have to keep an eye on that sketchy old duffer. Last year, during the Fenerbahçe-Galatasaray match, he had tipped his table over, filled with food and drink, when Galatasaray scored a late winner. Yusuf had banned him for a month and had to warn him before every big match to not act like a dickhead.

Before the penalty was taken, the young woman stood and departed, flicking a wave at Yusuf as she opened the door and braced herself for the cold. At least she had put on a big comfy hat and coat. That was proper winter-wear. Once you learn how to layer up, you can manage living in a cold country and almost feel pride at being able to survive the Nordic winter.

The bearded man had finished his coffee. He stood but waited to watch the penalty being taken on the television. The Beşiktaş player skied the ball over the bar and cheers rose around the café. For a moment, Yusuf was transported back to life in Istanbul on one of the big football derby days and he couldn't stop himself from smiling. The two men in the window had not even glanced at the television despite the sporting drama.

The man with the beard put his coat on, which was

definitely not warm enough for this weather. He nodded thanks to Yusuf and departed the café. Yusuf noticed the guy had forgotten his bag. He shouted towards the bloke but he didn't turn around. He was walking to the tram stop outside his café as a tram was pulling in.

Yusuf edged towards the doors separating the kitchen from the café when, for a surreal brief moment, all of the air and noise was sucked out of the café. Before Yusuf could work out what was going on, everything turned unfathomably loud as a ripping noise filled every sense and Yusuf's world turned black.

2

Oslo, Norway
Sunday November 13 - 20:54 CET

The leaden Oslo night sky was a vast canvas, painted by the first major snowfall of the winter. It was a fearsome sight, the sky looking like one giant grey snow flurry. Einar Simonsen stood frozen in awe, staring out of the large office window. The roofs of the suburban houses stretching into the distance were gradually whitening and the whole city would be swamped with fresh snow by morning.

Simonsen was alone in the office and the lights were turned off so he could enjoy the full majesty of the snowstorm. Voices could be heard in the office next door where an armed robbery investigation was building to a conclusion with an impending raid on a disused warehouse in Visperud.

He had forgotten what it was like to be on the front line of an investigation and actually going out and catching some criminals. As an Interpol advisor to the National Criminal Investigation Service in Norway - or Kripos as it is popularly known - most of his days involved liaising between different offices and attending meetings. Over the last two decades, he had been at interminable forums and conferences about organised crime that never seemed to result in many arrests but kept enough people in employment that there was no real inclination for anyone to rock the boat and push for more enforcement action.

Simonsen bent and stretched his left leg as he was taught to by his physio but with the weather on the verge of turning extremely cold, his knee was hurting. It was only going to worsen over the coming months and he was troubled by the thought. He was dreading another long winter of constant knee pain sitting in neverending meetings about Albanian people traffickers or Hells Angels dealing guns and drugs across Scandinavia.

He moved away from the window, glanced at the clock on his desk and saw that his shift had ended five minutes ago. He picked his mug up to finish his coffee when he noticed it was already empty. He placed it down and instead picked up his car keys and mobile phone off his desk. They were his only personal items on the desk, any visitor would assume it was a hot desk for anyone to sit at.

He had worked at this desk for five years now and he assumed he would remain for a further two years before retirement. The behind-the-scenes jostling to replace him had already begun. Simonsen had to admit that he derived a certain joy in winding up his colleagues by crafting elaborate lies about their competitors, making them even more determined to ruin each other's chances. This was a dream job for ageing coppers, a cushy, risk-free number before retirement.

Simonsen left the Kripos office and shuffled over to his car, enjoying the fresh snowflakes brushing against his face and greying beard. Once inside the car, the tiny moment of exhilaration had passed and he turned the engine on and allowed the heater to start warming up the car. He tuned to the news on the radio and drove out of the car park with the headlines being announced.

More fighting in Iraq as the country teetered on the brink of yet another civil war after the failure of recent peace talks. Tension was rising on the streets of Russia as the run-off presidential election race entered its final week and there had been a violent carjacking in broad daylight in the centre of Oslo, the third in a fortnight.

The news returned to the Russian presidential election.

One of the candidates, a man called Maxim Golitsyn, had apparently received proof that his rival was going to reinvade Ukraine in the event of winning the election. Einar turned off the radio and thought both candidates would probably launch another invasion of Ukraine if it enriched them somehow. If living in Russia had taught Simonsen anything, it was not to trust a single word uttered by anyone with a smidgen of power in that country.

Simonsen steered his car onto the Ring 3 toll road and powered his electric Audi up to 70km/h. He enjoyed maintaining the exact speed limit for as long as possible as a test of his driving and his eyes constantly flicked from the road to the speedometer trying to balance the pointer exactly on the 70 line without it dancing away to 69 or 71.

The new Vålerenga stadium snapped into view on his left hand side and Simonsen pledged to watch at least one match there next season. If he couldn't make the fifteen minute walk from work to the stadium, there's no saving him but he had to concede that it had been quite a few years since he had been to a live game.

He sped past the rapidly transforming Grünerløkka, brimming with new-build offices and warehouses before the Lego block towers of Sandaker and Åsen preceded his entrance into the Tåsen tunnel. Simonsen made his customary leftward glance at the wonderful view of Oslo bay, glistening in the snowy light, before entering the tunnel.

Driving through the tunnel always made Simonsen feel like he was a secret agent on a mission at night in some big American city, the blurred lights and speeding cars never seemed Norwegian to him but he enjoyed the sensation even if it only lasted a fleeting minute.

The car blazed out of the tunnel and Simonsen spotted the speedometer was touching 72km/h so he eased his foot off the accelerator as he passed the Ullevaal national football stadium. The University Hospital was on his right and he saw the sign directing him to pull off into the suburbs towards his home. Simonsen slowed the car down as he navigated his way through the low-rise buildings of Slemdal until the uniform urban landscape began to be replaced with tree-lined, low-rise suburbs.

Within five minutes, he had reached his home in the hills of Holmenkollen and the snow was dropping out of the sky like a million smashed pillow cases. He swept the car into his driveway and exited as quickly as he could and scrambled into his house.

Simonsen took off his coat and placed it on the back of one of the high kitchen chairs. He grabbed a bottle of beer from the fridge and sat in the luxurious office chair in his study. At 13,000 kroner, it was easily the most expensive item in the house. Using his good leg, he propelled himself off his desk to face the window so he could watch the snowstorm. Ever since he was a boy, Simonsen was obsessed with watching the snow fall.

The mesmerising weather was lulling Simonsen into a trance which was sundered when the landline telephone on his desk rang. He spun around in his chair and banged his bad knee straight into the table leg.

"God almighty!" Simonsen yelled and rubbed his knee which had been hurting already and he picked up the receiver.

"Yes?" Simonsen said. He had no time for politeness for late night callers at the best of times but particularly not when he had cracked his knee into the bloody furniture.

"Einar? It's Peter," the voice replied and Simonsen suddenly switched to professional mode. Peter Kelsey-Moore was the Head of Criminal Investigation at the Norwegian branch of Interpol, and the father of a current British cabinet minister.

"Yes sir,"

"There's been a rather messy incident," Kelsey said in his clipped English tones, a man born a century too late for his general demeanour of brusque condescension to anyone who doesn't speak English, "There's been a bombing at a café in Bislett this evening. I require you to attend and provide support to Kripos,"

"A terrorist attack?" Simonsen's stomach lurched at the prospect of having to deal with this.

"It's too early to confirm, but my sources indicate it is looking that way,"

"Why do they need our assistance?"

"Personally, I don't think they do but the Director called me requesting I deploy someone to help them with the investigation. The first victim had a Russian identity card which said his name is, bear with me a moment, please. The name of the victim is Pavel Zhyrgal,"

Pavel Zhyrgal. Once more, Simonsen's belly flipped over. He presumed Zhyrgal was already dead. A name that had cropped up many times when he worked in Russia. He didn't realise he was in Oslo, or what's left of him anyway.

"Is it definitely him?" Simonsen said.

"I retain a healthy scepticism when it comes to Russian gangsters but Kripos have requested a Russian expert," Kelsey-Moore said, "And I'm only aware of you from our office that can speak the language, so you'll have to do,"

Damning with faint praise, as always, Simonsen thought.

"Benny Karlsson is expecting you, he can provide you with the location. He said you two have eaten there before you went to watch some athletics meet,"

"What about Becker? Isn't he on shift this evening?"

"Einar, I need a Russian speaker. Becker is busy working on another case. Please correct me if I'm wrong, but I don't think you have retired from the service as of yet?

"No, sir,"

"Right-o, so it has to be you, is that clear?"

"Of course, sir. I'll head over now," Simonsen replied and he carefully placed the telephone back onto its base. He stood and winced as pain travelled down his leg. The severe drop in temperature this week was playing havoc with his leg and he wanted only to sit at home, keep warm and watch the snow fall. Simonsen drank his beer in one long gulp before putting his still-warm coat back on and heading out of the house, into his car and back into the whitening Oslo night.

3

Moscow, Russia
Sunday November 13 - 23:39 Moscow Standard Time (MST)

Dimitri Bolkonsky banged both his huge, calloused hands on the desk and everyone in the room flinched. It didn't take much to rile him up at the best of times but he was in as foul a mood as his staff had seen before. He stood behind his desk with his fists bunched on the top like a prizefighting dog. Once more, he smashed one of his hairy hands down on the desk and nearly put a hole through it.

Bolkonsky turned and marched towards one of the windows facing the Moskva river where a radio was perched on the ledge, broadcasting today's news. He was watched by Colonel General Ivan Zakatov, the head of the GRU, responsible for Russian military intelligence and a couple of GRU bodyguards.

"Did you hear what that arsehole said? Who the fuck does he think he is?" Bolkonsky closed his eyes and took a deep calming breath. After he exhaled, he lifted up the radio and hurled it at the opposite wall where it smashed into pieces, little black chunks of plastic remained embedded in the wall like sunflower seeds on a bread bun.

"Minister," Zakatov said, moving towards the wall and kicking the pieces of smashed radio into a small pile, "He's saying nothing of note. Golitsyn is on the backfoot, he's lashing out,"

Bolkonsky stared at Zakatov who continued:

"It's a huge day for the campaign tomorrow. There will

be a huge media presence so the onus is on you to change the narrative,"

"What, I tell the media 'I don't intend to invade Ukraine on my first day in office?'" Bolkonsky replied, not even bothering to mask his scorning tone. Zakatov winced and shook his head.

"Don't even mention it, Dimitri," Zakatov said, holding his fingers to his forehead, "The three planks, stick to the three planks - nationalising industries, fighting corruption and the job guarantee scheme for the youth. If you mention Ukraine in your speech tomorrow, I am moving to China and becoming a fisherman,"

Bolkonsky chuckled and sat down at his desk. He picked up a sheet of paper and immediately placed it back down.

"The media repeat everything he says without criticism. The moment I open my mouth, the rats start nibbling away at every word,"

"We know the media supports Golitsyn and we know the reasons why that is the case. That is why you have to maintain a disciplined narrative,"

"A 'disciplined narrative'? I don't remember you using phrases like that when I first met you,"

"I'm older and wiser now. Or maybe I've been hanging around with politicians for too long,"

"Are we expecting a good crowd?" Bolkonsky said, moving to within a metre of Zakatov and placing a hand around his elbow.

"It's St Petersburg, so it's hard to tell," Zakatov replied, "We've drafted a lot of GRU boys to attend but remember that the message is for the media tomorrow. The big crowd will be in Moscow on Thursday. That's the one where you can rouse the people. Tomorrow is all about policy and statesmanship, don't forget that,"

"Yes, I know, it's about 'narrative discipline'. How could I forget?" Bolkonsky glanced at his watch, "It's late. Please, go to bed, Ivan Vladimirovich. We have a big day ahead of us. Thank you,"

"Good night, Minister,"

Zakatov walked out of the office and Bolkonsky considered leaving too but thought he would check in with Oksana Devina, the current Prime Minister and head of the Security Council overseeing the Presidential election. He realised the phone in his office was lying in pieces after smashing it up this morning when he had read a profile in a newspaper that called him 'a moronic farmer-soldier pretending to be a statesman, a foul-mouthed gorilla in an ill-fitting suit'. He grabbed his mobile from his pocket and called her up. She picked up after about ten rings.

"Hello? Is that you Dimitri?" the low voice of Devina came through the line.

"Ah, yes it is. Sorry for calling so late, I hope I didn't wake you?"

"No, I was reading some briefs. Can I take a wild guess at why you are calling?"

"You can," Bolkonsky laughed, "Did you hear what he said today?"

"Yes, it's the same script he is using every day. You shouldn't let it bother you,"

"It doesn't bother me in the slightest. I am simply amazed at his barefaced cheek to lie like that. Can you imagine being that dishonest all the time?"

"Honesty is the rarest of commodities in politics, Dimitri. You know that as well as anyone,"

"The latest polls show me ahead by three points. He's panicking,"

"Maybe so," Devina said, "I hope you can refrain from using some of your more incendiary lines in your speech tomorrow. It's hard enough organising an election in this country without scandalous claims of foreign invasions and mafia regimes polluting the airwaves,"

"Oksana, I've not said one word that is a lie. I know and you know that Golitsyn is bankrolled by that pig Saratov. He's a fucking puppet for that piece of oligarch shit,"

"Maxim is a popular man with a lot of people, with or without the backing of Sasha Saratov. You could learn from him, rather than belittle him," Devina said.

"I'm almost convinced he doesn't possess a brain. Do people enjoy having their noses pulled by an aristocratic clown in an expensive suit? You can almost see Saratov's fingers manipulating his circuits, programming his pet robot dog,"

"Have you been drinking, Dimitri?"

"Not one drop today," Bolkonsky replied and they both laughed.

"God, that makes what you're saying sound even more crazy. Take yourself to sleep, that's my advice,"

"When I win, I won't forget the support you have offered me over the last few months,"

"Thank you Dimitri. I guess we will have to wait to see who will be moving into the Kremlin. No point making promises you can't keep. Good night Dimitri, I'll watch you on the television tomorrow,"

"Good night Oksana, I'm hoping to receive some news from a friend in Scandinavia too that might make a little difference in the race,"

"Sounds very alluring, but I have to go bed now before I fall asleep on my sofa,"

Bolkonsky ended the call and thought about Oslo. Hopefully by tomorrow evening, he would have concrete evidence that could bury that cancerous wretch Sasha Saratov once and for all. And once he is buried, Golitsyn would be next in the ground.

4

Oslo, Norway
Sunday November 13 - 23:03 CET

Simonsen parked his car directly outside the entrance to the famous Bislett athletics stadium, taking a moment longer than expected to peel his stiff hands from the steering wheel. He exited the car and immediately noticed how acrid the air smelt. It must have been some explosion, he thought. Every horizontal surface was covered with at least an inch of snow and the temperature can't have been far off minus ten degrees celsius.

One of the seven streets leading off the roundabout outside the stadium was subject to a police cordon. Two fire engines and at least five police cars with flashing lights but no audible sirens were present outside the smouldering ruins of the kebab shop on Thereses Gate. A string of nosy pedestrians in bulky coats bordered the cordon and Simonsen gently guided one woman out of the way as he approached it.

Simonsen waved his credentials at a disinterested, freezing young cadet who allowed him to pass through the cordon. Ahead, he saw Benny Karlsson, an old friend who was an investigating inspector for Kripos. If it was now a Kripos case, there was a good chance Benny would be running the show.

"Einar," Karlsson opened his arms in welcome, "Did you come for the barbecue?"

"You know I can't resist a mixed grill," Simonsen replied, giving his friend a firm, gloved handshake, "What's on the menu?"

"Three dead so far, a couple of retired Turkish chaps who were unfortunate recipients of shrapnel to their heads. They were taken to the hospital but didn't even last the journey. Not what they expected when they trotted out for their evening meal. The other victim is a man called Pavel Zhyrgal. It appears he is a Russian national. I've got his passport here,"

Karlsson passed over an evidence bag to Simonsen. The cover of the passport was burnt off and the stark face of Zhyrgal stared back at him through the transparent bag.

"Christ, it must be over twenty years since I last saw his ugly gob," Simonsen said, "He doesn't look any older. Or younger. Never could tell how old he was,"

"You know him?," Karlsson raised an eyebrow, "Who is he?"

"I've met him before in Russia, he operates in the shadows. He's connected to a lot of unsavoury guys in Moscow but was a highly regarded *mafiozi*. He had something between his ears unlike a lot of the thugs from those days. He'd occasionally act as a go-between with his bosses and the authorities, precisely because he wasn't a complete moron. I assumed he was dead as virtually nothing has crossed our path about him for at least a decade, the man's a ghost,"

"He is now, anyway," Karlsson said.

A memory of arriving at the hulking concrete Hotel Leningrad in Makhachkala two decades ago flashed into Simonsen's head. It was almost as if someone had won a competition to design a hotel to look as unpleasant and unwelcoming as possible. It wasn't a surprise that the hotel guests were a rum bunch of criminals, politicians and journalists, it was like a Soviet pirate tavern. Simonsen regularly saw Zhyrgal in there sipping a vodka which he would nurse for a couple of hours whilst waiting for instructions from his bosses.

"Are we sure it was him who died?" Simonsen said.

"They took the body away five minutes ago and he was a

bit crispy, but I'm confident it was him, the face was relatively unmarked. Most of the impact hit him from behind. We should hopefully find out in the morning when he entered the country and obtain some footage from the airport cameras. That should confirm that it's definitely him one hundred percent. Any idea why he would be in Oslo?"

"No," Simonsen was puzzled. A lot of old Russian gangsters are on Interpol watchlists including Zhyrgal. They rarely venture out of Russia, simply because it was too much hassle. Why would this guy be at a kebab shop in a backwater suburb of Oslo?

"Any survivors?" Simonsen asked, walking towards the burned out café. The sign for the Iskender Café was hanging off at an almost vertical angle and looked like it would fall off any second, "This is a pretty serious job,"

Simonsen could see four members of the Kripos forensics team working inside the café. All of the windows and frames had been blown out, shards of wood and glass spread out across the pavement and road. The quartz countertop had sheared away and was now lodged in the back wall as though it was flung there by an irate giant. The cheap, green plastic chairs were half melted into the floor. If this was in an art gallery, you might think Damien Hirst was exhibiting. Karlsson joined Simonsen in front of what used to be one of the main windows.

"Yeah," Karlsson said, "A few other men have been taken to hospital with a range of injuries including the guy this Russian feller was with. He may have been lucky as first impressions indicate his friend took the brunt of the blast,"

"Who's that guy?" Simonsen pointed twenty metres away from the café towards a tanned man with a bandage around his head, sitting on the steps at the back of an ambulance.

"The owner of the café, I've eaten here a few times. I tried talking to him when I arrived about an half hour ago but he was zonked out after cracking his head on the ground. He should have come round by now. Let's go have another chat with him,"

As Simonsen and Karlsson approached, the owner offered a small smile to them which fell away when he turned his attention towards his burnt-out business. Simonsen could see that apart from the bandaged head, he appeared pretty unscathed from the incident.

"Yusuf, is that your name?" Karlsson said whilst pulling a pen and notebook out of his coat pocket.

"Yes, my name is Yusuf Efe. What the hell has happened to my café?" Yusuf said.

"Good evening, I'm Chief Detective Simonsen. We were hoping you would be able to help us with that," Simonsen replied, "Do you want to tell us what you can remember?"

Yusuf rubbed the back of his head and took a few seconds to compose his thoughts.

"The football was on, a few locals were inside watching the game. The place was busy,"

"Did you know the names of everyone in there?" Karlsson said.

"A couple of young lads, Ömer and his mate Mehmet. Ömer is my second cousin. And there was some annoying old prick called Aydın. Never shuts up. A woman, she looked about twenty, came in earlier and drank a coffee and spent half an hour pissing about on her phone. She left a few minutes before the place exploded,"

"Anyone else?"

"Two other guys, they work for the council gritting the roads, a Kurdish man called Sammi and his pal Tayyip. They come in most evenings for some food. There were two other guys, they spent the night arguing like a husband and wife going through a break up at a restaurant. Trying not to argue in front of people but you could tell something was up,"

"Have you seen either of the men before?" Karlsson said.

"No, never,"

"Could it have been one of those men who carried the

bomb?" Simonsen said.

"They both had cases with them. No, the bald man had a briefcase, the big guy had a sports bag, like he had come straight from the gym,"

"Have you seen the bag?" Simonsen said to Karlsson.

"I don't think so, maybe it was taken to the hospital with the big guy?" Karlsson said to Simonsen before switching his attention back to Yusuf, "Anything else that struck you as suspicious? Strange noises or smells?"

"I don't know, my head is pounding,"

"We can let you rest Yusuf, but we will want to speak to you again tomorrow morning," Karlsson said.

"Oh, there was the other guy, come to think of it," Yusuf said.

"Another customer? Did you know him?" Karlsson replied.

"Never seen him before. He could have been an Arab, with a huge beard and quite a big boy. He left moments before the explosion and got on the tram,"

Simonsen and Karlsson exchanged a look. Yusuf chuckled.

"I see you already think it's the guy who you Nordics think looks like a terrorist,"

"I would venture that it's him leaving seconds before the bomb went off which is more suspicious," Simonsen said, "You've never seen him before?"

"No, I don't think so. He seemed freezing cold so he drank a coffee and then left the café,"

"Did he say 'bye' to you?" Karlsson said. Yusuf put a hand to his head and scowled.

"Yeah I think so, but...yeah that's it, he forgot his rucksack so I shouted at him but he can't have heard me,"

"He left his rucksack," Simonsen said, a statement rather than a question.

"Yeah," Yusuf's face visibly changed within a second as the reality of his statement hit home, "After he left I went to go take it to him but that's when my café exploded,"

5

Oslo, Norway
Monday November 14 - 03:12 CET

Simonsen's nostrils quivered with miasmic memories, reeling his mind back to car-bombings and gun battles on sunny Moscow boulevards. The smell of burnt flesh melted into machine wreckage was an experience that every cop learned to handle in Russia in the late nineties.

Witnesses to these atrocities would claim to have seen nothing when they spoke to the police but they allowed their minds to compartmentalise what they had actually seen into a locked room and carry on with their lives, only rarely allowing themselves time to reflect later. Simonsen could recall with pinpoint clarity, the day he was lying on a warm pavement with his knee doling out indescribable pain as the shooters fled in the black BMW they had arrived in seconds earlier, destroying his life in a handful of seconds.

He was troubled by the thought of Islamic terrorists bombing cafés in Norway. Norway didn't have the resources or experience to handle a determined and experienced cell of terrorists, reared in the conflict crucibles of the Balkans, Middle East and the Caucasus. But if it was an Islamic radical, why would they attack a café owned by a Muslim? Was it the Russians who were the real target? The presence of a known gangster made him wonder if Russian gangs were trying to expand into new territory or if they were making a deal with a group of radical Islamists to the displeasure of a rival group.

Simonsen pulled into the University Hospital car park and he could feel his palms sweating. Spending time in hospitals was bottom of his list of things he enjoyed doing. With his office role, he was fortunate that he rarely needed to enter any medical facility. Simonsen ambled into the hospital entrance and the whiff of antiseptic and perspiration was almost enough to make him turn on his heels and flee.

Simonsen stopped walking and closed his eyes, allowing himself to become accustomed to the smell of the hospital. He opened his eyes and walked over to the reception but couldn't hold back the memories of interminable days spent in the Central Clinical Hospital in Moscow at Mariya's bedside. Simonsen wanted to leave this place as soon as possible. He flashed his badge and went through the rigmarole of prising information out of the nurse on the main desk.

After a long series of back-and-forth questions which appeared to consist of her repeating the same question to him with slightly different wording, Simonsen was directed to the correct floor and ward. Simonsen headed to the stated location and met the doctor in charge of treating the patient. A wiry, small man with a pursed face, he reminded Simonsen of a mouse in a lab coat.

"Hello doctor, I'm Chief Detective Simonsen from Interpol, I believe you were expecting me. Is the patient under guard as requested?"

"Doctor Hansen," replied the mouse doctor, "Yes, they haven't left since he arrived,"

"Do we have a name yet for him?"

"Not yet, we think he's Russian but he only came around about twenty minutes ago,"

"I will need to speak to him as soon as possible,"

"You can go in now, he's in better shape than we expected. I don't think this has been his first rodeo,"

Simonsen showed his badge to the two cops standing guard by the door to the ward and they nodded curtly back at him. Simonsen entered a large ward which would normally hold eight patients but tonight only contained the bomb victim. The only sounds in the room were beeps from the machine the patient was hooked up to and low, husky breathing from the man.

Simonsen walked over to the bed and immediately recognised the face of the patient. Simonsen uttered a strange, audible exhalation. For the second time in the evening, he saw the face of a man he first met in the Hotel Leningrad. Simonsen placed a steadying hand on the bar at the foot of the bed and took a few long breaths.

The man was Abdulatip Narimanov. When Simonsen arrived in Dagestan as the Russians invaded to expel the Chechen rebels at the tail end of the last century, Narimanov held his arm and warned Simonsen that he could trust no one in Russia. Although an exaggeration, Simonsen barely made a dent in the organised criminal operations in Russia at the time. In fact, his whole time in the country was at best a pointless professional endeavour and at worse, an excoriating disaster that ruined everything in his life.

Narimanov's face was already scarred from previous battles, the new ones were simply a top-up. He was laid out with his left arm and right leg in casts and a multitude of tubes exchanging fluids between his body and the machines next to him. It made Simonsen queasy to even think about the ins and outs of the liquids.

Narimanov caught his gaze and lifted his eyebrows which made Simonsen jump, not realising the patient was awake. Narimanov allowed himself a wry smile and a wink.

"Mr Narimanov, it's Einar Simonsen," Simonsen said in Russian.

"I remember you," Narimanov could speak but the words struggled to be heard, like listening to smoke, "The Norwegian crime-fighter, the blonde crusader,"

"Who did this?" Simonsen gestured to Narimanov's body. The reply was not immediate, Narimanov lips began moving but he couldn't force the words out.

"They lied to us," Narimanov almost spat the last word out.

"Who lied to you? Zhyrgal?"

Narimanov tried pulling himself up in the bed using his one working arm but he failed. Simonsen slid an arm over Narimanov's chest into the crook of his arm and shoulder and heaved up the big man.

"I don't know," Narimanov said after taking a minute or so to gather his breath, "You think you know the game but they change the rules without telling you,"

Simonsen didn't ask a follow-up question yet. Narimanov was struggling to focus on him, his eyes darting around in different directions. He clearly needed a rest and Simonsen decided to allow him to sleep. He could catch a few winks too.

"Where is my coat?" Narimanov asked.

"I think it's on top of the bag here," Simonsen walked over to the opposite side of the ward where Narimanov's charred holdall was inside a clear bag on top of the bed opposite, "What do you need?"

"My key," Narimanov said but Simonsen was too far away to clearly hear him so he walked back over to his bedside, "The key to my hotel room. Actually, forget my coat. The key is inside my shaving bag. There is something I want you to look after until I'm out of here,"

"What is it?"

"A video tape,"

"A tape of what?"

"Watch it if you want. It might help to explain why I'm here,"

Simonsen opened the shaving bag and amongst the toiletries he located a hotel room keyfob which he took out and placed into his trouser pocket.

"I'll let you sleep, and we can chat again in the morning,"

"OK," Narimanov replied, his eyes drooping, "There's a dossier,"

"What?"

"A secret dossier, that's why they went after us,"

"What does it contain?" Simonsen said but he received no response as the patient had fallen asleep still in the upright position. Simonsen lowered him back to a lying position and sat in a chair to the left of Narimanov's bed and he immediately felt drowsy. A female nurse entered the ward and nodded at Simonsen who mumbled a response. Simonsen closed his eyes and thought back to arriving by military aircraft into Dagestan in the summer of 1999.

Simonsen had wangled himself on to the flight as a favour from the Russian police for helping to crack a major drug ring in Cheryomushki earlier that year. Simonsen thought the heat in Moscow could be sticky in summer but as the plane doors opened and the passengers disembarked, the Caucasian heat immediately coated him in claggy moisture. The soldiers who were on board began lifting their kit off and were already dripping in sweat and loudly bemoaning the conditions.

Dagestan was the death of many people that year and for Simonsen it killed off his hope that he could change things for the better. Every copper is idealistic when they first begin their career but even he could not have foreseen the swing that clubbed his idealism deep into the ground.

But as he arrived at the airport at Kaspiysk, about ten miles south of the Dagestani capital Makhachkala, Simonsen was confident that he could find evidence that organised criminals were secretly trying to sell arms to the Islamist rebels. Snippets of gossip were spreading amongst Moscow journalists but no one had yet named a potential suspect.

Simonsen rode in a decrepit taxi along the road from the airport to the city. A barren, treeless view from every angle dotted with occasional crumbling farmhouses and factories. It was only after arriving into the city that the first trees sprouted out of the ground along with concrete apartment blocks. It was almost like a normal city scene if not for the constant presence of military vehicles. Lines of tanks, personnel carriers and rocket launchers were travelling in all directions.

The streets remained busy with locals but Simonsen couldn't help feeling like the military presence bore the appearance of a colonial invasion rather than a counter-terrorist mission. Simonsen's taxi arrived at the Hotel Leningrad without breaking down once on the journey, which he thought was pretty miraculous.

After checking in and taking a quick snooze, Simonsen headed down to the bar. Unlike the fabulous Moscow bars that had sprang up during the years of Yeltsin's reign as money flowed into the capital, the hotel bar in the Hotel Leningrad was a relic of a forgotten era.

A square room covered in drab grey-pink wallpaper with a functional wooden bar at the far end brought no inspiration but the low ceiling and cloying fug of disgusting tobacco smoke made Simonsen immediately feel dirty and needing a shower. He walked to the bar where he had arranged to meet a colleague who had recently been redeployed here a few months ago. It was only once he reached the bar that he could make out the face of Gennady Rozlov.

"I thought you were ignoring me," Rozlov said, sipping vodka. He was a touch unsteady on his feet and Simonsen realised Rozlov had probably been propping up the bar all day. His drinking was one of the reasons he had been cast out to the Caucasus by his bosses in the capital.

"I can't see anything in this place, don't they have any air conditioning?"

"The lights in the bar are being run off a generator, I don't think they could stretch to powering an air conditioning unit too. Do you want a drink, old pal?" Rozlov waved his arm through the steamy fog attempting to garner the attention of a barman.

"A beer, please," Simonsen said and Rozlov managed to catch the eye of the barman who served up the drinks with neither a fuss nor a smile.

"Here you go," Rozlov handed the beer to Simonsen, "This place is fucking chaos. I thought Moscow was bad at the moment but here is another world,"

"It doesn't seem too bad, it's rundown and poor. Moscow feels more dangerous,"

"Wait until you venture out of the city centre. Jihadi groups are luring units out into the suburbs and the villages and setting off bombs. Our soldiers are then taking it out on the locals. I've never seen anything like it and I served in Afghanistan for a year," Rozlov finished his vodka before starting to drink the one he bought, "I heard a young lad boasting to his mates about a guy he pulled out of a house and shot him in the head. God knows if the guy he shot was a terrorist, or a separatist or both. If you came looking for action, you're in the right place,"

"I'm here as we've heard that Moscow gangsters are trying to sell weapons to the Chechen rebels. Have you heard anything?"

"I thought the gangsters were funding our own troops?" Rozlov cackled loudly, "The country is on its knees and the government isn't far off bankrupt. Yeltsin is letting the gangsters do what they want in exchange for funding the army,"

"So you haven't heard any rumours to support that they are betraying their own side?" Simonsen said and Rozlov suddenly appeared to sober up, his eyes lost their glaze and his mouth turned rigid.

"I will tell you this once, and not again and nothing else after this," Rozlov slid an arm around Simonsen's shoulders and brought him close, speaking in a low voice, "There is a man called Boris Ivanovich, do you know him?"

"No, I don't think so,"

"You would be blessed if that remains the case,"

"Who is he?"

"He is an FSB agent but according to the grapevine, he has diversified into both legitimate business and crime, like half of the FSB. It's all the old KGB guys, they are trying to claw back their power they lost since the end of the Soviet Union. But this Ivanovich, people are fucking terrified of him. Muscovites won't say a word about him but some of the locals have mentioned that he has been seen behind enemy lines. If there is one man behind this, he's the one,"

"Where can I find him?"

"You'll see him soon enough. As soon as he steps inside here, the atmosphere turns to ice. Listen son, if you value your life, I would leave this one well alone,"

"I can't do that," Simonsen said and Rozlov pulled away from him and began walking away.

"I had a feeling you would say that, old pal," Rozlov said, and at that point he looked about as sad as any person Simonsen had seen before.

Simonsen woke with a start and remembered where he was. A fleeting memory of Mariya holding his hand as they walked through a park entered his brain but the thought was replaced by the sound of the nurse whistling something Simonsen couldn't place. Simonsen opened his eyes and saw the nurse checking the drips. He closed his eyes again and finally drifted off to sleep, tiredness overwhelming his memories.

6

Oslo, Norway
Monday November 14 - 07:42 CET

Noisy chatter woke Simonsen from his slumber. He opened his eyes and saw two men in white coats speaking to each other over Narimanov. One of them was Dr Hansen that he had met yesterday. They were whispering at each other at quite a rapid pace. Dr Hansen caught his eye and Simonsen roused himself out of the chair.

"How is he?" Simonsen said, his morning voice sounding harsh and stretched.

"Not great," Dr Hansen said, rubbing his murine face, "He passed away overnight,"

Simonsen's stomach turned over and his head started to swirl. He knew colour was draining from his already white face. He sat down again in the chair out of fear that his legs would fail him.

"Jesus Christ, he was fine," Simonsen said, holding one of the bars on Narimanov's bed, "We were speaking last night,"

"He may have had internal injuries that we didn't realise," the other doctor, a barrel-chested young man who gave the impression that he was a circus strongman in his spare time, "Obviously, we won't know until the post mortem but he was only metres away from the bomb blast zone. Sometimes, people appear to be getting better then they slip away,"

"When is the post-mortem?" Simonsen said.

"Later today," Dr Hansen replied, "The police prosecutor

has already given consent for us to proceed,"

"OK, can you request that the coroner emails me the report as soon as possible?"

"Of course,"

Simonsen stood and was thankful his legs didn't betray him. He surveyed Narimanov's lifeless body. Whenever he had seen Narimanov in Dagestan, it was almost like he was built for action. It wasn't simply his size, but his athleticism too. He moved with the grace and ease of a tiger. He was not someone you wanted to cross but he displayed a loyalty and honesty to people that Simonsen could only admire.

Simonsen had called time on his investigation after five weeks in Dagestan probing underworld links to powerful businessmen culminating in a terrifying run-in with his prime suspect, Boris Ivanovich. With no evidence and the explicit threat of violence hanging over him, it was pointless proceeding. The complete lack of support from his bosses didn't help either. They were only too eager to recall him to Moscow and forget about the accusations of arms sales to the terrorists.

Narimanov had driven Simonsen to a beach bar a few miles outside of the Dagestani capital city, Makhachkala. With the waves gently lapping on the shore and the sound of excited kids playing in the sand, Simonsen almost imagined he was somewhere else. Anywhere but a far-flung province of Russia.

Simonsen laid out his overarching theory about *mafiozi* supplying weapons to the Chechen rebels and Narimanov laughed and told him it was probably all true but where was the evidence?

"I'm waiting for my source to supply stonewall evidence," Simonsen said, "Once it comes through, I can bring them all to justice,"

"How long have you been waiting for?" Narimanov replied and Simonsen said nothing. Narimanov placed a hand on his shoulder, "I tried helping you but you paid no notice. I told you when you arrived here that you'll never find what you wanted,"

"Maybe, "

"In Russia, one day you run away from a wolf but around the corner is a bear. How long have you been here, two years? Why are you still in Russia?"

"I don't know. Are you trying to suggest that I shouldn't try and stop criminal behaviour? All I want to do is help people,"

"Help? This isn't going to help anyone or create a better life for normal people. I think you might have a death wish, pursuing these people. I think you underestimate the levels that they are willing to stoop to. You should go home,"

"You're probably right. It's time for me to go back to Moscow," Simonsen hadn't told Narimanov about his unexpected encounter with Boris Ivanovich in a meat chiller.

"I don't mean Moscow. I mean Norway. I don't see a man drinking with me, all I see is a man staring into shadows. Listen to me, copper: you cannot trust anyone in Russia. Anyone who has anything, whether it be a little money or a little power will use it to exploit and destroy anything that comes near them," Narimanov said, repeatedly jabbing his finger in Simonsen's direction.

"My life is in Moscow now, my girlfriend is moving in with me," Simonsen said and Narimanov scoffed.

"You're a clever man and I'm guessing your girlfriend is no fool either. Take her back to Oslo, you can have a fantastic life. If you stay in Russia, bad luck will fall on you like it falls on everyone. My brother is fighting for the other side, did you know that?"

"Are you serious?"

"It's not something I would joke about. I love my brother but if I see him again, I will kill him. He wasn't brought up to follow these religious nuts with their medieval ideas. Our father ensured we were both educated but he still chose to follow that path,"

"Why?"

"Who knows? Maybe the promise of a wonderful afterlife outweighs the possibility of having a good life in the present. I wonder if you feel the same?"

Simonsen shook his head and walked out of the ward holding a desire not to be near anyone else. Narimanov's words had always stayed with him and he often felt as though he himself was a converted Muscovite. He would have been happy to have stayed there with Mariya for the rest of their lives. Ultimately, Mariya's life did end there and much more prematurely than he could ever have envisaged.

Back in Oslo, Simonsen decided that keeping a safe distance from people meant they couldn't end up as collateral damage like Mariya. Simonsen rushed out of the hospital and was gulping heavily by the time he reached his car and sitting in the driving seat, a mix of grief and terror stirring his insides.

He looked at his phone which informed him it was not yet eight in the morning. Simonsen noticed that he was gripping the steering wheel and released his fingers and tried to breathe at a regular tempo to bring himself to an even keel.

Simonsen drove back towards the Kripos offices still trying to process the fact that the death of Narimanov occurred less than four hours ago. He tried maintaining the speed limit along Ring 3 but his foot kept overstepping the pedal and no matter how hard he tried, he couldn't keep the speedometer at a level pace.

7

London, England
Monday November 14 - 13:20 Greenwich Mean Time (GMT)

Anastasiya Mazepa walked whenever she needed to clear her head of distractions. It was a habit she had stuck to since she was a little girl and her brother Oleg would pester her when she was drawing or writing stories. She would silently walk out of the cosy red dacha in Usovo and walk in circles in the garden until stupid Oleg tired of shouting insults at her and went back to picking up beetles and pulling their legs off.

She had walked by the river for an hour but nothing could stop the ceaseless repetitive drilling into her brain of the news she had heard earlier. She stopped and rested on a rusting barrier and watched a team of four female rowers roll past on top of the murky Thames.

An hour earlier, she had been making black bread at home when she read on the Reuters app that there had been an explosion at a café in Oslo that had claimed four victims. The most recent death was of former Russian soldier Abdulatip Narimanov and vivid memories immediately jabbed at her brain like irate woodpeckers.

Mazepa closed her eyes and she could smell his odour, a mix of sweat and camomile. It was a strange feeling to be so physically subservient to a man and she hated it. Yet she unquestionably loved being protected by Abdulatip and his giant bear arms. If Mazepa's university friends had known about their relationship, they would have been appalled. But, it wasn't simply the carnal lust that allowed him to devour her but his inherent sensitivity. Abdulatip was attuned to her moods and intentions in a manner her husband had never grasped or was capable of grasping.

To have your heart pulled in opposite directions empties your soul. Mazepa accepted her ethics were corrupted and tried to make peace with the fact that she was a terrible person. But what is even worse is the shame of hiding that fact and every once in a while, there is a reminder of the person you were and of the person you are now.

That is before the ego is taken into consideration. What the clever person hates more than anything is to be outwitted. Once you are reminded that you are not the smartest; logic informs you that you're also not the kindest, the funniest or the most caring either. It can be hard to accept. To counterbalance the knowledge that there is nothing about you that makes you special, it also helps you understand the truth about human weakness and thus should produce an accompanying empathy.

Mazepa was weak and she still struggled to accept it. For a journalist like her, commenting on the behaviour of others meant you should try and maintain some semblance of moral consistency. Yet, overshadowing every article she wrote, Mazepa knew she was ethically compromised because she had slept with a man who was not her husband with the sound of fighter jets passing overhead.

Mazepa had arrived in Makhachkala, the capital of the febrile Russian republic Dagestan, in the last week of July 1999. She had hoped to be one of the first reporters on the scene of an impending war. Shamil Basayev and his band of Islamic terrorists had taken over the Chechen state next door with surprising swiftness and were preparing to invade Dagestan to create a merged Islamic republic. They aimed to expel the Russians as had occurred in the Baltics and other parts of the old Soviet Union in the first part of the decade.

The First Chechen War in the mid-nineties had tried to

follow the template of the newly independent ex-Soviet states but the Russian military brutally put down the secessionists. The Second Chechen War was instigated by Islamist rebels who had taken advantage of the chaos caused by the first war. The instability in the region was proving infectious and the sclerotic Russian state was on its knees following the crash of 1998.

Mazepa had caught the train from Moscow which had taken two days and nights. The train was filled with soldiers and the journey passed against the background of their boisterous chat, mix of accents and prolonged drinking sessions. They only became subdued as the train passed through northern Chechnya and into Dagestan. The landscape was bleak, barren and washed-out, with snowless mountains jagging out of the ground.

The train arrived at the station in Makhachkala at eight in the morning and Mazepa was tired and anxious. She exited the station and was met by a wall of humidity and chaos. A local cop informed her that a car bomb had exploded a hundred metres from the station less than an hour earlier. Luckily there had been no deaths but there was an overwhelming security presence with local police, Dagestani officials and Russian military all on the scene.

Battered *marshrutka* minibuses were further clogging up the streets with street vendors taking their chance to block any free pavement space. The heat made everything appear to move ten per cent slower than normal, sluggish lorries were kicking up dust which seemed to float through the air with the same lack of urgency. The sense of everything being slightly off-kilter made Mazepa's head spin.

Every ethnic Russian passenger who disembarked appeared in shock at their reception to Dagestan whilst the returning locals nonchalantly walked past the ambulances and met up with family members picking them up in rusting VAZs and Ladas. Mazepa entered the first taxi she saw and soon realised it was a mistake when it took twenty minutes to travel ten metres in a vehicle with no air-conditioning and leather seats which she could feel herself sticking to.

After finally escaping the clogged tumult outside the station, the driver negotiated his taxi through narrow, poorly-paved streets before turning onto what Mazepa soon discovered was the main boulevard of the city, Prospekt Rasula Gamztova. After a couple of minutes, the two-storey buildings lining the avenue were replaced by bigger buildings until they arrived at her hotel. She paid the driver and exited the car when her eyes were drawn continuously upward.

The Hotel Leningrad was a hulking slab of grey concrete rising fifteen storeys high, jarring in comparison with the general low-rise atmosphere of the city. She knew one of her friends from university, a reporter for Novaya Gazeta, had arrived last week and informed her that there was work for her here for the newspaper if she could find her way to deepest Dagestan. With no regular job and sparse freelance work since graduating, Mazepa needed no second invitation.

Mazepa walked into the hotel lobby and was reminded of the two months she had spent travelling around the former Warsaw pact countries in 1993. All these giant brutalist hotels in Warsaw, Sofia and Ukraine featured interiors that were already badly dated when they were built in the 1970s. The lobby took up a large area of the Hotel Leningrad but its low ceilings combined with the tens of people milling around inside smoking and shouting, made her feel immediately claustrophobic and nervous.

She had taken a glimpse around the reception area but she couldn't locate her journalist friend. As she queued up to check in behind about seven other people, each on their own and all appearing lost in thought, she spotted what could have been the biggest man she had ever seen.

A giant hairy bear of a human was speaking to a clean-shaven man with close cropped brown hair and glasses. He must have been over two metres tall and almost the same width. Mazepa's stomach lurched and she could sense herself reddening when he looked over and smiled at her. Mazepa hurriedly checked in, walked past another desk offering travel packages and reached the lift.

She glanced around and saw that the big man was shambling towards her. At first glance, she thought he was in his forties but as he approached she could see he was probably not far off his late-twenties, like her.

"Good day, is this your first time in Makhachkala?" The man's voice was a lot softer than she expected, speaking Russian with a heavy local accent.

"Is it that obvious?" Mazepa replied and smiled.

"You have a look I have seen many times in the last few days," the man chuckled, "My name is Abdulatip Narimanov,"

The man held his hand out and Mazepa shook it gladly, holding a look with the man that was slightly longer than she intended which was especially unbecoming for someone married for less than a year.

"If you are working in Dagestan, I am helping a few journalists with travel and translation. If that is of any use to you, please let me know,"

"Thank you, Mr Narimanov," Mazpea said, "I may well require your services but at the moment, I have to take a nap. Two nights sleeping on the train from Moscow is not beneficial to my sleeping patterns,"

"I can imagine," Narimanov said and chuckled again, "You'll find me around here quite a lot so I shouldn't be too hard to spot,"

Mazepa smiled again at him and then entered the lift when the doors opened. As the doors closed, the two of them once again held each other's gaze. Her room was on the top floor. The room was tiny but had a balcony and Mazepa was stunned at the view of the Caspian Sea from her room, barely three hundred metres away. What is fleetingly beautiful is often staggeringly corrupting as she would discover in her time in Dagestan.

Mazepa opened her eyes and the only water she could see now was the Thames. She had the sense that the bombing possessed the unmistakable Russian stench of self-defeatism, unwarranted violence and corruption. She knew that the bombing had to be linked to her homeland but for what reason and why now?

The sun was out and the morning cloud had almost dissipated. A late autumn morning in London may be the most gratifying time in the city's bodyclock but Mazepa was anxious. Not only had her lover been killed but it was seventeen years to the day since her brother Oleg, barely out of his twenties, was killed in a Moscow nightclub after drunkenly starting a fight with the wrong person who shot him twice in the chest.

Mazepa checked her phone and after skipping through a dozen messages from friends including Alex asking her round for food later, she read that Maxim Golitsyn had narrowly pulled ahead in the polls to become the next Russian president. Mazepa wanted to do her part to contribute to the blossoming media output in Russia but not when she wasn't sure if she was being followed by thugs linked to one of the presidential candidates.

Was it paranoia? Mazepa didn't know but she remembered a phrase by a Russian poet, was it Bulgakov? It had been a long time since she studied the great poets at university. The words became a mantra as she headed back home, 'Rust and stardust, manuscripts don't burn'.

8

Oslo, Norway
Monday November 14 - 14:59 CET

"Is that him?" Simonsen pointed at the monitor, even though Karlsson knew who he was looking at. Karlsson hummed in agreement as Simonsen removed his finger leaving a smudged fingerprint on screen.

They were watching excellent quality CCTV footage of the number 18 tram heading towards central Oslo. The bearded suspect stood behind the double doors with an impassive look on his face. The other passengers were in a silent frenzy talking to each other and phoning friends in the midst of hearing the bomb go off as the tram pulled away from the Bislett stopping point.

Simonsen studied the suspect's face, his eyes refusing to budge from staring out of the window. He was holding the upright bar and for the first thirty seconds of the journey, there was absolutely no movement from him. Finally, he bowed his head and started surveying the scene on the tram. Although there was no sound on the clip, Simonsen was left in no doubt that there was a frantic commotion on board.

"Counter-terrorism upstairs should have a name very soon if he's got a record," Karlsson said as they spotted the suspect step off the tram at the Tinghuset stop in front of the district court. Ironic, as that might be where he will be making an appearance in the near future if they grab hold of him.

"Anything released online?" Simonsen asked. If it was an attack linked to a terrorist group, there would be a chance that they had confirmed it was them online.

"No, nothing on the usual outlets. We could be looking at a lone wolf," Karlsson replied.

"But that's not common for an Islamic terror attack is it?"

"No, so that's why we need to find out who this guy is. We could be facing more attacks if he has a network,"

They continued watching edited footage of the suspect as he walked past the courthouse on to Teatergata and then left onto Akersgata past Trinity Church where he continued northwards. He slipped right down St. Olav's onto Akersveien and that is where the footage stopped.

"I think he got off the tram at Tinghuset to fool us," Simonsen said. The man's movements seemed both completely normal yet very suspicious. After an incident like that, wouldn't an innocent man go to the police and tell them what he knew?

"Probably, but I want to know why a Muslim terrorist decide to bomb that specific café, the same day as two Russian mobsters are in there?"

"I don't know, in my time in Moscow, there were rumours that one businessman was happy to sell weapons to the Chechens. They could be a pretty fanatical bunch. It could be that a deal went wrong or they were seeking revenge,"

Karlsson's phone vibrated on the desk. He picked it up and read the message before nudging Simonsen in the ribs.

"We've got his name and address. We've got a raid to attend to. I'm guessing you've got nothing better to do, come on,"

"I can't wait, I hope he's expecting visitors," Simonsen said. Both men rushed downstairs. Simonsen's heart was pounding and they had barely left the office. He couldn't remember the last time he had taken such an active role in an investigation. The two men entered Simonsen's car and drove out of the car park.

"Where are we heading?" Simonsen said.

"Avoid the Ring, we're going to Grünerløkka, he lives

next to Birkelunden park. It probably makes sense to follow the sirens," Karlsson replied, and it was a very good point as Simonsen realised they had joined a convoy of police vans speeding towards the target.

"That park is nowhere near Tinghuset. He was fucking us over," Simonsen said. The convoy barrelled through industrial estates and identikit office blocks. Simonsen was focused on the road and ready for a rumble. He couldn't remember the last time he had chased a suspect through the city streets, probably when he was a beat cop chasing window-smashing pissheads through Oslo on a Saturday night in the early nineties.

"Nadim Alaoui, twenty-eight years old," Karlsson read from his phone, "A criminal record since he was a teenager, sent to prison for six months for wounding in 2012. Fucking hell, he flew to Syria in 2014 to fight for Islamic State,"

"That's quite a jazzy CV,"

"Yes, isn't it?"

Simonsen drove through the street of the gentrifying Grünerløkka, filled with drab apartments, winding streets and howling snow-gusts. After less than five minutes, they reached Birkelunden park and Karlsson pointed ahead to a cordoned off street and a blaze of emergency service lights.

A fleet of police vehicles were parked up on Toftes Gate. The suspect, Nadim Alaoui, lived in an apartment in the middle house on the block, next to a spiritualist's shop covered in gaudy multicoloured artwork. The main door was open and the counter-terror police had already burst into the flat. The leader of the armed operation walked up to Karlsson and Simonsen and advised that the suspect was not there.

"Let's take a look at his place," Karlsson said, pulling one of his team members towards him and telling them, "Bangoura, release that CCTV photo of him to the press now,"

The female officer, Anita Bangoura, hurried off and left the two men to investigate the apartment.

The apartment was clean with a distinct lack of

furnishings. It was about as minimal as minimalism gets. One of the two bedrooms was completely empty. Two desktop computers were being taken away by the digital forensics team. One of them turned to Karlsson and said:

"Password protected, we'll have to crack into them at HQ,"

Simonsen placed latex gloves on his hands and made his way into the other bedroom which contained a bed, a couple of wardrobes, a chest and a bedside cabinet. On top of the cabinet was a large hardback copy of the Quran. He opened the book at a bookmarked page. The left hand pages were in Arabic with an English translation on the right.

One sentence was underlined with ink: *"Every soul will taste death. Then unto Us will you be returned."* Simonsen placed the Quran down and Karlsson entered the room.

"It's almost like he was moving out, there's hardly anything left in the kitchen and the fridge is empty," Karlsson said.

"Yeah, it doesn't look like he spends much time here," Simonsen said and started rifling through the drawers of the chest, finding only clothing. The bottom set of drawers was empty save for a photo. Simonsen lifted the photo up and showed it to Karlsson. It was of two men, one presumably Alaoui, in military gear with another man, both wrapped in the black flag of ISIS.

"Interesting souvenir," Karlsson said, Simonsen kept looking at the photo and couldn't pull his eyes away from Alaoui, with the same inscrutable face that he had seen on the tram staring back at him.

9

St Petersburg, Russia
Monday November 14 - 17:12 MST

"Turn on the news now, for fuck's sake," Colonel General Ivan Zakatov directed his ire towards one of Bolkonsky's aides who, with no delay, scampered off to the television to turn it on.

"Is it my speech?" Bolkonsky said. He was striding around in large circles in the backstage area of the Gazprom Arena. He thought his speech had gone down well despite the arena only being half full. Bolkonsky and Zakatov had given firm guidance to the director to not show a single empty seat on the broadcast and he was eager to see if they had been listened to.

"There's been an incident in Oslo," Zakatov said and pointed to the small screen in the corner of the dressing room, usually filled with ice hockey players or pop stars, not politicians and their entourage.

"...a scene of utter carnage. Two Russians are confirmed dead. Pavel Zhyrgal, fifty seven years old of Moscow with links to organised crime who has recently been working as a bodyguard for presidential candidate Dimitri Bolkonsky and Abdulatip Narimanov, a former Russian soldier who once fought in the same unit as Bolkonsky..."

"What the fuck is this?" Bolkonsky's feet were frozen as his eyes flicked from watching the television and to Zakatov's eyes. Zakatov was speaking but the words appeared to be emanating from a motionless mouth.

"Everyone out," Zakatov commanded the hangers-on and assistants who began looking at each other, "Don't make me fucking ask again,"

The lackeys hurriedly exited the changing room and Zakatov switched the television off. He pulled up a chair and gestured to Bolkonsky to sit on it but the presidential candidate stood still, as if caught in a hypnotic trance..

"Sit down, Dimitri," Zakatov grabbed another chair for him to sit on and scraped it along the floor so it was positioned opposite to the chair he had offered to Bolkonsky. A few moments later, Bolkonsky emerged from his catatonia, sat down and met the gaze of Zakatov.

"You sent Zhyrgal to the meeting you told me about?" Zakatov said and Bolkonsky nodded gently.

"He's not my fucking bodyguard. He was a lowlife nobody. Do you know who leaked that shit?"

"It's almost certainly Saratov who spread that news to the media,"

"And now Zhyrgal is dead. Was he meeting up with Narimanov? I remember that sleazy *chernaya-zhopa* from years back. I thought he was dead already,"

"Did you know Zhyrgal was in Oslo?" Zakatov said.

"I knew the meeting was in Oslo but I didn't know where exactly the meeting was going to be or who he was meeting. They are not details I needed to know,"

Zakatov and Bolkonsky both sat back in their chairs in almost perfect synchronicity. Zakatov's eyes were boring holes into the ceiling whilst Bolkonsky had his eyes closed and sweat dripped down his cheeks. He picked a towel off the floor and wiped his face with it.

"It has to be Saratov," Bolkonsky said, "That fucking rat,"

"I would assume so. I've received a message from a Norwegian contact saying they think it was Islamic State," Zakatov said.

"He sold weapons to the fucking Chechens. He'd have no hesitation in paying some fucking terrorist *tsurban* to do the job,"

"That's true. Did you speak to Zhyrgal before the meeting?"

"No, I told him not to say anything to anyone apart from me and not to use his phone as Saratov could hack it wherever he is in the world,"

"I don't think he can do that, Dimitri,"

"It doesn't fucking matter now, does it?" Bolkonsky stood up, "My son called me yesterday and he has said there are rumours flying around in London that there may be some explosive shit regarding Saratov and Golitsyn and a dodgy visa. I'll call Oksana and find out if she knows anything,"

Zakatov stood up and checked his mobile phone. Bolkonsky stared at him, anticipating more bad news.

"Golitsyn has released a statement saying you have questions to answer about the bombing and your links to both men," Zakatov said, head bowed.

Bolkonsky uttered a throat-strangling roar and lifted the television up over his head. For a moment, he appeared perplexed about what to do before he hurled it against the door where it shattered into innumerable pieces. Zakatov quietly left the room and Bolkonsky sat down again in the empty dressing room. He pulled out his phone and called his son Alex.

"Dad?" his son said in English before switching to Russian, "Are you OK?"

"Of course I am, son, I am about to become the next President of Russia," Bolkonsky laughed.

"What happened in Norway? The British press are blaming you for it all,"

"My boy, it's a daily onslaught from the Saratov's gutter-rats. It's skin off this old man's nose. My security chief has information that Sasha Saratov is working with ISIS and that they blew up the café to embarrass me,"

"Wasn't one of the guys your bodyguard?"

"It's bollocks, lad. I knew him from years ago. Don't forget it used to be my job to know who the bad guys were. I've not laid eyes on him in years. Did you find anything about the email that was sent to you about Oslo in the first place?"

"No Dad, it's an anonymous email account that anyone can set up from anywhere. Do you think Saratov set this all up?"

"It has to be him,"

"So he knows there's a dossier about him?"

"Perhaps he does, we know how ruthless he is. He wouldn't be bothered about killing a few civilians to get his hands on it,"

"What are the polls showing?"

"Golitsyn has pulled ahead in the last one but it's the only time he has been ahead since the date has been set for the run-off,"

"I can't see him winning, he doesn't look like someone the Russians would vote for,"

"Are you saying they only vote for former soldiers with big hands and deep voices?" Bolkonsky laughed again, "Remember that text you sent me about the visa and the British minister a couple of days ago?"

"I don't know much more than I was told, it's a rumour going around the community here in London,"

"We need to hit back, place that story in the press,"

"There's no evidence, Dad. These types of rumours are always there, like mosquitoes circling around the Londongrad swamp,"

"What if I could find the evidence?"

"What do you mean?"

"If I could obtain proof for you, would they print it in your newspaper?"

Silence permeated the conversation.

"The election is big news here, I know they'd print it but wouldn't it look suspicious with my name on the byline?"

"We can worry about it later. Would you do this for me, Alex?"

"Of course Dad, I'm always here for you. You know that,"

"Yes," Bolkonsky said, "I'll send the documents to your

email as soon as I grab hold of them,"

"OK Dad, I'll speak to you soon,"

Bolkonsky ended the call and recommenced pacing the dressing room. A female ministerial assistant walked in and he immediately waved them out. His phone was in his hand and he dialled up the one number he hoped would save his campaign.

"Dimitri, I was wondering when you would call today," Oksana Devina said and laughed.

"What did I tell you about Saratov and his lies? He is spreading more shit about me saying I bombed that café,"

"Stop letting him infect your brain, Dimitri. I've told you countless times,"

"This election is too important. If Golitsyn wins, it means that Sasha Saratov will run the country pulling the strings of that little puppet,"

"You have the art of melodrama down to a tee,"

"You call it melodrama, I call it realism," Bolkonsky lowered his voice despite being alone in the changing room, "Oksana, I need the evidence about Saratov's visa waiver,"

"It may put my source in trouble,"

"It is too important,"

"OK, Dimitri, I will email it to you but you have to ensure my name is kept out of all of this. You are in danger of undermining our democracy and I don't say that lightly. After the drama of the last few years, all Russians want is a fair election not a media fistfight,"

"That's the problem. It isn't a fair fight. All I am doing is levelling the playing field,"

10

Simonsen sat watching Karlsson speaking on the phone. Karlsson stood hunched over his desk, mumbling occasional affirmations. Simonsen looked out of the window and the sky was a dirty slate grey, promising more heavy snow. After a couple of minutes, Karlsson hung up the phone and turned to Simonsen.

"No real leads yet," Karlsson said, "None of his phone contacts have triggered anything,"

"If he had another phone, he's probably got it with him,"

"Yeah, the people who we've spoken to say Alaoui is quiet, serious, dull. A real humourless bastard by all accounts,"

"A possible lone wolf," Simonsen said, stretching his legs out.

"I'm leaning to that at the moment rather than a cell but until we catch him, the city will remain on high alert. Are you OK, Einar?"

"What?" Simonsen said, "Yeah, I'm fine,"

"You look like shit,"

"I'm not used to this real policing lark,"

"No, I suppose not. Listen, take yourself home and go to bed. If there's any updates, I'll let you know. I want you with me when we catch hold of this guy. You might be able to help us work out why the two Russians were there, "

Simonsen nodded and stood up, wincing at the jolting pain in his knee which was worsening by the hour. Outside, another hefty snowstorm was descending on the city and he decided against taking the car into the centre of Oslo. He caught the train from near the Kripos office at Brynseng on its journey underground to the Jernbanetorget stop outside the central train station.

It had been a long time since he had arrived in the centre of Oslo and Simonsen was hit by an odd feeling of being a stranger in his own city. Night had fallen but outside Central Station the colours were vivid and it was thrilling him.

Tower blocks and billboards lit up the night and multiple construction cranes were peeking out behind buildings from various directions. The streets were packed with shoppers and drinkers, blue trams and the stealthy red electric buses fizzed around. All the views were obscured by the snow giving every vista the look of an old painting.

There was a spring in Simonsen's limping step as he veered left from the station and onto Dronning Eufemias Gate. He marvelled at the mini Manhattan that had sprung up in old Bjørvika. An arboreal avenue was flanked by towers rising nine or ten storeys into the sky. Absurdly large for such a low-rise city, thought Simonsen.

Simonsen tried to remember the last time he had been around this end of town but he couldn't recall when it was. It must be at least ten years and Simonsen slowed down wondering where the years had gone. So many years, so few memories. On his left was the Thon Hotel Opera. Narimanov's room key indicated that was where he was staying.

Simonsen walked into the hotel and his eyes surveyed all corners of the lobby. It was colourful, roomy and almost decadently beautiful. Compared to his monochrome apartment, it was alive with colour. Simonsen decided not to go straight to Narimanov's room and headed left to the bar which was full of women in business attire attending a conference about female empowerment in the workplace.

"A small Ringnes, please," Simonsen said to the barman. A smart young man with blond hair who barely looked old enough to shave, never mind serve him beer, started pouring a fresh drink. The man placed a beer on the bar and Simonsen handed over a hundred kroner before the barman could ask him.

Simonsen took his beer and walked off towards the corner of the hotel bar with a good view of the lobby. As he sipped his beer, he was trying to think of a reason why Narimanov would give him the room key. What was on the tape? Who would it expose? If the person or people that could potentially be exposed knew he was here, then it meant it was very dangerous for him to be in this hotel.

He had known enough Russians who gleefully wallowed in the ruthlessness and savagery that symbiotically accompanied organised crime in that country. Simonsen had witnessed the grisly results of car bombs and street executions. He had attended the aftermath of scenes of torture that would make Torquemada blush. He pondered how long he would last if he was interrogated by one of those sadistic bastards. He sipped his beer and almost laughed out loud at the thought.

His knee was now firing bolts of pain up his thigh and Simonsen decided to follow Karlsson's advice and head home. He had learned the hard way that poking your nose into Russians' business could be a dangerous game. It was dangerous for a man in his late twenties. At fifty-three, it was stupid and embarrassing.

He downed the remains of his beer and headed towards the hotel exit. The days of rummaging into the rancid underbelly of Moscow's criminals were over. The automatic doors opened but Simonsen hesitated. Leaving now would not only be cowardly but an abrogation of his duty. For a policeman to turn a blind eye to crime is to break an oath and no cop wanted to ever do that. He turned around, cursed out loud and made his way up the stairs to the third floor.

The third floor was silent, the carpeted floor masked his usually heavy footsteps. Outside of Narimanov's room,

Simonsen listened for voices beyond the door. He couldn't hear anything so he slid the room card into the electronic slot. A beep and a green light flashed above the slot and he heard the door unlock.

Simonsen pushed the door back and there were no armed gangsters ready to shoot him dead in the room. It was a well-presented but small room with a double bed backing onto a floral-printed back wall. Simonsen pondered where Narimanov would keep the tape. He carefully searched the room which didn't take long. Narimanov was clearly a light traveller with no luggage in the room. Simonsen remembered that the holdall was at the hospital, why did he take that to a meeting?

He made his way to the wardrobe which was empty except for a room safe. The safe also laid empty. There was nothing under the bed or in the bedside drawer. He couldn't see anything in the front room resembling a tape so he huffed his way into the bathroom.

A Spar carrier bag was next to the sink so Simonsen opened it up and saw a VHS tape. Simonsen lifted it out of the bag and wondered how long it had been since he last held one of these in his hand. He took the tape out and went back to the bedroom to see if the television had a tape slot. Unsurprisingly, it didn't have one as the year was no longer 1987.

With the tape in his possession and nothing else of note in the room, Simonsen decided to leave the room. He exited the room door and glanced to his left where he saw a sandy-haired man exiting the lift. Simonsen turned to his right and chose to play it safe by heading down the stairs. As he opened the door to the staircase he was sure he heard a shout of "Hey!".

Simonsen didn't look around and entered the staircase where he raised his descending pace by missing every second step. At the bottom of the stairs he burst through a door into the lobby and attracted a few glances from people. His heart was thudding in his chest and his knee was on the verge of seizing up. The lobby was very busy and Simonsen's eyes struggled to focus, causing him difficulty scanning the room for signs of trouble.

Simonsen spotted one man with a shaved head and mean countenance watching him over a copy of *Aftenposten*. Simonsen slunk across the lobby and flicked his eyes repeatedly between the man and the exit. For a brief second, they locked eyes. Simonsen thought the man said something but his eyesight was not up to scratch to say for definite.

With the pain in his leg making him wince and almost well up, Simonsen left the hotel and turned right, back towards Oslo city centre. He looked back into the hotel and could see the sandy-haired man enter the lobby. He maintained vision and saw the man look in the direction of the skinhead with the newspaper, who in turn gestured with his head towards the hotel exit.

Simonsen upped his pace despite the unceasing stinging pains throughout his leg. At the first opportunity, he headed right towards the South entrance to the central train station. As he entered the doors he turned around and saw the sandy-haired man from the hotel no more than thirty metres behind him. Who the hell was this guy?

It's annoying being right all the time, thought Simonsen. He knew that involving himself in this caper would prove to be a big mistake. The station was as bland and unwelcoming as Oslo could offer. For a moment, Simonsen felt utterly out of place in this station with its low, grey ceiling and overpriced chain cafés. Simonsen turned left and through into the old East station hall with its cavernous roof reverberating with conversations and footsteps of hundreds of people.

Simonsen jogged down the travelator and at the bottom cut back on himself, heading into a newsagent's shop. He picked up a book off one of the shelves and kept an eye on the moving walkway. He saw the sandy-haired guy walking around the hall displaying no subtlety whatsoever as he searched the area for Simonsen. Simonsen enjoyed a giddy sensation that he had eluded the guy, who clearly thought he would easily be able to follow a limping old feller.

Eventually, the man walked up the staircase at the opposite end of the hall and departed out of sight. Simonsen realised he was clutching the book so hard it was bending the pages. A female staff member had approached him and was staring at him with concern.

"Are you OK?" she said.

Simonsen nodded, placed the book back on the shelf and the girl turned and wandered back off to chat with her colleague. Simonsen rubbed his face and noticed that he was crying.

"Fucking hell," Simonsen whispered and kept his hands over his face, trying to mask his hysteria. Simonsen didn't want the shop girl to see him like this and he walked off back up the stairs. Running off with tears streaming down his face made him feel like he was back at school, being shouted at by his English teacher for pushing a classmate as they queued up to enter the classroom. Simonsen waited in the concourse for a few more minutes before catching the train back to the Kripos office where his car was located. Now all he needed to do was find a way to watch this tape.

11

London, England
Monday November 14 - 19:37 GMT

Mazepa had walked from her apartment in Battersea to Kensington across the Thames. The evening had turned chilly but she was wrapped up well and warm enough. Council workers were on cherry-pickers installing Christmas lights on to the tops of mucky lamp-posts. She would be forever puzzled at how early the English would start celebrating Christmas each year. Ten weeks of boozing and buying stuff they don't need for people they don't like or want to spend any time with.

It made her wonder if there was a chasm in the souls of the inhabitants which they tried to fill with presents but it seemed to her that it was like trying to fill up a sinkhole with more dirt. It simply keeps ebbing away, leaving the exposed soul still seeking nourishment. The Brits didn't know how lucky they were to live where they did.

They were mostly free of corruption and a compromised state apparatus where you weren't thrown in prison for your political beliefs. Yet, the majority of the citizens looked miserable and the only time they didn't look glum was when they were drunk. No wonder they spent as much time as possible boozing their misery away.

The demise of Putin and the short, forgettable reign of his successor had allowed what had been dubbed a "New Russia" to flourish. The media had cast off the shackles of authoritarianism and had been engaging in brutal, withering criticisms of the political class. The competitive wrangling to assume power meant that no one was in a position to impose their will on the media and Mazepa's friends were delighted with the way things were proceeding.

However, from her perch in Londongrad, Mazepa was still wary. The first candidate, Dimitri Bolkonsky, was a former soldier who had previously been the head of the GRU. That was enough reason for her to never contemplate voting for him. The other candidate, Golitsyn, appeared close to many of the oligarchs who still controlled large swathes of the Russian economy. On balance, he was less likely to invade neighbouring countries or abuse term limits to his advantage.

The precipitous situation in Russia unnerved her in all kinds of ways. It was only here in the maze of streets in London that she felt safe, even if many of the oligarchs who had siphoned immense wealth out of Russia also spent most of their time here too. Mazepa loved the area around where Alex lived with its stunning townhouses surrounding the square.

She arrived at Alex Deyneka-Bolkonsky's flat which was located above an antiques shop near Kensington Square Gardens. She buzzed his flat number, heard the click on the door and walked up the stairs where Alex stood in the doorway, grinning.

"Nastya, always a pleasure," Alex said, holding his arms wide, inviting her inside. Mazepa followed and Alex gestured to her coat, "You know you're the only person in this city that I actually speak Russian with,"

"You've turned native, Alex," Mazepa took her coat off and handed it to Alex. He hung it on the coat rack next to the front door and she took her shoes off, casually leaving them strewn on the floor, "You'll be talking about the weather and who was murdered on Eastenders next,"

"Don't you watch Eastenders? I thought you liked gritty real-life dramas about the uncultured natives fucking and fighting each other?"

"I'm a journalist, not an anthropologist. What's for dinner, Alex? I've not eaten all day," Mazepa walked into the kitchen with Alex and sat on one of the high chairs next to the central island. The kitchen was gloriously fitted with marble worktops and more electrical appliances than an entire Siberian village. One of the perks of having a Russian government minister for a father, Mazepa thought.

"You're wasting away, Nastya," Alex grabbed her arm and waved it around, "There's nothing on you. I demand you finish this delectable lamb khinkali I have slaved over for the last two hours,"

"I won't waste a single one, I promise,"

"You best not do, or I won't tell you my secret,"

"Oh Alex, don't do that. You know I have an unquenchable desire to know everything, no matter how trivial or banal,"

Alex giggled and began serving the dumplings into a plate for them both.

"Did you hear about the explosion in Oslo?" Mazepa said.

"Yes, terrible," Alex said, without taking his eye away from his serving spoon.

"Have you spoken to your father?"

"The man calling himself the next President of Russia? Of course," Alex brought the plates to the central island and sat opposite Mazepa. Alex opened a bottle of Beluga vodka and poured a couple of big servings for them both. He downed his drink and quickly poured another.

"Does he think he's going to win?"

"You know what he's like. He thinks there is a grand conspiracy fighting to prevent him winning the election,"

"It's Russia, there are probably three grand conspiracies a week forming to stop him,"

Alex laughed and gestured to Mazepa's glass. She sunk her drink and he poured them another one each.

"Dad thinks it was Sasha Saratov that orchestrated the bombing," Alex shook his head.

"So do I,"

"Are you fucking kidding me, Nastya? It's some Islamic

terrorist who fought for ISIS. His name is all over the news. Don't become one of those nuts. Jesus, don't end up like my father seeing conspiracies everywhere. It's been hard enough dealing with all the anti-vaxxers in the last couple of years,"

"These khinkali are delicious Alex," Mazepa leaned over the sink and washed her hands as they were now covered in garlic juice, "I'm convinced he was behind it,"

"Like I told my Dad, if I see some evidence I might change my mind,"

"Zhyrgal was your father's bodyguard,"

"He claims that isn't true. And Narimanov worked for Saratov in the past, so it proves nothing,"

"Narimanov had history with your father too, not only Saratov. He only became one of his enforcers recently and I don't know how much say he had in it,"

"What do you mean, history?" Alex's face would have been amusing if the subject matter wasn't so serious.

"I'm saying Saratov could have organised it to have them both killed," Mazepa switched to English, "Two birds with one stone,"

"He's corrupt but I've never heard anyone apart from my Dad say Saratov is a killer. He's a ruthless businessman but that doesn't mean he bombs takeaways in Norway,"

"He was a businessman in Moscow in the nineties," Mazepa's tone was a touch more strident, "You don't become a billionaire in Russia by sticking to the rules. He's only different because he's a lot cleverer than those other KGB thugs who became oligarchs,"

"Maybe not as clever as he thinks," Alex said, delivering an over-exaggerated coy smile, "My father mentioned earlier today there might be a dossier about Saratov. I thought it was nonsense but then I received an email from his contact, take a look,"

Alex opened his laptop which was perched on the island and spun it around with a dramatic flourish. Mazepa read a hand-written letter on screen from Ian Kelsey-Moore, the British Immigration Undersecretary. It was addressed to Maxim Golitsyn, the other Russian Presidential candidate. Mazepa noticed the letter was written on official UK Government-headed paper.

"He fast-tracked British citizenship for Saratov because of Golitsyn's recommendation?" Mazepa intoned, mainly to herself.

"That's right,"

"Didn't the UK government refer all oligarch citizenship requests to the Prime Minister's office after they passed that bill last year?"

"Again, that is true,"

Mazepa downed her vodka and poured herself another one.

"I've written the story and the editor at the *Journal* is going to print it on the front page,"

"Don't do it, Alex," Mazepa said, "Stay out of this battle,"

"My father asked me to do it,"

"Your father also pretty much banished you from Russia in case you embarrassed him,"

"It was a different time ten years ago, he didn't understand who I was. He's not the same man,"

"Your father is a former soldier who was appointed as the head of the GRU by Vladimir Putin. He knows how to handle himself without involving you,"

"You don't think I can stand up to these people, Nastya?" Alex banged his hand on the table, "I've heard it all my life. You're not like your father. My mother says it all the fucking time. She's absolutely delighted that I'm not like him. 'Oh this is why I brought you to London, I don't want that life for you',"

"I'm saying you're an arts journalist, not a war correspondent,"

"There is no war, it's an election,"

"In Russia, there is no difference between those two concepts,"

Mazepa poured another vodka and stood up before

walking around the island to Alex. She sipped her drink and rubbed his back.

"You should have spoken to me, you don't realise how dangerous Sasha Saratov can be,"

"The story will be on the front page of a major British newspaper in the morning. It will be my first front page story. Anyway, it's too late for him to do anything about it,"

"The dossier, I've heard from a source that is real. Alex, there are documents that prove real wrong-doing, not a little visa issue,"

"The election is days away, surely now is the time for this to come out? If Golitsyn is Saratov's puppet, don't we need to do something?"

"If the files were released about Saratov, it would bring him down but have you wondered why they haven't come out yet?"

"I don't know,"

"People are afraid of him. And with good reason. That's why I ask you not to file your story. Take the setback and the bollocking from your editor and move on,"

"Too late now Nastya, I've already sent it to my editor,"

Mazepa placed her arms around her friend's waist and rested her cheek on his back.

"Come on, you know I've faced worse," Alex said.

"I'm not sure you have," Mazepa said, knowing that Alex had lit a match in a tinder dry forest.

Alex poured another vodka for them both with Mazepa still clasped to his back. She eventually released him and sat back down again.

"Why haven't you written much about the election?" Alex said.

"I can't do it anymore," Mazepa said, the anxiety of filing any story about the Russian political class was becoming increasingly acute. The act of sending a story to the subs caused her to break down in tears.

"Why not?" Alex said.

"I'm thinking about writing a novel," Mazepa said, which was partially correct as she would need to write something if she could no longer perform as a journalist. She couldn't tell him that submitting her articles terrified her.

"Wow, that's great," Alex said, "It's a real shame that your source won't tell you the whereabouts of the dossier about Saratov, isn't now the ideal time to strike?"

Mazepa didn't respond and her vodka-infused thoughts began to jumble. Alex wandered off and she saw him writing something down and then pouring more vodka. Alex smiled at her and pointed towards his living room.

"Hey, go in there and find us a film to watch. If you can't find anything, stick on Eastenders,"

12

Oslo, Norway
Monday November 14 - 21:30 CET

Simonsen pulled his car into the driveway of his home in Holmenkollen. He refrained from getting out for a few minutes. Simonsen's guard was up and he wanted to ensure no one had followed him home. He had spent the evening at Kripos HQ researching the background of their suspect for the bombing, Nadim Alaoui and the whole situation at the hotel had him on red alert.

There was nothing but silence around but he remained in the car. He had a brief moment of panic when he wondered if there was a car bomb attached to the underside of his car which would explode once he opened the door. But he soon realised that car bombs tend to go off when you enter a vehicle and not when you get out. He turned the radio on and the presenters were once again talking about the Russian election.

That was his prompt to finally exit the car. He trampled over fallen snow leaving footprints which would be filled in by morning as fresh flakes were falling again. Simonsen knew there would be another white coating across the city. He unlocked his house and entered gingerly, fearful of intruders. As he closed his front door and bolted the door, he cursed his timidity and strode off to the kitchen.

Simonsen appreciated his central heating which meant his home was very warm. He quickly took off his coat and carefully placed it on the back of one of the kitchen chairs. He retrieved Narimanov's tape from the inside pocket of his coat and placed it on the table. Simonsen wondered if he knew anyone who still had a VHS player until he realised he was that person.

Simonsen went into one of the spare bedrooms which was now a stockpile for junk. With barely any furniture in any of the other rooms in the house, this spare room was a Grand Bazaar of discarded electronics, broken furniture and unused gym equipment.

He began checking empty boxes but none of them contained their stated products. There was a toaster with no dial in an old shoebox, an MP3 player stuffed into an old Nokia phone box and a bunch of wires snaking around the bottom of a damaged microwave on a pristine treadmill.

Simonsen moved a collection of his old kitchen chairs that he never managed to throw away and found himself in the eye of the junk hurricane. On the window ledge was the VHS player. Unfortunately, on top of the player were metre-high piles of atlases, textbooks and old case files. He lifted the books off and dumped them onto one of the chairs next to him. There were no cables so he ended up bringing not only the tape player but also every cable he could lay his hands on.

He brought it all into the front room and switched the television on. It flicked to the news where the newsreader was talking about the suspect in the Iskender Café bombing still being on the run. The footage of him disembarking the tram and wandering the streets of Oslo was being shown to the viewers. Simonsen knew that in this weather, it was only a matter of time before he was caught, did something stupid in a moment of cold panic or simply froze to death.

The cable connecting the video tape player to the wall socket was easy enough to slot in but it took ten minutes of messing about to find the right cable to connect it to the television. Eventually, Simonsen found the red, white and yellow cable to slot into the TV and he pressed a button on the remote to bring up the VCR image on screen.

A blurry saturated image of sun-baked concrete popped up on screen which was marred by tracking lines. The TV remote also acted as a remote for the VCR so Simonsen pressed rewind. Whilst the tape was rewinding, he stood up and walked over to the fridge and pulled out a beer which he cracked open and drank a big mouthful. Simonsen heard the tape click and walked back over to the television. He pressed play and sat on his sofa to see what Narimanov was so adamant he should watch.

After about thirty seconds of blackness, a picture emerged of a couple of soldiers who began speaking to each other rapidly in Russian. It took a few moments for Simonsen to understand their accents and what they were saying.

"...definitely. It's payback time," one of the soldiers said. They both looked very similar with crewcuts, dark marks under their eyes and bad skin.

"Let's do this, the Captain says it's OK to film it,"

The two young soldiers laughed and walked across what appeared to be an empty factory lot, the sky was a rich, gorgeous blue and the sun was blazing down on tarmac. Simonsen could almost taste the heat off the screen.

As the two recruits walked inside the factory, ahead was another bunch of five or six soldiers who Simonsen presumed were also Russian. Shouting and good-natured jibes between them all confirmed it. As the two soldiers reached the bigger group, the camera panned round to highlight about ten people, hooded and kneeled on the floor.

"He's here," a voice said, in the background. The loud chatter dropped to near-silence.

The camera moved its attention from the detainees to an officer who had walked into the empty factory floor flanked by another four men. The man looked like a bruiser, Simonsen thought, and by the time he was in good shot of the camera, anyone could see the man was a genuine hard nut. A few of the soldiers greeted the man but he waved away their words.

"Good day Captain," a voice off camera said to the big man who didn't respond to the greeting.

"So, these are the fuckers who ambushed us?" the

Captain said, kneeling beside one of the suspects.

"Yes sir," the same off-camera voice said.

One of the men who had knelt on the ground began speaking. One of the soldiers knelt down to the same level and grabbed the hooded man by the throat and bawled some incomprehensible words at him for thirty seconds before backing away.

"Your Allah won't save you now. You assumed your stupid God would protect you from the power of the Russian state?"

The camera panned to the Captain and it dawned on Simonsen who the man was. Like at the hotel earlier when he knew he was being followed, Simonsen's stomach turned inside out.

The Captain, despite being at least twenty years younger, was unmistakably one of the Russian presidential candidates, Dimitri Bolkonsky. Was this the reason Narimanov was in Oslo? And was it also the reason the two men meeting about the tape were blown up?

"What do you want to do with them?" said a low voice, which to Simonsen's ear, also sounded recognisable but he couldn't place it.

"I will teach those Chechen fuckers a lesson in how to win a battle," Bolkonsky said and pulled out a TT-30 service pistol and delivered a head-shot to the prisoner kneeled in front of him.

Bolkonsky then went to each man one by one removing their hoods. A couple of the men began begging when they saw their comrades dead on the floor. Simonsen tried not to look but he held his gaze on the screen.

"Please sir, don't kill me," a voice could be discerned off camera, weak and youthful. The camera darted to the sound of the voice and it turned out to be a scruffy young boy, no older than fourteen.

Bolkonsky slowly walked over to the boy. The man next to the boy maintained a stone face and turned to the boy.

"It's OK, son," the man said.

"How old are you, boy?" Bolkonsky said.

"I am twelve years old," the boy said, the camera zooming to his face, smeared with muck and canals of tears weaving their way through the grime. Pure terror was in his eyes.

"Why are you fighting? Do all Chechens boys fight?"

"I don't know, please don't kill me,"

"If twelve year old boys are fighting, we can take no chances in this war," Bolkonsky turned to his troops and addressed them, "I've told you before. Treat every single Chechen male as an enemy combatant. They want us dead, that is their only wish. If you remember that, you will survive this war,"

Bolkonsky brought his pistol up to the boy's face and pulled the trigger. The camera jolted at the sound of the weapon discharging and thankfully turned away from the boy to the man next to him.

"Was that your son?" Bolkonsky said.

The murdered boy's father was trying to be stoical but he was understandably losing control. His shoulders were juddering like pistons and as the camera remained on his face, the hope in the man's eyes was extinguished. Simonsen could see a man who knew his time on earth was coming to an abrupt end.

The shot exploded and it was so loud, for a moment Simonsen thought it was inside his own house. Simonsen stopped the tape and sat back on the sofa occasionally gulping from his beer bottle.

Thoughts were racing through his mind. How the hell did Narimanov obtain this tape? It must have been taken in the Caucasus, maybe even when Simonsen was there in '99. Is this the only copy of the tape?

Simonsen decided to pull another beer from the fridge and walked towards his desk and sat down. He began making notes about the tape and its potential origins. His phone buzzed in his pocket. It was a message from Benny Karlsson asking Simonsen to call him. He immediately dialled the number and it was answered before it had fully rang once.

"Einar, this case is becoming more curious by the hour," Karlsson said, his voice crystal clear. It sounded off-kilter to Simonsen after being engrossed in the sickening Russian video.

"Have you found Alaoui?"

"No, but we have found Narimanov's phone amongst the wreckage of the café. There is an email address telling him where to go for the meeting,"

"Right. OK, any helpful details?"

"It's an anonymous email address but it was sent through a basic Gmail account and not a secure email provider. The boffins have traced it to England,"

"England?"

"That's not even the strange part," Karlsson paused and Simonsen allowed him this moment of drama, "It came from the Houses of Parliament,"

"Why am I not that shocked?" Simonsen said.

"What if I told you, it came from the office of the cabinet minister Ian Kelsey-Moore?"

"You must be joking,"

"This is not a joke. If it was made-up, do you think I'd make up something like that? If I was going to lie, I would have definitely said it was Prince Andrew,"

"Does my boss know?"

"Not at the moment, the big cheeses at Kripos have said this needs to remain under wraps,"

"Jesus,"

"I need you to go to London and investigate, Kripos have given authority,"

"I'll book a flight for tomorrow. Keep me posted,"

Simonsen hung up and pulled out his home laptop to book a flight. Before he had the chance, his phone buzzed again.

-        EINAR, MEET AT OPERA HOUSE. V IMPORTANT - ASAP

Simonsen scrolled down to the sender. It was Peter Kelsey-Moore.

13

Moscow, Russia
Monday November 14 - 23:51 MST

Dimitri Bolkonsky had arrived back in Moscow from St Petersburg an hour earlier. From his window at the Defence Ministry building, he had spent most of that time staring out across the river into Gorky Park. Moscow was awaiting the first snow of winter and it had been unseasonably warm for the last week. A few couples were ambling along the promenade enjoying the remnants of the Muscovite autumn.

Bolkonsky's phone vibrated in his pocket and he snatched it out, entering his password incorrectly a couple of times. After unlocking the device at the third attempt, he read a message from his son, Alex:

-        check The Journal website.

Bolkonsky typed in the newspaper title into his phone and it loaded the homepage of his son's employer. He would often check for his son's pieces about the London art scene even though none of the articles made much sense to him, even less so when translated into Russian.

There was a headline and despite barely speaking any English, Bolkonsky recognised the names of both Saratov and Golitsyn in the Latin alphabet so he clicked on the story and translated it into Russian:

SARATOV VISA ILLEGALLY FAST-TRACKED BY MINISTER AFTER GOLITSYN INTERVENTION.

"How do you like that, you fucker?" Bolkonsky punched a hand in the air and shouted to an empty room before he read the translated article in full. He kept walking and pumping his fist into the air like a maniacal robotic cheerleader.

"You corrupt rats, you fucking bastards," Bolkonsky whispered and he typed out a message to Colonel General Zakatov to inform him of the good news and also one to Oksana Devina to see if she had any more dirt on Golitsyn.

Bolkonsky almost skipped out of the office. As he entered the hallway, he immediately noticed that the two GRU guards who were supposed to be guarding him had nodded off, which was damned unprofessional.

"Hey," Bolkonsky shouted and clipped one of the guards on the side of the head. The guard nearly jumped out of the chair, and was panicking in the way only people who have been woken up against their will can do, "If I catch you asleep on duty one more fucking time, you'll be cleaning out the shitters in Nizhneyansk,"

"Sorry, Minister," the soldier replied, trembling whilst the other soldier displayed fine logic and kept silent, staring forward, directly through about twenty walls. Bolkonsky kept his eye on the other guard but he maintained his countenance and he flipped his attention back to the sleepy guy.

"You're supposed to be fucking *Spetznaz*," Bolkonsky dragged the guard out of his chair and brought his face to within centimetres of his, "This whole fucking country is brim full with complacent clowns. When I am President, there will be changes, I will pick up all of the fools that waste oxygen in this country and fucking throw them in the trash. If I ever see you with your eyes closed again, I will personally throw you in the fucking river,"

Bolkonsky continued to glare at the sweating guard with their faces separated by a centimetre of air and by a vast chasm of power. Bolkonsky turned and stormed down the corridor. The two guards traipsing behind him exchanged looks at each other and also with the guards at the end of the corridor. The guards opened the huge, ornate double doors that led to the staircase. Bolkonsky glided down the stairs at a fast clop before bursting out of the office towards his black Aurus Senat ministerial car.

The dozing guard managed to finally overtake Bolkonsky and opened the back door of the vehicle. Another guard sat in the back with Bolkonsky on the short drive back to his city centre home. Bolkonsky spent the journey continually re-reading the article and occasionally spitting out chunks of translated excerpts to the silent guards.

The car was now crossing water which reminded him that only a little over six months ago, on another mild, flat evening in Moscow, Dimitri Bolkonsky met with Maxim Golistyn on the Bolshoy Moskvoretsky Bridge. The new President had died less than a year after replacing Vladimir Putin and both men were considered by the media as major contenders for the top job.

"I can't believe he's dead," Golitsyn said, his suit looking immaculate as they both gazed over the Moskva River, facing towards the Kremlin.

"The old fucker looked like a corpse anyway. I'm not convinced he was alive when he won the election," Bolkonsky said, spitting into the river.

"He didn't win anything did he?"

"No, and I don't think anyone believes otherwise,"

"The newspapers are sure you must be the favourite to take over, Dimitri," Golitsyn said, arching a well-defined eyebrow.

"Oksana may run, maybe even that Kamchatkan turd, Volkov. He's been in front of the media every day, spouting shit," Bolkonsky made the sign of a mouth chattering away with his fingers.

"I think you are still the man to beat,"

"You probably say that to everybody. Were you saying the same thing to Oksana Devina in that meeting yesterday.

What happened, did she turn you down?"

"The meeting was a standard briefing as part of my new Ministry. I'm not only the governor of Moscow Oblast now, I'm the Energy Minister now that Volkov has been appointed Foreign Minister. We need to keep the lights on, Dimitri,"

"I'm sure the meeting was completely above board. What I don't believe is that someone like you would be championing a GRU man like myself. I saw a quote from one of the newspapers yesterday saying you believed the military shouldn't be involved in politics,"

"Come on, it was an interview with *Novaya Gazeta*. It's a standard line. I respect you Dimitri, you are honest and a true patriot,"

Bolkonsky said nothing and spat in the river again. He could sense Golitsyn flinching in disgust each time he did it.

"I can garner a lot of support, especially in the media. I could support your bid to become President,"

"And what do you get out of it? Don't beat around the bush, man. Tell me,"

"I would like to be Prime Minister,"

"Aren't you a little inexperienced, Maxim?" Bolkonsky said and he saw his acquantaince's cheeks flush.

"I'm not an idiot. You're not an idiot. You know a pact would make sense,"

Bolkonsky slowly nodded his head. Golitsyn was right. He knew that an electoral pact would bring the liberals in the big cities to his bid and that the newspapers would also probably offer support.

"The Dream Team, as the Americans say. It is an intriguing offer, Maxim,"

Bolkonsky pulled himself upright and began to walk off when Maxim called out to him:

"Don't wait too long to decide, Dimitri,"

Bolkonsky had walked off back towards the Defence Ministry thinking that he was about to make a deal that would place him as the firm favourite for the election. By the time he had arrived back at the ministry, an exclusive story and interview in Sasha Saratov's fledgling television channel All-Russia News announced that Maxim Golitsyn was about to launch his bid for the Presidency.

Not for the first time, nor the last, Bolkonsky rampaged through his office hurling items at walls and stamping his foot through chairs, potted plants and a large printer. His aides hid until the storm had passed. Bolkonsky had telephoned Zakatov and explained that the campaign was not going to be as straightforward as they had hoped.

The campaign had been brutal with battles on the stump and in the papers but finally Bolkonsky intuited that things were beginning to move in his favour. As the ministerial car pulled up at his house, Bolkonsky was happier than he had been in a long time.

14

London, England
Tuesday November 15 - 01:13 GMT

Mazepa was cocooned from the patented English drizzle in the back of the cab as it trundled over the spindly Albert Bridge. She was unable to shift the image of Alex's face when he told her he had filed his story about Maxim Golitsyn and Sasha Saratov's visa application. It was the look of a defiant child who was clearly petrified underneath the bullish demeanour. Or perhaps she was projecting her own fright onto her friend's countenance.

Making the decision to involve yourself in Russian politics is to understand that you will immediately have to learn how to dance between cobras ready to attack at any point and from any angle. Mazepa had more than two decades of experience in the cauldron of these competing combustible ingredients.

A few weeks ago, she had decided that it was too dangerous now and that was why she would begin writing novels. She had secrets hidden away for so long and at some point, your luck always runs out.

Battersea Park was on the left hand side and Mazepa looked into the dark trees and wished she could disappear into them. Since the death of the President, a sense of sickly foreboding had attached itself to her and would not go away, anxiety relentlessly gnawing at her. The taxi driver was speaking constantly into a bluetooth headset in an incomprehensible language and that only made her worry more. She had lived for years wondering when the dark forces would take action against her.

Mazepa had used words to strike against targets who weren't the extremely dangerous ones. She had used what she thought was her rational mind to choose wisely. She had once poked the rocks where the cobra lay and pulled her hand away in time to prevent being fatally bitten. Her sense of self-preservation was too high to risk attacking the most dangerous men in her homeland.

She was disappointed in herself. Her reputation in Russia as a fearless reporter was not deserved, she had held back from exposing the real villains because she was scared and embarrassed. In London's journalistic circles, she was celebrated. Her fellow writers saw her as the new Anna Politkovskaya but in truth, she was little more than a hack, albeit a hack who could write well and disguise her cowardice with well-chosen words.

"Left here," Mazepa instructed the driver as they approached a crossroads. The cab turned onto Prince of Wales Drive, "Here is fine,"

The cab pulled up and Mazepa paid using her debit card and exited the vehicle. The rain was becoming more insistent and within seconds, Mazepa was soaking wet as she approached her apartment building.

She still couldn't shake her worries about Alex and she jumped when the communal door opened. A pretty young woman with a mousey-brown pixie haircut and leather jacket walked out at exactly the same time. They exchanged smiles and Mazepa checked her postbox. Nothing in there except an advert for a Chinese takeaway and a reminder to pay her TV Licence. Her apartment was on the first floor and she climbed the stairs cursing the British weather, which was liable to change at a minute's notice.

At her apartment door, Mazepa noticed something amiss. Every time she left any place she was staying at, there were a few measures she would put into place so she would know if someone had been snooping. Mazepa looked down at the floor and the doormat was exactly parallel to the door. She would usually leave it at an angle of about ten degrees. If someone came round, it would create doubt on how it initially appeared, thus they would normally straighten it out.

Has someone been here this evening? The lock on the door didn't appear to have been touched and the key slotted in and turned with no issues. You're going mad, Mazepa told herself and slowly opened the door.

The tennis ball that she placed without fail behind the front door when she leaves was still next to the door. Perhaps no one had been in or perhaps the potential intruder had placed it back there by curling their hand around the door and placing the ball down before closing it like she does every day.

Mazepa closed her front door and walked into the kitchen, trying to remain as noiseless as possible. The thought that someone might be in here was causing her heart to beat hard. Can someone hear my heartbeat, she pondered and the patheticness of the thought appalled her.

She opened one of the drawers and pulled out the handheld RF scanner that she bought off the internet about ten years ago after reading an article an old pal had written about Mexican police departments who took on the drug cartels. She did a full sweep of the house for bugs and other devices that may have been planted.

Yet again, this came up with nothing and Mazepa began to relax. For a final check she went to her desktop computer, nestled snugly in the corner of her living room. The mouse should be resting on the Aeroflot mouse mat snuggled exactly inside the Russian letter F - ф - as she left it every time she had finished using it.

The mouse was instead placed over the second letter O near the end of the word. Mazepa was now sure someone had been in the house. Her hands were trembling as she placed the mouse in its rightful position.

She told herself she should have invested in that home

camera kit but at the time it seemed like a waste of money. She remembered Abdulatip once told her that you can't be too careful as it only takes one moment before your world falls apart. The best soldiers do not let their guard down ever. Is that why you're now dead, my dear? Did you drop your shield?

If someone had been sanctioned to break into her house and she had more than a suspicion that people involved in the Russian presidential election were the likely culprits, then it would only be a brief step up towards using violence.

The puzzling thing was why had they chosen her? Had they been listening in at Alex's house? That was a distinct possibility and she felt a flash of anger that Alex's incautious article could jeopardise her safety. If anyone had taken the time to read her articles (and she was convinced that Russian security services do read every article), they would mainly see musings on Russian history and only generic remarks and insinuations about current politicians.

Mazepa had a good idea what the intruder was searching for and it was unlikely to be linked with Alex's recent story. They were looking for the Saratov dossier under the wild impression she had a copy. Mazepa was certain that there was no copy of the dossier on her computer, or anywhere in London, in fact.

However, they were right in assuming Mazepa was the author of the dossier and she did have a copy that was in a very safe place. Mazepa wanted to live so the dossier must remain hidden. Mazepa told herself that if she remained alive, no one would know that she was the compiler of the dossier. The dossier was originally intended to bring down Sasha Saratov but it had become a life insurance policy. As long as the dossier existed, it should keep her safe. Even though the dossier was locked up far away, it still weighed on her mind like a ticking bomb.

15

Oslo, Norway
Tuesday November 15 - 01:22 CET

Another new experience in Oslo for Simonsen, it was certainly a week of new adventures, he thought. He was standing on the summit of the white granite opera house, overlooking the whole Oslofjord from the rooftop.

The snowfall was cascading from the night sky and Simonsen felt like a man trapped in a snowglobe being shaken by a particularly heavy-handed child. His insides were tumbling around and even with the hood up on his coat, his brain was freezing.

Simonsen turned to his right, facing the city centre, lit up by thousands of streetlights, headlights and office lights. He had never been up here before and it was something he now realised he had missed out on. It was so beautiful atop the roof gazing at the capital city, even on a cold and snowy Tuesday night. He was the only person here and for this period of time, it was almost like he was the High King of Norway, ruling his kingdom of ice and electric light.

"Einar," a voice sailed across the roof and Simonsen turned back around and saw Peter Kelsey-Moore walking up the slope to join him on the roof which took him about a minute. Kelsey-Moore was taking his time, his walk confident and unrushed.

"Hello, sir," Simonsen said. Neither man attempted to exchange a handshake, they simply stood facing each other with hands buried in their pockets, distanced by about four metres.

"Sticky old mess, this bombing," Kelsey-Moore drawled, shaking his head. Simonsen hummed his assent but said no more, "How is Inspector Karlsson's investigation going? I've not had the chance to shoot the breeze with him yet,"

"We're confident we know who the bomber is,"

"Ah yes, the Muslim. Not a big surprise is it?" Kelsey-Moore looked freezing, his long woollen coat wasn't suitable for this weather.

"It's a matter of finding him now. Oslo isn't a city that is easy to hide in,"

"Indeed. I wouldn't like to be on the lamb in weather like this,"

"I agree, sir. I'm confident he will be apprehended very soon, the investigation is proceeding at a good rate,"

"I assume Inspector Karlsson has no more use for you now?" Kelsey-Moore said. Simonsen was waiting for this moment and he tried to remain stoic, with no idea how convincingly that was coming across.

"On the contrary, sir," Simonsen replied, "We have a potential lead to the Russian community in London, he has asked me to travel there tomorrow and pursue the lead,"

"Dearie me," Kelsey-Moore grinned, "More Londongrad conspiracies. Christ above, I hear these tales every day. If I had a pound for every conspiracy featuring Russians in London, I'd be a very rich man," Simonsen made no mention that Kelsey-Moore was already a very rich man, thanks to inheriting from his father a company that owns multiple commercial properties across Europe.

"Of course, sir. It's better to be sure either way. As two Russian nationals are involved, it requires investigating," Simonsen said and shrugged his shoulders.

"You're an intelligent man, Einar. Surely you can't believe this is a good use of your time?"

"It is better to be safe than sorry, as you've said to me many times, sir,"

"Of course, rigorous probing of the facts is the very lifeblood of law enforcement. I wouldn't want to interfere in a fast-moving investigation. I'm simply puzzled at how a homegrown Islamic terrorist can be linked a bunch of Russians in another country,"

Kelsey-Moore walked towards the edge of the roof and scanned the city. After a few moments, Simonsen joined him and they listened to the hum of the city at night. To Simonsen's ears, the rhythm of the traffic moving around the city was like the sound of your heartbeat thrumming away gently in bed at night.

"You don't need me to tell you what sticking your beak into the business of some of those Russia chaps can lead to,"

"I know the risks, sir,"

"You thought you knew the risks when you lived in Moscow,"

Simonsen knew he would mention Moscow and his stomach tightened even further.

"I was asked by the head of Kripos to chase a few leads. I'm sure it'll all turn out to be nothing in the end,"

"If Inspector Karlsson believes it is the right thing to do, then follow the lead but everything is pointing to the immigrant. Make sure you don't lose sight of that. More often than not, the simplest explanation is the correct one,"

"I know sir, you can count on me,"

"You know I can't protect you from certain elements if you rattle the wrong cages,"

The insinuation to Simonsen was obvious and Kelsey-Moore eyeballed him when a double-beep popped out of nowhere. Kelsey-Moore pulled his phone out of his coat pocket and turned away from Simonsen to read the message.

Simonsen watched him run a hand through his receding, thin grey hair. Kelsey-Moore turned back around to face Simonsen. He had the look of someone who had received harrowing news. It didn't need a copper's experience to know that.

"Everything OK, sir?" Simonsen said, very intrigued about the contents of the message.

"Yes, of course," Kelsey-Moore started to walk off back down the slope when he turned back round to Simonsen, "Finish this in a couple of days and we can talk about your retirement plans,"

Simonsen nodded and Kelsey-Moore walked down the long ramps back towards ground level. Simonsen desperately wanted to find out what that message said. He hoped that the revelation about the origin of the email sent to Narimanov hadn't leaked out. He doubted that would be the case as Kelsey-Moore would have insisted he was taken off the case. Simonsen stayed staring at the city for a good half hour before finally heading back home to pack for his flight to England.

16

Oslo, Norway
Tuesday November 15 - 05:58 CET

Simonsen leaped up from his bed, still dreaming of hearing gunshots and a woman calling his name. Simonsen's bad knee buckled and he collapsed onto his bedroom floor clanging his right arm off the bedside cabinet. His mobile phone was ringing from atop the cabinet and after taking a moment to gather his thoughts, he saw it was a call from Benny Karlsson.

"Benny," Simonsen answered the phone, dragged his body up and sat on the edge of his bed.

"Did I wake you up, Einar?" Karlsson said and started laughing. It was too early for such jollity, thought Simonsen.

"What's going on?"

"We've caught him,"

"Alaoui?"

"*Mais oui*, Monsieur Simonsen. Come down here and we'll interview him together, let's see how much Russian this guy knows,"

"I'll be there in half an hour," Simonsen hung up the phone and buzzing with energy, jogged to the bathroom to shower.

In less than half an hour, Simonsen had raced to the Kripos HQ in record time where the prisoner was being detained in a holding cell. Dozens of police vehicles were outside on the streets ready to obstruct any journalists from poking their noses in, once word inevitably escaped regarding Nadim Alaoui's arrest.

Karlsson was outside HQ, smoking a cigarette and scrolling on his phone when Simonsen arrived. He waved with his phone in his hand before he pocketed it and smirked as Simonsen approached.

"Christ, this must be your earliest shift ever," Karlsson said, "Do any of you Interpol guys ever start before midday?"

"Piss off, Benny," Simonsen clapped Karlsson on the shoulder, "Where was he hiding?"

"Spotted in St. Hanshaugen Park," Karlsson chucked his cigarette in a bin and gestured inside and both men entered the building, "Two cops thought he was a vagrant and were about to give him a kick up the arse when they caught him sleeping beside a warm air vent behind some building. No resistance and he was in a pretty bad way thanks to the cold. Let's have a chat with him before his solicitor turns up,"

Simonsen and Karlsson slalomed their way through the Kripos offices which were bustling at this early hour. The atmosphere was tremendous but both Karlsson and Simonsen knew that despite the cliché, this truly was where the hard work would start. They descended stairs to where the interrogation rooms and holding cells were located. There were only a handful of cells in the Kripos basement but they were usually used for sensitive cases and counter-terrorism suspects.

Karlsson and Simonsen entered the room adjoining the interrogation room and saw the suspect through the double-sided mirror. Karlsson began collating some documents and Simonsen walked right up to the glass.

The suspect, Nadim Alaoui, was shivering so much that he appeared to have no control of his body. He repeatedly attempted to drink his plastic cup of coffee but he couldn't lift it without spilling it. He finally gave up and placed his head in both of his hands. Simonsen couldn't tell for sure amongst the shivering, but Alaoui seemed to be sobbing.

"Are you ready?" Karlsson said and Simonsen nodded. Simonsen went to the drinks machine and filled a mug halfway full of coffee and the two men walked in silence into the interrogation room. Both men sat down and Alaoui pulled his hands away from his face to stare at his interviewers. The tape recorder remained untouched as Simonsen slid the mug of coffee towards Alaoui who gave a slight nod.

"Mr Alaoui, I am Investigating Inspector Karlsson and this is my colleague from Interpol, Agent Simonsen. Are you able to answer a few questions for us?"

"I didn't blow up the café," Alaoui blurted the words out and spittle rested on his lower lip. He stared at the cops for a few seconds before lowering his eyes and wiping his lips with the back of his hand.

"Let's start at the beginning before the bombing took place," Karlsson leant back in his chair and opened his arms, "Why did you go to the Iskender Café on the evening of Sunday 13 November?"

"I go there occasionally. I sometimes have a cup of coffee after work,"

"The owner has said he hasn't seen you before,"

"That's not true, I must have been there at least ten times, it's always busy so he might not recognise me," Alaoui's North African accent was strong and Simonsen struggled to understand his Norwegian when he spoke fast.

"Where do you work?" Simonsen said.

"I work for a tech company. The office is on Pilestredet, it's near to the café,"

"NorSoft?" Karlsson read out loud from his notes.

"Yes, I'm a programmer,"

"How long have you worked there?"

"Maybe five or six years,"

"It says four years here," Karlsson lifted an eyebrow from his notes towards the suspect, who was still shaking in his chair.

"Yeah, that's probably right,"

"Why did you say six years?"

"I don't know, I was estimating,"

"Estimating, OK. What were you doing six years ago?"

"Isn't it written down on your paper?" Alaoui said, folding his arms. Karlsson continued looking down at his notes for a few seconds before meeting Alaoui's gaze.

"Almost six years ago to the day, you deserted from ISIS and handed yourself in to a brigade of Turkish troops near a place called Kobanî," Karlsson said.

"Is that a question?" Alaoui said.

"You fought for ISIS and then came back to Norway where you joined a deradicalisation programme established by the government," Karlsson said and this time Alaoui remained silent.

"So, you underwent this de-radicalisation," Karlsson continued, "And trained as a computer programmer which is a very good job to have, let's make no mistake. Nadim, please tell me why would a programmer, who has supposedly undergone this deradicalisation, bomb a Turkish café?" Karlsson said, placing his palms on the table.

"I didn't bomb the café, or any other café. So, I am unable to answer your question," Alaoui said, taking another sip of his coffee with much steadier hands than earlier.

"You didn't bomb any cafés in Syria?"

"Of course not. This is ridiculous,"

"Wasn't that the kind of thing ISIS did in Syria and Iraq? Before I came in here this morning, I had read about some of the things ISIS fighters got up to on tour. Mass rapes, torture of non-believers, ethnic cleansing, massacres, destroying historic monuments, forced conversions, organ trafficking, enlisting of child soldiers. Did you take part in any of those activities, Nadim?"

Alaoui lowered his head and didn't say anything. When his head rose again, his eyes were moist. Karlsson's eyes remained focused on the suspect.

"So, I would say that based on your experiences, that it isn't a ridiculous idea that four people are dead from a little café bombing in which one of the patrons was a former member of ISIS,"

"I could have been one of them people, stop accusing me of doing it,"

"Why did you leave ISIS?" Simonsen said. Alaoui's mouth opened as if caught off-guard by Simonsen's intervention. Alaoui closed his mouth again and Simonsen wasn't sure if his suspect would speak.

"It was...," Alaoui said and paused for a few seconds, "Have you ever done something and straight away thought 'I've fucked up here'? I travelled with my friend Hisham and we knew within days of arriving in Syria that we had made the worst decision of our lives,"

"How did you manage to enter Syria?" Simonsen said.

"It was easier than we thought it would be. We had made a few contacts online and we flew to Turkey. No one questioned us, no one stopped us and the two of us hired a car and drove down to the border. We were smuggled over with about twenty other men and women and bang, we were in Syria,"

"And then what?"

"It didn't seem real. We had left Oslo and now we were in a war zone, we didn't know anything. Neither of us had fired a weapon before. We trained in some godforsaken village in the middle of nowhere for a few weeks before we went on border patrol near Raqqa. We saw a lot of bad stuff. We kept our heads down and tried to avoid trouble,"

"Sounds convenient," Karlsson said.

"Believe what you want. We didn't take wives or go round killing people. From the day we arrived, we were waiting for the right moment to escape,"

"You must have believed the ideology before you went? You can't have been that naive?" Simonsen said.

"We were in a hole in every way, me and Hisham. No qualifications, no jobs. We used Western wars of aggression and anti-Americanism as an excuse. I'd like to say I was an innocent kid caught up in it but I wasn't. I didn't rush the decision. I thought I made a rational choice but I didn't, I made the choice of an unworldly man,"

Simonsen nodded and all three men in the room were staring into space. Simonsen wondered if these were the words that he had heard on the de-radicalisation programme and whether Alaoui actually believed them.

"What happened to your friend Hisham?" Karlsson said.

"He was killed,"

"Who killed him?"

"Our commanding officer shot him in the head,"

"Why would he do that?" Simonsen said.

"He refused to obey a command," Alaoui replied, hands shaking, "Hisham was a good guy, they wanted him to shoot a young boy who had been stealing from our supplies. He wouldn't do it, he would never have shot a kid,"

"And because he refused, your officer shot your friend?" Karlsson said.

"Yes," Alaoui said, tears glazing his eyes.

"What did you do after your commanding officer shot your friend?"

"Nothing, I did nothing. I was frozen to the ground. I was sure I was going to be next but instead he shot the little boy who nicked from us right there in the street. That was it. Our unit had to clean the bodies of Hisham and the boy off the road. I couldn't do anything, I was in shock. I left Kobanî that night, stole a car and drove up to the border,"

Alaoui erupted into a fit of sobbing with his head in his hands. Simonsen and Karlsson both scrutinised him as he bawled. They allowed him to continue crying for a full five minutes.

"It is certainly an interesting story, Nadim," Karlsson said and he picked up his notes and held them up, "We believe two Russians may have been the targets for the bombing. A couple of nasty mafia-types. Pavel Zhyrgal and Abdulatip Narimanov. Do you know any reason why they would have been targeted?"

"I don't know who they are. I don't know any Russians. I wouldn't know who they are even if you showed me pictures,"

"They were sitting in the window of the café, about three metres from where you drank your coffee,"

"I don't remember, all I wanted to do was warm up. There was a football match on and I was watching that,"

"Zhyrgal fought in Chechnya in the nineties, he probably killed Muslims. He was known for his hatred of Muslims,"

"I have already told you, I don't know him. What the fuck has Chechnya got to do with me? I don't even know where the fuck Chechnya is,"

"Zhyrgal and Narimanov both fought in Chechnya against fundamentalist Muslim terrorists. And you were a fundamentalist Muslim terrorist too,"

"You're talking shit. None of these things are related,"

"Not on a first reading, no,"

"What was the name of your commanding officer?" Karlsson said.

"Abu Hussein. We called him Abu Hussein,"

Karlsson showed his notes to Simonsen and pointed towards a line which Simonsen stared at and made him immediately queasy.

"Abu Hussein was the *nom de guerre* of Nurakhmat Narimanov, the brother of one of the victims of the bombing," Karlsson said.

"I didn't bomb the café," Alaoui was weeping again. He repeated his assertion that he didn't bomb the café a couple more times.

"So we are to believe that it is a coincidence that the brother of a man killed in a café was the man who murdered your best friend in cold blood?" Karlsson said, "It appears to me, Nadim, that these things may be related after all,"

17

Zelenograd, Russia
Tuesday November 15 - 11:13 MST

"Where are you, Dad?"

"I am in the manager's office at a semiconductor factory in Zelenograd," Bolkonsky was on the phone with his feet up in a cramped office with faded posters of Soviet actresses haphazardly plastered on the wall. Bolkonsky was speaking to his son and simultaneously admiring a picture of one of his favourites when he was younger, Tatiana Somoilova, "The story has had a huge impact here in Russia. It's the major story on all the television channels. Well done, lad,"

"I hope it helps, what are they saying?" Alex said.

"A lot of it is saying that he thinks he is the cat that got the cream. The average citizen can't relate to a man like that. Working-class folk could accept that he was rich, as long as he remained clean-cut. But now he's been caught with the cream around his lips, hasn't he? A couple of papers have come out said it's time to vote for me, the incorruptible voice of the people,"

"That's a good line, did you feed that to the paper?"

"Of course not, I am not a man of words, as you well know,"

"My friend was worried when I told her I was about to print the story. She said I was putting my head into the lion's mouth,"

"Which friend is this? A Russian?"

"Yes, she's a journalist too, Anastasiya Mazepa. She was

very concerned,"

"I remember her. She fled to the comfort of London, sniping away on her typewriter from a thousand kilometres away. That's the problem with a lot of our people these days. They are too scared to take action, to stand for what they believe in,"

"I think she's concerned about me, that's all,"

"Let me worry about that and not some floozy who can't hold down a job in Russia so she has to slink off to England,"

"Like I did?"

"That was your mother's idea. Not mine,"

"You were happy to see me leave though, weren't you?"

"Don't be silly,"

"I know what happened, you told her you didn't need a gay son jeopardising your political career,"

"I never said that,"

"Not in those words but mother isn't a fool, Dad. She might not have a university education but she knows people,"

"She thinks she knows people. There's a big difference,"

Alex snorted, "She knew that you didn't want us around,"

"Maybe I didn't at the time. What do you want me to say? I won't apologise to your mother. Ever,"

"You exiled us both. I know why you wanted me out of the picture. I still don't understand why you wanted rid of her,"

"Listen son, your mother talks a lot. I admit I was focused on my career and that's what pissed her off. She craves attention and money and I told her that. She didn't like to hear the truth so she took you away,"

"You could have stopped us from leaving,"

"Yes, of course I could but I can't change the past. I was a stubborn man and I wasn't going to back down,"

"Isn't it a bit childish?" Alex said and his father said nothing, choosing silence over a big argument, "What will I do if someone tries to attack me for the article?"

Bolkonsky paused, knowing that his son would stand

no chance against a professional hoodlum sent by Saratov.

"Your friend, the journalist. What was her name? Anastasiya Mazepa? Let me tell you about her, son. She is unreliable, untrustworthy and not someone whose opinions I would listen to,"

"She's a friend and someone I respect and she is the first person I would solicit help from. She says there's more information out there about Saratov,"

"I've heard this bullshit from her before. She was spouting this kind of rubbish when you were still at school and never backed it up. She demands attention so she says these controversial things. She's a typical bourgeois provocateur. If she had anything on Sasha Saratov, she would have written it by now,"

"Maybe she's following her own advice?"

"Or maybe, she's a past-it old hack trying to impress a young journalist whose father is about to become the most powerful man in Russia with some invented stories about a man everyone with a working brain knows is totally corrupt?"

"Any other person who has dirt on Saratov and you're all over them,"

"Son, I give everyone a chance. Everyone. She blew her chance in Dagestan,"

"Dagestan?"

"Like I said, this conversation about a dossier came up over twenty years ago. She said she had the dynamite ready to explode Saratov's empire. She had nothing,"

"You've spoken to her before?"

"That man who died in the bombing, Narimanov, was working for me during the Dagestan conflict. He used to be a soldier in the mid nineties but was a fixer for journalists and the military during the Second Chechen War. He passed on a message from her to me about some files she had that could bring down Sasha Saratov. I didn't know much about Saratov until Dagestan and he was swanning around like he was the King, spraying cash around and boasting that he was funding the war effort. Everyone was fawning over him and telling him how great is,"

"What did this have to do with you? I don't understand,"

"This was a different Russia, it was before the Twin Towers, before Putin became all-powerful. The military could see that the oligarchs were trying to take over and we couldn't stand for it. The media and the foreigners thought the armed forces were the bad guys but we were the ones trying to stop the assets of our nation falling into the hands of jumped-up little bandits backed by unemployed KGB spies.

"I met that journalist in the gardens of a huge mosque in Makhachkala. She told me she was in the process of obtaining proof that Saratov was selling arms to the Chechen rebel leaders. I couldn't believe it, if it was true, we could slam the fucker in prison for years. I learned a lesson from that day, I knew I could never trust anything that comes out of the mouth of a journalist. And by that point, I had bigger fish to fry,"

"What happened?"

"My unit was called to the frontline about two weeks later to relieve a brigade who had been dug in for a week. At midnight, our trucks arrived at a farm outside of a town on the road to Khasavyurt. We piled out and tried to get our bearings. We would occasionally hear gunfire but we could see absolutely fuck all,"

"Were you scared?" Alex said.

"A lot of my men were scared," Bolkonsky said, unable to tell his son about the fear that coursed through his body on that night, "Most of them were young kids. Well trained but inexperienced in a real combat situation. As the night wore on, the attacks increased on our position. Rockets were dropping short of our position and all we could do was respond with small arms fire. It was coming from the town but we had no intelligence. We were easy targets with no idea where the fucking attacks were coming from.

"We dug in and gradually started to repel the attacks and as the sky started to light up, we had survived the night. Well, two young lads didn't survive. Two of my privates, still in their teens. They were dead. By the time morning came, we scoured what was left of the farm and found some brand new Russian spent shell casings that hadn't come from our side. From what that journalist said, I knew. I knew it. They had to have come from Sasha Saratov and that he had sold the missiles that killed our own troops,"

"I can't believe I've never heard this before,"

"It's not something you can bring up over some *borshch* at the dinner table. I defended our country so I could keep you safe. I put my body on the line for Russia and when I arrived back in Makhachkala a week later, I met up with your friend. She said she had no evidence. I couldn't believe it and I still can't. I told her what I had seen and all she could do was shrug her shoulders and walk away,"

18

"He said he didn't want the solicitor?" Simonsen was sipping a coffee and leaning on a filing cabinet in one of the open-plan offices at Kripos. Karlsson was standing next to him and a bit too close for Simonsen's liking, it was making him edgy.

"No, I don't think it will take much to crack him," Karlsson whispered.

"Why no solicitor?"

"Fuck knows. It's his funeral,"

"We need more evidence," Simonsen shook his head. There was something not right about not having a solicitor. It meant that if he was part of a cell, then the other members were already proceeding with their roles and his part was complete. The thought of that made Simonsen shudder. The alternative was that Alaoui was so convinced of his innocence that he didn't need a solicitor and that unnerved Simonsen even more.

"That will come, we have the motive. Did you see his face when we dropped that shit about Narimanov's brother on him?"

"Let's go, I've got a flight to catch,"

"Are you still going? We may not need you to go now,"

"Yeah, Kelsey-Moore warned me off but with that story about his son doing the rounds, you never know,"

"Your boss is an absolute prick," Karlsson said.

"Don't I know that? I've had him over my shoulder in

Moscow and Oslo. I'm sure the main reason you want me to go to London is simply to spite him,"

"You're a better detective than I give you credit for," Karlsson said and both men laughed, "We can decide after our little chat with Alaoui. Let's go,"

Alaoui was sitting in the same chair as the earlier interrogation and appeared a lot calmer. He turned down the offer of a drink and even mumbled "Hello" to both officers.

"Nadim," Karlsson said, "Tell us more about Nurakhmat Narimanov, or Abu Hussein, as you knew him,"

"There's not much to tell, people like him aren't very chatty,"

"Did you meet him when you first arrived in Syria?" Simonsen said.

"No," Alaoui shook his head, "After a few months at the border post, we were sent to a command outside of Manbij. We fought there in a regiment of soldiers that came from other European countries before we ended up in Kobanî and placed under Abu Hussein's command,"

"What did you do in Kobanî?"

"We were at the rear after the siege. Abu Hussein was a pretty high-up guy. I didn't see him take orders at any point. Mainly we were upholding the law, petty stuff,"

"Petty stuff like shooting shoplifters and selling women into slavery?" Karlsson said and Alaoui's face twitched.

"Yes, stuff like that," Alaoui said with a grimace plastered to his face.

"Did you ever speak to him?" Simonsen said.

"Not really, maybe late at night we would speak about home. He never said where he was from,"

"He didn't discuss his brother or his hometown?" Karlsson said.

"He may have mentioned a brother, I can't remember,"

"I thought soldiers would reminisce about their childhoods and sweethearts when they were on campaign?"

"It was safer not to say anything. There was always

a divide between the guys who grew up in Western Europe and the Arab-born and the guys who fought in Yugoslavia. I planned to escape but I knew if I did, they would find me,"

"In Norway?"

"Yeah, why not? We were winning at that time,"

"We?"

Alaoui made a strange gargling noise and slammed a hand down on the table.

"You know full well what I mean, don't twist my words. I live every single fucking day of my life thinking those nutjobs are going to find me and kill me,"

"You think you're on some sort of hitlist?" Simonsen said.

"Of course I am, and I didn't even change my name. It's like that bombing, all it needs is one lunatic and boom, you're history. I know you released my name so they will be after me now. My life is in danger no matter what happens now,"

"Do you know anyone who is after you?"

"I have no idea but I boarded that tram and didn't say anything because I was terrified,"

"Terrified of being caught?" Karlsson said.

"Terrified of losing what I have built in my life since I came back. I've got a job, I'm happy. I know you think I'm irredeemable, a Muslim terrorist unworthy of a place in your perfect Scandinavian society but it's not true. I've done bad things, probably a lot worse than most and all I can do now is try and be a good person,"

"It's a nice speech," Karlsson said and Simonsen could tell from his face that he didn't believe Alaoui.

"So you went on the run thinking that you were the target?" Simonsen said.

"Of course. And with you saying Abu Hussein's brother was in the café, it all adds up," Alaoui said.

"It adds up if Narimanov was carrying the bomb but nothing indicates that was the case. And also the small matter of him being killed by the explosion," Karlsson fixed Alaoui with a glare, "Why would Abu Hussein send a hit squad to Bislett to take out a guy who was basically a traffic warden in Syria?"

A knock at the door caused all three men to spin around. A female face popped into view as the door opened.

"Boss?" Anita Bangoura said, "Can I borrow you?"

Karlsson pressed the stop button on the tape recorder and both he and Simonsen exited the room. A uniformed cop exchanged places with them in the interview room.

"What is it?" Karlsson said.

"There is a woman at the front desk claiming to be Alaoui's fiancée," Bangoura said, "She says he didn't come round like he usually does and she turned on the news and there he was,"

"Is she a piss-taker?"

"Looks legitimate, Boss. She's got photos of them doing 'coupley' things,"

"Why didn't this clown mention her?" Karlsson said. Simonsen had never seen his mate look so agitated. Karlsson started pacing in circles in the corridor.

"God knows," Simonsen said, "But it may explain why his apartment looked barely lived in. Is she white?"

"Yeah," Bangoura said, "A science teacher and your textbook lovely Nordic blonde,"

"Fuck," Karlsson said, "We need to interview her now. Find out if she is an accomplice,"

"Or that he is innocent," Simonsen said and Karlsson's eyes told him what a nightmare that would be to explain to his superiors.

"Bangoura, come with me," Karlsson said, "Simonsen, jump on that plane and bring me back something I can use,"

19

London, England
Tuesday November 15 - 13:30 GMT

Mazepa was sitting on her tired brick-coloured leather sofa in the living room refusing to move. On days like this, Mazepa wished she lived in the same country as her husband. He had returned to Moscow last year, hailed as a symbol of the country's new start, as the figurehead of what they hoped would be a new cultural openness. There was no such openness within the marriage.

For Mazepa, there was no compulsion to head back to Russia. She told her husband Mikhail that she would stay in London as that is where her career was now. She couldn't face admitting it was because she was scared to be part of the cultural renaissance that they so longed for. And hidden even deeper was the shame of living with a good man who she had secretly betrayed.

There was unrelenting dread stewing her stomach. She wanted to be sick, both literally and figuratively. She needed to purge her fear, her shame and also that fucking dossier. Perhaps, it would be safer in the hands of Alex. If his father wins the election, he will have a measure of protection. And from that stance, he could bring down Sasha Saratov and free both her state of mind and the oligarch's increasing stranglehold on Russian life.

She was stunned by the reaction in Russia to Alex's story. Her phone had been beeping all day with messages from all over the motherland chatting about it. Some of her

Russian friends were seeing it as the first sign that Saratov's empire was crumbling. However, a large number held opposite opinions. They were concerned that Dimitri Bolkonsky was on the verge of becoming President and that he would crack down on anyone of a liberal persuasion.

For Mazepa, her patriotism was personally wounded by the deep regard that a large number of Russians held of macho leaders from Peter the Great to Stalin to Putin. Was it the vastness of the country that led people to believe only a strong man could keep them safe? At some point, the populace needed to grow up, take some personal responsibility and accept more from their politicians. Reverting to Bolkonsky would be a retrograde yet unsurprising step. However, Golitsyn was clearly Saratov's preening marionette, a vain man, obsessed by status being manipulated by an oligarch with a despicable moral code and endowed with the real understanding of where true power lay.

Doing nothing was Mazepa's preferred option but something was tugging at her soul, as if fate itself was creeping out of the shadows and pulling her into a story she didn't want to engage with. The dossier would provide inarguable proof of Sasha Saratov's criminality and treasonous behaviour.

However, the dossier was not in England. She had left it in a safe place in 2015 before she took on a job as the UK correspondent for the *Izvestia* newspaper. Mazepa had only visited the hiding spot three times since, to add more material to it. Each time she had returned to Moscow to bulk up the files, it shredded her nerves. She feared that she would be unable to summon the courage to access it one more time and pass the poisoned chalice to Alex.

Mazepa dragged herself off the sofa, taking off her pyjamas and putting on gym wear. She rarely attended the gym now but she wore the outfits as a lame sop to remaining part of the fitness clique. For a woman in her fifties, she thought she still looked good. She was tall, slim with greying blonde hair. She cleaned her teeth and examined her face, self-pity smothering her objectivity.

Staring at her reflection in the mirror had always made her wistful. A duality of emotions flowing in her mind from memories of her youth interlaced with thoughts about the future. Now she remembered finding out she had been successful in her first job interview after graduation, the sense that she could make a difference as a journalist. A laughable naivety, looking back, but she had to harness that sentiment and use that juvenile courage for a cause bigger than her. The 1990s was the only time akin to a Golden Age that Russian media had experienced.

After throwing on her blue Burberry coat, she left her apartment after completing her security checks. She carefully took extra time to place the tennis ball behind the door before closing it successfully without chopping her arm off. She made her way downstairs and outside where the sun was shining so much you could mistake it for late summer.

Mazepa's feet sped along the street until she reached Battersea Park underground station, boarding the first train towards the Oval where she would switch lines and head to Moorgate. Mazepa's thoughts drifted back to Abdulatip Narimanov and the journey they took in Dagestan to meet a friend of his who had allegedly obtained photos of a highly sensitive nature.

She had agreed to meet the source following a tip-off from Narimanov himself. Narimanov picked her up outside the Hotel Leningrad in his brand new Lada Niva, its blood-red exterior gleaming in the sweltering Caucausian heat. Mazepa entered the passenger seat and she couldn't help but laugh at the bear of a man at the wheel who looked like a Barbary pirate trapped in a tiny, poorly-built motor vehicle.

They drove out of Makhachkala engaging in low-key yet comfortable conversation about how she was finding life in

Dagestan. Mazepa slowly found herself being entranced by the scenery as they rumbled southwards. After an hour or so, the terrain turned from barren hills to gigantic pewter-coloured mountains and wide, inviting lakes.

The landscape was majestic and Mazepa was fascinated by the villages perched on hillsides, looking as though some deity had hurled houses into the side of the mountain, hoping they would stick. Their progress slowed as the bumpy single track roads wound dangerously around ridges and peaks.

After around three or so hours, they entered a village high up in the Caucasian mountains. They parked up beside a run-down house,

"This is my home village, Gunib," Narimanov said.

Mazepa assumed the house may have been Narimanov's family home but he didn't make any further comment and he walked off after they exited the car. Mazepa had to jog to catch up with him.

"I can't believe people can live here," Mazepa said, causing Narimanov to laugh.

"Not everyone wants to live in a concrete *panelka* two kilometres into the smoggy sky,"

"I don't mean that. It's so isolated that it must be so hard to see the doctor or go to school. But the views are unlike anything I have seen before,"

"Beauty can often be a burden when jealous suitors come calling,"

"This man we are meeting is your friend?"

"Yes, we grew up together. He was a soldier too but he was discharged on medical grounds a couple of years ago,"

Narimanov and Mazepa strode uphill to a viewing point marked by a huge concrete sculpture. Mazepa ignored the awful statue and gazed at the view. The village of Gunib lay on two levels with a higher level on their right and a lower level below them in the centre of their view. The village was hemmed in on both sides by huge mountains and the valley stretched off into the distance with Tolkienesque peaks as far as the eye could see. The scale was immense and Mazepa again thought that it was surely beyond the capabilities of humans to live in such a place where you are reminded every day how fragile and insignificant you are in the face of such outsized natural wonders.

A man arrived holding onto a walking stick, wearing a tattered grey suit and a tight, wizened face. Narimanov ran over and slammed him into a bear hug. The other man appeared taken aback by the ferocity of the greeting. Narimanov pulled him over to meet Mazepa.

"Anastasiya, this is my friend Khabib. We played on these hills when we were boys, pretending to be soldiers,"

"Good afternoon," the man, Khabib, said rather formally and bowed, "I much prefer the version when we were children, it is not so much fun as an adult,"

"What happened to you?" Mazepa asked Khabib, flicking a look at Narimanov who appeared a touch embarrassed by the directness of the question to his pal.

"I fought in the First Chechen War and my leg was blown half to bits when we tried taking Dolinskoye," Khabib rapped his leg over his trousers which made a hollow sound, "I made it out alive so I'm thankful to Allah for that, a lot of my friends weren't so lucky,"

"And now we are about to go back to war with the Chechens," Narimanov said.

"Not about to, we are doing. Locals in the East are fighting the Islamists already and taking heavy losses. Abdulatip, my friend, where is the Russian army?"

"You know what the bureaucracy and logistics are like, the support will be there soon,"

"I'll tell you where they are. They are selling weapons to the people they are allegedly fighting," Khabib said, spit spilling out over his bottom lip down his chin.

"The Russians are selling weapons to the Chechens?"

"I was there when they did it, I drove for them last week and did some translation. Some rich businessman met with

Shamil Basayev near Khasavyurt and sold them all kinds of shit,"

"Who was he?" Mazepa said and Khabib turned his attention to her.

"I don't know who, nobody told me his name. He had a fucking platoon with him, a whole platoon. Can you believe it? I thought they were engaging with the enemy not selling them their guns,"

"I'm not sure we can write a story without a name,"

"I took some photos of the meeting. Do you want to see them?"

Mazepa didn't say anything and simply nodded. Mazepa and Narimanov moved nearer to Khabib as he pulled out a packet containing photos from the inside of his jacket pocket. He handed them to Mazepa who immediately recognised the businessman shaking hands with the head of the Chechen rebel government, Shamil Basayev.

"Isn't that Sasha Saratov? The guy who started that new bank in Moscow, Sarabank?" Mazepa said.

Narimanov didn't say anything but walked over the barrier with his head bowed.

"What's up?"

"He's a fucking traitor,"

"How do you know him?"

"He's paying my wage and…" Narimanov was struggling to say the words, "And he's underwriting half of the army's costs. He is good pals with the politicians in Moscow. And he's selling us out,"

"Never trust an oligarch," Mazepa said and snorted, "I've seen him at the hotel a few times,"

"You've probably seen him with me," Narimanov said.

"Can I take these photos?" Mazepa asked Khabib.

"Of course, I want you to bring down that treacherous rat. Are we all little pawns in his big chess game?"

Mazepa and Narimanov were unable to respond. Khabib was right, the private motivations of the powerful were demonstrably opposed to the goals of the state. Saratov was covering the costs of the war for the excellent PR and offsetting it by trading with the enemy. It was as depressing as it was predictable. In the Russia of the 1990s, if she made it public, she could have brought down Sasha Saratov.

Mazepa disembarked the train at Moorgate and headed towards the Barbican estate. She was astounded by the amount of construction work in the area. New offices were popping up all over and she wondered how many were funded by Saratov, one of the ten richest men in Europe, with all his English pawns and knights doing his bidding.

It had been a few years since she had last been here but she traversed the immense concrete estate with ease. Mazepa still felt uneasy and she looked behind her and saw only a couple holding hands and a woman with blonde hair walking with a backpack on. The girl was staring at her but didn't look away when Mazepa looked at her. No threats here but the size of this place meant you never know who is watching from one of the windows or through some foliage.

She entered the entrance of Shakespeare House and as always, swooned at the sleek, modernist look of it. She pressed the lift button and waited, rapping her fingers on the wall and checking the entrance to see if anyone followed her. No one did and the lift doors opened.

The lift shot up to the 23rd floor, the doors opened and Mazepa headed onto the cramped corridor. She jogged to Narimanov's apartment and pulled the spare key she had out of her bag and entered his place. It was amazing how spacious it was. From the outside, you see the hulking brutalist outer and you assume it would be tiny inside.

Narimanov had told her that she was the only person in the world who knew about this apartment and she hoped he was telling her the truth. Being in the apartment brought another bout of sudden heart-rending grief and Mazepa had to visit the bathroom where she dry-retched over the toilet bowl.

She rolled on to the bathroom floor and started to cry, pulling a towel off the rail to dry her eyes. She could smell his scent on the towel and she held it against her face for a long time until she had expelled all the tears she had.

Mazepa stood up and the crying actually seemed to have dissipated her torment and her mind was suddenly clear. She headed to the bedroom where she had spent many a wonderful evening with Narimanov. She pulled the large double bed away from the wall with little difficulty. She needed to pull up a floorboard but had to pop to the kitchen to grab a knife to do it.

After obtaining a large chopping knife, Mazepa returned to the bedroom and knelt down and pried at the boards. After some vigorous jabbing, she managed to pop the board out. She pulled out a small, burgundy jewellery box engraved with the eagle from the Dagestan coat of arms.

She opened up the box and pulled out the only contents, a key and electronic fob and was reminded of a Tolstoy quote: 'Rummaging in our souls, we often dig up something that ought to have lain there unnoticed'.

Mazepa stood up and placed the key and fob in her handbag and stared at the bed. She thought back to that evening in Gunib when Khabib had departed. Narimanov and Mazepa had watched the sun set over the town without speaking for a long time. As night fell over Dagestan, he took her back to the family home and they made love for the first time on a ramshackle bed in a house with no working electricity. It was perhaps the best night of her life.

20

London, England
Tuesday November 15 - 17:50 GMT

Simonsen peered out of the aeroplane window and saw a patchwork of fields below. Simonsen used to travel to London at regular intervals in his first few years at Interpol but it was probably over a decade since he last visited the city. An air hostess walked past collecting litter at the same point as the pilot advised they were beginning their descent. He noticed an English newspaper in the seat pocket of the man sitting next to him, dressed in a sharp suit with his eyes closed.

"May I take the paper please?" Simonsen spoke in English, gently nudging the man's arm.

"Sure," the man said and didn't bother opening his eyes. Simonsen lifted the newspaper and it was a copy of the *Journal* with a headline stating 'THE MINISTER, THE CANDIDATE & THE TYCOON' and a subtitle 'VISA SCANDAL ROCKS RUSSIA & UK'.

Simonsen scoured the article which went into detail about how the son of his boss Peter Kelsey-Moore had interfered in Sasha Saratov's application for a UK visa when he was the Immigration undersecretary. The copy of the letter was printed in full inside the newspaper. It was from Ian Kelsey-Moore, now appointed as Minister of State for Borders & Immigration to Maxim Golitsyn actually thanking him for recommending Saratov's visa.

The British opinion writers were scathing about Ian Kelsey-Moore's behaviour at a time when visa applications for Russian citizens had been frozen by the British following a strengthening of Magnitsky sanctions as relations between the countries refused to thaw despite the end of Putinism. Saratov's application was waved through in a week and also backdated enabling him to qualify for certain tax rebates.

Simonsen knew that the English press could be relentless in their character assassinations and they weren't holding back in this case. The editorial called the Moscow-born Ian Kelsey-Moore a traitor who should be stripped of his job and arrested. Another article said "his first language is Russian, and clearly also his allegiance," which was an astonishing thing for a British newspaper to say about a government minister.

Simonsen checked the window and they were now flying over London. His mind swirled as he tried, and failed, to pinpoint any landmarks. The IP address had been traced to Ian Kelsey-Moore's office and that's where he planned to head after a phone call to check in with the UK Interpol office. Simonsen thought they'll be secretly very happy with Ian Kelsey-Moore being investigated. Law enforcement officers hate nothing more than corrupt politicians.

The plane landed with zero issues and Simonsen waited until everyone had disembarked before following them off the plane. He had called ahead and was being expected by UK police, who would fast-track him through passport control. Simonsen felt a keen burst of joy as he was prioritised through customs by the border force.

After bypassing the crowds of passport-wielding members of the public, Simonsen arrived into the heaving Terminal 2 arrivals hall. It was very busy as the post-coronavirus travel boom showed no signs abating and Simonsen scoured the hall, looking for a sign to indicate where the taxis were.

He stopped in front of a map board and tried to forget about the loudmouth tourists filling the cavernous room with noise. Simonsen learned the rank was outside the terminal building and over the road. He began turning around when a young blonde woman knocked into him and grabbed his arm to stop herself from falling. She was fleetingly familiar and Simonsen was confused for a moment until she giggled and said "sorry" in English to him. People here are always apologising, even if they aren't at fault. Simonsen mumbled something and headed out of the airport terminal.

Simonsen entered the taxi at the front of the rank and asked the driver to take him to his hotel in the centre of the city. They were soon riding along the M4 above the suburbs of London and Simonsen made a couple of phone calls. He rang the Interpol UK bureau in Manchester as a courtesy. The Norwegians had already been in touch and there were no issues in Simonsen investigating in the UK on behalf of Kripos. The guy on the other end of the line even provided a direct, non-public line to the office of Ian Kelsey-Moore's personal parliamentary secretaries.

Simonsen called up the first number he held for the office and he was stonewalled by the switchboard operator so he then dialled the number provided by the Interpol agent. It rang about five or six times before being answered.

"Home Office, Borders & Immigration department, who is speaking please?" a very soft female voice spoke.

"Good evening, my name is Einar Simonsen, I am an investigating agent for Interpol in Norway,"

"Excuse me, sir," the woman interrupted, "We have had a very busy day here so we are not in the mood for foolish pranks, how did you obtain this number?"

"Like I said, I am an Interpol agent investigating a major incident which recently took place in Oslo and I would like to speak to members of your office as quickly as possible,"

"What incident?" the woman sounded frightened to Simonsen's but it may have been the softness of her voice making him think that.

"There was a bombing in Oslo of a café two evenings ago,"

"Oh yes, I saw that on the news. But what does that have to do with us?"

"Our inquiries indicate someone in the office may possess some knowledge that could help the investigation. I simply would like to come in tonight or tomorrow and have a chat with you all,"

"Oh, I see. We've had such a day, I've been in a constant tizzy. Please feel free to drop in tomorrow. Lunchtime is probably the best,"

"Will the Minister be there too?"

"I don't know, he left early today. I think he had a meeting with the Home Secretary. Do you want to speak to him too?" the woman said and Simonsen thought, damn right he'll be in a meeting with the Home Secretary after those newspaper articles.

"If he's there, it would be good to speak to him. I think he'd prefer to know about our investigation,"

"OK, Mr...?"

"Simonsen. Einar Simonsen. I am staying at the Park Plaza near Waterloo station so if you need to contact me, please feel free to leave a message at the front desk,"

The driver must have been overhearing the discussion and he piped up immediately after the phone call ended.

"Are you investigating the bombing?"

"Yes, I am,"

"It's bloody awful pal, it gives all us Muslims a bad name. I was reading about it earlier, fucking ISIS bastard,"

Simonsen didn't say anything as the taxi weaved through the deadening London streets, gloominess settling up around the Albert Hall. Rain was falling and with the greying skies, Simonsen could only think how miserable the city looked in this weather.

The taxi eventually arrived at the Park Plaza.

"Cash or card?"

"Card please but I need a receipt. Thanks," Simonsen entered his card in the reader and entered the PIN.

Simonsen exited the taxi and started to walk off to the hotel entrance when he heard a shout.

"Hey mate, don't forget your receipt," Simonsen spun around and the driver was waving a flimsy strip of paper.

"Oh, thank you," Simonsen said and plucked it out of the driver's hands who sped off within half a second.

Simonsen placed the receipt in his coat pocket when he noticed another receipt was in there. He was momentarily puzzled and he fished out the scraps from his jacket as he slowly made his way into the hotel foyer with the doors parting. A man in a business suit narrowly avoided bumping into him and he heard the man tut at him but Simonsen was in a world of his own.

His taxi receipt was the first thing he saw and he carefully placed it in his wallet, failing to smooth out the creases after he had shoved it in his coat pocket. The other snippet of paper was a note written on high quality paper and folded neatly in half. Simonsen had never seen this before and stared at it blankly for a few seconds. It comprised a name - Alex Deyneka - and a UK mobile telephone number.

Who was Alex Deyneka? For the second time today, he had the sensation that he already knew the answer. Simonsen checked into the hotel but his mind was elsewhere wondering where the note had come from.

Upon entering his pleasant room, Simonsen chucked his bag on top of the desk where the television and coffee machine were located and pulled out his mobile phone. He typed the name from the note into the search bar on his phone and the first result confirmed that he had seen the name before.

The story in the *Journal* about Maxim Golistyn and Ian Kelsey-Moore was co-written by Alex Deyneka. Simonsen continued scrolling through results when an article from another UK website contained a story with the headline: 'CANDIDATE'S SON PAINTS HIMSELF A NEW CAREER'.

The details of the story highlighted that his full name is Alexander Deyneka-Bolkonsky who moved to London about a decade ago. One article claimed that his mother walked out on Dimitri Bolkonsky because her husband had shunned their son due to him being homosexual. His mother appeared to be a bit of a publicity hound, there were a lot of stories about her, which mostly consisted of her slating her ex-husband, although nothing too recent.

Simonsen was no novice with regards to the shadowy world of Russian politics and he played around with the motives that people would have for pushing him in the direction of the candidate's son. Was Golitsyn trying to hint that Alex Deyneka knows something about the bombing, possibly as a punishment for his father rejecting him because of his sexuality? Or were the allies of Bolkonsky trying to obtain more dirt on Golitsyn and Saratov and a police investigation would aid their smear campaign?

Either way, Simonsen could see no reason not to speak to the author of the article that had inflamed Russia and the United Kingdom this morning. Simonsen poured himself a coffee and dialled the number from the note with a shiver of nervous excitement making his arms tingle with goose pimples.

There was no answer so he hung up and sent a text message stating his name and reason for calling. Simonsen stared out of his window sipping a sickly coffee concoction he had crafted. He could see the newly restored Big Ben, the symbol of British democracy, from his viewpoint it looked like it was rising directly out of the River Thames. Simonsen's phone rang and it was Alex Deyneka's number.

"Hello, is that Alex?" Simonsen said.

"It is Alex, how did you find this number? It's my personal one and only about ten people know it," the voice spoke in English with an unmistakable Russian accent.

"Someone planted a note in my pocket today. I have no idea who did it or when they did it but it seems to be the real number,"

"And you claim to be investigating the bombing in

Oslo?"

"Yes, I am investigating the bombing. I am an Interpol officer supporting the Norwegian police as I am a Russian speaker and some of the victims are Russian. Our enquiries have led us to London so I am following them up,"

"I thought you had caught the man who did it?"

"We have a suspect in custody but we are continuing with enquiries,"

"Into Sasha Saratov?"

"What makes you say that name?"

"My father thinks he was behind it. But he also thinks he is behind every bad thing that happens in Europe. He would blame Saratov for Russia not winning Eurovision,"

"But you don't believe he is responsible for the bombing?"

"I have no idea. My father thinks he is a monster. I think he is jealous of his success,"

"Can we make an appointment to discuss the case?"

"Why would I want to do that?"

"You could help solve a major crime?"

"I don't see how I could,"

"There's also something I need to tell you about your father but I would rather tell you face-to-face,"

"Nothing could shock me about him. You could tell me now,"

"Yes but it is very sensitive and you never know who is listening to these phones,"

"Now you are sounding like my father. I'm sorry but I doubt I will be able to meet you,"

"That is a shame Mr Deyneka, as I was hoping to pick your brains regarding a dossier about your father's nemesis, Mr Saratov,"

"A dossier?"

"Yes, we have intelligence that the bombing may be linked to a rumoured dossier about Mr Saratov, the Russian businessman," Simonsen said and there was a long pause on the other end of the line.

"I'll text you my address, you can pop round in the morning," Alex Deyneka said, and hung up the phone.

That went better than expected, Simonsen thought. Is Bolkonsky's son the author of the dossier? There was a good chance that was the case but why hadn't he released it if that was the case? Is he on his father's side or working against him?

21

Moscow, Russia
Tuesday November 15 - 20:32 MST

"...the airwaves and newspapers are filled with propaganda, with lies, with deceitful slurs designed to hurt me and my campaign. You are all aware of the other candidate, Dimitri Bolkonsky. You know him, he's the big, bad spy who spreads his tentacles of duplicity and fear throughout the media ecosystem. We have had enough of this environment of terror, it is time for a..."

"He is undoubtedly a colossal prick," Zakatov said. He was perched on the edge of the desk alongside Dimitri Bolkonsky in the Minister of Defence's office. They were both watching Maxim Golitsyn's speech on the television, precariously placed on a chair a few metres in front of them.

"It is astonishing how lies fall out of his mouth like shit out of a dog's arse," Bolkonsky looked at his acquaintance who nodded in return, "Listen to it, it's nonsense,"

"Have I done something I regret?" Golitsyn's speech continued on screen, "No? All I did was help one of our citizens during a time of fraught relations with our friends in Britain. I am sick of the poor bonds we have with our European neighbours. If I am elected, I will repair our connections with our nearest trading partners so our economy starts to boom.

"Sasha Saratov is one of the biggest employers in the country. Every single one of you will know someone who works for one of his companies and every single one of you will know that he pays vast amounts of taxes that fund public services, that employ nurses, police officers and teachers.

"My opponent sits in his gilded, palatial ministry over the river and he has the gall to accuse me of being elitist and out-of-touch. I have worked all my life and earned a fair living like all of you sat in front of me today. I have not sat in an office or a van with blacked-out windows spying on our own citizens, arresting people for having what he or his secretive friends deem the 'wrong' opinion.

"And I will not tolerate it anymore. He can instruct his son to write scurrilous stories about me, his son that he banished from Russia because he was ashamed of his lifestyle choices. Is this the man we want to lead the new Russia? A modern nation state reintegrated into the global system…

"Turn it off, Zakatov," Bolkonsky said, standing and pouring them both a vodka. Zakatov flicked the television off using the remote and gratefully received his glass.

"He knows he's losing, he looks flustered with that red face," Zakatov said.

"I agree. It's not a good look for him, he looks like a spoiled brat whose father has told him to shut up and go to bed,"

"What are the latest polls saying, Dimitri?"

"He's only dropped a point on average but the gap is pretty decent now. He will need a miracle now to beat me,"

"He's desperate. Keep your focus now, Dimitri. Let him snipe and rave, you've got the moral high ground now. The people want a man who won't crumble and cry on the TV because a naughty journalist wrote a bad story about him,"

Bolkonsky's mobile phone started ringing and he noticed it was Oksana Devina.

"Good evening, Oksana. Have you been watching Maxim's tantrum?"

"Yes I have, are you still watching the news?" Devina said.

"No, why?"

"There are riots in St Petersburg,"

"What? Ivan, turn that television on again," Bolkonsky yelled at Zakatov who immediately leaned over and turned on the television before resting his backside onto the desk again.

They watched as security forces clashed with protestors. A couple of youngsters were being repeatedly clubbed by riot police as their comrades tried to pull them to safety, taking a few hits themselves.

"Who the fuck are they?" Bolkonsky shouted into the phone.

"Students from the State University," Devina said, "They have gathered on three of the main bridges. I've had to permit OMON troops to intervene,"

"What are they rioting about? The needn't worry about Maxim Golitsyn, his goose is cooked,"

"They are sick of the tone of the debate, Dimitri. You need to appeal for calm or you won't have a country to run. There are smaller, similar incidents in Kaliningrad and Voronezh which we are monitoring but if you don't take a firm grasp of matters now..."

"Don't worry Oksana," Bolkonsky interrupted her, "I will make a speech tomorrow calling for unity, he's close to caving in,"

"That's all I ask for. You know how febrile the country has been over the last few years. Stability doesn't come solely from the application of brute force,"

"It's nearly over, I know it and you know it. By tomorrow, Golitsyn will know too,"

"We shall see, Dimitri," Devina said and ended the call.

Bolkonsky grinned at Zakatov.

"I'm sure she thinks Golitsyn still has a chance," Bolkonsky said, walking over to the television and muting the sound.

"Until the votes are cast, she's right. We can't be complacent, we need to ensure turnout is high. The higher the turnout, the better are your chances,"

Bolkonsky was watching the television footage of

rioters and police engaging in scuffles. Violence can be contagious and if there is one thing Russians can't abide, it is political instability.

"I know that, Ivan Vladimirovich. My head is clear. We are taking back Russia for the people. Once the people are convinced by that idea, we will storm the election. And once I am President, we can deal with our enemies in the most appropriate manner,"

22

After the toil of the day's exertions at the Barbican, Mazepa lay on her side in her bed clenching one of her pillows up to her chest. She stared at the message from her husband on her phone:

-        Heading to protest in town

This was something else to worry about. Mazepa was watching news footage on her laptop of street battles between students and police in St Petersburg. The loosening of the government's grip on the media over the last year or two meant that protests like this were being screened without filter to the whole nation. The police didn't seem to be aware of the impact the images could have on the populace. State-sanctioned brutality was no longer accepted yet the authorities appeared ignorant of the new reality.

A couple of young women were being hit with batons on their legs and screaming in pain. Another clip that was being shown repeatedly was a van of cops driving through a group of protesters near the Obukhov Bridge which caused multiple serious casualties. The live footage was showing huge numbers of people at Palace Square chanting and holding placards, although the police were sensibly allowing the people to gather and were not cracking skulls there.

Mazepa started to weep, her country was in turmoil and she was here in London, cowering away while Mikhail would be at the forefront of the protests. Her mind blazed with worries that someone was going to break in and kill her, or even worse, take the key she had obtained today.

Simply seeing Narimanov's flat today was a reminder of the rare evenings he would visit London and they would blot out the world and dedicate their time to each other. They would drink vodka and survey the London skyline as night would fall. Their time together would simultaneously last forever yet pass in no time.

She also was concerned that she had seen the blonde girl from outside Narimanov's place again on the tube ride back to her neighbourhood. Was she one of Saratov's goons? Or was she imagining that she was being followed? She could be offered a million pounds to head to the Barbican to obtain that key again and she would turn it down.

This was why she couldn't do this job anymore. Her time as a journalist was on the verge of being over. Once this election is over, it will definitely be time to retire and write some novels, or maybe a book on Russian history. Could she face returning to Russia? Probably not if people like Bolkonsky and Saratov and their wretched behaviour still dominated society.

Mazepa had only one person she could turn to in these times. Not many people had the telephone number of the woman who was supervising the Russian election and nominally their temporary Head of State but Mazepa and Oksana Devina went back years since their days at university together.

"Good evening Nastya," Devina's articulate, low St Petersburg accent was unmistakable.

"Oksana, thanks for answering," Mazepa said.

"Is everything OK?"

"I don't know, my head is all over the place. What is happening in Russia?"

"It's not as bad as it looks, a few isolated incidents but nothing we can't handle,"

"You sounded like a politician for a moment there," Mazepa said and both women laughed. Mazepa was unable to stop clutching the pillow to her breast.

"Things seem to have a habit of appearing in the press these days so it pays to be careful, even with my old dorm friends. How is London with all the press stuff about Golitsyn?"

"They are going in hard on him, I don't see how he survives this,"

"He has a lot of backing here in the cities. Muscovites favour him so if they turn out in big numbers he could snatch it,"

"Saratov will probably have paid half of them,"

"Most likely he has, I can't disagree with you on that point. If the towns and villages vote in big numbers, then Bolkonsky wil cruise it. Turn-out is the crucial factor but after two decades of rigged elections, no one has a clue if the polling is accurate. Oh, did you know Saratov's close pal has travelled to London today?"

"Who?"

"'The Vampire', Boris Ivanovich,"

"Boris Ivanovich?" Mazepa repeated, her voice strangulated. She sat up in the bed and pulled her knees up to her chest, squeezing the pillow even tighter to her body.

"Yes, he travelled over today into London,"

"Why would a Deputy Prime Minister travel here a few days before the election?" Mazepa said, trying to sound more like a proper journalist and not a scared little girl.

"That's something I would like to know too. Why would Saratov's old consigliere travel here unless something big was popping up?"

Mazepa felt blood and heat drain out of her body. She knew Boris Ivanovich was capable of limitless harm. She knew he had murdered enemies on the streets of Moscow with brazen disregard for the law. She also knew that he was the black hand behind Saratov's business dealings, blackmailing and threatening people into silence. Mazepa had first hand knowledge of this and it was something she would never be able to forget.

Was the woman who followed her earlier linked to him? And what about the break-in the other day? Mazepa's brow tingled and she knew she was sweating despite the apartment being chilly.

"Are you still there Nastya?" Devina whispered.

"Yes, I was thinking about what you said. Why would he come here? You know his reputation, maybe he was behind that bombing in Oslo,"

"I'm not sure. According to the immigration ministry, he hasn't left Russia since 2013 when Saratov appointed him the CEO of Sarabank,"

"He doesn't need to leave the country to sanction the bombing,"

"True. Some of the staff here in the Kremlin say that when he walks through a park, the grass dies beneath his feet,"

"That doesn't surprise me, you know he's a murderer,"

"You've told me that before. I don't remember you letting the police know about it,"

"I don't think I'd leave the station alive if I did that,"

Both women chuckled and Mazepa's blood slowly returned to her face.

"I'm coming back to Moscow," Mazepa said.

"Oh, that's great news,"

"Yes, I have an article to write for the *Journal* about the election, to give it a spin for the English readers,"

"I'm delighted you'll be here for such an historic occasion, we should meet up for dinner one evening,"

"Yes and hopefully I can grab a word for the article,"

"I'll refer all queries to my press office, I don't want to be misquoted. Sleep well, Nastya,"

"Good night, I'll speak to you soon,"

Mazepa left her bed and went to brush her teeth in the bathroom. The thought that Boris Ivanovich was in London freaked her out. Perhaps Alex was right about Saratov being behind the bombing of that café in Norway. Brushing her hair with one hand, she texted Alex with the other hand asking if he was OK.

She returned to bed and suddenly a wave of tiredness hit her. Her phone pinged and she looked at the message from Alex:

- I'm fine. I remember my old lecturer at uni said how could I live and have no story to tell? I've told my story now! Alex x

23

London, England
Wednesday November 16 - 09:53 GMT

Simonsen crossed Westminster Bridge and wondered if he had stepped into the middle of a film set. The view of the Palace of Westminster from the bridge was so iconic that it didn't feel real to him. Everyone else traversing the bridge at this time in the morning was also staring at Big Ben and the Houses of Parliament. It was like a beautiful woman in a bar, everyone would look at her whether they were male or female, hopeful lover or jealous rival.

The austere, almost Russian-looking facade of the MI5 building, the UK's domestic security service, could be seen on the left over another bridge. Simonsen pondered how much activity was going on there in response to recent events involving a British cabinet minister and his Russian friend. The morning newspapers were again eviscerating Ian Kelsey-Moore as they jumped on the bandwagon. Once you are under the wheels of the British media juggernaut, it's only a matter of time before your body is flung out as a chewed-up carcass.

The purchase of the venerable *Chronicle* newspaper a decade ago by Sasha Saratov had not gone down well with many people in the UK. Some of the articles Simonsen read this morning did not hold back from denouncing Saratov as a potential security risk and stating that the *Chronicle* should be seized from him. An hour earlier, a brick had been thrown through a window at the *Chronicle's* office in Kensington injuring a security guard who had the misfortune to take receipt of the flying brick square in the mouth.

The *Chronicle* was ignoring the Russian aspect of the story which was quite difficult considering it comprised more than a fair chunk of it. They were devoting pages to the corrupt British political class and the threat posed to the nation if Dimitri Bolkonsky was elected. Fanciful claims that he wanted to militarise the moon were almost beyond satire but some readers probably lap up this nonsense, Simonsen thought.

Simonsen reached the other side of the river but he didn't cross the road to enter Parliament. He intended to visit there later. Instead, he dipped down into the underground station and descended the escalator where giant metal tubes and metal sheets seemed to take up every available space making him feel like he was trapped inside an enormous washing machine.

He boarded the Circle Line train towards Kensington which chugged along the line for ten minutes before it arrived at Kensington High Street. Simonsen exited the station and the early morning sunshine had already given way to grey clouds and drops of rain. Delivery vans were racing along the compact high street and he wedged himself between a bin and a lamp-post so he could check his map on his mobile phone.

Foot traffic was as equally dense as the vehicular kind and it was slow going trying to overtake the gangs of well-dressed, pushchair-pushing mothers and doddering old people even on one bad leg. Simonsen continued along the high street becoming more and more puzzled at the off-kilter ratio between humans and pavement space which was also peppered with other street furniture such as rental-bikes and stands. This was not a city designed for the modern urban human who simply wants to walk down the street.

At long last, Simonsen turned right onto a pedestrianised street lined with pavement cafés amidst the alluring, corrupt heart of Londongrad. He ended up outside a park surrounded by beautiful townhouses of a type that you don't see in Oslo. How much ill-gotten wealth had been taken out of Russia and invested here, Simonsen wondered, and the British authorities had simply turned a blind eye to the origin of the funds for years and years until Putin had reinvaded Ukraine.

Simonsen reached Thackeray Street as the rain began thundering down despite the rays of sunshine piercing through the fossil-grey sky and hitting the buildings. He was looking forward to escaping the rain now and cursed the English weather stereotype that had turned out to be true on every single occasion he had been here. It was utterly impossible to dress for the weather in this bloody country as it changed three times a day.

He crept into the alcove where the apartment numbers were listed on a metal panel and hit the button for Alex Deyneka's flat but there was no response. He tried once more but again, there was no response. He didn't want to go back into the rain and find himself even more soaked so he texted the number asking where he was. After a minute or two of no response, Simonsen contemplated finding a café to dry off in when he saw the main door open. A coarse-faced old woman with hair covered in a see-through bonnet was about to leave the building.

"Yes, what do you want?" she asked, blocking the doorway and staring at Simonsen as though she was a duchess and he was a nineteenth-century ruffian asking for some money to buy some soup.

"Hello madam," Simonsen said, pulling out his Interpol identification. "I have an interview with somebody here but they are not answering their phone,"

"Well, that's not my problem. You will need to leave this building at once, it is residents-only,"

Simonsen reeled for a moment, who the hell did she think she was?

"Excuse me but if you do not let me in this building, I will consider that an obstruction of my investigation into a terrorist incident. I need to enter that building now and if possible, without causing a scene. If you proceed with this obstruction, you may be arrested by my Counter-Terrorism colleagues at the Metropolitan Police,"

The woman's face did not crack. She simply stood aside and held the door open for Simonsen who walked inside. Welcome to London, Simonsen thought. He headed up the stairs and after a bit of corridor-wandering, found the flat number he was looking for.

The door was ajar and Simonsen's policeman's senses tingled. He carefully pushed the door open with his jacketed elbow, trying not to make a sound. The hallway contained a well-used coat stand and shoe rack and the lights were on. Simonsen edged into the apartment and arrived at the door to the living room which led into an open plan kitchen. His fingers were tapping on invisible keys and he knew he should try and find a weapon to defend himself if necessary.

Nothing came to hand except a laptop so he picked it up anyway and made his way to the side of the kitchen area where a corridor led off it, also lit up. Simonsen moved along the corridor and arrived at the entrance of another fully lit room, hoping that he wouldn't have to whack someone with the laptop. He entered the bedroom and emitted an audible gasp.

Simonsen saw that on the bed was a bloodied, naked man bent over on his knees with arms flailed out and his half-turned head buried into a pillow. Simonsen had to turn away for a few seconds to compose himself, bending over and trying to calm his breathing. There was a dense stench of warm blood that made him feel sick. He stood erect again and saw that there was blood everywhere, especially around the man's genitals and anus and also where it appeared he had been handcuffed to the bed, his wrists had clearly been streaming with blood. The mattress was soaked in the dark substance too with some blood droplets on the cream carpet.

Simonsen moved to the side of the bed towards the body and saw the victim was a young man, his face frozen in shock. There was no visible trauma on the front of his body that he could see. On the drawer at the side of the bed was a glass half-full of a powdery pale substance, some pills and a small bottle of lube.

Simonsen assumed he was examining the body of Alex Deyneka-Bolkonsky. He searched on the internet browser on his phone and found images of the man which helped him confirm that the dead man was definitely the son of Dimitri Bolkonsky.

Shit, Simonsen thought, this was huge news. Once this becomes public knowledge, it is going to cause a massive shitstorm. His thoughts turned to who killed him. Behind the glass was a wallet emptied of cards and cash, leaving only a couple of photos of Alex with some friends at a bar and a supermarket loyalty card.

Simonsen was almost certain it was the work of Russians, most likely unhappy at the story he wrote about Maxim Golitsyn. The nature of the hit was either the work of amateurs in a hurry or professionals, who had set it up to deliberately appear rushed.

A few moments of analysis indicated it was the second option. The open door, every light on in the house, it was too convenient to be anything but a planned assassination. The staged nature of the body's pose showed that the killer or killers had time to set this up. The front door was left open on purpose, the body was meant to be found as quickly as possible, clearly to send a message.

Did the person who placed the note in Simonsen's pocket at the airport kill him?

He paused for a moment, thinking that he needed to see if there was any dossier inside the apartment. He opened the laptop that he still held in one hand and opened it up as he walked back into the kitchen. The screen was locked and Simonsen lacked the technical know-how to unlock it. He tried a few combinations but he soon gave up that course of attack.

Simonsen realised that the victim's father was the head of the Russian military spy service, the GRU. If anyone would know where to hide important things, it would be this guy. Hell, even Interpol agents had a few tips and tricks they would use. Simonsen headed to the bathroom first and started going through medicine bottles. Nothing came from that so he moved into the front room again and dismantled the backs of photo frames to no avail before reassembling them.

Simonsen scoured the kitchen drawers and again came up blank when his eye was caught by a pack of cards leaning on an empty bottle of vodka. Simonsen once received a note by that method in Dagestan when he was investigating reports that the Russian mafia was selling weapons to Islamists.

He lifted the pack up and opened it up, he allowed the cards to slip out and checked the inside of the case which came up with nothing. He flicked through the cards one by one when he noticed one of the cards had a touch more sheen than the others. He carefully scratched at the corner and he could see the card was in two parts, stuck together with an adhesive.

Simonsen pulled the two halves apart and a block of text was written in tiny handwriting. Most of it was written in English about the story he had broken about Ian Kelsey-Moore, but scribbled at the bottom was a new note in slightly bigger letters.

Mazepa may have a copy of the dossier about Saratov!

Email - abddocs@rosmail.ru

Is Mazepa a codeword? Something about the word clanked a bell in Simonsen's head but for the life of him, he couldn't think what it related to. Simonsen pocketed the card and realised he had to leave here as soon as possible as he had an appointment at Parliament. He telephoned the police and reported the murder.

24

Moscow, Russia
Wednesday November 16 - 13:41 MST

Bolkonsky could hear the rising tumult behind the curtain. He could sense the size of the crowd as if by some bizarre form of aural osmosis into his body. He wasn't sure if the human body could generate electricity but he was almost certain that if you plugged him into the grid, they would be able to power homes from Moscow to Vladivostok.

He snapped his head to the right in the direction of Zakatov and bellowed a sound of incomprehensible defiance. Zakatov was looking at his mobile phone. Even he is fucking obsessed with staring at his mobile phone, Bolkonsky thought. Zakatov looked up and locked eyes with Bolkonsky and he had the strangest face - strained and white. He had never seen him look like that before.

Bolkonsky couldn't worry about that now. He took a deep breath and raised his arms, the cue for the curtains to spread and the roar of the thousands of people packed into Red Square hit him like a nuclear bomb.

The sound was not something Bolkonsky had received before. He had struggled to achieve big crowds until today. This was raucous, loud and loving. Any tiny doubts he had harboured about his election run were now utterly vanquished.

Bolkonsky strode around the stage pumping his fists like he had scored the winning goal for Spartak in the last minute at the Luzhniki stadium. He raised his arm into the air thinking there were more people here than when Paul McCartney turned up. It was utterly intoxicating. In Bolkonsky's mind, the sight of the massed people with the domes of St Basil's as their backdrop indubitably conveyed that he was the right man; the Godly choice to lead the Russian people into a new era.

He gradually lowered his arms and approached the solemn, burgundy lectern embossed with a discreet Russian coat of arms. The crowd noise dimmed but it was still a lively atmosphere and Bolkonsky spent a few more seconds basking in the adulation.

"People of Russia, I am at your will. Grandmothers and grandparents, farmers, soldiers, teachers, factory workers, students and street cleaners. Thank you for your attendance here today, at what is the most important juncture in Russian history since the tragic end of Communism and the Soviet Union.

"The tragedy wasn't the demise of the Communist Party, who after years of failing to listen to the people, deservedly fell. But the tragedy is the loss of the firm ethical compass that our people shared with everyone else in the nation - from the dockers working in the ports of the far East, to the loggers and truckers crossing the forests of Siberia and to the factory workers toiling in the industrial heartlands of our country.

"But, my friends, our country is broken. It is broken in terms of our dilapidated infrastructure, it is broken in terms of struggling businesses and shops but most of all, it is broken due to the disgusting debasement of our moral values because of the actions of a tiny elite who have siphoned our money - no! What am I saying? They have siphoned your money away to London and Malta, to New York and Dubai.

"Mother Russia has been sacrificed at the altar of consumerism, moral depravity and obscene wealth. I tell you today that no more shall our elderly suffer with meagre pensions. No longer shall our children learn in rundown, freezing schools. No longer shall the Russian people work hard for little reward whilst rich embezzlers live in luxurious London mansions surrounded by servants off the back of your labour.

"The other candidate falsely claimed that I want a war with the West. He couldn't be more wrong. I don't want war with the West and I don't want another war with our Slavic cousins in Ukraine. But I do want a war with the oligarchs and bloodsuckers. That I will not deny.

"Once I am elected, I pledge to you a campaign of mass nationalisation of our assets. Oil companies, mineral mines and gas fields will be brought back into public hands. And not into the hands of a select group of greedy officials but into your hands. It is you who descend into the mines and quarries and dig out the coal so it is you who should reap its rewards.

"Peter the Great once said that nothing is too small for a great man. I would like to say that no Russian is too small for a great nation. It is time to end the tyranny of the billionaires. Destiny rides with us on election day! Long live our glorious Motherland, her liberty and her independence!"

25

Einar Simonsen sat facing the River Thames on a bench at Victoria Gardens in the shadow of the Palace of Westminster. He had solved the mystery of 'Mazepa' and was almost certain it referred to a journalist called Anastasiya Mazepa. She was a respected Russian journalist who was based in London, like Alex Deyneka-Bolkonsky.

He had placed a request with the Interpol office in Manchester asking for contact details for her and he was waiting on them to respond. It was a nice respite sitting by the river watching the world go by in the midst of the craziest investigation he'd even been involved with. His all-encompassing loneliness had been placed on the back-burner for the first time in years.

He was able to think about Mariya without descending into a pit of gloom. He thought about their time together and how they would waste days in bed together. At the time, he thought that it was wrong to take joy in such pleasures, the consequence of a dour Lutheran upbringing by his humourless parents. Now, Simonsen recognised those days as the most important and life-giving moments of his life.

Those days holed up with Mariya filled his soul with pure joy and the relationship was so important to him that Simonsen still struggled to comprehend that it only lasted a year of his life. In the grand scheme of things, it's barely a page in a book but for Simonsen it was the key tome of his life, in a similar way that the importance of the stories in the four gospels overwhelmingly outweigh the rest of the New Testament.

It had been so many years ago since he spent time with her that in many ways it didn't feel real. He had never been able to fill the cavity that was in his soul as he had never been able to pinpoint what it was until now. The hole in his soul wasn't so much the lack of Mariya but the absence of what she represented to him. Together, they exceeded the sum of their parts and that was the magical thing. Without, he was completely diminished. He had mourned her for over two decades but had never tried to heal the hurt caused by his loss.

Simonsen became aware of a man aged about forty wearing a grey, sports rain jacket watching him. The man was sitting on a bench about thirty metres to his right. He first noticed him in Kensington suspiciously close to the murder scene. He had also noticed an older man in a grotty bottle-green coat who had been following him as he made his way back into the centre of London. If this was the quality of Russian surveillance these days, he thought, no wonder the country is falling apart.

For the last twenty years, the thought of these people tracking his every movement would have sent him into a nervous despair. But Simonsen was working this investigation with a previously absent serenity. He was still terrified but he knew the people he was trying to catch were also living in fear. The serenity puzzled him but Simonsen was not going to argue.

Simonsen stood and stretched out his leg for a good two minutes, today's exercise had caused his knee to stiffen. He strode off towards the House of Parliament where Ian Kelsey-Moore's department had moved to last month following a fire at the Home Office HQ in Bermondsey. Simonsen didn't bother to check if he was being followed as it was a pretty safe assumption. It's unlikely they would enter parliament unless they had a guy on the inside.

After going through the process of obtaining a lanyard and security clearance, Simonsen was escorted to the relevant departmental office by a young girl barely out of school. They reached a door which the girl knocked on, and gestured to Simonsen to walk through.

As he entered a tall, blonde-haired woman in a tight cream blouse and red pencil skirt stood up to greet him. She was also very young and Simonsen wondered if a bunch of kids were running this country?

"Ah, Mr Simonsen," the woman said, giving him a perfunctory handshake, "We spoke yesterday on the telephone. Please take a seat,"

She pointed at the chair in front of her desk and sat down again. Simonsen sat and examined her face. She was trying to betray no emotion but the corner of her lipsticked mouth kept pulling away in a twitch.

"Thank you," Simonsen said, pulling out his notebook and pen.

"My name is Charlotte Hornsea-Reed, I am the Personal Parliamentary Secretary for the Minister of Borders and Immigration. We are so glad to be speaking to you and I've advised all the staff to give you as much time as you require,"

"That is very much appreciated," Simonsen said, "I hope my English is at an acceptable level for you all. Is the minister here today?"

"Oh, he was here earlier, I think he's attending a meeting at the moment across the city,"

"OK, that's no problem. What I would like to discuss is whether any staff members here have any connections to Norway or to Russia,"

"Can you clarify what you mean by 'connections'?" Hornsea-Reed said and Simonsen felt the cold diplomatic chill of the UK civil service blow around the room.

"Do any staff members have family linked to those countries or do they regularly visit there?"

"Obviously, I can't speak for all of the staff here Mr

Simonsen but I am not aware of anybody with 'connections' to those countries," she said, with Simonsen thinking the unspoken ending of that sentence was 'except for my boss'.

Hornsea-Reed's mouth suddenly dropped open as though Simonsen had rudely exposed himself in front of her. She stood up and ignored Simonsen as she walked around the desk.

"Minister, I wasn't expecting you back today," she said. Simonsen slowly turned around and saw Ian Kelsey-Moore holding his ministerial case. He was young and good-looking although visibly balding, a victim of inheriting his father's thin hair.

"Oh, I thought I am of more use here. You know, keep myself busy,"

"This is Mr Simonsen, he is an Interpol agent," Hornsea-Read said, directing the minister towards Simonsen who had stood up.

"Hello," Kelsey-Moore said, without offering a handshake.

"He is investigating the bombing in Oslo a few days ago," Hornsea-Reed added, her countenance angsty as if she was grassing up a schoolpal to a teacher.

"Oh right, I see. Why don't you come through to my office for a chat?"

"Sir, we have important ministerial business to attend to, do we honestly have time for this?"

Simonsen didn't say anything, Ian Kelsey-Moore made a noncommittal grunt and waved away the secretary and hooked a finger indicating Simonsen should follow him. They entered a white-walled office, with documents and folders piled high on the floor.

"Try to ignore the mess, we still haven't completed the move. In all honesty, it's a bit of a shitshow," the minister collapsed into his chair behind his desk and gestured to Simonsen to sit down opposite. Simonsen wasn't sure which shitshow Kelsey-Moore was referring to.

"I know this is a difficult time and I'll try not to take up too much of your time," Simonsen said and Kelsey-Moore laughed.

"You know what, Mr Simonsen? I think I may have quite a bit of time on my hands soon. I assume you have read the news today?"

"Yes, Minister. The press don't hold back over here, do they?"

"No, but we wouldn't want it any other way, would we?" Kelsey-Moore said, a stock answer from politicians in every democracy but his eyes told Simonsen the exact opposite, "What brings you over to London, my secretary said it relates to the bombing in Oslo the other day?"

"Yes, that's right. A couple of the victims were Russians so I have been drafted in to assist with the investigations as I can speak the language,"

"I think you went the wrong way. Russia is East of Norway," Kelsey-Moore said and laughed at his own joke, Simonsen smiled in reciprocation.

"That is true but we have reason to believe that someone in your office may have knowledge that could assist us,"

"If that is correct, it is indeed very troubling. Naturally, you are aware that I have links to Russia. In fact, I attended the British International School for a few years as a teenager thanks to my father working in Moscow and I worked in Moscow after graduating from Cambridge. But none of this is new information. It feels like I am being accused of being a Russian mole simply because I used to live there with absolutely no evidence to support it,"

"I have to ask about your connection to Maxim Golitsyn?"

"You have to ask? I thought you were investigating the bombing? If I'd known you were looking into the visa issue, I would have brought my solicitor," Kelsey-Moore laughed again and to Simonsen, it seemed genuine, "I don't have a relationship with Maxim, I've only met the man a couple of times,"

Simonsen thought that was a strange response considering there was a high chance he was about to be sacked and possibly face a criminal conviction for helping him.

"Can I ask why you helped him with the visa application for Sasha Saratov if you didn't know him that well?"

"Mr Saratov is a personal friend of my father's, I've known him since I was a young boy," Kelsey-Moore replied and Simonsen's mouth went dry. His boss was long-time friends with Saratov, no wonder that he wanted the investigation to stop. Kelsey-Moore was staring at him like he was amused by his reaction.

"Unlike the ravings of a few unhinged looney-left journalists and that barbarian running against Maxim, I can assure you Sasha Saratov is not the devil incarnate. He is a very successful businessman in Russia and also here in the UK. You know he owns one of our national newspapers, right?"

"Yes, I was reading his newspaper this morning, they don't appear to be big fans of Mr Bolkonsky either,"

"Freedom of the press is a wonderful thing," Kelsey-Moore said and he chuckled. Simonsen wondered if he was actually a little drunk which would explain his candour.

"Saratov's visa application had been stuck in limbo for years. When they appointed me as Minister, I investigated and there appeared to be no good reason why it wasn't given the thumbs-up. I didn't fast-track any application, all I did was give the green light to an application that had been awaiting processing for bloody years and now these press hounds..." Kelsey-Moore's voice tailed off before he said how he honestly felt about the British press.

"Do you know Abdulatip Narimanov?" Simonsen said as he became more sure that his interviewee was half-pissed.

"Never heard of him,"

"An email was sent to him from this office stating the location of a meeting in Oslo. The location was the Iskender

Café where the bombing took place. Can you tell me how it is possible for the email to be sent from this office?"

"I have no idea," Kelsey-Moore said and Simonsen held his gaze for a few seconds.

"Did you send the email as another favour for Sasha Saratov?"

Simonsen watched Kelsey-Moore shake his head, unable to utter a denial, tears visibly welling up in his eyes. Simonsen said nothing and allowed the silence to pressure Kelsey-Moore.

"The prince of darkness is a gentleman," Kelsey-Moore said with a rueful smile, "Now fuck off out of my office,"

26

Moscow, Russia
Wednesday November 16 - 15:09 MST

It didn't seem possible to Dimitri Bolkonsky but the noise at the end of the rally was even more rapturous. In fact, pockets of the crowd were bordering on mania. Bolkonsky thought that if he was a weaker man, he could have mistaken himself for a messiah.

He had always appreciated the sense of power which only increased as he rose through the GRU ranks. People had respected him and he had marshalled large groups of men but this was different. This was the kind of power that could change the world. It was scary on one hand but exhilarating on the other.

Bolkonsky bounded off stage and Colonel General Zakatov's face was ashen. Bolkonsky was irked that Zakatov was looking so bloody miserable after such a triumphant display. He was about to give him a quick bollocking when he saw Oksana Devina standing next to Zakatov. Why was she there? He was certain she couldn't be seen attending his rally, as it would appear that she was favouring him over Golitsyn. Hers was a delicate balancing act as she was the Prime Minister and head of the interim security council overseeing the election.

"Dimitri," Devina said, placing her hand gently across his left arm.

"Oksana, what are you doing here?" Bolkonsky said, alarmed at the pallid faces of his acquaintances. His exuberance was being swiftly replaced by dread.

"It's Alex," Devina said, slipping her hands around Bolkonsky's wrists, "He has been found dead at his apartment in London,"

Bolkonsky stood motionless, he didn't need Devina's grip to hold him steady. Zakatov began speaking but Devina cut him off with a look. Bolkonsky had the random notion pop into his head that she would be an excellent teacher or manager; she must have learnt these skills when she was at Harvard Business School.

"Dimitri, the police in London say he has been murdered. It's too early to jump to conclusions,"

"What?" Bolkonsky whispered, then he shook off Devina's grasp and raised his arms aloft and shouted:

"Don't jump to fucking conclusions? Are you utterly insane? A retarded Pole knows who is responsible and you tell me not to jump to conclusions?"

"News is creeping out, Dimitri," Zakatov spoke quickly and quietly, "The crowd is already scrapping with the police out there. Shops are being looted on Stoleshnikov Pereulok. I'm hearing a unit of FSB units are cracking your supporters' skulls across the south of the city. I've sent troops in to restore order,"

"You need to calm the situation, Dimitri," Devina said, once again trying to hold his arms but he batted her attempts away, "We can't have rival security services acting like paramilitaries on the streets of our cities, this isn't Syria,"

"Have you spoken to the rat?" Bolkonsky said, turning to face the wall with shoulders hunched, "Well?"

"I spoke to Maxim a few minutes ago,"

"Did he send best wishes?"

"We talked about de-escalating this conflict. It's in no one's interest for this to spill over into violence. The whole world is watching Russia, Dimitri. This is bigger than you two,"

Bolkonsky spun around and swiped his hand across a table filled with drinks and snacks. He dropped his hand full force into one of the tables which didn't crack which seemed to infuriate Bolkonsky even more. He lifted the table up and ran with it as though it was some postmodern take on a pole vault routine. He slammed the table through a window and it sailed towards the ground below where it landed with a thump and an accompanying shower of glass shards.

Zakatov ran over and grabbed Bolkonsky and attempted to hold him still. Bolkonsky's face was blood-red and his fists were tightly balled up. He shouted over the shoulder of his companion towards Devina, spittle flying from his mouth.

"Bigger than us, Oksana? Is my son's life worth the Presidency? Golitsyn and Saratov have gone too far this time,"

Devina walked over towards the two men who were in an uncomfortable embrace. She stroked Bolkonsky's cheek.

"Please Dimitri, if you go off the rails now, there will be no Russia to rule anyway. You can seek revenge after you win the election. They have done this solely for the purpose of making you lose your mind,"

Bolkonsky bobbed his head and Zakatov eased his grasp and stepped away pulling out his phone. Devina hugged Bolkonsky and stroked his cropped hair.

"I'm so sorry about your loss, Dimitri, he was a fine young man,"

"What would you do in my position? I know you wouldn't sit back and take this lying down,"

"Nobody knows anything yet. Our people are investigating but the British have locked it down and nothing is leaking. Their government will release information to suit their interests, not ours. Let's wait until the morning. I'll speak with Maxim again tonight but please don't inflame the situation today. Don't make any public remarks until you've spoken to me or Zakatov. OK?"

"I understand, Oksana. Thank you," Bolkonsky said, his arms hanging loosely by his side now as he slouched on the smashed window pane. Devina nodded and walked off, accompanied by her aides.

Zakatov walked towards the window where Bolkonsky

had lobbed out the table, he popped his head out of the window and took a look down outside. A crowd had gathered around the table that his friend had hurled out of the window. A few people pointed up towards the empty window frame. Zakatov pulled his head back in and held a gaze with Bolkonsky for a few seconds.

"It's a declaration of war," Bolkonsky said.

"Devina is right about not making any rash decisions,"

"It's a declaration of war, we both know it,"

"I agree. But the next steps are vital, we can't fuck this up,"

"The response needs to be proportionate,"

"Yes but it also requires pinpoint accuracy. They will be anticipating a counter attack so the plan needs to be solid," Zakatov squeezed Bolkonsky's shoulder and his old friend reciprocated.

"If Saratov thinks he will win this election for his pet toy, he is living in another world. I don't think he realises what I'm capable of,"

27

London, England
Wednesday November 16 - 16:32 GMT

Simonsen laid on his extremely comfy hotel bed and stared at the message he had received from his boss, Peter Kelsey-Moore.

-       Urgent, call me when you receive this!!

It didn't take a group of Nobel Prize-winning scientists to work out that Ian Kelsey-Moore had spoken to his father after their chat earlier in the afternoon. The government minister had all but confirmed that he sent the email to Narimanov confirming the meeting details which must have come directly from Sasha Saratov.

The implications of that were immense and he had already telephoned Benny Karlsson on his way back to the hotel to advise him of what Kelsey-Moore had told him. The realisation of how big this conspiracy was turning out to be was hard for his friend to hear. What the information didn't do was provide a context for the bombing. How would Alaoui know that the brother of his old commander would be in the café? The more the investigation progressed, the less likely it was that Alaoui was guilty therefore the more plausible explanation was that he was an innocent caught up in the midst of something much greater.

Simonsen had been expecting contact from his boss and he noticed that his hand was shaking as he held the mobile phone in front of his eyes. He scrolled to Peter Kelsey-

Moore's number in his phone and pressed 'Dial contact'. It was answered before the first ring.

"Yes, is that you Simonsen?" Kelsey-Moore's voice was a touch higher than normal.

"Yes sir, you asked me to phone you?" Simonsen said.

"I wanted to keep you updated on the case from our side. I spoke with Anita Bangoura at Kripos and we believe that a decision to charge Alaoui is imminent,"

"Oh really? What about his girlfriend and her story?" Simonsen was surprised that Kelsey-Moore was starting with such a bold lie.

"It seems she is a fantasist. You know how these oddballs come out of the woodwork during big investigations. There is nothing to corroborate her tall tales,"

"What about the photos of them as a couple?"

"Tall tales, tall tales. You know how easy it is to photoshop pictures to make them look how you want?"

Simonsen said nothing and allowed the silence to hang over the line.

"So, based on that information," Kelsey-Moore spoke again, "It is probably best that you return to Oslo as soon as possible. Your assistance is no longer required but I would like to pass on tremendous thanks from the top brass at your diligence and dedication to this matter,"

"Well sir, I have to say that there are still a few avenues to pursue. Naturally I will return as soon as my enquiries have concluded. Thank you for your support in this matter,"

Simonsen added the last line as a deliberate antagonism to his boss. He could almost hear his stiff upper lip curling up.

"Simonsen, I think you are misunderstanding what I said. Your time in London is up,"

"With respect sir, I am still under secondment by Investigating Inspector Karlsson and he is yet to inform me that my services are no longer required," Simonsen said and another long silence hung over the line.

"I see what you are trying to do, Simonsen. You think

tarnishing my son's reputation and trying to tie him up in this inquiry is fair game, do you?"

"There is no evidence to suggest your son is linked to the bombing, sir," Simonsen said and it was true. He was clearly involved in Narimanov's attendance at the meeting but obviously he had nothing to do with blowing up the café.

"Of course there isn't evidence, you stupid little man. Don't you realise that the act of simply questioning him, a British government Minister, is outrageous enough? And without legal representation too, Jesus. I know you're not as moronic as you make out. I know your game, I know there is despair at the heart of your soul. Well, let me tell you now Simonsen - not only is your time up in London, your time is up in Oslo too. You're done, Simonsen, you'll finish your time at Interpol in Belarus arresting dissidents on behalf of the government,"

"Sir, I believe I have adhered to every regulation as an Interpol agent. If you want to go down the route of attacking my professional integrity, I will be back in the office soon and we can discuss it then. If there is a disciplinary process to follow, I will gladly cooperate. As I said previously, I await contact from Benny Karlsson who is running the investigation,"

"I genuinely can't decipher whether you are a naive, idealistic idiot or a man with a death wish,"

"Why would I have a death wish?" Simonsen said and he could almost hear Kelsey-Moore spitting his derision at his remark.

"This is your last chance, Simonsen. Return home tonight or face the reality that you will be seen as a legitimate target by certain unsavoury actors. I won't be able to protect you if you proceed down this road,"

"Who would see me as a target? Your old pals in Russia?"

"You want me to say it out loud but I don't need to. If you make it out of England alive, I would recommend not setting foot in Norway again,"

Peter Kelsey-Moore hung up the line and Simonsen dropped his phone on the bed, turned his face into the pillow and screamed. He screamed until there was no breath left inside him and he flipped onto his back and stared at the ceiling, drenched in sweat.

The ultimatum was stark. Stop investigating or you die.

Simonsen picked his phone up again and saw there was a text message received during his bout of yelling.

-       Einar Simonsen, this is Sasha Saratov. I would like to meet with you for dinner this evening to discuss the incident in Oslo. I will be at Zhizhu at 8pm.

Simonsen held the phone and scowled at the message for what felt like hours but was probably only a few seconds. A phrase his mother used to say seemed very apt - *'Fra asken til ilden'*. From the ashes into the fire. Simonsen replied to the message:

-       Yes, I will see you there

28

London, England
Wednesday November 16 - 17:52 GMT

Mazepa woke up with her head full of violent dreams. She rarely dreamt but now her head was full of images of soldiers with chopped-off limbs and exploding buildings with the sounds of screaming children piercing her ears. The image of Khabib's sad face as he realised that the New Russia of the 1990s was defined by corruption, self-interest and treachery would not leave her mind.

She threw a look at the clock and she couldn't believe it was nearly six in the evening. She supposed that barely sleeping for the last three nights can make you pretty tired. This whole situation was crazy and every time she thought about catching a flight back to Russia, her stomach did somersaults.

Mazepa grabbed her mobile and saw she had thirty missed calls and the same amount of unread messages. Her stomach dropped and she hated herself for knowing it was going to be bad news. This was typical for a journalist when a terrible story was breaking, the messages would fly in. She opened the first message sent by Oskana Devina at midday:

\-   Alex has been murdered.

Mazepa arched her back and screeched, her neck muscles straining, a gutteral outpouring of terror and grief. She screamed and screamed until her energy had dissipated and she flopped back on to the bed.

"No, not Alex, not my friend," she said and started whimpering.

She read the other messages and a few more were from Devina stating that he had been killed last night, possibly by a lover. Mazepa was puzzled at this news as she knew Alex had no boyfriend and wasn't dating anyone. She would be one of the first people he would tell about a new beau.

First her lover had been killed, next it was the turn of her close friend. Mazepa was now certain that someone knew that she was closely linked to the dossier about Sasha Saratov. She was also certain that the person who knew this fact was Sasha Saratov and he had sent Boris Ivanovich to London to find out and deal with it. Did Alex give her identity up as the probable compiler of the dossier before he died?

Alex wasn't a hard man, he was a tender, sweet boy who was happiest hanging out with his pals and drinking in the bars of London. He was not the type of man who would withstand a brutal interrogation or even torture. She warned him about wedging himself into the machinations of the political class. Alex had no appreciation of the stakes of the power game. He had led a coddled life which in comparison to most Russians, was very easy.

When Mazepa analysed the power held by people like Sasha Saratov due to their extraordinary wealth, it was terrifying. Saratov is a man who, by virtue of his affluence, can own other human beings. People became enslaved under the cushion of regular cash payments and the underlying threat of extreme violence. Anyone who interferes in that is liable to be terminated, that is the brutal truth of an oligarchic society. A few powerful men exert their poisonous influence upon the world and everyone else has to live with the consequences of it.

Mazepa's flight to Moscow was due to leave at nine o'clock tomorrow morning. She called the airline to see if there was a flight back today but they informed her that it was already fully booked. A lot of people wanted to return for the election, whether to vote or simply to witness history of what should have been a peaceful transition of power.

Mazepa packed her bag anyway, placing the key and fob she had obtained at Abdulatip's apartment inside an empty pack of condoms and putting it at the bottom of the case. She started searching online for hotels near the airport where she could stay tonight if she didn't want to stay at her place. Fearing one or all of her devices may have been hacked, she booked hotels near Heathrow, Gatwick and London City airports on her mobile, laptop and desktop computer.

She was unable to remove the thought of Alex being murdered from her mind. He must have been terrified. One stupid decision to try and help his awful father and this was his reward. Does his father even care? Mazepa would bet money that his first instinct would be to maintain that the election was his number one priority and not his son's death.

Mazepa could vividly imagine Bolkonsky's reaction to his son's murder. The stories of his temper are legendary in political circles. She searched for clips of his speech from today on her laptop and he was conveying the exact amount of righteous fury without sounding too much like he would be ushering in a new era of pogroms and persecution.

She could see why people would vote for him. His indignation about corruption and the power of the oligarchs was sincere and people related to him. He genuinely looks like he worked in a tractor factory for a couple of decades. Mazepa could see why people liked Bolkonsky for his relatability, but in darker moments they would also appreciate the indignation and quick recourse to savagery whilst mounted upon a moral high horse.

The danger in electing a man who holds such binary views in a democracy is that a lot of people suddenly turn out to be 'anti-Russian' and the people experience déjà vu when the prisons fill up with political undesirables, the wealth concentrates at the top and the media is silenced.

Mazepa sent a reply to Oksana Devina confirming she would be heading to Russia in the next day or so. Within a few seconds, her phone started ringing:

"Nastya," Devina's voice came through as though she was sat right next to her, "I can't believe what has happened to Alex,"

"It's terrible. I feel partly responsible," Mazepa replied, "If I had been firmer with him, I could have persuaded him to pull the story,"

"Don't say that. He did it for his father, I'm not sure there was anything you could have done to stop him,"

"It angers me, Oksana. Why was he always seeking affirmation from his horrible dad, the fucking homophobe?"

"I don't know, maybe every boy wants their father to be proud of them. I'm not sure we are the ones to ask, neither of us have kids,"

"How has Bolkonsky taken the news?"

"Not great. I watched him throw a buffet table through a window earlier,"

"He's going to raise havoc,"

"Probably. Hopefully Zakatov will calm him down, he's done a good job so far in managing him through the campaign without exposing his more, how shall we say, draconian tendencies,"

"Zakatov is another GRU goon. They'll be plotting something,"

"Oh, I don't doubt that but the longer they hold off from acting, hopefully it won't be too substantial,"

"It makes me weep for Russia,"

"The Russians will survive, we always do but will the nation be diminished yet again in the eyes of the world? Whoever wins needs to show some statesmanship which is distinctly lacking,"

"Can't you do something to stop them acting like clowns?"

"I can only advise and manage the internal situation. I am doing my best to prevent this country from collapsing and I will do whatever it takes to do that. You have my word,

Nastya,"

"Any word on Boris Ivanovich?"

"Nothing, he has slipped off our radar completely,"

"I have a feeling he's coming after me, I can't shake it,"

"Why would he do that?" Devina said and Mazepa knew she couldn't allude to the dossier.

"I don't know. I met him years ago in Dagestan and he threatened me when I was going to write an article about him. Maybe he still bears a grudge,"

"I'm sure you'll be fine, he's a deputy Prime Minister now so he can't go around killing folk on foreign soil. I'll speak to you when you land in Russia. Stay safe, Nastya. Don't worry, I'll keep you from the wolves when you are back home,"

Her father would always say that if you're scared of wolves, don't go into the forest. Too late for that Dad, Mazepa thought, I am heading into the forest ready to be devoured, armed only with a key.

29

London, England
Wednesday November 16 - 19:53 GMT

Simonsen's earlier serenity had dissolved. It wasn't replaced by fear but by a form of otherworldliness in which it seemed everything was moving as if on rails. He was in the midst of a story that was being written and he had no control of the narrative. Simonsen was now a character in a novel and all he could do was buckle up and experience the disconcerting ride.

Simonsen had refrained from travelling by taxi and had walked to Soho from his hotel. No one would kill him on his way to meeting the most powerful man in Russia. Although with recent events, maybe they would. Simonsen weighed it up and thought that would be a shit way for his novel to end, shot dead in a gutter without finding out anything interesting or meeting Saratov, the enigmatic antagonist.

He arrived at Zhizhu, 'one of the capital city's finest Asian-inspired eateries' according to their website. A barrel-chested man of average height with a shaved head, who was clearly one of Saratov's goons, immediately approached him as he came through the entrance. Simonsen could tell he was the type of man capable of squashing your head with his bare hands. Simonsen called out a cheery "Hello!" in English and the man motioned with his head that he should follow him.

The shaven-headed man and Simonsen slalomed through the busy dining area before passing through a velvet burgundy curtain behind which a smaller dining room was located. There were about eight tables in this space but they were empty save for only one that was located in the middle of the room which had one person sitting at it.

Simonsen saw a man rise, signalling to him to sit down. He was probably the same height as the shaven-headed man with very closely cropped, greying hair and rimless glasses. He was dressed in a simple, well-tailored dark grey suit with a black shirt buttoned all the way to the top and no tie. His face conveyed neither friendliness nor hostility and Simonsen obliged him and sat down before he also sat back in his chair.

"Mr Simonsen, thank you for joining me this evening," the man said in English with a deep, pleasant voice with only a hint of a Russian accent, "My name is Alexander Saratov, my friends usually call me Sasha,"

"What does everyone else call you?" Simonsen said.

"I suppose it depends," Saratov turned his head to the side as though deeply pondering the question, "My enemies call me a pernicious influence on Russian politics. What do you think, Mr Simonsen?"

"I don't know enough about you or Russian politics to comment,"

"I think you are being too modest, I imagine there is a lot going on in that head of yours. I don't think you reach your rank at Interpol without being imbued with a good level of intuity and wisdom," Saratov's eyes penetrated Simonsen, uncomfortably so, "It's eight o'clock which is the time I eat every evening. I wasn't sure if you would turn up on time, so I took the liberty of ordering for you,"

As he spoke a couple of waiters turned up and laid plates of food down for the two of them. Simonsen wasn't entirely sure what was on the plate but it looked like something the Hobbits would have eaten in the Lord of the Rings films.

"Don't worry, Mr Simonsen. I haven't poisoned the food, I can assure you of that. It is tempura spring onions with an onion and garlic purée,"

Simonsen continued to poke his food with the fork and wasn't completely swayed by Saratov's assertions that he hadn't laced the food with some exotic toxin.

"I am a man of business and extraneous chit-chat is not my style. I will be direct in my language so please don't be offended. I ask that you treat me as an intelligent man, Mr Simonsen and not some *gopnik* from the streets. I appreciate honesty, and in return you will receive only candid responses,"

"Did you arrange the murder of Alex Deyneka-Bolkonsky?" Simonsen said, putting the elephant in the room squarely on their dining table.

"There is absolutely nothing to be gained for me, by murdering that young man here in London. Other people may have something to gain, but not me,"

"By saying that, are you not suggesting his father is responsible?"

"You are not a clown, Mr Simonsen. I can see that. It is reasonable for you to assume that is what I am insinuating. But what do you know of the relationship between Dimitri Bolkonsky and his son?"

"Very little,"

"Have you wondered why his son is living in London and not in Moscow?"

"I don't know. Maybe for the same reasons you are?"

Saratov laughed and it didn't suit him, thought Simonsen. He looked like a man who very rarely indulged in such a habit.

"Very good, very good," Saratov's merriment was over as soon as it began, "Dimitri Bolkonsky moved to London in 2004 and became the GRU station chief here. He brought his family over including his charming, down-to-earth wife with a mouth like a toilet and also his son who began enjoying the nightlife of London as any nineteen year old son of a government apparatchik would do.

"It was then that Bolkonsky began harbouring ambitions of a political career. He slowly and very successfully, stuck himself as far up Putin's arse as possible and within a few years he was recalled to Moscow to become the head of the GRU. He became the Colonel General with a place on the Security Council with his close pal Ivan Zakatov following closely behind.

"Unfortunately, his son had built a bit of a reputation for causing a scene in some of the city's unwholesome nightspots. So the Colonel General ordered his faggot son to stay in London when he came back to Moscow. His wife wasn't happy as she quite fancied becoming a rich Muscovite housewife spending her days spending her husband's salary. So she left him and stayed with the boy who delighted in allowing himself to act like whore with any African man he could pick up,"

"You don't approve of homosexuality?" Simonsen said.

"It's not that I don't approve, I simply don't care about any of that kind of thing. My father was a very pious Muslim man and I'm afraid certain prejudices may pass down the family line. I can only apologise if I have offended your liberal Scandinavian sensibilities,"

"I'm not sure how any of this relates to his murder,"

"You have asked if I am responsible for the boy's death. All I am suggesting is that his father was not happy with the prospect of his gay son coming back to Russia and jeopardising his chances during the most important week of his life. He is the most ruthless man I have ever met,"

Simonsen thought back to the videotape of Bolkonsky executing the Chechen rebels. There was no denying that Bolkonsky appeared to have a wicked streak of self-righteous brutality. Does that ruthlessness stretch to sanctioning the murder of his son? Could any father be so callous?

"Do you recall Pavel Zhyrgal from your time in Dagestan, Mr Simonsen?"

"Yes, I remember him. How do you know him?"

"Oh I was there at the same time as you, helping the war effort. I was born in Dagestan so preventing those terrorists from taking over was, how would you say…a personal mission for me,"

"You helped the war effort?"

"Indeed. You must remember the government in Moscow at the time? No money, no ideas and led by that clown, Yeltsin. I spoke with Putin who was one of the Deputy Prime Ministers at the time and I offered to subsidise a large portion of the costs for war,"

"In return for what?"

"I'm a patriot, Mr Simonsen. I have seen what fanatical religious beliefs do to people. Prayers don't put bread in the mouths of children,"

"Pardon my cynicism, but I can't believe you did that out of pure altruism. And what does that have to with Zhyrgal?" Simonsen said, his irritation at Saratov's soundbites growing by the second.

"He was rumoured to be involved with the Chechens trying to negotiate secret arm sales with certain high-ranking Russians,"

"Would a man named Bolkonsky be one of the 'high-ranking Russians' involved in that?" Simonsen said, unable to prevent a smile reaching his lips.

"I remember hearing gossip around the Hotel Leningrad that seemed to indicate he was up to no good. And of course, in Moscow it was common knowledge that he killed a lot of people investigating this type of corruption. Many of the journalists realised it was safer to give him a wide berth. It was a wild time back then wasn't it?"

Simonsen bowed his head and was momentarily transported to the hospital in Moscow, agonising pain in his legs and...

"Yes, you know the head of the GRU is Ivan Zakatov. He is Bolkonsky's right hand man. He was the man who gave the go ahead for some terrible shootings in Moscow twenty years ago. In the next day or two, I may even be able to obtain proof that Zakatov and Zhyrgal were behind the shooting of your girlfriend Mariya,"

Simonsen's composure began to desert him. Surely,

there is no evidence that Zakatov was behind the murder of Mariya? It was too good to be sure, this man is the modern equivalent of the ferryman on the River Styx. What would be the price for this information?

"How would you be able to find that evidence after all this time? I know there's video evidence of Bolkonsky's alleged war crimes," Simonsen said and it took all of his energy to keep his voice even, more so when he realised he was letting slip to Saratov about the existence of the massacre tape.

"Mr Simonsen, I am not sure if you are aware or not but there are rumours about the existence of a dossier about me containing all types of wild and inaccurate slurs," Saratov was staring at him and swirling his fork in circles in the air, "The person behind the dossier is hoping to negotiate a trade for information. By tomorrow, both myself and subsequently you, may be in possession of these files and the real truth will come out,"

"What is in the dossier?"

"Who knows? It is probably Dimitri Bolkonsky who is behind it all, or maybe Zakatov - he's the brains behind the throne. I believe that the meeting in Oslo was an attempt by Bolkonsky to obtain the dossier and use it to discredit me as part of his pathetic bid to become president. Have you heard anything that could implicate him in the terrible attack?"

"I can't discuss an ongoing investigation, as you well know. Isn't he the favourite to win the run-off?"

"No," Saratov batted an imaginary fly away with his hand, "Russians don't need another brainless ex-Commie thug in charge. The people are ready for a candidate who will engage with the world. It's time for Russia to come in from the cold. Unfortunately, military men like Bolkonsky and Zakatov believe brute force is the only way to win a battle.

"If you can help me in any way to retrieve this dossier, this litany of falsehoods, then I give you my word that when Golitsyn wins the election, Zakatov will be arrested for the death of Mariya,"

Each mention of her name stabbed him in the chest, reminding him what a waste it had been of a beautiful life. Saratov was offering him a quid pro quo but Simonsen had to keep telling himself that it was virtually certain to be a lie simply so Saratov could claim the dossier.

"It has certainly been an interesting evening Mr Saratov. And potentially, it could be the beginning of a fruitful relationship between the two of us,"

30

Moscow, Russia
Wednesday November 16 - 23:10 MST

Glass shattered and Bolkonsky woke up with a start. He realised that he had dropped his own vodka glass onto the hard wooden floor that he had been holding when he must have fallen asleep. His head pounded and his office was black, save for the city light casting a strange grey glow over a portion of the room.

He stood and was momentarily on the verge of falling when he put a hand out to steady himself, slicing his hand open on the jagged base of the glass. He lifted his hand up and saw blood seeping out of the wound and then put it to the back of his mind as he remembered his only son had been murdered less than twenty-four hours ago.

Bolkonsky picked up the bottle of vodka he had nearly finished off earlier in the evening and walked to the main window of his office and stared out at the river. The snow had begun to fall this afternoon but it wasn't at the stage where it would settle. The night was still but Bolkonsky's grief was pulsating through him.

Golitsyn and Saratov had gone to the ultimate length to try and disrupt his bid to become the nation's leader. To murder an innocent young man by virtue of his father was a low trick. Bolkonsky swigged straight from the vodka bottle between muttered obscenities about the killers.

What people do to gain power is insane, he thought. It troubled him because he was guilty of the same thing and knowing that, it made the grief unbearable. The all-consuming lust for power that energised him during the rally was still propelling him now, when he should be mourning his only son. How could that be the case?

In his low points during his political career, his mind would always drag him back to an empty warehouse in a shitty village in Dagestan and to the boy who he shot in the head.

"Do all Chechens boys fight?"

"I don't know, please don't kill me,"

The conversation, along with the smell of sweat and weaponry was etched perfectly in his mind. He could see the boy's face clearer than any memory of Alex and that only made everything worse.

The first night on the frontline had seen a huge escalation in violence in this sector after Bolkonsky's platoon had relieved the previous troops. Mortars were being fired at their positions they had taken at a ramshackle farm. Each time they attempted to counter the attacks, the enemy stepped up the ferocity of their own attacks. Their adversaries didn't try to advance and take their position at the farm, they were seemingly content to simply ground the Russians down in deep defence with a constant barrage of missiles.

Bolkonsky made repeated requests for air support on the radio and each time he was told that there were no planes available. His men were terrified, most were raw recruits who had been thrown in the deep end and were keeping their heads down, trying to find cover in the darkness and Bolkonsky didn't blame them. They had been thrown to the wolves by the top brass.

Bolkonsky heard shrill screams from behind the largest of the three barns, the top of which was now on fire. He crawled his way there and it took a few minutes for him to arrive as he waited until there were breaks in the barrage before moving. The back half of the barn had been blown to pieces and what was left of the roof was ablaze. He couldn't work out what angle the missile had come in from. They're hitting us from three fucking sides, he thought.

Bolkonsky pulled his body alongside the injured young private, a lad called Krushnikov. He had stopped screaming and was whimpering. His legs had been blown off and he was lying in a huge circle of blood. Bolkonsky held the boy's head in his lap and told him everything was going to be alright. He couldn't see the boy's eyes so he didn't know if he heard Bolkonsky speaking to him. Seconds later, he ceased breathing and Bolkonsky checked his pulse which confirmed the inevitable.

Bolkonsky picked up the private's rifle and started shooting in the direction he assumed the attack must have come from. He kept firing until the ammunition was exhausted. He unholstered his own gun and heard no further fire from the enemy. The sun was starting to peek out of the hills and it was the first time he could rest.

As light filled the valley, Bolkonsky was able to survey the damage. The surrounding land was devastated, the attacks on their position had been indiscriminate and mostly off-target. The surrounding hills were scorched and pock-marked. He was stunned that there was only one death apart from Krushnikov. A Junior Lieutenant who had been obliterated by a shell. They could only find out who it was that had died after taking roll call.

Bolkonsky pulled his advisor Narimanov to one side.

"It came from everywhere, we were like sitting ducks," Bolkonsky said.

"All the villages here must be under Chechen control," Narimanov said, "Why didn't they tell us yesterday?"

"Fucking hell, they don't know what's happening. I was told it was just that one village to the east. What is the name of the village there at the foot of the valley?" Bolkonsky was pointing to the area where he assumed the barn strike that killed Krushnikov had originated.

"That's Mekhelta or Tlyarata," Narimanov had pulled out a map for them both look at but only resulted in both of them realising they had no idea where they were attacked from, "Where was our air support?"

"God knows, this was supposed to be safe territory. I don't know why they didn't send in planes when I asked for it. This is bullshit,"

"Maybe they fired here in error,"

"Our troops have been in this spot for a week so they know we are Russian," Bolkonsky called over his captains, "Gather all the men, we are heading into Mekhelta,"

An hour later, Bolkonsky and his unit arrived in Mekhelta. He issued orders to pull every adult male out of their houses and put them in one of the Ural-4320 trucks they had arrived in. Bolkonsky's mind was blank as his men dragged out a collection of men from nearby houses.

At one house, a man was hauled out of his shabby stone cottage with his screaming wife holding on to one of his arms. Bolkonsky headed towards the woman and grabbed her by the throat and she immediately dropped her grip on her husband. He was taken by surprise by how light she was and as he pinned her up against a wall, he noticed a young lad running out of the house. The lad started whacking him on his arms which had virtually no impact on him.

"Take him as well," Bolkonsky ordered to no one in particular. One soldier grabbed the boy and gave him a couple of slaps around the head before dragging him away by the scruff of his t-shirt. His mother started wailing and Bolkonsky delivered a stinging punch to the side of her face and she fell unconscious to the floor.

Bolkonsky ordered half of his platoon to take the men to a warehouse they had passed earlier, near the entrance of the village. The other half were ordered to remain in place in Mekhelta with orders to shoot to kill anyone who they thought posed a threat. Bolkonsky reminded them that at this point everyone in this village was considered a threat and left the implication hanging in the air. Anyone who stepped out of their house would be at risk of being shot by his men.

Bolkonsky strode through the village enveloped in a fug of retribution. He could not stop thinking about Krushnikov dying in his arms last night and the urge to punish the locals pushed him forward towards the warehouse. It was baking hot on the streets but Bolkonsky's decision-making was ice cold. The men of this village had allowed rebels to base themselves here.

Bolkonsky entered the warehouse and was greeted by a few of his men who advised that the prisoners were waiting for him. He heard some men trying to speak to him but he shushed them with a downward arm movement. A row of ten people were kneeling down in the middle of the empty warehouse.

"So, these are the fuckers who ambushed us?" Bolkonsky said and no one responded. He knelt down next to one of the hooded suspects. Another of the hooded men started speaking and Bolkonsky turned around. One of his men ripped off the hood of the man and started shouting at him before moving away when he saw Bolkonsky looking at him.

Bolkonsky stood over the man and they locked eyes. The man looked at Bolkonsky with defiance. He wanted to smash the guy's face in for his temerity to meet his gaze.

"Your Allah won't save you now," Bolkonsky whispered to him, "You assumed your stupid God would protect you from the power of the Russian state?"

"What do you want to do with them?" Narimanov said.

"I will teach those Chechen fuckers a lesson in how to win a battle," Bolkonsky said. He unholstered his pistol and shot the man in the head. A dual sense of relief and power swept through his body. He was sure this was the justice for the men he had lost and a righteous punishment for traitors against the Russian state.

Bolkonsky took off the hoods of each man in turn and

killed them. He heard a voice of one of the prisoners and he took the hood off the boy who had been trying to attack him earlier. The father of the boy was next to him and he said something to his son.

"How old are you, boy?" Bolkonsky said, ignoring the father.

"I am twelve years old," the boy replied. He was crying and Bolkonsky understood that the lad was perplexed that his normal day had turned into this situation.

"Why are you fighting? Do all Chechens boys fight?" Bolkonsky said to the boy.

"I don't know, please don't kill me,"

Bolkonsky looked at the soldiers and he saw that they shared his anger. Every one of them was holding their weapons as though ready for combat and a wave of pride washed over him at the loyalty of his troops.

"If twelve year old boys are fighting, we can take no chances in this war. I've told you before. Treat every single Chechen male as an enemy combatant. They want us dead, that is their only wish. If you remember that, you will survive this war,"

Bolkonsky turned around back to face the young lad and he shot him in the face.

"Was that your son?" Bolkonsky said, moving his gaze to the father who was barely able to keep his composure. His shoulders convulsed but he said nothing. Bolkonsky watched as the man processed the death of his son before ending the man's misery and sending him to hell to join his son.

"Kill the rest of them," Bolkonsky said and Narimanov and a couple of other men blasted the remaining prisoners. Bolkonsky walked to Belanov who was holding the camera and demanded the tape. He called over Narimanov who was standing over the body of the villager he had killed.

"Hey, make some copies of this video," Bolkonsky said, handing the tape over, "Make copies and ensure everyone in this valley sees it. Warn them that any cooperation with the enemy will result in the exact same thing happening to them,"

"Understood," Narimanov walked off with the footage and Bolkonsky returned to the village centre to gather his troops and lead them deeper into the valley.

Bolkonsky killed the men and that boy in cold blood for what reason? Nothing that stands up to any scrutiny. He didn't even know if the villagers were guilty of anything. Perhaps they were storing arms for the rebels. Maybe they allowed them to fire shells from their village. He didn't even know for definite if any of the rocket fire from that night had come from that direction. The lack of military intelligence and air support were a sign of weakness of the army and he couldn't allow his own troops to be infected by the incompetence of those higher up the chain of command.

He had to kill them for the message it sent. It was a warning to not only the rebels, but to anyone who collaborated with them, that the Russians were not a walkover. A new generation was in charge now unscarred by the Afghanistani War embarrassment.

He did it so his troops would fear him, respect him and most importantly, kill for him. It sounds harsh but in a warzone, you need people willing to kill, and to die, for you.

That poor boy's face was frozen in time. Bolkonsky chose death for that little lad and the decisions he had taken during his adult life had now resulted in death for his own blood. His son was killed as a rebuke to his ambitions.

Zakatov had recommended avoiding instant retribution for Alex's murder but he agreed retribution was required. Bolkonsky wasn't sure he had ever seen his companion so irate as the more the news sank in, the more belligerent he became. Bolkonsky had told him to calm down whilst in the presence of Oksana Devina. The last thing he needed was for her to think he was a loose cannon and flip her loyalty to Golitsyn.

There would have to be a reckoning for Saratov and his puppet but it would need to be clever. Zakatov had agreed to put military units on standby outside the biggest cities in Russia ready to deal with civil strife or direct action from the KGB/FSB animals.

Bolkonsky had never played chess, he never had the patience or the brains for it but he knew his next move would have to leave his opponent in checkmate.

31

London, England
Wednesday November 16 - 21:47 GMT

Simonsen took a long shower after arriving back at the hotel following his meeting with Saratov but it wasn't enough to feel clean. Being in the man's presence for an hour was enough for him to believe his body was now tainted with iniquity and conspiracy, a fetid spirit tainting everything in its sphere. A menace that was gradually spreading across Europe fuelled by blood money.

Simonsen found himself enraptured during his conversations with Saratov. He had a remarkable ability to tell you what you wanted to hear and simultaneously convey absolutely nothing. Was it a mistake to allude to the existence of the tape? Most likely it was and with a man like Saratov, he will be intent on finding the evidence as soon as possible. With the election days away, he would be intent on obtaining that at any cost.

Saratov was portrayed almost as a cartoonish bogeyman in the media in the UK where genuine fear of him wasn't as pronounced as it was in Russia. Since he had returned to his hotel, Simonsen had been reading articles about journalists in his homeland who had disappeared soon after publishing defamatory stories about Saratov.

He was a shadow operating his own dark regime beyond the range of the law and societal norms. Yet there was virtually zero hard evidence against the man. Everything was circumstantial, in fact you could probably make a decent case that a lot of the claims were blood libels against a dedicated businessman. But Simonsen was not as naive as that. There may be a lot of violence in Russia but there was always a reason, no matter how debased or ridiculous it was.

The tape of the massacre was now a burden and he was unprotected. When he analysed the situation, he had nothing over Saratov. He didn't have any evidence of crimes against Saratov, only mild suspicion based on his link with Ian Kelsey-Moore. The mention of Mariya had weakened him, causing him to let slip about the tape.

He could assume that Saratov knew where he was staying considering how easily he had obtained his mobile number. It would take very little effort for some of his thugs to break into his room now and retrieve the tape. They wouldn't even need to kill him. Simonsen had told nobody about the burden at the bottom of his case. He knew couldn't stay in his hotel room tonight.

Simonsen dried himself off and dressed in jeans and a black shirt. He had received no response from his voicemail or texts to Anastasiya Mazepa. He was heading back to Oslo in the morning and he had to see her tonight without fail and tell her about the existence of the tape. He put on his thick winter coat even though the weather in England was much too warm to warrant it. However, he could stash the VHS tape in the inside pocket with ease and it wouldn't be noticeable.

He left the hotel room and another shot of pain went through his knee. He had done a lot of walking in the last couple of days but the occasional bouts of pain still shocked him when they struck. He half-walked/half-stroked his knee as he made his way along the corridor. If someone was watching him, they would think he had superglued his hand to his leg.

He descended in the lift and much like after leaving Narimanov's hotel room in Oslo a couple of days ago, he was on high alert. He hobbled the short distance into Waterloo station and it took him barely twenty seconds to spot the old man who had been tailing him outside parliament earlier today. Saratov hadn't mentioned Anastasiya Mazepa during his conversation with Saratov so he had to arrive at hers without being followed.

He entered the station and descended the escalators before walking to the end of the platform so he could see if anyone was approaching. The platform became increasingly busy with drunken Brits heading out for the night and tourists heading back to their hotels. He couldn't see the old man anymore and he was thankful when the train arrived.

Simonsen took a few moments to check his map as he had chosen not to travel west towards Kensington and south to reach Battersea. He planned to travel on the overground past Vauxhall to Queenstown Road where he would be within walking distance of Mazepa's place.

He scanned the train and multiple groups of lads were drinking cans of lager despite the alcohol ban on the public transport in London that he remembered from his last visit here. A man sat down and caught his attention in a manner he couldn't describe. Simonsen's first thought was that it was his policeman's sixth sense transmitting an urgent bulletin to him. He scrutinised the profile of the man who was sitting down on one of the seats that backed onto the windows.

The man had receding dark brown hair and a large hawk nose. His mouth was concealed by a huge beard like he was the reincarnation of Rasputin. And that's when the realisation hit him straight in the gut causing him to violently exhale.

Simonsen was adamant that the man was Boris Ivanovich. He was the fixer for Sasha Saratov back in the late nineties and had now somehow wangled his way to becoming a deputy prime minister in Russia. In Dagestan, he had witnessed Ivanovich doing something unspeakably barbaric to a man in a meat chiller.

The screams of his victim now echoed through his memory and Simonsen felt the same hopeless fear that he had back then when Ivanovich spotted him and asked him how his investigation was proceeding whilst holding a cleaver dripping in flesh blood. Was this maniac going to recognise him after so much time? Of course he was, it was not a coincidence that he was on the same train as him.

Simonsen didn't want to stare and bring attention to himself but he was hypnotised at the thought that Ivanovich was on the same train as him. The voice over the tannoy announced the next station would be Vauxhall. Simonsen couldn't peel his eyes away from Ivanovich, a man hewn from abject darkness who always seemed to be lurking in the background when he lived in Russia. He was sitting motionless, looking ahead out of the window.

The doors opened on the train and Ivanovich spun his head round and stared directly at Simonsen. Simonsen gasped and his chest constricted. Simonsen's decision-making process crumbled and he stumbled off the train, displaying the appearance similar to that of half the drunkards also disembarking the train.

Simonsen grabbed a barrier and tried to descend the stairs out of the station. Each step was difficult due to his knee pain flaring up along with him struggling for breath. Simonsen turned around and saw Ivanovich following him down the stairs. Simonsen was wheezing as he exited the station.

He knocked into a group of camp men standing outside the station entrance who started loudly berating him. Simonsen couldn't understand a word they were saying, his hearing was muddy and he hoped this wasn't the onset of a heart attack. He edged backwards keeping an eye on the station exit when his foot slipped off the pavement and he felt a solid thud from a moving vehicle that jolted and planted him on the floor.

Pain ripped through his left side, he lifted his head and saw that the contact was from a taxi which had struck him firmly on the hip. Simonsen rose to his feet, powered by adrenalin and started shambling off over the road. The pain was excruciating but Simonsen moved at a pace that he hadn't in years, heading off down a street lined by little terraced houses.

He quickly turned his head around and saw Ivanovich marching about thirty metres behind him like a fucking bearded Terminator. Simonsen swore and tried to gather his thoughts but with the lack of oxygen, it was proving difficult. At least his hearing was back to normal and he could hear the buzz of a large crowd.

He followed the sound and a couple of minutes later he saw a stadium up ahead. There was an event on and Simonsen walked through the open gate and then through an unmanned turnstile where he arrived at what appeared to be a sporting event crossed with a carnival. There was a cricket match taking place on the round pitch and a party atmosphere on the terraces as the fans were on their feet singing and dancing. He wondered why they were playing cricket at this time of year.

As chants of "Eng-er-land" rang around the ground, Simonsen weaved his way around the seats. He dared not turn around lest he catch sight of Ivanovich. Every glimpse of that man removed a litre of oxygen from his lungs. Simonsen slowly made his way through the crowds to the front of the stands where a huge conga line of people of all hues weaved its way along the front.

Simonsen joined the conga line as it snaked around the front of the terraces before exiting and turning right where he saw a huge sign advertising this was the Oval stadium. He stopped before departing and rotated around. He couldn't see Ivanovich but he knew he wouldn't be the only one following him.

His eyes moved to the action on the pitch where he watched a man dressed in blue hit a huge shot out of the stadium. The noise from the crowd was ear-shredding and he saw the players celebrating on the pitch. The fans were manic now and some began to leave the stadium so he joined the throng.

Outside the stadium, the streets were quickly filling up

with people heading home or to the pubs. Simonsen spotted a taxi and he tried to increase his pace but the pain coursing through his lower half prevented him reaching the taxi before a group of young women.

The girls entered the taxi and Simonsen took a moment to consider his options before entering it as well.

"What the fuck are you doing, you dickhead?" a skinny dark-haired girl in a replica England football shirt yelled at him.

"Please, I am injured. Can you take me a little further and I will get out?" Simonsen said.

"You cheeky bastard, we've already paid for this," another girl said.

Simonsen stayed in the car hoping they would cave in but a third girl started batting at his arm shouting "Get out!". Simonsen stepped out of the car in a writhing agony. He bent over to catch his breath and looked up and saw Boris Ivanovich walking towards him from barely twenty metres away.

"Fuck," Simonsen said. He turned around and kept limping forward. The sounds of Caribbean instruments and singing only added to the bizarre situation. Simonsen was dragging his left leg now and he saw a bus parked at a bus stop. Please don't drive off yet, he thought. The bus didn't drive off and Simonsen jumped on the bus and it pulled away within seconds of Ivanovich reaching the doors. The two men locked eyes for the first time in more than twenty years. Simonsen saw nothing in the eyes of Boris Ivanovich, no anger or frustration, simply a void of humanity.

The bus trundled off and Simonsen walked to the back of the bus and couldn't see Ivanovich amongst the blizzard of people that were now exiting the stadium. Simonsen finally relaxed and he disembarked in Clapham before catching a taxi to Battersea Park. He easily found Mazepa's apartment and almost started crying as he pressed the buzzer. There was no response after twenty seconds so he pressed it again. Eventually, he heard a crackle on the speaker.

"Hello?" a female voice said.

"Hello, is that Anastasiya Mazepa?" he said in a hoarse, trembling voice.

"Who is calling?"

"My name is Einar Simonsen, I am an Interpol agent and I need to speak to you about the Saratov dossier,"

Silence. Then the door zizzed and Simonsen entered the apartment block.

32

London, England
Thursday November 17 - 00:01 GMT

Mazepa peered through the spyhole of her apartment and the man she assumed had spoken to her on the intercom entered her view. He was running his hands across his face. He didn't have the appearance of a hitman, more that of a dishevelled accountant whose contract was recently terminated by his employer after they uncovered that he was implicated in a massive pension fraud.

Did he have an accomplice? She didn't know but something about the man indicated he wasn't here to kill her. In any case, her lawyer would pass details of the dossier to Oksana Devina in case she was murdered so she opened the door and allowed the man to enter. He almost fell into her apartment and made some off-putting wheezing sounds as he did so.

"Thank you for letting me in," the man said as he sat on her sofa with a huff.

"No problem," Mazepa replied. He looked terrible, sweat had matted his light hair to his red face, his jacket was too big for the time of year and he smelt like a musty dog, "What did you say your name was again?"

"Simonsen," the man said and reached out a hand and Mazepa shook it and could feel grime on her hands. She must have pulled her face as Simonsen looked at her slightly abashed.

"Do you have any painkillers? I was run over earlier

tonight," the man said, with eyes closed.

"Yes, I'll bring you some," Mazepa entered her kitchen without trying to think about who ran over this strange man and pulled out some high-strength tablets and a big glass of water which she brought back to the man. He guzzled six pills and drank the whole glass of water.

"Six pills, you'll sleep well tonight," she said, lifting up the glass to take back into the kitchen.

"I'm not sure I will but thank you for this," the man replied, grimacing. "I didn't think I was going to escape him,"

"Escape from who?"

"A man called Boris Ivanovich," Simonsen said and Mazepa stepped back and dropped the glass on the floor, shattering it.

"Is he near here?" Mazepa said, her voice tremulous as she stared towards the front door.

"No, I managed to shake him off near a cricket stadium a few kilometres away. No-one followed me here, I'm sure of it,"

Mazepa brought out a dustpan and brush and cleared the glass off the floor. She thought again about the quote about the grass dying after Ivanovich stepped on it. That man was a vacuum of devilry.

"I heard he was in London," Mazepa said, "I was hoping it wasn't true,"

"I've not seen him in a long time. I hoped I never would see him again,"

"What was he doing? Was he trying to kill you?"

"I assume so, he chased me across the city tonight, with a manic look in his eyes. Fucking hell, I was terrified,"

"Why would he want to kill you?"

"I'm investigating the bombing of the café in Oslo on Sunday night with my colleagues from the Norwegian police. I received a message from Sasha Saratov to join him for dinner this evening. So, I met up with him and he told me Dimitri Bolkonsky was responsible for the bombing and for killing his own son,"

"Oh, my Alex," Mazepa said and grief unexpectedly swept back into her heart, "His father is a violent moron but he wouldn't have murdered his son,"

"I discovered your friend's body this morning," Simonsen said, repeatedly rubbing his injured hip, "It looked staged. Are tomorrow's newspapers out yet?"

Mazepa pulled out her laptop and opened up the *Chronicle* front page on the browser. The two of them sat huddled next to each other and read the main story on Saratov's newspaper website.

"Have you read that? The lying bastards," Mazepa was switching between English and Russian which she would do at moments of great excitement or anxiety.

The headline was 'BOLKONSKY SON MURDERED BY RENT BOY' - the story claimed that Alex Deyneka-Bolkonsky was murdered in a lurid drug-fuelled sex romp. Mazepa was disgusted at the story. She opened up the web pages of other English newspapers which led with similar articles.

She moved onto the Russian press websites and the Saratov-owned media were even more brutal with their lies and slurs.

"His father is going to explode," Mazepa said, her grief morphing into trepidation.

"Mission accomplished for Saratov and Golitsyn, in that case," Simonsen said and Mazepa threw him an angry look.

"He was a young man who wasn't involved in Russian politics,"

"He probably shouldn't have wrote that story then, because that involved him in Russian politics,"

"Why on earth were you there?" Mazepa said, wondering who on earth this stinking Norwegian grim reaper was sitting next to her.

"I received a tip off that he would know something, I called him up yesterday and agreed to visit him this morning,"

"I still can't wrap my head around the fact he has been murdered,"

Mazepa stared at Simonsen and examined his face, his lips were chapped, stern and unmoving but his blue eyes told a story all by themselves.

"It's such a fucking waste, it turns my stomach inside out thinking about it," Mazepa said.

"His death may help us solve the bombing and we may be able to prevent more deaths," Simonsen said.

"Do you honestly believe that?" Mazepa glared at him and she could read his eyes, a readable script of cynicism but with an underlying sense of goodness.

"I found your name at his house, he had hidden it in a deck of cards along with a password,"

"It doesn't make sense to write my name down, everyone knows we are good friends,"

"The note said you may have information about the Saratov dossier,"

Mazepa laughed and Simonsen looked confused. Isn't that what this is all about, she thought, obtain the dossier and bring down Saratov? Is there any hunt for justice for Alex, a young man murdered to pursue political ambitions?

"What is the password for?" Mazepa said.

"I have no idea. I thought you may know?" Simonsen shrugged.

"It could be his personal email address, he used to tell me that if he died prematurely, to delete all the porn from his computer. Let me try it out,"

Mazepa picked the laptop up and placed it on her lap. Simonsen leaned over and she almost gagged on the pungent odour he was lathered in. Mazepa tried not to make it obvious and concentrated on entering the password correctly.

"Wow, it worked," Mazepa said and for a moment, they both sat there blankly. Eventually, Mazepa began manoeuvring through the inboxes. There were a lot of emails to and from colleagues at the paper but nothing of real interest. Especially nothing that could bring down a government.

"Hmm, try the junk folder. It says there is an email in

there," Simonsen said.

Mazepa opened the junk folder and there was an email from an address made up of a jumble of letters received twenty-four hours ago. The title of the email stated "Smoking Gun" and contained only scanned images.

"What is it? A screenshot of a visa?" Simonsen said as they opened up what looked like a UK visa document for a woman named Svetlana Popovskaya.

"Yes it is, it looks like mine after I applied for one. Let's scroll to the next page," Mazepa moved her fingers on the trackpad and a screenshot of a web page popped up.

"And what's that?" Simonsen said.

"Don't be coy, Mister," Mazepa replied, "It's an escort listing from a website. Is it the same girl from the photo?"

They flicked back and forth between the solemn passport photo and the raunchy images from the website. Mazepa was pretty sure it was the same girl. She kept scrolling and they saw another three Russian girls and their respective escort listing pages on screen.

"I thought your friend was gay? Keep going," Simonsen said and moved his own grubby finger onto the trackpad, smearing it with grimy sweat.

A letter on Russian government headed paper popped on screen.

"Oh," Simonsen said and Mazepa chuckled and shook her head, "Is that genuine?"

Mazepa opened her hands in a non-committal gesture and read the letter from Maxim Golitsyn asking the UK government minister Ian Kelsey-Moore to fast-track four visas for Russian students, their names all matching the ones on the passports.

Mazepa cackled and couldn't stop, laying back on the sofa holding her belly. A blessed relief after such a terrible day. Simonsen moved through more documentary evidence.

"Hey, look," Simonsen said, grabbing Mazepa's arm, "Someone has hacked the escort website and found emails to the girls from Golitsyn's government email address,"

"He used his ministerial email to book four hookers?" Mazepa said and laughed hard again.

"If it is genuine," Simonsen was rubbing his chin, "We have his campaign in our hands,"

33

"Do you have a VHS tape player?" Simonsen said, finally taking off his coat. He noticed how much he smelt of sweat and grew self-conscious. The woman, Anastasiya Mazepa, was attractive in the intimidating way that tall, confident women with a good education can often be, where he found himself unnerved and feeling stupid and clumsy around her.

"I do, I used to use it quite a lot with my work. I will need to dig it out. You smell pretty bad. Do you want to take a shower?"

"Yes please," Simonsen laughed and appreciated the Russian directness from Mazepa. Simonsen was guided to the shower room and he gladly took possession of a towel. The shower was packed with power and he was instantly refreshed.

The documents they had seen blew his mind. How often do you ever see evidence like this crop up? Was Alex killed to prevent this coming out? Quite likely, and Simonsen didn't like himself for thinking it but if he was in Golitsyn's position, the logic of murdering Alex Deyneka-Bolkonsky was hard to argue with. This *kompromat* would be lethal for his campaign.

He dried himself off and heard Mazepa shout that she had left out a spare t-shirt he could wear. It was a tight fit but better than his grimy shirt and underpants which he chucked in the bin. After putting on his trousers he headed back to the front room where Mazepa had hooked up the VCR.

"I have a tape that proves that Dimitri Bolkonsky

committed a war crime in Dagestan in 1999," Simonsen said.

"In ninety-nine? That was when I had a meeting with him. I was the one to inform him about Saratov selling weapons to the enemy,"

"I met him at the same time. He didn't name him when we met up but now it makes sense. So it was Saratov who sold the weapons to the Chechens? Saratov told me earlier that it was Bolkonsky,"

"Well, he would say that wouldn't he?"

"Bolkonsky said he would give me the proof to convict an oligarch but he never did. He said the guy was close to the government. At the time, I didn't believe one of them had betrayed Russia, especially when Bolkonsky couldn't supply the evidence,"

"Promises didn't count for much in that environment," Mazepa said, picking up the remote control and throwing it to Simonsen.

"It looks like both candidates have a lot to hide. This video is tough viewing, I have to warn you,"

"I'm an investigative journalist, not a virgin princess, Simonsen. Show it to me,"

Simonsen placed the tape in the recorder, switched to the correct channel, rewound it back to the start and played it.

They watched the video in silence. Simonsen was already struggling to focus on the screen knowing what was about to occur. The video reached the point where Bolkonsky shot the young boy and Simonsen and Mazepa both flinched.

"Jesus," Mazepa said, her eyes fixed on the carnage.

"I know, it's bad," Simonsen replied.

The tape carried on and Simonsen realised he hadn't watched the full tape. He saw an old face appear on screen. Abdulatip Narimanov was dressed in dusty military fatigues and was holding a Mosin-Nagant rifle. Narimanov's face betrayed no emotion as he put the gun to the head of another prisoner and pulled the trigger. The man's head exploded and flecks of blood spattered onto the camera lens.

"No!" Mazepa shouted, and began wailing on the couch.

"I'm sorry you saw that, it was very graphic," Simonsen said as Bolkonsky and Narimanov finished off the remaining prisoners. Bolkonsky began giving a speech on the Russian character as Simonsen turned off the tape.

"It's not that. It's…" Mazepa trailed off and Simonsen was puzzled by the strength of her reaction.

"Did you know Narimanov?" Simonsen asked.

"Yes, in Dagestan, he was my fixer and driver. He was… a good man,"

Simonsen rubbed Mazepa's back as she sobbed with her head encased in her hands.

"Yes, I always liked him,"

"He wouldn't have done that, he wasn't capable of that,"

"Men are capable of anything on a battlefield,"

"It wasn't on a fucking battlefield, was it? It's in a bloody warehouse. How old was that boy?"

"I don't know. Barely a teenager,"

"Where did you find that tape?"

"Narimanov told me where to find it. I spoke to him on his deathbed,"

"I'm sorry? I thought he died in the explosion?"

"No, he was taken to hospital and I spoke to him. I fell asleep in the chair by his bed but when I woke up, the doctors said he had died,"

"You spoke to him and then he died? How does that happen? Why the fuck are you always there when people die?" Mazepa said, her eyes blazing and wide.

"I don't know, I don't know. The doctors said it was probably an internal injury. I'm still awaiting the coroner's report, "

"Sounds like bullshit to me. But why would he tell you about the tape? It doesn't make sense in publicising the fact he shot dead prisoners in cold blood,"

"Before I returned to Moscow, I spoke with him after my case fell apart and Bolkonsky's claim turned to dust. He held my face in those giant paws and said 'There are things I cannot discuss with you. Remember, you can never trust anyone in Russia,'"

"He's probably right," Mazepa said, and she appeared to much calmer, "I'm Russian and I've felt that way for a long time,"

"Perhaps it was guilt, that by allowing this tape into the public domain, we could prevent Bolkonsky becoming President,"

"That sounds like a good reason for Bolkonsky to arrange bombing the café to me. If Bolkonsky could destroy that tape and find out where the dossier is, then there would be nothing to stop him,"

Simonsen nodded and was even more confused. The more time went on, both candidates were outing themselves as irredeemable amoral thugs who would quite easily have blown up a café or killed a journalist to protect their own reputations.

"He was the first person to mention the dossier about Saratov," Simonsen said.

"If the dossier exists," Mazepa said.

"Saratov himself mentioned it too, this evening,"

"Does Saratov know about me?"

"Not that I am aware of,"

"What makes you think I am linked to the dossier?"

"I'm an Interpol agent, all the evidence points that you know something about it,"

Simonsen studied Mazepa through the exchange and she tried to strike an inscrutably insouciant pose but he wasn't buying it. He didn't know to what extent she was involved with the dossier, but he was certain she had some part in it.

"How long did you live in Russia?" Mazepa said. Simonsen acknowledged the change of subject with a wry smile.

"I moved there in ninety-seven. I only planned to stay a year but I met a woman and I decided to stay,"

"Who was she?"

"Her name was Mariya," Simonsen spoke quietly, "She had recently graduated and started working for a bank in Moscow. Things were great and I went off to Dagestan thinking I could unravel a weapons-trafficking conspiracy. I failed to do that and not long after, she was killed,"

Mazepa nodded. Simonsen hesitated but carried on:

"We were eating breakfast at a café near the Bolshoi Theatre, you know where I mean? It was a normal day, the sun was out and life was going OK. Then, a car pulled up, the windows wound down and machine gun shots were fired at me. I was hit in the knee and I collapsed off the chair. I looked at Mariya and saw her on the floor too, holding her chest trying to stop the blood.

"The doctors managed to stabilise her but she was hooked up to a machine for months. She never regained consciousness or showed any signs of improvement so in the end her father and I agreed to turn the machines off. I had spent every day there with her but there was nothing I could do. And in a moment, everything turned black. She was gone,"

Mazepa's head was bowed.

"They were targeting you?" she said.

"Yes, I was investigating organised crime at the time and I was an easy target. Naivety, idealism, call it what you will but at that age you don't even contemplate death,"

"That is terrible,"

"I stayed in Moscow for seven more years but I was living like a zombie. Eventually I moved back to Oslo and for the life of me, I can barely remember anything from the last twenty years. Every day is the same,"

"A part of you died then too," Mazepa said. Simonsen thought it was the sort of line that a journalist would write in a story about Mariya. Wrong and right in equal amounts. It wasn't that a part of Simonsen died that day, it was that he discovered the fragility of life at the worst possible time.

"What should we do with the Golitsyn documents?"

Mazepa said and Simonsen stood up and stretched his legs.

"Print them, write a story. Do what you do. I'm too far in this now to back away,"

"What about the tape? I'll make a copy and we can decide later what to do,"

"I am returning to Oslo in the morning. I'll take the original and you can make as many copies as you want. We still need to see if the bomber that we have in custody is the man who actually did commit the crime,"

"I am going to write the story now, my flight to Moscow is early too. Are you coming to Moscow?"

"I don't know," Simonsen said. He would head back to Oslo and hope his time on this case was over. If Bolkonsky was to be exposed as a war criminal, that would be the end of his campaign. Saratov would be content that his candidate would win the vote and should call off his dog Ivanovich from murdering him.

Simonsen went to the spare bedroom and had an inkling that the dossier must be in Moscow. His thoughts about what was in the dossier began turning murky and he could feel the bullet fly into his leg and the pain course through his body. All he could see in his mind's eyes was the beautiful, uncomprehending face of Mariya as she lay on the pavement and that same face day after day in the hospital.

Why the fuck are you always there when people die?

Simonsen wished he knew the answer.

34

Mazepa sat at the seat nearest to the airport gate for her flight with her laptop open. She wasn't typing or browsing but she was using it as a proxy shield against malign forces. The flight to Moscow was delayed by an hour and she was succumbing to the belief that the delay was planned by Saratov or Bolkonsky. Perhaps Maxim Golitsyn had written one of his official missives on government-headed paper to Heathrow Airport asking them to hold the flight until the meddlesome journalist had been apprehended.

She re-read her open email, addressed to the editors of most of the major English newspapers, her finger ready to press "Send". It contained all of the information she had discovered with the help of Simonsen, the Interpol spook who had turned up at her place like the dishevelled uncle no one wants to speak to at a funeral.

She feared seeing Boris Ivanovich so much it was twisting her stomach muscles. Constant cramps passed through her lower belly and not for the first time this week, she was transported back in time to the end of the Dagestan conflict and the last occasion she had been up close and personal with him.

Russia was victorious after a brief, harsh offensive and the cessation of hostilities provoked celebrations at the Hotel Leningrad. Cigar smoke and singing crackled through the air as the generals basked in the glory of war. Bottles of vodka were being passed around and the politicians were revelling in the success of their troops and boasting to the journalists of their role in the triumph, no matter how minor or false their claims happened to be.

Most of the journalists were ecstatic to be returning North, back to the civilised world and out of the wretched Caucasus. Mazepa had mixed feelings. She wanted to return to her life in Moscow, to visit friends and galleries and not live in the fear that terrorists would fire rockets at the hotel.

Yet she didn't want to be parted from Narimanov, their bond had grown strong but he had been away for a week with only the occasional message left at the front desk being her sole contact. She stayed at the hotel after the celebrations and most of the other journalists had returned home. Mazepa remained to interview locals about the area for a book she had conceived about Dagestani culture.

Dagestan had seized her heart in unexpected ways, the friendliness and hospitality of the locals caught up in yet another warzone. Every time Narimanov and Mazepa ventured to remote villages, they would be taken in by the locals and fed and put up for the night, if required.

A week after the end of the war, most of the journalists and other hangers-on had departed. She was sitting at the hotel bar one evening, cycling through the photos of Saratov's arms sale to the Chechens. She was amazed that Saratov felt so comfortable at bringing a platoon of soldiers with him to back him up as he sold arms to the people they were fighting against. What must the soldiers have thought about that? They probably didn't have a clue what was going on.

Out of nowhere, two men pulled up chairs to her table without asking her permission. Her stomach lurched when she saw it was Sasha Saratov and his fearsome deputy, Boris Ivanovich.

"Anastasiya Mazepa, the doyenne of war correspondents, please allow me to introduce myself," Saratov said, his voice forceful yet balanced. His rimless glasses gave him the air of an intellectual but the eyes behind the lenses were dark and probing.

"I know who you are, you're a traitor," Mazepa said, with an unusually strident tone. The brazen perfidy of the man had rumbled some untapped source of patriotism inside her.

"Those photos," Boris Ivanovich said, his voice rasping through his immense beard, "They need to be destroyed,"

"You're too late. I have made copies. They are in Moscow by now," Mazepa said, struggling to hold the gaze of Ivanovich, whose own eyes burned with hatred. When this was allied with his constantly flaring nostrils, he gave off the impression of a man capable of violence at the minutest provocation.

"No, you don't. The man who supplied them to you said there were no negatives and we have kept a close watch on you. We know you haven't made copies,"

"What man?"

"A man named Khabib," Saratov said, "He provided us with information before his untimely death,"

Mazepa's throat tightened and she didn't dare say anything. They can't have murdered Khabib, Mazepa thought, please, it can't be true.

"You can't print those photos," Saratov continued, "As it would present a national security dilemma for the government in these challenging times. The last thing the people want to read about after a decisive military victory are the petty conspiracy theories of a publicity-seeking journalist,"

"They are proof that you betrayed our country," Mazepa said, fists clenching under the table at the audacity of this man trying to tell her not to do her job.

"Keep your voice down," Ivanovich snarled at her. His nostrils flaring to an even greater extent than before and he bore the appearance of a wild animal rather than a human being. A fear grew inside her, a genuine foreboding of serious harm caused by this psychopath next to her. It took an immense effort to keep her emotions in check.

"I will be printing these when I return to Moscow tomorrow, if you would like to make a comment, I would be pleased to place you both on the record," Mazepa said.

Ivanovich growled and Saratov laid a placating arm across his companion's chest without taking his eyes off Mazepa.

"Yes, you could attempt to print those photos," Saratov opened a briefcase and pulled out some photos of his own, flinging them across the table, "But we would then be compelled to send these to your husband and your friends and to all of your prospective employers at Russia's most prestigious newspaper offices and television studios,"

Mazepa picked up the photos and she saw that she was the subject of the images. They were photos of Narimanov and her engaging in lovemaking from her hotel room. Mazepa's world teetered on the brink of collapse and she had to hold the table to steady herself. How the hell did they take these photos?

"You went full native, didn't you?" Ivanovich said, "You fucking slut. Cheating on your husband with a big hairy Muslim gorilla. It's not the done thing amongst the liberal scum who go to the posh restaurants in Tsentralny is it?"

"What would your illustrious husband say? What poetic words would Mikhail Mazepa use to paint the disgusting betrayal that his breathtaking and lustful young wife had perpetrated?" Saratov arched an eye towards Mazepa.

Mazepa could say nothing and all she could do was hand over the photos to Saratov. He forced her to hand over her room key and Ivanovich visited her room to remove any other potential evidence of wrongdoing by his boss. Mazepa remained seated in the hotel bar for hours, for the first time in her life believing she was a failure.

For Mazepa, that incident in Dagestan was almost like being stabbed in the heart. What Saratov didn't know at the time was that Khabib had stuck to his principles even when being tortured by Ivanovich. He had lied about the negatives which were in the possession of Narimanov who would later print the photos for her to place in the dossier. Saratov's vanity meant he couldn't countenance that someone could outsmart him, especially a poor, crippled soldier.

Mazepa glanced at the clock on the Heathrow departures board which was ticking towards 8am. And then she saw him. Boris Ivanovich was walking along the terminal towards her gate, towards her. Mazepa hovered her finger over the button on her laptop to send the email.

Ivanovich strode to within five metres of her, his intense bearded face causing her insides to slush about. He stared directly down into her eyes making her blood run cold and Mazepa faced the sudden stark realisation that her life was about to end.

But her life didn't end. He maintained eye contact for as long as he could without looking foolish and sat down about ten metres away from her. Mazepa was trapped, she couldn't leave now. She would be trapped on the plane and trapped once she landed in Russia.

Her finger was still a millimetre away from sending the email. She looked down at the screen and paused. She had not been murdered at Gate 4 by Boris Ivanovich, so she held off from sending the email. After what she saw on the tape in the early hours of the morning, the thought of Dimitri Bolkonsky becoming Russian president made her queasy and conflicted.

Simonsen had said men are capable of anything on the battlefield and she couldn't shift the words from her mind. She knew Narimanov was no angel, but for a man as kind and considerate as him to willingly engage in the massacre of civilians, it astounded her. What prompted him to fire a bullet into the head of an unarmed man? There were multiple soldiers there who were presumably itching to do the same but instead he was consumed by the urge to commit cold-blooded murder. Mazepa thought about the amount of times they had made love after that and she had to push out the thought or she would lose her mind.

The battlefield was now the Russian electorate. Golitsyn was guilty of organising visas for prostitutes. If this was the worst thing he had done, he would still have the cleanest hands of any post-Communist leader in Russia. He was undoubtedly sleazy, vain and corrupt, but Mazepa couldn't imagine him picking up a gun and blowing a child's brains out.

Fundamentally, releasing the tape that Narimanov had held for over two decades would torpedo Bolkonsky's campaign. The motive was there for Bolkonsky to arrange the bombing in Oslo. He had connections to murky people who would not shy away from the act. Zhyrgal was an ex-GRU grunt and it was logical that he would send him to obtain the tape no matter the cost. Perhaps he was caught up in the explosion by accident? Or was the bombing plan B in case Narimanov refused to hand it over?

The call to board was heard around the airport gate, prompting shuffling and barging to board the aircraft. Mazepa slammed her laptop shut, jumped up and was at the front of the queue ready to show her ticket and passport. She bent her neck around and saw Ivanovich sitting down vacantly staring at nothing. Mazepa passed her documents to the air hostess who checked and returned them to her. Mazepa walked along the air bridge on the aircraft and prepared to return home.

35

Moscow, Russia
Thursday November 17 - 11:29 MST

Dimitri Bolkonsky sat frozen at his desk in his Defence Ministry office. Staff who normally walked on eggshells around him, were now tiptoeing on air. He had not slept during the night and had spent half the time in the early hours on the phone to his ex-wife who used the majority of that time to scream down the phone at him, blaming him for Alex's death.

He hadn't admitted any responsibility to his former wife for what happened to their son. In the end, he hung up the telephone on her during the middle of one of her obscene rants. As the morning wore on, the sympathetic faces from the female staff and the avoidance of eye contact from the men ground him down. Bolkonsky wasn't generally the type to drink much, never mind to excess. He preferred to keep his mind clear but he had already drunk a couple of straight vodkas this morning to try and keep his emotions on an even keel.

The first one he drank was seconds after he read the headlines of the newspapers in the morning. The staff had tried hiding the papers from him, claiming they hadn't been delivered yet. It took a mighty bollocking for them to hand them over so he could see exactly who wrote what. After reading the headlines and gulping down a large vodka, he compiled a list of the names of every journalist who cast a dirty aspersion or wrote a complete libel against him or his son.

Lurid tales spewed from the pages about his only son. The Saratov-owned papers had gone to town claiming his son was raped and killed by a Ukrainian rent boy, another one said Alex had hosted an orgy where he had taken drugs with some American soldiers, one of whom later murdered him.

The story that got to him the most was in a paper not linked to any of Saratov's publications but was situated in the usually independent Moscow Today. Their front page was a purported exclusive stating Bolkonsky had arranged for his son's death because he was ashamed of his lifestyle and that this was the prelude to removing civil liberties for vulnerable and minority groups if he was to be elected.

One thing was for sure, Bolkonsky thought, the journalist who wrote that article would certainly find life very difficult in his new Russia. If a free press means carte blanche to write spurious lies, then they should be prepared to face the repercussions of that freedom.

Bolkonsky read all of the newspaper articles about his son. Alongside the names of the journalists he had jotted in his notepad, he also added the names of the editors of each publication. Stalin said you cannot make a revolution with silk gloves and Bolkonsky was intent on using this maxim to craft a new country, built on integrity, hard work and a zero tolerance for the media when they spouted their despicable falsehoods.

One of his assistants, a useless lump of flesh called Zuzana, entered his office with a bouquet of flowers as he read a text message from Zakatov asking what he planned to do now.

"Sir, these arrived moments ago, shall I place them in a vase?" Zuzana gingerly edged towards Bolkonsky, as though she was keeping her distance partly out of fear that he would whack her round the face or that his grief was contagious.

"No. Give them here to me," Bolkonsky stuck out a hand and grabbed the bouquet from her, and she stood there like a fool, "What are you waiting for? Piss off,"

She fled the office like an Olympic sprinter. Fucking idiots, Bolkonsky thought, I hope the staff at the Kremlin are more competent than these clowns. The first thing he intended to do after he won the election would be to revamp the entrance exams for civil service applicants. The people working to run the country should be the best that the nation can offer and not a bunch of slack-jawed dunces and power-hungry braindeads.

The bouquet was a mix of black and white flowers, Bolkonsky had no idea what type of flowers they were. There was a note nestled in the bouquet written in neat hand-writing which he read out loud.

Death does not take the old but the ripe. Thinking of you at this difficult time - Alexander 'Sasha' Saratov.

Rage. An unfiltered, abominable rage filled Bolkonsky. He screamed at the uppermost volume possible and flipped his desk over, office equipment flying off in multiple directions, the mayhem bringing no catharsis. His primeval utterances caused a couple of guards to enter his office.

"Get out now!" he hollered at them and they quickly scarpered. He lifted up the hefty chair behind his desk and hurled it through the window of the office, the sound of screams could be heard amongst the smatterings of glass raining onto the pavement.

"That fucking piece of shit," Bolkonsky whispered and as quickly as the rage had erupted, he was becalmed within seconds. He called Ivan Zakatov's number.

"Ivan," Bolkonsky said, "It is time for action,"

"At last," Zakatov replied, a happy tinge to his words, "What are your plans?"

"We are going to hit Saratov hard and big. I demand maximum shock and awe. I want that cockroach screaming for mercy by tomorrow night,"

"It's about time we fucked over that piece of shit. Sir, the power of the GRU is available to you and we will follow your orders to the death,"

"I'm proud of you Ivan Vladimirovich, you are a loyal patriot of the motherland. This will not be forgotten by me,"

"Dimitri, I have received word that the private airfield Saratov usually flies into is expecting a private jet from London. It's scheduled to arrive in the early hours of tomorrow morning. We've checked and it's definitely one of his planes. We don't know if he will be on board yet but it's a good bet,"

"Good, instruct your men to keep their eyes on him at all times. I have a plan that will blow his mind,"

36

Moscow, Russia
Thursday November 17 - 16:23 MST

Mazepa was at the bustling passport control at Sheremetyevo Airport where the customs officer was taking his time examining her passport. She had rushed off the plane and was the first to arrive at the passport control queue.

She occasionally looked around trying to spot Boris Ivanovich to no avail. The officer was watching her and Mazepa knew she was acting suspiciously. However, the fear meant she had no option but to keep checking for Ivanovich's presence, no matter how dodgy this made her appear.

The officer stamped her passport and handed it back to her, then flicked his hand to indicate she was OK to enter the country without saying a word to her. Mazepa walked past the checkpoint and spun her head round to make a final check of passport control and a small wave of relief passed through her as she couldn't locate Ivanovich.

Mazepa was carrying two pieces of hand luggage and she was glad she didn't need to claim any baggage. She entered the arrivals hall and she was taken aback by how busy it was for a midweek afternoon. The election was bringing back people in huge numbers sensing change on the horizon. If only they knew what I know, Mazepa thought.

Her initial plan was to catch the train into the centre of Moscow but with the looming shadow of Saratov's terrible lackey firmly lodged in her mind, Mazepa decided to catch the first possible taxi despite the extortionate cost thanks to mafia taxes. She walked out of the airport and headed left, remaining under the covered entrance towards the taxi rank. As she neared the first taxi, another set of airport doors opened and Boris Ivanovich walked out in between the taxi and Mazepa.

Mazepa's legs almost buckled and she carried on moving as if she had only learned to walk this morning. Ivanovich turned and spotted her. He gave a short wave and approached her.

"Anastasiya Mazepa," Ivanovich said and held out his hand, "Welcome back to Russia,"

"Hello," Mazepa said, her brain switching to autopilot as she met the handshake, giving it a firm shake. A chill passed up her arm in response to the touch of a man who had killed with those hands.

"It's always good to see one of Russia's most prominent journalists back where she belongs. Russia is changing and we are delighted you are here to witness history in the flesh,"

Mazepa said nothing, she was most puzzled at the change in his voice. When she met him twenty years ago, he was an uncouth rasper, now he had the rich timbre of a seasoned politician.

"I believe you are a deputy prime minister now, Mr Ivanovich. Would you be willing to give me an interview?"

"I would be delighted to. In fact, I may have a little exclusive for you," Ivanovich said, and then made an overripe show of conspiratorially looking around for covert listeners, "Did you hear about the terrible bombing of that café in Oslo?"

"Of course," Mazepa said, unsure whether Ivanovich was being wilfully ignorant of her relationship with one of the victims or that he was being dismissively spiteful because of the fact.

"Hard evidence has come to light that Dimitri Bolkonsky was behind the bombing. I would be happy to provide this to you tomorrow if you are available?"

"Maybe, where would we meet?"

"At the Sarabank headquarters in the Moscow-City

business district. The documents are there waiting to be released to a writer with the required gravitas and ability,"

"Why would you give it to me? Why not release it now to the media?"

"We could do that but as you know, our friend Maxim Golitsyn needs a helping hand with the election. We feel the impact of the story would be greater if it came from a journalist with an impeccable reputation, who is not...how would I put it?"

"Not a propagandist mouthpiece for Sasha Saratov?"

Ivanovich opened his arms in a gesture of reluctant acceptance.

"That's not for me to say but I don't think you can deny that if the story came from you then it would make a much bigger splash,"

"I look forward to seeing what evidence you have," Mazepa edged towards the taxi and opened the back door as the driver placed her baggage in the boot, "I shall see you tomorrow. Will the esteemed Sasha Saratov be there at the interview?"

"He will be there," Ivanovich waited for Mazepa to sit in the taxi before closing the door, where she opened the window, "He's been keeping a close eye on you over the years,"

"I'm sure he has," Mazepa closed the window and advised the driver of her destination and he began speeding away.

She pulled out her phone and texted Einar Simonsen about what had happened with Ivanovich in one long paragraph without punctuation.

The dull drive from Sheremetyevo into Moscow city centre gave her time to think. There was something odd about Ivanovich's behaviour. It was almost like he had no idea who she was nor any knowledge of the threats he uttered to her at the Hotel Leningrad over two decades ago when he genuinely looked like he would kill her if Saratov hadn't calmed him down.

Now he was masquerading as a politician. The crazy thing is that he's not the mayor of a shitty town in the middle of nowhere but a deputy prime minister. What a fucking country, Mazepa thought, where a lunatic like him can be appointed to one of the most powerful positions in the country. If Golitsyn wins the election, Ivanovich would be a shoo-in to become Prime Minister meaning Saratov's puppets would control the two most powerful offices of state.

If Ivanovich wanted Mazepa dead, he could have killed her at Heathrow or upon arrival in Russia but he hadn't done that. Based on that, the scale of probabilities indicated that he may actually have evidence to support the allegation that Bolkonsky was behind the bombing of the Oslo café. Paired with the tape of the butchering of the Chechen civilians, she would be able to destroy his election bid.

The logical follow-on would be that as the woman who helped Golitsyn into power, she would be protected by Saratov. The thought partly reassured her. And you never know, Golitsyn could prove to be his own man, an instinctive liberal who wouldn't stifle debate and would enact the reforms required to modernise the nation.

Mazapa's mobile phone buzzed in her hand and she noticed that the city had come into view, concrete rectangles jutting out of the earth with the sky, which itself was barely a lighter shade of grey. She looked at the text message reply from Simonsen:

-       If he had the evidence, why didn't he hand it over to you at the airport?

Simonsen's Scandinavian logic was hard to criticise. Why would she need to go to the Sarabank headquarters when Ivanovich could have handed over any relevant documents at the airport or even sent them to her in London?

The words of her former lover that Simonsen had said to her last night came right back into her head. Don't trust anyone in Russia. She could be walking straight into a bear trap tomorrow.

Mazepa opened her laptop up and opened up her mail browser. She clicked on the draft of her email to the various newspaper editors and double-checked its saucy attachments. She paused for a second before hitting the send button.

37

Oslo, Norway
Thursday November 17 - 17:00 CET

"When most people visit London, they go look at those shit waxworks at Madame Tussauds or go to the Zoo," Karlsson reclined on his office chair with his big, shoeless feet resting on the desk, "But somehow you manage to discover a dead body, get chased around a cricket stadium and chance upon the evidence that at best, might swing the Russian election and at worst, might bring about World War Three. Good work, Einar,"

"Thanks," Einar smiled and took comfort that he was back on safe ground at the Kripos office, "And in all my time away having adventures, you haven't even charged our prime suspect,"

"Don't remind me," Karlsson grimaced and pulled his feet down off the chair, "You are positive that there are no links to anyone in London?"

"Nothing,"

"But you think one of the candidates in Moscow ordered the hit?"

"I'm almost certain of it but there isn't a shred of evidence to tie them to Alaoui,"

Karlsson slipped his shoes on, stood up and stretched. Simonsen thought his friend looked tired, which wasn't a surprise for the lead investigator on such a high-profile case. Karlsson had the personality where he could handle the pressure from the media and his bosses but this case was on a much higher scale than anything else he had investigated. This was easily the biggest criminal investigation in Norway since Anders Breivik's awful terrorist act in 2011 and the scrutiny on Karlsson was intense.

"I thought we had him," Karlsson muttered under his breath, "I fucking hate innocent people,"

"Thank you for not taking me off the case, Benny,"

Karlsson laughed and walked round to Simonsen and patted him on the back.

"Your boss called me three times asking for you to be removed from the case. The bloke is fucking compromised, my bosses think he's an arsehole. I know he's a corrupt arsehole,"

"It's no wonder I didn't get anywhere when I worked in Moscow. It's clear now that he was working against me,"

"You don't think he was involved when you were shot?"

Simonsen said nothing and waved his hand in a non-committal way. The more Simonsen contemplated the idea that Peter Kelsey-Moore was involved in the attack that killed Mariya and left him a limping coward, the more it unnerved him and if he was totally honest, it disgusted him.

He had always hated conspiracy theories, they gave people an easy, convenient explanation of difficult subjects. They would often absolve people of responsibility for their actions. Yet, when you examined the evidence of this case, it looked like there were multiple conspiracies on the go. A collection of particularly cunning snakes couldn't organise the type of stunts that some of these Russian politicians were capable of.

"What about the coroner's report on Narimanov?" Simonsen said.

"Inconclusive," Karlsson said, "It appears that the explosion didn't kill him but they are waiting on toxicology results before they will give a definite verdict,"

"Sir," a female voice spoke along with a brisk rap on Karlsson's open office door. Both men turned around and Simonsen saw Anita Bangoura, in a stylish royal blue suit standing in the doorway. Simonsen was now at the age where he thought most of the police officers looked like they should still be at school. He remembered her from outside Alaoui's place barely five days ago. To Simonsen, that felt about five years ago now.

"What's up, Bangoura?" Karlsson said, stretching out his arms and back.

"I think I've found something strange," she said and beckoned them out towards the open plan office where Karlsson's staff were working. Karlsson sped off after her and Simonsen stood up and slowly followed them. Bangoura was at her desk and Karlsson had already pulled up the spare chair to her desk. Simonsen crouched between the two of them.

Bangoura was pulling up some CCTV clips in separate windows on her screen. She pressed play on the first snippet.

"Right, this clip is from a couple of minutes before the bombing," Bangoura pointed at an image of a young woman on a subway train.

"Who is it?" Karlsson said.

"That's the woman from the café who left a minute or two before Alaoui,"

"You've found her? She's the last one from the café we have to identify. Do we know who she is?"

"Well, that's when things start to get interesting," Bangoura said and turned to each man with a raised eyebrow.

"OK, Saga Norén, you're not starring in the new series of *The Bridge*, get on with it," Karlsson said.

"She walked for a couple of minutes to Majorstuen station. And this is her heading back to Oslo on the subway pretty much at the time of the explosion," Bangoura said, moving the mouse pointer to another video file and pressing play, "And she rides it all the way back to the Central Train Station,"

Simonsen watched the video, transfixed. It was always fascinating to see how modern technology can monitor someone so effectively in urban areas. A seductive but potentially abusive technology. In this instance, he found it incredible. He watched as the woman left the station through the same exit that he did when he obtained the videotape from Narimanov's room. Instead of walking towards the Barcode Project towers, she hailed a taxi. Within seconds, she was in the taxi driving off.

"We lost her a couple of times on the CCTV but the taxis in Oslo are fitted with location tracking devices and after chasing down the taxi company for the last few days, they have finally supplied us with the information so we managed to track her journey. She paid in cash and got out at Aker Brygge where she went into of those flash new apartments,"

"Why did she go back on herself?" Karlsson said, "She could have got off at the National Theatre. I mean she could have walked straight from the café anyway, it's not that far is it?"

"I reckon it would take twenty minutes or so to walk but it was pretty bad weather so understandable for her not to walk it," Bangoura said and brought up another clip, "But, travelling back the way she came rang a few alarm bells, so I wanted to track her movement prior to arriving at the café if I could. It took a while but I managed to locate her at a coffee shop in Frogner at about seven in the evening so I guess she walked from there to the Iskender Café.

"From there, she took another taxi - again, we have confirmation of the journey, back to Majorstuen where we see her outside McDonalds. They have supplied this clip from their CCTV," Bangoura opened another clip and which showed the back of the woman in a big grey puffer jacket and red woolly hat, "Also note she has a little black backpack over her shoulder,"

Bangoura opened yet another clip which showed the woman walking through the main street through Majorstuen before slipping down a side street and hovering out of view.

"That is the last we see of her, she presumably reached the café where she ordered a coffee, according to Mr Efe's statement,"

"OK, now what?"

"If we go back to the clip of her leaving the area," Bangoura brought the first clip back to the front of the screen, "You can see that she is on the train with a different hat. The red woolly number has been replaced by a white bobble hat,"

Simonsen and Karlsson both hummed in unison and exchanged glances.

"But, more importantly, this is her walking out of the Central Station. What else do you notice?" Bangoura said and for a few seconds there was silence until Karlsson started patting the desk in front of him.

"You have got to be fucking kidding me," Karlsson spat out the words and leaned back in his chair.

"She no longer has the backpack," Simonsen said and Bangoura grinned at him.

Simonsen studied the image of the woman and was certain he had seen her before. It was on the tip of his tongue, agonisingly out of reach.

"Who the fuck is she?" Karlsson said.

"The apartment she rented is a typical short-term let, the name she used is Jana Schmidt but it's almost certainly false. Johnsen spoke to the agent who said he didn't meet her, he gave instructions on how to obtain the key and she paid via bank transfer. We are getting no joy out of which specific bank it was but we know it was sent from a Russian bank,"

"Are you sure?" Simonsen said and Bangoura nodded, "Benny, I've seen her before, I'm sure of it,"

"In Oslo?" Bangoura said.

Simonsen realised he had seen her in Oslo and he began groaning. He paced up and down the bank of desks with Bangoura and Karlsson staring at him.

"I saw her on the night of the bombing," Simonsen said.

"You are taking the piss now, Einar," Karlsson said, "You know her?"

"No, it was at the hospital, when I went to visit Narimanov. She was the nurse who came into his room. I was falling asleep in the chair and she came in and was whistling and adjusting his drips and things,"

"And when you woke up, he was dead," Karlsson said and Simonsen was struggling to process the realisation that this woman had murdered Narimanov when he was four metres away.

"Bangoura," Karlsson said, "Gather everyone in. See what you can find out about Narimanov's death, find all the footage and start sharing the images around Europe. She could be anywhere. This is good work, Bangoura, fucking excellent work,"

Bangoura started texting her colleagues and Karlsson strode off back to his office. Simonsen followed him in. Karlsson banged his hand against the side of one of the metal filing cabinets.

"We're back to square one," Karlsson looked forlorn, "Alaoui didn't do it. This little waif has managed to bomb a fucking café and finish off one of the victims in hospital whilst he's under armed guard. Who is she? A Russian hitman? Or should I say hitwoman? I don't fucking know,"

"I'll fly to Moscow, there's a flight at midnight. I think Moscow is at the heart of all this,"

"You're probably right, no wonder you went nuts working there. I'm going to find out who she is, and I'm travelling over there myself if needs be to arrest her. And I'll tell that corrupt shit of a boss of yours that you are going to Russia on my orders,"

Karlsson lifted his blazer off the back of his chair and put it on.

"Stay safe in Moscow, Einar," Karlsson said as he headed towards the door, "Now I'm off to tell my bosses that we picked up the wrong guy and that the real suspect is a twelve year old Soviet schoolgirl assassin,"

38

Moscow, Russia
Thursday November 17 - 20:11 MST

The explosive rage had gradually morphed into a ball of festering fury, settling deep in the gut of Dimitri Bolkonsky. Every little noise or annoyance in the office caused spasmodic grunts and increased blood pressure. He wasn't able to stay in the office with the nattering and clattering of the cretins inside the ministry.

He had walked out of the office, ordered his security detail to leave him alone and crossed the Pushkinsky Bridge before heading into Gorky Park. And thus Bolkonsky sat on a white bench staring at the calm water of the Golitsyn Pond as a light snow fell around him. The irony of the name of the body of water wasn't lost on him.

Bolkonsky leant over his legs and held his head in his hands. All the years of fighting, arguing and settling scores would culminate in the poll on Saturday. In a couple of days, Bolkonsky thought, I will be the most powerful man in Russia; I will be the man who will set the nation back on the right path after the stagnation of the last decade.

The tension reminded him of the night he spent in that Dagestani farm being bombarded by rockets. He didn't want his men to know that he was scared of dying on a mountain in the middle of nowhere. It wasn't how he pictured a soldier's death and when the young private, Krushnikov, died in his arms, it only confirmed it. Dying from the shock of your legs being blown off by some grubby peasant firing stolen rockets from a godforsaken hillside was not the way a soldier should die.

It wasn't a battlefield where he was part of ten thousand men prepared to die for his homeland against the massed ranks of French or Prussians. That night at the farm, he was alone and he realised all of his men were alone too. He always maintained a brave front, but that night was the closest he had come to mental collapse. It was only the urge to protect his remaining men that prevented him from curling up in a ball and praying to make it through the night.

Bolkonsky's phone started to ring and he was initially annoyed that he hadn't left the damn thing back at the office. He saw it was Oksana Devina and answered it.

"Good evening Oksana," Bolkonsky said.

"Dimitri, I've been trying to reach you all day," Devina said.

"I've been busy, thank you for the flowers,"

"I was very fond of Alex, he was a credit to you,"

"He certainly didn't deserve what happened to him. What can I do for you today?"

"I wanted to speak to you and make sure you are OK?"

"No, I'm not in a great place but there is an election to win and nothing is more important than winning that vote. I will put my grief on hold in the service of my country,"

"Did you know that the investigation into the Oslo bombing is pointing to a link with Moscow?"

"I didn't know that. Are they closing in on Saratov at last?"

"I'm not sure, but there is an Interpol agent who has been snooping around London. I think he is trying to link the bombing to the election,"

"That makes sense, Saratov is behind it all. He's a spider, he controls cops all over Europe,"

"The agent is a Norwegian man named Simonsen. He is due to board a flight to Moscow that arrives first thing in the morning. I've sent you a photo of him, check your phone,"

Bolkonsky pulled the vibrating phone away from ear and clicked the notification advising that he had received a photo message. He opened it up and saw a nondescript man with sensible greying blonde hair in a big coat entering a restaurant.

"Is that him?" Bolkonsky said, moving the phone back towards his face.

"Yes, he was on his way to meet Sasha Saratov for dinner,"

"Excuse me, what the fuck are you telling me? This cop met Saratov in London?"

"Yes, last night,"

"Why would he meet Saratov?"

"It's hard to say, but I've had it confirmed that he is definitely investigating the bombing."

"That's a bold move to meet one of his own snitches in public. He must be desperate to cover his role in the bombing,"

"I don't know but he was there for an hour or so with him and now he's heading here. Dimitri, is this cop going to unearth something that connects you to the bomb?"

"I don't like this one bit, I had nothing to do with the bombing. That prick Saratov has sent him on a wild goose chase to harass me,"

"It's the police's job to follow the trail. But there is one odd thing though. That Interpol guy, Simonsen, he was also the man who called the police to tell them about your son's murder,"

Bolkonsky didn't say anything for a few moments, pondering what she was insinuating.

"He was there?"

"Yes, he phoned the local police and gave a statement. I'm trying to obtain a copy of the statement, it is potentially a matter of state security,"

Bolkonsky again went quiet, the implication that this cop might have murdered his son hung heavy over the line.

"I'll speak to you soon, Oksana," Bolkonsky said and ended the call. He stood up and began walking back through the park to his office. He kept his phone open and called Zakatov, who answered within a couple of rings.

"Ivan, how are preparations going?"

"We are ready for action. I've called two of our best special forces units into the city. They are at safe houses tonight,"

"And firepower?"

"It's at one of our warehouses in Khodynka. I'm heading there now to inspect it. Everything is going to be fine. Short, sharp and effective,"

"I hope so, Ivan,"

"Dimitri, are you sure you want to proceed with the plan? I don't want to go ahead if you are not fully behind me,"

"I'm not changing my mind. We need to hit Saratov hard. I know he organised my son's murder and I think I know who did it,"

"Are you serious? Who was it?"

"I won't find out until tomorrow morning," Bolkonsky said, with plans running through his head on how to extract the truth from the Norwegian cop, "I'll speak to you later,"

Those Chechen rebel collaborators realised the cost of fucking with him, and by extention, the Russian state. After he had left the warehouse that afternoon, Bolkonsky had walked back to town where he was due to meet up with the other half of his platoon.

The high temperatures and his heavy uniform should have weighed him down. However, Bolkonsky's inner self was serene and light as a handful of feathers. He was not weighed down by guilt but actually felt giddy at how easy it had been to shoot those Chechens.

Bolkonsky thought about all the training it had taken to become a Captain in the Russian army. He wasn't a natural student but reading about great Russian military heroes was the hook that had engaged him. From Zhukov's defence of Stalingrad against insurmountable odds to Skopin-Shuisky's use of ski-troops as part of the campaign to remove the Polish-backed False Dmitry II as Tsar in the early seventeenth century, Bolkonsky had wanted to write his own name in the annals of Russian history.

He was now in this wretched part of Russia where a bunch of goatherds thought they could tear apart his country. Well, they were wrong and Bolkonsky would shed no tears for bringing order back to these uncivilised areas. What he had done today was in the name of the Motherland. It wasn't a matter of choice to shoot those men but an obligation to protect the integrity of the state.

"Everything OK, sir?" one lad said to him as Bolkonsky joined up with his troops in the main road through Mekhelta, "We heard shooting,"

"Don't worry, that was from our side. Any issues here?"

"No sir," came the reply and Bolkonsky noticed how quiet it was. No sounds of humans, animals or machinery came from the village. You could be mistaken for believing the village had been abandoned.

"Excellent," Bolkonsky stood in the middle of the road and addressed his troops, "Lieutenant General Shamanov is sending two divisions to support us today. Air support will be on the way too, better late than never, eh? They will be striking targets from North of here towards Khasavyurt and Shamonov's men will arrive from the East from the same direction we arrived.

"Half of the platoon will remain here with Lieutenant Zhyrgal guarding the road to Chechnya and the other half will come with me to the junction at Tlyarata until reinforcements arrive. Well done today, lads. I want to tell you that every single one of you has fought with honour and I will never forget that. In years to come, you'll tell your grandchildren about what happened here and I want you all to be proud of what you have achieved.

"I understand the difficulties we have faced with our shitty equipment and the lack of support from those cowards fifty kilometres behind the front lines but you can be proud of what you have done here. Now, let's get back to work,"

A loud cheer arose from the men, Bolkonsky was shocked at the response and he noticed a few of his men were crying. This was the exact point when Bolkonsky understood what true leadership was. He knew his life would change from that point and that one day he would try to enter politics with the ultimate aim of leading a whole nation.

In Dagestan, Bolkonsky realised that not only he had the skill set to lead men but he also had the expertise to wage war. Saratov has declared war on me, Bolkonsky thought, but he has never come under fire in the dead of night. Bolkonsky entered his office and was clear in his intention that if it's war Saratov wants, then he will bring the war straight to him.

39

Oslo, Norway
Thursday November 17 - 21:48 CET

Simonsen had left the Kripos office an hour earlier, leaving a workplace where morale had taken a battering following the release of Nadim Alaoui. He was sorry for his friend Benny Karlsson, as the case against Nadim Alaoui had collapsed and there was no sign of the real suspect. The press were going to hammer him over this. The news of Alaoiu's release had already spread via the internet and the morning papers would make grim reading over Karlsson's breakfast.

Most of Karlsson's staff had remained at the office, pulling in overtime in the hunt for the woman who was now the main suspect in the bombing of the Iskender Café. They were a loyal bunch and they knew Karlsson was a good cop who was caught up in something bigger than your average crime.

Simonsen had driven to the tip of the Aker Brygge district, an expensive, gentrified neighbourhood jutting out of the south of the city centre into Oslo Bay. He had travelled there to investigate the room where the woman stayed but after finding nothing linked to her there he wandered off to the water's edge to look across the bay at night, entranced by the flickering orange lights.

He sighed and realised his flight to Moscow was in about four hours' time so he turned around and walked back past the busy waterside restaurants where people scoffed their food protected from the freezing temperatures by heated verandas.

He had parked up opposite the Nobel Peace Centre and he entered his car and turned the heaters up to full blast in preparation for the journey home.

After a couple of minutes, his car was warm enough and he could see out of the windscreen, so he moved off and waited at the junction to turn left onto Dronning Mauds Gate. Simonsen was feeling a little sleepy and he hoped he would be able to sleep on the flight.

He glanced to his left and saw a silver Jaguar had pulled up parallel with his vehicle which was strange, as they had parked on the pavement. For a moment he thought he recognised the face in the driver's seat. The other driver's window began to descend and he realised who the man was.

Peter Kelsey-Moore was the driver and he was drawing out a pistol and aiming it at Simonsen.

Simonsen froze momentarily and with vital timing, ducked his head down with millimetres to spare as a bullet smashed through the driver's side window and through the other side.

"Jesus!" Simonsen shouted, raising his head so he could see outside the windscreen. He saw there was no traffic so he stepped on the accelerator and immediately dragged the steering wheel to the right, and then harshly braked to jive through a couple of road signs onto the pavement outside the town hall. He blazed the car down the pavement for about fifty metres before yanking the vehicle back onto the road.

He jerked the steering wheel rightwards, accelerated for about fifty yards before pulling another right turn and then a left to bring himself onto Rådhusgata. He flattened his foot down on the gas again and raced down the road.

Simonsen checked his rearview mirror and he could see Kelsey-Moore's Jag steaming up behind him. He elbowed the remaining glass from the driver's side window so he could see his side mirror and maintained a high speed as he approached the roundabout ahead.

Simonsen pulled the handbrake and skidded his car

around the Glove statue, the official centre of the city of Oslo. His car barely made it round as it started skidding sideways towards the café at the side of the road.

The car clipped the flower boxes and clattered through the lightweight tables where the diners had already leaped out of the way. Simonsen shouted as though his voice would stop the car crashing into the café. The car actually stopped barely a few centimetres from the large front window and Simonsen allowed himself a long exhalation. Before he could praise God for the miracle, he saw Kelsey-Moore's Jag heading to the roundabout too and straight for his car.

Simonsen hit the accelerator again and his vehicle shot off the mark and evaded his boss's car by centimetres. He drove back onto Rådhusgata and yet again, the chasing car was closing him down like it was being driven by Nikki Lauda. At the town hall, he slammed on the brakes and pulled a hard-right turn.

Simonsen guided the car around the arcing street outside the town hall before bursting down towards the Stortingsgata junction. He had to almost stop due to the busy traffic and he heard another gunshot thumping against the back of his car.

He turned the wheel left and darted off down the wrong-way street past the National Theatre. Multiple cars approaching them were honking their horns and were forced to veer out of the way of the two racers. Simonsen could smell the tires burning from his car and wondered how long his car would hold out. He circled the roundabout without checking for other cars and up the road towards the royal palace. As he accelerated, yet another gunshot cracked into the back windscreen, disintegrating it.

Pedestrians flung themselves out of the way and Simonsen kept beeping his horn to alert others. As the palace hoved into view, Simonsen made as if to turn left and then pulled the car sharply to his right.

Simonsen thought he had nailed the turn but then

struck a patch of black ice and the car spun around. His stomach lurched and he cracked his head off the door frame as glass from the shattered window dribbled over him. Simonsen's car came to a stop at the foot of the stairs towards the palace as the statue of King Karl Johan looked on unimpressed from atop his bronze horse.

Kelsey-Moore's car had pulled up behind him. For a few moments, there was no movement from the other car. There were still a few isolated people but most of them had run off now after hearing gunshots. That was when he saw Kelsey-Moore exit the vehicle. His normally detached demeanour was not on show as Simonsen watched him cursing and slamming his car door, his other hand holding the pistol with the barrel facing the ground.

Simonsen's head was fuzzy, the idea that his superior was about to shoot him seemed silly and unreal. A light-headedness started to cloud his brain and a passing thought came to him that it wouldn't be such a bad exit, one bullet and then he would be back with Mariya.

Kelsey-Moore's feet scrunched on the slushy snow and he stood level with the driver's side window. Simonsen momentarily thought, not me; please not me right now.

Silence fell and Simonsen prepared for death. He heard the shot and instantly realised he was still alive. A face then bumped into the space where the window used to be.

It was Peter Kelsey-Moore and there was a hole in his forehead where a bullet had gone through. His body crumpled to the floor and Simonsen opened the door pushing the body away. He dragged himself out of the car and collapsed onto all-fours. He noticed he had pissed himself and lifted his head up as he tried to locate the shooter.

He couldn't see anyone except a woman with long black hair about fifty metres away who was crouched over, packing a rifle away into a case.

"Hey!" Simonsen shouted. The woman raised her eyes and stared at him and they both stood like that for a few seconds before she finished packing her rifle up and standing up. She took one more look at Simonsen before running off into the trees and within seconds she was out of sight.

40

Moscow, Russia
Friday November 18 - 05:44 MST

"Poor little Maxim. Poor little man," Bolkonsky was drinking a mug of black tea and reading the first editions of the day's newspapers.

Revelations that Golitsyn had arranged for visas for his prostitute pals were on the cover of every paper. If there was any balm to his grief, this was it. The fury had not yet ebbed away but the schadenfreude was undeniably delicious. Even the Saratov-owned newspapers were leading on the story even if they were trying to blame the British government for leaking it.

Bolkonsky had already spoken to his press secretary and they had issued a condemnation of Golitsyn's behaviour. He had railed against his rival's utter lack of moral rectitude and the shame he had brought upon the great nation of Russia. Usually he would listen to his advisors trying to dampen down the insults but not today. He had called his fellow contender a corrupt fraud, a moral black hole and a harbinger of unprincipled governance, although that last line was written by one of his interns.

He was surprised that Golitsyn was going to proceed with his final rally at Red Square today. A last push but surely it was too late to salvage his campaign? Doubt, usually cast aside so easily by Bolkonsky, was pushing into his brain. Anyone normal would concede by now unless he had a plan.

Did the plan involve the Norwegian Interpol guy? Bolkonsky was sure that Saratov would have filled his head with nonsense that he was responsible for the bombing and any other crime he could pin on him from the death of JFK to the sinking of the Titanic.

"Fucking bastard, I'll deal with him later," Bolkonsky said out loud to an empty room. His wish for a cathartic attack on Saratov's interest was keeping him going. But who was this cop, Bolkonsky thought, and who the fuck does he think he is coming to my country to investigate me?

And that was when it struck him. Bolkonsky had to sit down to help him remember but once he did he could remember everything. He recalled meeting Einar Simonsen in the Anzhi Bazaar during the Dagestan conflict. Bolkonsky had been told that Sasha Saratov had been selling weapons to the Chechen scum and he was irate. The gobshite journalist Anastasiya Mazepa had approached him and said she was building a file of evidence against Saratov. She filled his head with all kinds of sordid treachery about Saratov that had polluted his mind for over two decades.

Bolkonsky was only too keen to grasp his hands on the curious dossier that the journalist had teased him about. In those days, the new Russia was struggling and he retained faith in the leadership to make the new nation a success. His belief in a strong, responsible state and as a major component of harmonious international institutions remained resolute and he made contact with an Interpol guy who had spoken to one of his men, Narimanov. He couldn't approach him directly with Saratov's moles everywhere in that horrible hotel where all the journalists and gangsters were staying.

Narimanov followed Bolkonsky's instructions and placed a note containing a location under Simonsen's room door at the Hotel Leningrad. For hours, Bolkonsky remained in his hotel room pacing the floor and checking the clock. An hour before the meeting was scheduled, he could wait no longer. He left the hotel and caught three different taxis to take him on a circuitous route through the city towards the bazaar. He arrived twenty minutes early and he was sure that no one had followed him.

The blazing sun was making Bolkonsky wish he hadn't worn a heavy jacket. He pondered walking inside the crumbling concrete market, shaped like an upturned washing machine drum but his note specified he would be at the entrance. He checked his watch and it was one minute until the meeting time.

He lifted his eyes, wiped away a line of sweat and saw the man he was due to meet. A blonde, solidly built man had left a taxi and was crossing the road. He could have walked it from the hotel but Bolkonsky guessed he wanted to ensure he made it on time in case he became lost or he had taken the same precautions and used multiple taxis to arrive here.

Bolkonsky nodded at the man and then they both walked inside the abandoned market hall where it was a relief to be out of the sunshine. Inside the deteriorating bazaar, the men stood ten metres apart not saying anything as they measured each other up.

"You are Captain Bolkonsky?" the Norwegian man said. His Russian was excellent with barely a trace of an accent which was quite impressive for a foreigner.

"Yes, I am Captain Dimitri Bolkonsky. My sources tell me that you are investigating organised criminals from Moscow?"

"It is true, there are reliable reports that members of the SoIntsevskaya group are trafficking weapons to the Chechens. There is a lot of pressure in Moscow to see if that is correct,"

"What have you found so far?"

"In all honesty, nothing," Simonsen replied, sweat patches visible on the armpits of his shirt. Bolkonsky saw a determined man standing opposite. He was someone who could help staunch the open wound of gangsterism infecting Russia.

"I am awaiting proof of the crimes that you are investigating. There is an oligarch who come to prominence recently in Moscow who is behind the sales of weapons to our enemy,"

"Is he the same guy who is paying for the war on the government's behalf?"

"Money is more important to bastards like him, not honour or patriotism,"

"And you can prove these accusations?"

"In a few days, I should be in receipt of evidence. If you can make the charges stick, I will supply you with everything you require,"

"I'll speak with my bosses. If they find out he has betrayed Russia, I'm confident that we could take him down. There is an appetite for a scalp back in Moscow,"

"I am heading towards the front line but you shall be hearing from me when I return," Bolkonsky said and walked out of the building into the blazing sunshine. That was the last time he had seen Simonsen until he saw the photograph of him today.

Christ, Bolkonsky thought, I'd forgotten about that meeting. After returning from the front and that bitch journalist Mazepa avoiding him, he had given up on bringing down Saratov at that point. Bolkonsky had been promoted to Major upon his return to Moscow and a few years later Putin had dispatched him to London to run the GRU station there.

This cop had not received the evidence he was promised so was now looking for revenge. He remembered that he appeared competent and determined at the time and Bolkonsky was never one to underrate an enemy. Knowing that he ruined Simonsen's case meant he had a personal reason to see him go down. Did that cop murder his son as part of the plan? It seemed unlikely but Saratov had the means to support people with money and means to fulfil their plans. Did Saratov offer him a deal?

It was not beyond the realms of possibility that Saratov

paid the cop to kill Alex and then he was going to pin the bombing on him unless he took action now.

Bolkonsky phoned Zakatov and instructed him to stop Simonsen from entering Russia and to keep him posted with regular updates about the interrogation. Bolkonsky thought that if he could get Simonsen to confess, he could also connect Saratov to the bombing. Once Simonsen was taken care of and Saratov dealt with by later today, winning the election should be easy.

41

Moscow, Russia
Friday November 18 - 08:20 MST

Simonsen didn't sleep on the flight over from Oslo. The absolute madness of the previous evening refused to shift from his brain. He still could not grasp quite what possessed Peter Kelsey-Moore to chase him around the streets of the Norwegian capital city and attempt to shoot him in public. It was an astounding level of mental disintegration and it was probably a good thing he missed the morning headlines about his son, Ian.

The disgrace of Ian Kelsey-Moore was now complete after he scanned the UK websites before he boarded. Every newspaper in England and Russia had printed the new 'visas for sex workers' revelations and pressure was mounting for Ian Kelsey-Moore to resign. Simonsen was pretty certain he would have departed office by the time he landed in Russia.

He didn't know when the news of his father's antics last night would hit the press. He had asked Benny Karlsson to try and keep it under wraps but the story was simply too big for it not to leak out very soon. He had updated Karlsson on what had happened on the way back to his apartment.

Karlsson wasn't too impressed when Simonsen told him that he was still heading to Russia after the little incident especially when it was capped off seeing the bomb suspect assassinate the head of Norwegian Interpol. Simonsen was adamant that he would be leaving for Moscow and that it would be up to Karlsson to stop him.

Karlsson didn't stop him and Simonsen knew that would be so. Karlsson had the scent for clues and everything was now pointing to Russian involvement. The bomber was likely to still be in Norway so Karlsson was focusing on that side of the investigation whilst Simonsen would attempt to discover who was the mastermind of the operation.

Simonsen had been queuing at passport control at Sheremetyevo Airport for over forty minutes. The low ceilings, slow moving lines and muttered Russian conversations that he could hear from every angle was making him anxious. He was struggling to push away a grim sense of foreboding. Something inside was informing him that he wouldn't be leaving Moscow alive this time.

Moving to Moscow had been a dream for him. Growing up in the dull suburbs of Oslo, he had never felt entirely comfortable in Norway. A misguided dislike of what he saw as a country crammed with stiff, parochial people. Simonsen would come to later appreciate the unthinking acts of kindness that people were capable of in his home country as he tried to rebuild his life. That the rebuilding failed was not due to his friends and colleagues, but to his own withering view of himself.

The portion of his life spent with Mariya was paradise, Simonsen thought, and that wasn't the sands of time scouring away bad moments. The best word to describe how he felt was 'fulfilled'. Fulfilment was something that he had never experienced until he first met her at a swanky party at a governmental office building. The party itself reminded him of something from a Hollywood film full of glamorous, well-dressed people in a beautiful mansion. She was there as a representative of the bank she was working for who were bidding for a ministerial contract.

They made immediate eye contact and for the first time in his life, he approached a woman with the intent to chat her up. Working in a job he loved in a fascinating new country made everything feel exotic, even himself. A couple of Mariya's male colleagues who were chatting with her soon departed when they sensed the connection between Simonsen and her.

They spent the night chatting, eventually going to a nightclub in the early hours, engrossed in each other. And that was how it remained for the next couple of years where they spent virtually every day with each other. Simonsen's trip to Dagestan would be the first time they had spent more than a night apart. Barely a few weeks' later, Simonsen and Mariya would be the victims of a shooting in broad daylight and his Muscovite dream turned to ash.

The queue was moving slowly and Simonsen's angst grew by the minute. His knee began to seize up as if the pain was linked to his brain and he had to constantly stretch it. The border control guards were scrutinising every passenger and interrogating them. The fear of agents provocateurs and foreign-based activists was scaring the country's leaders at this delicate time. The conversations he was overhearing were almost all about the upcoming election. Fears of violence on the streets was a common theme from his fellow passengers' conversations.

Simonsen and Karlsson had pulled a few strings to obtain a fast-track visa. Unlike in the UK, the Russians showed barely any positive inclination towards cooperating with an Interpol agent. He had informed the Russian Interpol office of his investigation and when he mentioned on the phone call about Saratov and Bolkonsky, he could almost hear their bollocks slapping against the floor.

His plan was to attend the Maxim Golitsyn rally to be held today at Red Square and try to worm his way backstage with the view of talking to him. Moscow was the bedrock of Golitsyn's support and Simonsen wanted to see what the size of the crowd was going to be today after the torrent of revelations against their man.

Simonsen finally reached the front of the queue and he noticed he was tightly squeezing the handle of his holdall. He placed the holdall on the floor and checked that his documents were in order. He scanned around the hall and saw a bunch of high-ranking military officers and border staff engaged in a heated discussion. It doesn't take much in Russia to set the pulse rate going and watching armed soldiers arguing didn't help calm Simonsen's nerves.

Simonsen was beckoned forward by a stern faced young woman with a blonde bob.

"Documents," she said, Simonsen could tell she was still waiting for her diploma to arrive from the charm school. He handed over his documents. Simonsen looked across at the quarrelling officers and he was sure he saw one of them pointing at him.

"What is the purpose of your visit?" the woman said, inspecting Simonsen's face and comparing it to his passport.

"What, sorry?" Simonsen said, bringing his attention back to the woman.

"What is the purpose of your visit to Russia?" the woman barked the words at Simonsen.

"I am investigating a crime committed in Norway. The document at the bottom contains a signed confirmation from the head of Russian Interpol of my intentions,"

The woman began reading the visa document and the relevant remarks. She was a slow reader and Simonsen turned to look at the officers again. More of them were pointing at him now and suddenly they began walking towards him. Simonsen's stomach rolled at the prospect of detention into Russian custody when a piercing screech rattled around the customs hall.

"He's got a bomb!" a woman's voice rang out and Simonsen turned around and saw a huge commotion in the middle of the queue. People were scrambling away and pushing. The soldiers who were heading towards Simonsen stopped, unsure what to do. They decided to ignore Simonsen and piled into the panicking crowd.

Simonsen turned around to face the woman holding his passport and she appeared fascinated by the commotion in the background. She absent-mindedly passed the documents back to Simonsen and muttered:

"Welcome to Russia,"

"Many thanks," Simonsen chimed and claimed his papers with a flourish and headed straight through the customs gate into the airport. Simonsen had arrived in Russia.

42

Mazepa took a sip from her mug of coffee and looked across the Moskva River at the Russian White House. It was usually the Prime Minister's office but was now serving as her friend Oksana Devina's office in her role as head of the national security council overseeing the election. She knew it would be a scene of manic chaos in there now. The revelations that came out last night and then in today's newspapers had generated a huge seismic impact across the nation.

The stories carried the bylines of journalists employed by each newspaper. Her name was not attached to any of the articles. Golitsyn had yet to make a statement and he was scheduled to make a speech in Red Square. No word had come through that the rally had been cancelled. Security was high in the capital and out of the hotel room window she could see phalanxes of police vehicles heading towards multiple locations including outside the White House.

Mazepa's thirst for knowledge and gossip was as keen as any other journalist. She needed to know the inside scoop on what was happening so she dialled Devina's number in the off-chance she would be forthcoming with the inside track. She answered almost immediately.

"I've been waiting for your call," Devina said and started chuckling.

"You know me too well. Come on, tell me everything that's going on,"

"What, so it appears in the papers tomorrow?"

"Oh Oksana, such cynicism doesn't become you," Mazepa said, realising she missed speaking to her friend on a regular basis.

"It's bedlam here, Maxim isn't pulling out of his rally. He's adamant it's going ahead,"

"You're joking?"

"Sadly I'm not. I've spoken to him twice and suggested he should cancel and stop campaigning but he's as stubborn as Dimitri when he wants to be. Nastya, he still thinks he's going to win,"

"Rich men like him always suffocate in their own hubris. If he carries on, there'll be a bloodbath,"

"There are major protests already in the East. Vladivostok workers have gone on strike and police have waded in. The FSB know that their man is going down so they are stirring up trouble,"

"Jesus, Oksana. This is scaring me,"

"There's street fighting in Irkutsk and Krasnoyarsk, militias have sprung up and are shooting at police,"

"This is madness, where are they coming from?"

"The cynic in me would suggest Sasha Saratov is rolling his last dice, I don't see how anyone else would be able to mobilise armed groups at short notice,"

"He's going to burn the country down," Mazepa said this more to herself rather than as a response to Devina's remarks, "Can't you pull the rally?"

"It's not within my remit, Dimitri held his rally so Maxim will proceed with his,"

"What about the threat to public safety?"

"That would be the mayor's responsibility and he is a good shout for foreign minister if Golitsyn is the winner,"

"Somebody has to stop him,"

"Golitsyn or Saratov?"

"It's the same thing," Mazepa didn't have the time to philosophically ponder whether the two men were actually a bicephalic creature or not. If you count Boris Ivanovich, it could be classed as a three headed monster.

She was due to interview Sasha Saratov in less than three hours, she had been wavering about attending but she knew that if she met him, she could try and convince him to back off, however futile the gesture would be.

"What are you planning to do while you are back in Moscow?"

"I may have to see the rally at Red Square," Mazepa said. She couldn't admit to her friend that she was going to interview the man at the heart of the chaos swirling around the country. Mazepa couldn't even answer why that was the case. Was she ashamed or was it her journalistic brain automatically censoring her so she wouldn't ruin her scoop?

"Don't do anything stupid. It's a tinderbox, Nastya," Devina said and ended the call.

Mazepa was about to do arguably the most reckless thing in her career but there was no way she could pull out now. She would try and persuade Saratov to admit that his candidate can't win. If not, she may even bag a massive exclusive story. Her phone buzzed and she saw a news update stating that Ian Kelsey-Moore had resigned from the British government.

One down, she thought, now who's next?

43

Moscow, Russia
Friday November 18 - 11:37 MST

Moscow was as cold as yesterday in Oslo but the low sun was filling the streets with light. Simonsen had spent half an hour exploring the streets trying to reacquaint himself with the city he spent the most significant years of his life. Simonsen arrived at Revolution Square and readied himself for a confrontation with his past.

The café at Revolution Square where Simonsen was attacked in the late summer of ninety-nine and which left Mariya fighting for life was still there although re-branded. The café was busy and the nearby streets were packed. It was almost as though Simonsen expected everyone to be sitting in respectful mourning for his loss. Instead, it appeared that the entire population of Moscow was outside today.

The atmosphere outside the Bolshoi Theatre was crackling with festivity thanks to large crowds of people. Simonsen was witnessing the masses display their power. Flags were being held aloft adorned with the names of different towns and each group of people were singing their own songs, creating a cacophony of noise.

He wasn't sure why he had chosen to visit the scene of the worst moment of his life. Simonsen wasn't even labouring under the apprehension that it would be cathartic. But it wasn't grief or pain that he felt, more of a distanced sadness. To Simonsen, it was starting to feel like an experience he could now leave in his past.

The incongruity of the contrasting atmosphere only further wedged the memories somewhere deep below the surface. The urgency of the political situation here demanded his full attention and his pilgrimage to this spot was not the priority now.

The idealistic cop whose knee was obliterated by a bullet was not the same man as he was today. He could accept who he was now and stop hiding in the shadows. You can't solve every crime or catch every criminal but you can at least give it your best shot. People can only act with impunity if they are confident that there will be no negative repercussions. Simonsen walked towards the bottom of Revolution Square so he could cut through to Red Square to witness the rally in support of Maxim Golitsyn. The sheer number of people astounded him. Not only was the amount of attendees sky-high but so was the agitation level. As he reached Teatralnaya metro station, a group of riot police were recklessly attacking people. He couldn't tell what the reason was as they didn't appear to be an organised group of protestors.

As batons were being cracked on the heads of a group of young women, a mass of fifty or so men with shaved heads dressed in black bomber jackets waded into both the police and random strangers. It was the dictionary definition of 'indiscriminate violence' and for a moment, Simonsen's feet were stuck to the floor and he was unable to prise his eyes away from the violence. Simonsen swore and finally managed to move his body away from the incident as the sound of sirens and screams pierced the air.

Groups of Bolkonsky supporters were ceaselessly chanting his name and had taken up residence on the grass outside the Patriotic Museum. There were easily over five hundred people there and the size of the assembly meant Golitsyn supporters were making do with shouting abuse at them or throwing potshot punches at the less observant members of the rabble on the edges rather than engaging them physically in a mass battle.

Simonsen was fascinated by the verbal jousts that were taking place. The group of skinheads who had attacked the police moments earlier joined the Bolkonsky supporters on the strips of grass who, in turn, reacted with loud cheers. The arrival of the hooligans prompted the Bolkonsky partisans to go on the offensive. Fists were swinging and anyone was a target as they were clearly not checking if people were rival supporters before they unleashed their fists. Simonsen scurried away and his head was dazed at what he was witnessing.

As he marched past the side of the State Historical Museum into Red Square, the noise level increased tenfold. The sound was stunning in its raw power and made the jeers of the Bolkonsky supporters around the corner sound pathetic. He walked past the cordoned off stage that led into the Kremlin complex and as he reached the front of the stage, a wall of goons were standing watching the crowd. They were clearly handy fellers and probably some of Saratov's men who had been drafted in, due to the very high expectation of trouble.

Simonsen realised that his chances of accessing the inner sanctum to speak with Golitsyn were zero. It was so loud he was struggling to focus, he found a bollard next to a tree where he spent a couple of minutes trying to calm himself down. The blurred vision eventually passed so he pulled himself up onto the top of the bollard to obtain a full view of the square.

He saw masses of people filling Red Square all the way towards the domes of St Basil's but also large gaps amidst the crowds which was strange. Helicopters were flying overhead and it added to the commotion. There must be close to half a million people here, Simonsen thought. He climbed down and began jostling through the throngs of people.

He reached the outside one of the main doors to the GUM department store, which had wisely shut its doors until the conclusion of the election. Simonsen again stood on a raised plinth and was astonished to see that one of the gaps in the crowd was being caused by a huge line of police wading into the crowd. He couldn't make out the reason for the baton charges. But as soon as they cleared the space with brutal efficiency, the people responded with their own charge.

Despite a lack of tools they forced the police back into a defensive shape. About three hundred yards to the left of this incident, another similar scene was being played out. It was bizarre, there were multiple riots dotted around the square but in other areas of Red Square, the atmosphere was like a carnival with exuberant singing and flags flying.

Simonsen turned his head to the right, back in the direction where he had walked from and saw the group of skinhead-led Bolkonsky fans heading into Red Square. His stomach lurched and somehow sank even further when he looked left and saw another group of black-clad men enter Red Square from Ilyinka Street in a clearly-planned pincer move. These men immediately started to punch anyone they deemed a supporter of Maxim Golitsyn.

Red Square was now a battlefield. This was more than scuffles, it was the prelude to disaster if it continued in this manner. Saratov's goons guarding the stage were now engaged in a brawl with the skinheads. People were now trying to flee the square but there was danger on every corner. Simonsen weighed up his options and he decided to stay put for now. The chances of getting attacked would be greater if he headed towards the trouble. Hopefully they will have punched themselves out by the time they had reached the middle of the square.

44

Moscow, Russia
Friday November 18 - 12:03 MST

Bolkonsky was writing his victory speech in his living room with a pen and notepad. He had received a bunch of bullet points from his staff and he was trying to work the words out in a manner that sounded victorious but not overly triumphant. That was pretty difficult as the urge to rub Golitsyn's face in it was proving almost irresistible. He always liked to compose his own speeches. The content would be provided by his aides but he would phrase it in his own words. The words had to sound authentic to have the impact he desired and no one else knew him better than himself.

He had learned from an early age that if you shoulder the responsibility for your own life, then you have no one else to blame if things go wrong but also you don't need to owe your success to anybody else. His inner circle was small and contained, and generally, he had few real personal enemies. He saw himself as someone who gave everyone a fair chance and that hard work would always be rewarded.

Zakatov was ready to launch their attack at the heart of Sasha Saratov's empire. In a couple of days' time, there would be no-one capable of challenging his power. Bolkonsky was nervous, giving the go-ahead for Zakatov's mission was risky but the Russian people had always respected boldness and bravery. Yeltsin's popularity soared when he faced down the hardline coup and stood on the tanks outside parliament, back in ninety-three. Bolkonsky knew his own Yeltsin moment would arrive very soon.

Bolkonsky glanced at his watch, a tattered antique passed down from his grandfather, who fought on the streets of Moscow against the White Guards during the Bolshevik Revolution. Golitsyn's rally was scheduled to start a few minutes ago so he flicked the television on and switched to the state news channel.

The first image he saw was a close-up of a policeman slapping a young woman with a thick, gloved hand. The woman's nose exploded and blood spurted out as though from a broken sink. It was all caught in high-definition slow-motion. Bolkonsky dropped his pen and pad and turned the volume up and watched another replay of the shocking incident.

Footage switched to an overhead shot of Red Square which showed that an immense crowd had gathered. Bolkonsky was impressed at the size of the crowd Golitsyn had mustered considering today's revelations. The picture cut to the front of the stage and a huge fistfight between two groups of tough-looking men. There were casualties on the floor, some of whom were being kicked repeatedly. The kickers were then being set upon by angry comrades of the men lying on the floor. Blood was smeared on the ground in places where people had gotten up to start rucking again.

"What the fuck is going on?" Bolkonsky said out loud to himself. Outside Lenin's mausoleum, the police were engaged in furious exchanges with Golitsyn's supporters. The clashes were of a ferocity that Bolkonsky had never witnessed in the capital. The sheer amount of people involved made it look like a battle in a war, it was on the cusp of moving from riot to revolution.

A revolution was not what the nation needed. A revolution meant that his ascension to president was not a given. If the nation crumbled today, the election could potentially be postponed. He telephoned Oksana Devina but there was no answer.

Bolkonsky knew he needed to postpone the attack he had planned with Zakatov. If it goes ahead, it could be the drop of blood that breached the defences of the nation.

Bolkonsky muted the television, stood and dialled Zakatov. However, Zakatov's telephone was switched off. He tried again and again but Zakatov remained out of contact. The attack was going to go ahead and Bolkonsky's body became convulsed by shakes.

45

Moscow, Russia
Friday November 18 - 12:20 MST

Anastasiya Mazepa couldn't stop staring at the gleaming skyscrapers in the Moscow-City area of the capital. She had decided to walk along the embankment along the river from her hotel to the Sarabank headquarters. Messages kept beeping on her phone but she had to stop looking at them as they were making her anxious.

Violent scenes in Red Square between rival supporters and security forces had forced Golitsyn's rally to be postponed. If Mazepa kept reading about it, she would fall into a pit of despair. Why was there such a propensity for Russians to resort to violence? The two candidates were happy to fan the flames of barbarity with the agitation and lies simply so they could hold power, not for the betterment of the citizens.

She reached the Bagration footbridge and began crossing the river. It was like walking along a giant airport corridor. She couldn't decide if the bridge looked futuristic or tacky. This was the new Russia, where dubiously-acquired money controlled everything. The Moscow-City development contained more skyscrapers than anywhere else in Europe despite the fact that Russia's economy was barely bigger than Spain's despite having three times the population. The money was concentrated not only in tiny portions of the cities but also concentrated into the hands of very few people with very little disposition to redistribute that wealth.

She reached the end of the footbridge and her

destination was the nearest and most stunning building in the district, the Evolution Tower. Its twisting facade reminded Mazepa of a double helix DNA string. The tower was now filled with the workers of Saratov's most public-facing company, Sarabank. The company had gradually grown larger and larger and was now referred to as the Kremlin's bank and thus it was the bank of former KGB men who had taken hold of the country's assets during Putin's tenure.

Rivals had been bought up, usually after engaging in some brutal methods, Mazepa was aware of at least one director of a competitor being dangled out of a window in their previous HQ. He soon arranged for the sale of his shares to Sarabank. Another director of a small bank in St Petersburg was kidnapped, and forced to watch a live video stream of a gun being held at his wife's head until he signed over the controlling stake to Sarabank. Naturally, none of this was reported inside of Russia.

At the entrance to the tower, Mazepa looked up to try and take in the full scale of it. The winding structure and diagonal windows made her stomach turn over so she closed her eyes. Was going to meet Ivanovich and Saratov the wisest move?

All she could hear was sirens and cars honking. The city was in a febrile state and she was about to meet the two most dangerous men in the country.

Mazepa was greeted at the entrance by a young, very handsome man in a beautifully-fitted blue suit who said he would lead her to the meeting. The two of them entered a lift together, the offices were pretty quiet, perhaps they had been sent home due to the unrest in the city.

"It's quiet today," Mazepa said.

"Yes, most people were giving the day off because of the election tomorrow," the man replied to her in a quiet voice.

"Is Saratov in the building?" she asked and the man blushed.

"I'm unable to confirm that," he said and she knew that

was the line he was told to utter when he heard any mention of Sasha Saratov's name.

"Keeping you out of the loop, eh?" Mazepa said and winked at the man whose face remained either disappointingly impassive or frozen in fear, "I'm sure Sasha will give you that big promotion to the top table soon enough,"

The lift continued upwards and the man stared at the floor whilst Mazepa kept looking at him, enjoying him squirm. The lift arrived and the doors opened, the man pointed out of the door and Mazepa exited the lift. Her guide remained in the lift and only now did he possess the confidence to meet her eyes. Mazepa thought he looked terrified. She wondered if he saw that reflected in her eyes too.

Mazepa walked out into a large open-plan room surrounding a black circular wall about six metres in diameter and a couple of metres high. The room was a strange mix between a high-end apartment and futuristic space command centre. Beautiful modernist furniture adorned the room which was bathed in light. She recognised an Isamu Noguchi table that Sasha Saratov had won at an auction for an obscene sum last year which was the subject of a fawning article in the *Chronicle* about his artistic taste.

There was a huge Boca do Lobo desk that housed multiple screens and telephones. Sitting at the desk was Boris Ivanovich, dressed all in black, almost camouflaged by the ebony backwall. She couldn't stop herself from letting out a little gasp at the sight of Ivanovich. No matter how much he could change his voice and manner, he remained the most sinister man she had ever met in her life. He was smiling at her and Mazepa thought that only made him look worse. He had clearly spent years practising how to smile to enable him to stand for public office.

"Anastasiya, welcome to the hub of our global operations, loyally located here in the centre of Moscow. You are very lucky to see the inner sanctum. We thought you might like a tour of the top floor. This is where the most important business in the whole of Russia takes place," Ivanovich stood and walked around the table to meet Mazepa. He didn't shake her hand and to Mazepa's eyes, he looked tired and showing signs of age. God knows how old he was, she thought, surely he must be in his sixties now?

Ivanovich walked her around the apartment. Majestic views of the city could be seen from every window, it was impossible not to be impressed by it.

"It's not exactly a communal apartment in Khasavyurt, is it?" Mazepa said, referring to Saratov's bleak, far-off Dagestani hometown.

"Does it offend your bourgeois sensibilities that a man can come from nothing and end up here?"

"I'm only offended about the collateral damage on the way to the destination,"

"For a man to accumulate wealth in Russia, you will meet a lot of dishonest and violent people who try to prevent it. Sasha has only reacted in self-defence to any threats to his hard-earned fortune. It's nothing to be ashamed of, it's actually something that we are proud of,"

"He is accused of more than simply self-defence," Mazepa said.

"What kind of things do they accuse me of?" a low voice said and Mazepa turned around. Framed by a huge portrait of Peter the Great at Peterhof stood Sasha Saratov, the man who would be tsar of a new Russia. He was wearing a crisp white shirt and excellently-tailored gunmetal grey trousers. His intense eyes burned out of his glasses and Mazepa could only feel a pure terror in her heart.

"I never knew you were that naive," Mazepa said, her voice wobbling. She didn't know what to do with her hands which were dangling by her side and she felt like a little girl being told off at school.

"Please take a seat, come over here and we can look at the best view over the city," Saratov opened his arms and directed Mazepa towards a few backless sofas with views over the city.

She couldn't deny how amazing the view was. She trained her eyes on the domes of St Basil's but from here she couldn't see the battles that were raging on the square and its environs.

"Have you seen what is happening in the city? It's chaos," Mazepa said. She stared at Saratov and he appeared serene, like a boat bobbing on a lake in summer.

"Dimitri Bolkonsky has sent in his GRU mates to crack some skulls. Once the people see that and with the knowledge that he organised the bombing in Oslo, they will turn against him and they will see that Maxim Golitsyn is the only candidate who can bring stability and direction to the country. Finally, Russia is on the verge of becoming a great power once again. And not power built on the secret police or aloof elites but on democracy, economic freedom and respect for all cultures,"

Fucking hell, he likes to talk, thought Mazepa. This is what happens when you surround yourself for decades with yes-men.

"Can't you see that the country is disintegrating? If this continues, there will be no Russia left to govern," Mazepa said.

"Bullshit," Ivanovich piped up from behind her, "You journalists see what you want to see. Your preconceived ideas prove you are unable to see past your bias,"

"He's right," Saratov said, standing to survey the city from his open-plan altar, ready to continue his sermon, "You liberals are quick to predict the end of our nation but we always survive. The Byzantines, the Turks, the Khans, the Poles, the Nazis - they have all tried to destroy us but they haven't come close to erasing us from history. Maxim will be an excellent leader and business leaders are unified behind his candidature. You may not approve of my methods but everyone knows you have to break a few eggs to make that democratic omelette,"

A democratic omelette? Mazepa was sure this guy was a lunatic. Whatever evidence he had on Bolkonsky, it was bound to be damning if its veracity could be verified. However, the longer she spoke to him, the more it appeared that he was living in his own world, full of constructed conspiracies and with a deferential staff unable or unwilling to project some semblance of reality into his brain. Nobody has told this guy to shut the fuck up and stop talking shit in years, Mazepa thought, and sometimes that is what you need to keep you rational and normal.

"I know you are a busy man, Sasha. Let's get down to business. You are making strong claims about Dimitri Bolkonsky being responsible for the bombing of the Iskender Café in Oslo. A bold claim requires substantial evidence. Do you actually hold evidence?"

"I have always been a man of my word. You may not like what I say but I have never lied to you," Saratov said, the words dripping out of his mouth like poisoned apple juice.

"You're dissembling,"

"Many years ago, I promised you safety if you eased off on a false story you were planning to write,"

"The story wasn't false,"

"I am a patriot and I value honesty above everything else. Your honesty lasted as it took until you met a beefy peasant who you allowed to violate you,"

Mazepa could simultaneously feel her heart breaking again and her brain fogging over. She was being hypnotised by this psychopath and she was incapable of disengaging from his thrall.

"You are compromised as a journalist, Anastasiya, but nobody else knows it. The only people aware of your unsavoury carnal pursuits are us three in this room," Saratov gestured his hand towards Ivanovich who appeared in a world of his own, staring at his feet until he heard his name when he lifted his head and showed off that horrible smile again.

"The story outline is already written," Ivanovich grabbed a sheet of paper from a nearby table and handed it to Mazepa, "All you need to do is add the journalistic flair that befits one of our nation's most respected correspondents,"

"But the proof?" Mazepa said and knew straight away

that she was caught in a trap.

"We have seen the proof and that should be good enough for you," Ivanovich's dead gaze fused into her brain, "As Sasha told you, we are honest men. The notes contain enough for you to write a story which will be printed in the morning. It will be trailed on television later too,"

"I can't write the story without seeing the evidence. I am a journalist, not a propagandist,"

"You can, and you will write it," Saratov said, "Due to the unrest in Moscow, it is probably safer that you stay here and complete the task. You will not go wanting for food or drink and in the new Russia, we would be delighted to appoint you as our new head of state television,"

Mazepa was nihilistic, speaking to Saratov had drained her spirit. Her defences had been breached and she knew she would do the bidding of the grey-haired malevolence. She slowly nodded her head and slumped her shoulders. Saratov grinned at her, completely unable to conceal his perverse delight.

"I need to use the toilet, can you direct me to it please?" Mazepa said and pulled her eyes from Saratov to Ivanovich who once more, seemed distracted by something he was reading on his mobile phone.

"What? Oh, yes, it's the door next to the lift where you came in,"

Mazepa stood and fought to retain her composure so she could walk slowly towards the toilet. She reached the plain white door and entered the bathroom where a light and extractor fan both popped on. She entered a cubicle and sat down. She ran her hands over her face before grabbing her phone and dialling Simonsen's number.

"Simonsen, is that you?" Mazepa whispered.

"Yes, it's me. Are you alright?" Simonsen said, his voice calming her down straight away.

"I'm OK. Well, I'm not but I have to tell you something. I need to tell you where the dossier is. If I don't make it out of here, please release it somehow,"

Silence on the other end of the line. For a brief moment, she thought that Saratov and Ivanovich had tapped the line and cut her off but then she heard Simonsen's voice.

"Yes, OK,"

"The key is in my room safe at the Hotel Ukraina, room 539. Ask at reception and they will allow you in my room. The safe code is 4497 and the keyfob will tell you where to go. I have to go now. Goodbye, Simonsen,"

46

Moscow, Russia
Friday November 18 - 13:11 MST

"Hotel Ukraina," Simonsen hopped into the passenger seat of a yellow taxi and gave the order to the dark-haired driver who raced off from his rank on the Kremlin embankment. Police vans were lining up on the opposite side of the road and blood-covered protesters were streaming out of the area. The taxi driver appeared delighted to be fleeing the mayhem. For two hundred metres, it was an unbroken line of police vehicles. This was a city on the edge of collapse and Simonsen was caught right in the middle of it all.

Simonsen had managed to evade the trouble in Red Square which had plateaued to a stalemate as Bolkonsky's well-organised hooligans were driven back by sheer weight of opposition numbers. The police had also withdrawn and there was a defiance in the public mood. Golitsyn had taken a few steps on stage but immediately withdrew at the sight of the trouble, almost tripping over in his haste to depart the scene.

The driver swung the taxi past the statue of Vladimir the Great, the defender of early Russia, holding his great cross. They continued through the city and the driver was chattering on about the rioting, to which Simonsen ignored every single word.

Simonsen was overawed at the responsibility he had been given in obtaining the dossier that contained potentially explosive revelations about the most powerful man in the country. The sick feeling that had lodged in his belly when he obtained the tape from Narimanov's hotel room in Oslo was still there but was transforming into exhilaration.

The driver was hitting good speeds as they cruised along the fast lane of New Arbat Avenue. Yet more police vans were heading in the opposite direction and every car seemed to be driving faster than they would normally on a Friday afternoon.

The taxi approached the junction at Novoarbatsky Bridge, the colossal Hotel Ukraina proudly sat directly on the other side of the riverbank with the Moscow-City financial district located a kilometre further away in the background. Something told Simonsen to go to the Sarabank building to see if Mazepa was OK but he knew that he had to stick to the plan. Deviating from the plan to head into the wolf's lair would be a risky and potentially fatal move.

Suddenly, a huge explosion emanated from one of the skyscrapers in the far distance. The driver shouted and nearly drove the car off the bridge before he managed to regain control and haphazardly park up on the pavement. Simonsen glanced at the driver who appeared petrified before his gaze returned to the skyscrapers as another three or four blasts ripped into the towers in the far distance and the rumbles resonated across the city.

"Are we under attack?" the driver said, his Central Asian face had turned a strange off-white colour and he looked like he was going to puke. The driver seemed to be looking at Simonsen for answers but he was caught in two minds. Should he keep to the plan and head to the hotel or venture on to see if Mazepa was safe?

"Keep going," Simonsen said, pointing forward. He had to check to see if she was safe.

"Not a chance," the driver said and all the other drivers on the bridge seemed equally reluctant to move forward in the direction of the explosions. The bridge was now full of people out of their cars staring at the flaming tower, partially obscured by the Hotel Ukraina. The taxi driver kept staring at him, as if expecting Simonsen to tell him to clock off for the day and go home.

Simonsen's phone buzzed in his pocket and he pulled it out. It was a message from Mazepa:

-    under attack, help

"Hey," Simonsen shouted at the driver whose hands were glued to the wheel, "Listen to me. Drive!"

"I can't go any further. No, no, no," the driver had finally stopped staring at Simonsen. Now he was facing into the middle-distance as though in shock, an anxious mess caught up in a nightmare. Simonsen opened his passenger door and ambled around towards the driver's side. He shocked the driver by opening the driver's side door.

"What the hell are you doing?" the driver said, now as equally confused as he was panic-stricken.

"Police, I need your vehicle," Simonsen said, thinking he was the only policeman in real life who had ever used that phrase. The driver looked at him blankly and Simonsen dragged the man out of his car by the lapels of his cardigan and hurled him onto the floor.

The driver appeared terrified as Simonsen loomed over him. Simonsen was about to shout in his face but the driver was already cowering in a foetal position and all-in-all, was having a genuinely terrible day at work, so he left him in the middle of the street. Simonsen entered the driving seat and smashed his foot down on the accelerator, blaring the horn to move any humans out of the way of his commandeered vehicle.

Within seconds, he was weaving around cars, half of them still parked following the shock of the blasts. His original destination, the Hotel Ukraina rose dramatically to his right but his mind was now set on his new location.

He kept the foot down and the blocky buildings on either side of the avenue blurred into one. He reached the junction for the Third Ring Road and glided the taxi onto the bridge where the Moscow-City skyscrapers surged into view with sunlight fulgurating off the buildings like diamonds.

The Evolution Tower could be glimpsed at the right of the skyscrapers and he could see fires in a few areas of the building. Armed men dressed in black fatigues were taking shots at the windows, whether they were aiming at people they could see in the windows, he was unable to tell. The tower fell out of view as he moved the taxi around the back of the district. He pulled up about one hundred metres away from the rear of the Sarabank headquarters. Simonsen remained in his car lost for ideas on what to do now he had arrived at what could only be described as an active warzone.

47

Moscow, Russia
Friday November 18 - 13:32 MST

The first explosion struck the building as Mazepa re-entered
Saratov's office. A strange high-pitched whistle was perorated
by a thunderous blast. Ivanovich and Saratov watched her
enter the room at the same time as the world shook.

Both men dived to the floor, more in self-preservation
than as a result of the shockwave which had luckily not taken
place on this floor. Was it a bomb? Mazepa had heard a few
bombs going off in her time in Dagestan. Before she could work
out if it was a bomb, she heard even more explosions.

The first two were muffled so must have been on much
lower floors. By the time the third one had hit, Mazepa realised
it was rockets that were being fired at the building. She saw the
tip of one crash through a window behind where Saratov was
lying, it slammed into the top of the central concrete wall and
the noise was beyond comparison.

The whole floor shook and parts of the ceiling collapsed
along with huge amounts of dust and debris. Mazepa fell to
the floor and couldn't hear anything. She lifted her head up
and put her hands across her nose and mouth to keep the
dust out. She saw Ivanovich dragging up his boss by hooking
his arm under Saratov's shoulder and yanking him up to his
feet. She couldn't tell if either man was injured when another
rocket clipped the windows and exploded outside, shattering
whatever glass was still held in place.

Both men hurled themselves to the ground again, barely

three metres away from her. All three were laid on their bellies shaped like some odd human recreation of the Mercedes logo. Saratov met her gaze and for the first time, she saw fear in his eyes. It was the fear of a man who was always one step ahead but this time he had been caught off-guard and he didn't know how to react.

"Sasha, come on!" Ivanovich was already on his knees bellowing at Saratov who turned to face him like an ailing grandfather lying on his deathbed looking at his relatives one last time. Ivanovich again grabbed him under his armpit and jerked him to his feet with one hand. With his other hand, he had taken his phone out of his pocket and was barking instructions to someone at the other end of the line.

Mazepa was glad the rocket attacks had ceased, She remained on her belly as Ivanovich and Saratov ignored her. What a couple of ungentlemanly bastards, she thought, with little sense of surprise. Mazepa heard automatic gunfire and now she was scared. Rockets are fired from a distance but exchanges of gunfire meant armed men were very close. She pulled her phone out and texted a message of help to Simonsen, the crippled Norwegian cop who was her last, and rather uninspiring, hope.

Mazepa flipped onto her back and tried to remain calm. It was surely Bolkonsky's GRU men that were attacking the building. This was a direct armed assault on Saratov's empire and his FSB allies. With the security services at each other's throats at ground level, was it safe to leave or would she have a better chance of survival by staying here?

It was a big tower and she didn't think that the building was structurally compromised, despite being hit by missiles. She couldn't stay in this office though, there was a good chance that this would be the first place the attackers would head to if they breached the security downstairs. Mazepa got to her feet and was immediately lightheaded and wheezy in the dusty space. Her hearing was slowly coming back but the ringing in her ears still dominated her senses.

She didn't want to take the lift as she heeded all the stories over the years that asserted lifts aren't a good place to be in during a fire. It had indoctrinated her enough to try and find a stairwell. She walked around the office trying to locate a stairwell. On her route past Saratov's desk, she saw a mobile phone which she pocketed and kept searching for an exit.

Between two large bookcases, both filled with weighty business tomes, she saw a plain white door. She opened it and it led into a staircase which she tiptoed into. Mazepa allowed the door to close and noticed it had no handle on the other side and thus realised she was trapped on the outside of Saratov's office. She was forced to descend, the only way was down. She heard a couple of distant gunshots and realised that attackers may already be in the stairwell.

She raced down a few flights of stairs, her balance still off-kilter from her ringing ears. On arrival at each landing, she tried to open the door to access the floor but with no success. Panic was rising and Mazepa didn't want to keep descending and bump into a trigger-happy goon with a gun. She began mumbling words of encouragement to herself.

On the next flight of stairs, she pulled the door handle and it turned and opened. A flush of relief passed through her belly. She exhaled a long breath, entered the office and closed the door behind her. The office lights were all turned off but it was brightly filled with sunshine. She saw a sign stating this was the 47th level of the tower.

Now that she was inside this office, she had no idea what to do next. She stood in the centre of the office, her mind numbed by the explosions. The decision-making part of her brain was paralysed. All she could think about was the face of Sasha Saratov and the look of terrified incomprehension he displayed to her. Mazepa allowed herself a brief moment of pleasure knowing that Russia can be a dangerous place even for the most powerful.

48

Moscow, Russia
Friday November 18 - 14:09 MST

Simonsen's doubts about how to locate Mazepa were threatening to overwhelm any courage he had summoned on his drive to the Sarabank headquarters. Shots were still ringing out and the idea that reversing the taxi out of here and driving straight to the Hotel Ukraina was at the forefront of his mind. How was he supposed to find her in the midst of this chaos?

In some twisted policeman's logic, it was inconceivable that he could leave Mazepa in peril. Simonsen's brain was trying to weigh up whether the world would be in a worse state if the dossier wasn't released and Sasha Saratov, the maniacal puppeteer, could gain power and exert his toxic influence to a much greater extent than he does now.

Simonsen repeatedly slammed his hand down on the steering wheel and shouted a string of Norwegian curses in the empty, stolen taxi. He pulled his phone out and messaged Mazepa:

- I'm at Sarabank, where are you?

Simonsen chose to remain in his car as he wasn't sure if Mazepa had escaped the mayhem. As he awaited a response to his message, another colossal explosion ripped through the bottom of the tower. A wall of flame and glass burst out like a tidal wave and Simonsen ducked down below the steering wheel of the taxi. Shards of obliterated skyscraper material peppered the road and a disgusting intense heat passed over the car but within a few seconds it was gone.

Simonsen popped his head up and wondered what he was going to see. Charcoal-coloured plumes of smoke were rising up the frame of the tower. The bottom of the tower was engulfed in roaring flames and Simonsen's fears for Mazepa continued to increase. He checked his phone and received a message:

- On floor 47. Be careful, gunmen.

Simonsen uttered one more Norwegian obscenity before exiting the taxi. Immediately, he was shrouded in moist warmth and an awful acrid taste filled his mouth. He scanned for the gunmen Mazepa warned him about but saw no-one so he ran towards the source of the explosion.

As he reached the foot of the tower, a large delivery entrance door started to horizontally raise up. Once it was half opened, a yellow Ferrari edged out from under the door. Simonsen caught a glimpse of the driver, who despite blood running down his shaved head, was unmistakably Sasha Saratov.

Saratov flashed a look of incomprehension at Simonsen. He didn't stop but instead accelerated away from the scenes of carnage that had enveloped the area. As Simonsen entered through the gap where Saratov had driven out of, he saw an armed man dressed in black pointing his weapon at him.

Simonsen stood still, unable to run. The man shouted something but his mind had stopped working and he couldn't understand. The man approached him and Simonsen heard a bullet fly past his ear. The armed man standing in front of him suddenly had a hole in his forehead and he dropped to the floor, stone dead.

Simonsen realised he had pissed himself like he did after Peter Kelsey-Moore was killed last night and thought this kind of thing didn't happen to Bruce Willis in the *Die*

Hard films. Simonsen had no idea who had shot the man or whose side he was on but he didn't hang around to find out. He liberated the dead man's gun from his prone body and ran inside the tower.

Inside the parking garage were a string of supercars neatly lined up like a child ordering his toy cars into rows. It must be Saratov's private collection and was clearly worth a fortune. Half of the lights in the room remained on and he spotted a burning door with a man halfway inside calling out. Simonsen jogged over and pulled the guy out. It was Boris Ivanovich and he was in a terrible state.

His legs were smouldering lumps of flesh and Simonsen couldn't understand how the man wasn't dead already. Ivanovich's feet appeared to have completely burned off and a truly awful smell emanated from his charred body.

"Help me," Ivanovich's piercing eyes pleaded with Simonsen. There was no helping him, Simonsen thought and he looked for another way up. The stairwell appeared to be where the latest rocket had entered, so Simonsen decided it was off-limits. For a brief second, he considered putting Ivanovich out of his misery with a quick shot to the head but logic overrode compassion and he realised he may need all the bullets in the weapon on his mission to find Mazepa. Simonsen knew that spite also played a part in his decision but the time for ethical debate was not this precise moment.

A service elevator was about ten metres to his right and despite the risks, he knew it was the only way up to the forty-seventh floor. Simonsen edged over to the lift, his sense of alertness at its highest level. He pressed the button to call the lift and held the gun ready. It had been a good fifteen years since he had undergone his last weapons training when he was still with the Norwegian police but he felt confident he could handle this AK, knowing they are renowned for being easy to use and reliable.

The lift door opened and it was empty. Simonsen ran into the lift and pressed number 47 on the panel. The lift began to rise and Simonsen hoped more than anything that no one else had pressed the button. He wasn't sure he could handle having to shoot anyone. Simonsen had to battle to not think about whether he could shoot someone and to concentrate on the task at hand.

Every floor he passed, a wave of relief hit him hard. At long last, the lift arrived at the forty-seventh floor. The doors parted and Simonsen could hear his heart pounding as he expected armed company. However there was no one on the landing so he ran out towards the office door. It pushed open easily and he walked into a large open plan office filled with banks of desks containing identical computers and monitors.

Simonsen made his way slowly through the office, he was confident it was deserted but he didn't want to take any chances. He stood in the middle of the office and scanned around to see if he could locate Mazepa.

Almost on cue, he saw her head pop up like a meerkat. Her right hand also popped up and started waving and he couldn't help but laugh. He walked over to her and they embraced.

"Hello," Simonsen said and he was so glad to see her alive he started laughing.

"Simonsen, you took your bloody time,"

49

"Who is attacking the building?" Mazepa said as Simonsen yanked her by the arm back towards the lift. She saw that he had his eyes set forward watching the door he entered through. He pushed the office door open and paused for a few seconds before proceeding through it.

"I don't know. It has to be Bolkonsky and the GRU," Simonsen said as the two of them entered the lift. Simonsen pressed a button and backed up against the far wall. He lifted and aimed his gun at the centre of the doors.

"He's starting a civil war," Mazepa held her head in her hands and tried to settle her nerves down. The whole situation was insanity. That bastard Bolkonsky might be even crazier than Saratov. Madness was the only way to describe launching an armed assault on the headquarters of one of Russia's biggest companies.

The lift doors parted and there were no visible gunmen that she could see. Mazepa was trembling and she had to fight the urge not to press the button to close the lift doors again. They appeared to be in a parking garage and she watched Simonsen edge his way out of the lift with the gun raised up, his posture that of a soldier. Seeing him in that pose only terrified her even more.

"It's Saratov's private garage," Simonsen whispered, "Go check if any of the cars are unlocked, Saratov escaped from here a few minutes ago,"

MARTIN O'BRIEN

Mazepa forced her legs to propel her forward. She edged out of the lift and saw Simonsen pointing to his right so she scurried off in that direction. Mazepa saw a dead body with legs burned to a tapered tinder lying on the floor and she shrieked, the sound echoing around the garage.

Simonsen turned to her with a face that looked like he wanted her to either shut up or die. He made a slashing motion with his hand and Mazepa was irritated at the motion. You could have warned me about the body, she thought.

"Quick, try the cars," Simonsen said, his voice as tight as a bow. Mazepa realised his annoyance at her was simply a manifestation of his terror. Mazepa stepped over the body and she recognised that it was Boris Ivanovich. Even his lifeless corpse scared her shitless and she almost yelped again. Being this close to Ivanovich, however lacking in life and minus two feet, prompted her to speed up and she reached the first vehicle, a tiny red Ferrari. She couldn't even work out how to open the car door, never mind actually gaining access.

She crouched down and ran to the next vehicle, a bulky black Range Rover with tinted windows. She reached the driver's side door and was about to enter the vehicle when she heard a cry from Simonsen:

"Stay down!"

Mazepa threw herself to the floor and heard automatic gunfire rattle around the garage. The noise was incredible and she could almost taste the sulphurous discharge. The shooting stopped and she lifted her head up and was beyond relieved to see Simonsen, eyes blazing, stood with the AK-47 held upwards like a Jihadi at a Syrian roadside checkpoint.

"The door, the door!" Simonsen shouted to her in English. Mazepa pulled the handle and the door opened. She flung herself into the car clipping the top of her head off the roof causing her to shout out in pain. She hunted for a way of starting the car and panicked because she couldn't see anything. Simonsen stood about four metres in front of the car unleashing another hail of bullets at some unseen assailants.

Mazepa was mystified about what to do next. She was searching everywhere in the vehicle. She noticed something was under her foot so she lifted her foot up and saw a key fob. The sight of it almost made her cry. She plucked it off the floor, pressed the button and the car engine began rumbling.

Simonsen turned to her and his face looked confused. Mazepa looked at him and he was frozen to the floor staring at her. What the fuck was he waiting for?

"Come on, get in!" she shouted while beckoning him with both hands towards the car. Finally his reverie broke. Mazepa noticed a shape in her peripheral vision trying to enter the garage from underneath a large shutter door. As soon as she saw the gunman, Simonsen was shooting over the car towards the figure. A bullet careered into the top of the attacker's arm and sent him to the floor, dropping his weapon and clutching his injured wing.

Simonsen opened the passenger door and jumped in. He stank of piss and sulphur and his wild eyes implored her to get them out of here. Mazepa accelerated away and the car burst into blinding sunlight. She kept her foot down and heard more shots ring out including a couple of bursts that appeared to clip the back of the car.

The unreality of the situation was ridiculous, she turned to look at the dour cop who had metamorphosed into the Norwegian Rambo and she started to laugh. Simonsen looked at her and he shook his head at her and grinned with what could have been the most wonderful, life-affirming smile she had ever seen.

50

Moscow, Russia
Friday November 18 - 18:38 MST

Dimitri Bolkonsky was sitting at home watching the television news with a very large glass of vodka balanced on his knee. He had muted the sound as the noises were turning his mind to mush. All he could see was the frenzied skirmishes between rival groups on Red Square, overhead shots of huge riots across major cities and now the battle at the Sarabank headquarters that had ended a couple of hours earlier and left at least thirty people dead.

The footage was undeniably spectacular. RPGs scything through gorgeous blue Muscovite skies into the modern architectural towers at Moscow-City. People on the other side of the river bank had filmed footage of dozens of GRU units engaged in firefights with Saratov's armed men, half of them FSB agents. The scenes could have been pinched from a Hollywood blockbuster, but Bolkonsky knew this footage was only too real and also contained the seeds of his potential downfall.

Bolkonsky held his hands out in front of his chest and saw both hands were shaking. This was a new sensation. Bolkonsky was nicknamed the Bulldozer when he rose through the military ranks due to his ability to dust himself off from criticism and setbacks. And not simply setbacks, he had an uncanny mentality in which he did things he should be ashamed of but refused to allow guilt to even enter his head, never mind weighing him down.

It was only now that he realised the guilt he had kept completely subdued was finally rising to the surface and he had so much blame to accept. He was a man who was comfortable casting out his only son from Russia because of his sexuality. He was a man who could casually slaughter a bunch of peasants in the Caucasus and carry on as though these things were menial chores.

Bolkonsky was now encumbered by a shroud of compunction. Was it old age or the murder of his son that was now causing this feeling? Anxiety gnawed at him and the only thing that slightly mitigated it was sitting very still. He was a remorseful statue and he realised tears were dripping down his face.

"No," Bolkonsky said and drank a slug of vodka. He picked his phone up and saw he had dozens of missed calls. As he scrolled down the list of calls, the phone started to ring. It was Ivan Zakatov and with a quivering, vodka-soaked finger, Bolkonsky answered the phone.

"Dimitri," Zakatov's voice rumbled down the line, "Where the fuck have you been?"

"I'm at home," Bolkonsky said, and to his ears it sounded like a whimper.

"Ivanovich is dead." Zakatov said. Bolkonsky sat up straight on his sofa at the news, "His body was found half-burned to a crisp. He was still alive somehow when we found him. I put a bullet square through his fucking head,"

"What about Saratov?"

"He escaped. A few cars managed to drive out of the garage at the back of the tower. We don't know where the fuck he is but he's on the run,"

Bolkonsky should have been elated at the demise of Boris Ivanovich and the scurrying rat, Saratov, running scared. However, the anxiety gripping his body had numbed the pleasure sensors in his brain.

"We're nearly there, Dimitri. Russia is going to be ours," Zakatov said. Bolkonsky could almost picture him, puffed out like a peacock at the other end of the line.

"If there is a Russia left to rule," Bolkonsky said.

"What are you talking about?"

"Have you been watching the fucking news, Ivan? Every bloody station is calling it the start of a civil war. Mother of God,"

"Stop watching Saratov's TV channels, you're fucking obsessed with him. It's bullshit propaganda that we will put a stop to from next week,"

"It's on every channel," Bolkonsky said, placing his glass of vodka on the floor lest he hurl it at the wall, "There are protests and riots in every city, from Kaliningrad to Kamchatka, the country is on fire,"

"You're losing your bottle Dimitri, I never thought that would be possible,"

"I'm going to ignore that remark and assume you said it in the heat of the moment because I know you're not a complete moron, Ivan Vladimirovich,"

"Listen, Dimitri, my car is pulling up to yours in a minute. Let's talk about it like the old friends that we have always been,"

"OK, I'll buzz you through the gate when I see you," Bolkonsky said and he hung up the phone.

The cheek of Zakatov! A man who had grabbed onto his coat-tails years ago and held on as Bolkonsky rose the ranks. Now Zakatov had the gall to accuse him of losing his bottle? Bolkonsky chuckled at the conversation. Zakatov was a perceptive bastard and he could see straight through him.

He stood and at the moment he reached his window, he saw Zakatov's car pull up outside. He buzzed the gates to open and the car door opened and Zakatov exited the vehicle. His companion jogged up the drive and straight into Bolkonsky's house. Zakatov was wearing his combat fatigues and his usually impeccable short hair was a spiky mess. He looked exuberant and his chest was as ridiculously puffed out as Bolkonsky expected to see.

"You should have been there, Dimitri," Zakatov clasped his hands around Bolkonsky's wrists, "They weren't expecting it, and we overran them. Twelve of his men were killed included that bastard Ivanovich and thirty taken into GRU custody,"

"FSB men?" Bolkonsky said, fearing immediate reprisals.

"Some will have been, others are mercenaries. Either way, they are paid by Saratov and are traitors to the state. Fifteen branches of Sarabank have been raided too and dozens of staff arrested. We've not touched the newspaper offices, that can wait until next week,"

Bolkonsky almost fainted at the scale of the destruction. He walked off, lifted his vodka glass off the floor, drained it and refilled it. Zakatov joined him at the sideboard and poured himself a whiskey. He put his arm around Bolkonsky and pulled him closer.

"This is the final test, Dimitri," Zakatov met his gaze and held him tight, "Every great leader has these doubts. Do you not think Julius Caesar had misgivings before he crossed the Rubicon? The die is cast and we must stay strong,"

"It's election day tomorrow," Zakatov continued, he released his grip on Bolkonsky and shuffled to a chair, sitting down with a huff, "Within twenty-four hours, the results will come in and confirm that you are the new president,"

Bolkonsky remained facing the wall and forced himself not to cry even though his whole body was urging him to do it. But Zakatov was right. Bolkonsky knew that people don't understand what it takes to put yourself on the line. Summoning that courage, Bolkonsky had to keep reminding himself that only someone with ample reserves of guts could rule Russia.

"I'll see you before you head to the polling station in the morning. Not one step back, Mr President," Zakatov stood up, saluted Bolkonsky and departed the room.

Bolkonsky heard doors being slammed by the heavy-handed Zakatov as he made his way out of his house. Bolkonsky walked to the front window and watched Zakatov nodding his head as the gates opened. Bolkonsky decided he would keep Zakatov as head of the GRU. If he maintained sufficient loyalty, he could look to promote him in due course. He was loyal and his ambitions were not a threat to his position.

Zakatov reached the gate line where the GRU staff car was waiting. The driver's side door opened which was strange and within a couple of seconds, a woman with blonde hair dressed all in black stepped out of the car.

Bolkonsky's stomach dropped and he knew what was occurring before it actually happened. And as he foresaw, in one smooth moment, the woman raised a pistol up and planted a shot straight into the head of Zakatov who collapsed instantly. She fired two more shots into the prone body of Colonel General Ivan Zakatov and stared towards the window that Bolkonsky was standing at.

His feet were frozen to the floor despite the terror gnawing at his nerves.

"She's going to kill me?" Bolkonsky mouthed the words yet still he couldn't shift his feet. The woman stared at him for a few seconds and rather than approach his house, she moved back into the car with the pace of a cat and drove off.

"No, Ivan," Bolkonsky said and fell to his knees with his fingers holding onto the window ledge. He screamed for a long time before he realised that the head of the GRU being assassinated outside his house didn't burnish his security credentials too well. Bolkonsky scrambled on all-fours across the room and pressed the panic button underneath the television stand. GRU agents would be here within minutes. Bolkonsky picked up his mobile phone and called Maxim Golitsyn who answered within two rings.

"Maxim, things have gotten out of hand," Bolkonsky said at the exact moment the phone was answered.

"Good evening Dimitri, I thought you would be sat in a

tank outside the Kremlin to cement that military coup look that you appear to be going for,"

"All I have done is respond proportionally to your provocations and those of your boss,"

"My boss?"

"Don't play dumb. Your boss, Saratov,"

"Did you call simply to spout lies, Dimitri? I'm up early tomorrow, you know there's an election,"

"You can't win, it's too late. If you concede now, it will help pacify the country,"

"You actually believe the nonsense that comes out of your mouth, don't you? You blew up a café in Oslo to try and dig up dirt on Sasha Saratov, you have spread vicious slurs in the media about me and my family, you have arranged for gangs of thugs to attack my supporters and only hours ago, you fired rockets into one of the biggest companies on the Moscow Stock Exchange. Do you know what would pacify the country? If you withdraw your candidacy and retire from politics. You're sick,"

"You can believe what you want to believe, Saratov is finished,"

"I doubt that, I spoke to him only ten minutes ago and he is in full contact with the staff at his newspapers, websites and television channels. The media tomorrow is not going to be kind to you,"

"You're done for, Golitsyn. Everyone knows you are a corrupt puppet who organises visas for hookers. I saw you today running away from your own rally because you're scared of a bit of trouble. No one is going to vote for you tomorrow,"

"You could be right but nobody is going to vote for you either, you deluded fool," Golitsyn ended the call and Bolkonsky dropped his phone and sank to his knees. Finally, Bolkonsky started crying and he was bawling his eyes out on the floor when the GRU agents arrived at his house.

51

Moscow, Russia
Friday November 18 - 19:45 MST

Simonsen sank his fourth Smirnoff vodka miniature from Anastasiya Mazepa's hotel room minibar. His heart rate had barely settled down in the five hours since they fled the Sarabank headquarters in Saratov's stolen Range Rover. There was no sane way of computing what he had been through earlier from the violence and riots in Red Square to finding Mazepa in the smouldering tower and escaping out of there.

He had telephoned Benny Karlsson an hour ago and told him his tale without stopping. The more he talked, the more outlandish everything sounded and this only increased his anxiety.

"If it was anyone else telling me this tale," Karlsson had said, "I'd think it was complete bollocks. As it's you Simonsen, you're probably missing out half of the shit that happened,"

In a way, Karlsson had been right. Simonsen hadn't mentioned the dossier. Even he was succumbing to paranoia, assuming that every phone call was being monitored by at least one shadowy force. This was no way to live and Simonsen was not surprised the febrile atmosphere was polluting the whole country. Even in this hotel, there were raucous parties going off everywhere. It was like the last days of Rome.

Mazepa kept reading him articles about disturbances and protests in different cities and the information dissipated the moment it touched his brain. There was too much chaos and too much potential for worse to come.

"Are you ready?" Mazepa had dressed into a retro blue tracksuit and she looked both unfathomably pretty yet ridiculous, like she was attending a fancy dress party.

"Yes, when is the Opening Ceremony?" Simonsen said.

"Very witty, Simonsen. And here was me thinking you were another humourless Scandinavian,"

"I try my best," Simonsen said and walked with Mazepa out of the room door and towards the lifts to the lobby. After fleeing the carnage at the tower earlier in the afternoon, Simonsen had driven them back to his hotel so he could change out of his piss and blood stained clothes before they left the stolen car in a back street a few kilometres away and used the metro to arrive back at the Hotel Ukraina.

"We'll catch a taxi, I've already ordered one to pick us up," Mazepa said. Simonsen was impressed at how assured she was, considering what she had witnessed earlier today. In contrast, he was on the verge of travelling straight to the airport and flying back to Oslo. Although, he would probably have a few questions about the death of his boss outside the royal palace so any crumb of comfort in returning home was offset by that.

In the taxi, Simonsen attempted to rest his eyes and try to relax after the day's events but he was unable to settle down. He knew Ivanovich was dead but he still had the crazed idea that you can't kill him, that Ivanovich was not even human. Whether it was London, Moscow or Makachkala, every time he saw that man's face, devilment was close by.

The labyrinthine corridors of the Hotel Leningrad were hard to negotiate anyway but the constant fug of tobacco smoke that pervaded the place gave Simonsen an added kick of nausea to go with it. Simonsen was trying to dig up more information about a man named Boris Ivanovich, who had become the prime suspect in his investigation, the problem being that no-one would talk about him.

Every soldier, journalist and hanger-on would blanche upon hearing the name Boris Ivanovich. Simonsen had never seen anything like it, not only would people clam up but they would walk away from him as though he had a contagious disease. As the days passed on in Makhachkala, Simonsen began to wonder if he had a body odour problem as people he had spoken to previously, ignored him in the most obvious ways.

Earlier that evening, a minor breakthrough occurred which gave Simonsen the tiniest glimmer of hope in this mind-numbing case. He bought a small beer from the bar and sat next to his locally-based colleague Rozlov who it appeared had barely left the bar in the four weeks since Simonsen had arrived. For a few minutes neither man spoke before Rozlov's natural policeman's curiosity kicked in:

"How's the inquiry?" Rozlov snickered to himself as he already knew the answer.

"I think there's a national omertà in Russia when anyone mentions a certain name," Simonsen downed his beer in one swill before ordering drinks for the two of them.

"You're trapped into thinking this is about right and wrong, old pal. For people, this is self-preservation. And I don't blame them,"

"I'm not sure what else I can do. The army captain who said he had documents that could prove the link between a certain someone selling weapons to the Chechens has gone quiet on me,"

"You need to find someone who is willing to stand up to him. And that's a rare thing, someone actually spoke to me earlier and asked me to give you this," Rozlov subtly slid a folded piece of paper across the bar to Simonsen who slipped it into his jeans pocket without looking at it.

"Who gave you it?"

"Don't know his name but he's one of the fixers, I see him around here all the time,"

"What does it say?"

"No idea. I told you I wouldn't be getting involved in your Superman bullshit. You've got the note now so I've done all I want to do,"

Simonsen guzzled his beer down and left the bar area. He entered the large foyer and scanned for anyone suspicious. Simonsen couldn't decide if there was no one suspicious or if everybody in there looked dubious. He pulled the note out of his pocket and it read:

I have photos for you
Meet me in storeroom 7 this afternoon
- Narimanov

Thus, the note had preceded Simonsen's seemingly eternal jaunt through the bowels of the hotels. Larders and storerooms seemed to be in an inexhaustible supply. Half the rooms had no signs on them so he had no idea how he was going to locate the seventh storeroom. Simonsen wondered how many bloody storerooms does one hotel need?

He would hear occasional portions of conversation from the below-stairs staff but it was mostly deathly quiet. He was trying to make as little noise as possible as he moved around the hotel. He turned a corner and heard a grunting sound. Simonsen stopped so he could try and pin down the location where the sound came from.

For about a minute, there was no sound. He then heard a muffled voice speaking. Simonsen edged along the corridor and reached an open door. Simonsen paused and listened.

"...treat me like a fool," a rasping voice could be heard, speaking Russian, "You disobeyed me,"

"I didn't," a male voice whimpered and suddenly a slapping noise thundered around the room. Simonsen actually ducked from the sound because it was so loud.

"You disobeyed me!" the rasping voice shouted before returning to a low level, "We are all following orders. That's the way it is. And when one person breaks the chain of command, they must face the consequences,"

Simonsen drew a breath and poked his head around the door and saw the interior was a chiller full of animal carcasses hung up from the ceiling. He could see a few human legs underneath the meaty slabs. Simonsen heard a man sobbing and he edged inside the chiller where he hid behind a large frosty pig and carefully positioned his head so he could see what was happening.

A man was sitting on a chair, Simonsen could only assume he was tied to the chair as most of his view of the seated man was blocked by an imposing man with his back to Simonsen. The big guy was resting his hands on the shoulders of the man in the chair. He was whispering something to him but even from only a few metres away, Simonsen couldn't hear what he was saying.

The big man stood up straight, he must have been nearly two metres tall. He wasn't the broadest man but his demeanour oozed menace and Simonsen couldn't take his eyes off him.

"You think you only have to follow the instructions from the people you deem to be acceptable, yeah?"

"It's not like that. Please, please it's true," the man in the chair said and Simonsen realised he was potentially watching something very unpleasant unfold. The tall man clenched his fists as though he was disgusted by the man's response. The man had a thick beard and from the side profile that Simonsen could see, the realisation of who it was slammed into his mind. This was Boris Ivanovich. He had only caught a glimpse of him once since he had been in Dagestan but everyone said he was always nearby and that he had the uncanny ability to know everything about what people had been up to.

"You think you're better than me. I see it in your eyes. A little rich boy who thought he could fuck with the big boys. Let me tell you how it works, you little bitch. Order is only possible if you listen to instructions and follow them to their conclusions. You're not the only one who has orders to follow.

My orders today are simple. I was told to punish you for refusing to listen to orders that were given to you,"

Ivanovich pulled out a meat cleaver from his coat pocket and the man in the chair screamed. With barely a hint of hesitation, Ivanovich swooped in and grabbed the man's head with his left arm, hooking his hand around and grabbing the man's right ear before quickly slicing the ear off and tossing it away like it was a piece of discarded material. The man's screams continued but Ivanovich carried on to the other side of his head so he could synchronise the victim's lack of ears.

Simonsen's feet switched to autopilot as he tried to back out of the chiller. He stumbled and banged his knee into a trolley and the sound echoed around the chiller. Simonsen was by the doorway and turned around. Boris Ivanovich was staring at him and holding the cleaver upwards. Ivanovich smiled a terrible smile and Simonsen could only utter a light moan as they locked eyes.

"Good evening officer. Is your investigation going well?" Ivanovich whispered and Simonsen could only stare at the fresh blood glistening on the knife. Simonsen could only whimper like a puppy and he backed out of the chiller with obscene haste.

In the corridor, his ears were filled with the howls of pain and mocking shouts from Ivanovich. As best as he could, Simonsen tried to retrace his steps out of the maze of tunnels in the basement. He eventually found the ground floor again and he headed straight to his room to try and process what he had witnessed in the chiller racked with guilt that he had betrayed his police officer's oath to protect people in danger.

It was only looking back that Simonsen realised the words Ivanovich was using about following orders. At the time, he was sure that he was the boss but even then, he was under instruction from Saratov.

"Have you seen this?" Mazepa said.

Simonsen opened his eyes and saw dozens of people trying to force their way into an electrical store. He was torn between closing his eyes and watching the shops being looted.

"I shouldn't have taken this route," the taxi driver said, his tenseness palpable, "I'm sorry,"

Simonsen didn't know what he was apologising for, the whole city was in a revolutionary fever. He respected the driver for still trying to earn a living amongst the chaos of central Moscow. At the junction of Tverskaya Street and Pushkinskaya Street, hundreds of riot police were lined up and preparing to move in one group down the street to clear out the mass of pillagers who appeared to have temporarily stopped ravaging in order to goad the police.

To Simonsen, it felt like trying to squash water. The protestors would simply take their rage out on businesses in other areas of the city. It wasn't simply looters, protesters and criminals out on the street. Bystanders were filling the streets too, as though being in the midst of this disorder meant they were part of history being written. Simonsen knew that Russia would not be the same after this, the turmoil was immense and he thought this was probably what it was like in 1917, only this time everything was being filmed and broadcast to the world.

"We're here," Mazepa said, sounding tense. She paid the driver and they both exited the vehicle on an austere back-street which was free of people, seemingly the only road inside central Moscow which was empty.

The Sanduny baths were contained within a stone building with a typical Russian Neoclassical facade, with a door facing the angle of a T-junction. Inside the building, Simonsen was overawed at the beautiful interiors. It was ornate, over-the-top and superbly crafted. Bathing here would be a very enjoyable experience, Simonsen thought.

"Come on, you can admire it another day," Mazepa said, with the tone of a cosmopolitan lecturing the yokel from the countryside on his first visit to the big city.

Simonsen followed Mazepa as she flowed through the corridors. The place was almost deserted save for a few staff members spending their time chatting as people avoided taking a bath while the city burned. The last place you want to be if a gang of thugs turn up is in the tub or wrapped up in a towel sipping a cup of tea.

They entered a room filled with rows of old wooden lockers, each taller than a person. This room was also deserted but Mazepa peered round each corner like a cautious spy. Simonsen remained a few steps behind and said nothing.

At the furthest row of lockers, Mazepa stopped and pulled the key out of her tracksuit pockets. She threw one more furtive glance around herself before opening the locker. The locker was mostly empty except for a pile of folders placed neatly at the bottom. Simonsen heard Mazepa emit a sigh and she crouched down to lift the folders out. Each one she picked up and passed to Simonsen who stacked them into a small pile on a bench next to them. Simonsen and Mazepa stood looking at the five slim folders that they had placed their lives on the line to obtain.

"So this is the Saratov dossier," Simonsen said.

"You sound disappointed. Did you expect to see a sawn-off leg or a briefcase full of millions of dollars?" Mazepa said. She lifted the folders up and guided the two of them back towards the exit.

52

Mazepa couldn't fail to be amazed and disgusted every time she read through the dossier about Sasha Saratov, the most powerful man in Russia. Due to the riskiness of adding documents to the dossier, many of the things she read surprised her and she realised this was probably the tip of the iceberg, as Saratov's tentacles slowly constricted the body politic of the nation.

Simonsen was devouring the documents with his eyes, occasionally shaking his head and muttering what she presumed were Norwegian expletives. They were both sitting on the end of her bed going through all the information. Mazepa was reading about Saratov's investments in rare earth elements involved in the production of mobile phones. Based on the documents, virtually every single smartphone that was purchased in the world saw him make money.

Mazepa turned to Simonsen who was nudging her arm with his elbow. He was waving the photos of Saratov.

"Are these photographs of Saratov?" he said.

"Yes, this is the proof he was meeting the Chechens to sell them weapons. That guy he is speaking to is Shamil Basayev, who was the leader of the Islamist rebels. It's like Princess Leia selling lightsabers directly to Darth Vader,"

"Jesus, if I had this photograph back then, I could have taken that bastard down,"

Mazepa refrained from commenting, knowing that it

was her shame in her relationship with Narimanov that prevented this information coming to light. The shame once more welled inside her, mixing with the grief that she kept trying to suppress. But this time, she was unable to hold it in and she burst into tears.

Simonsen tried to put his arm around her but she pushed him off and stood up and then immediately sat back down again, the sobs racking her chest.

"I loved him," Mazepa said, squeezing the words out. She stared at Simonsen who looked blankly back at her. He has no idea, she thought, "Abdulatip Narimanov, we were together,"

His vacuous face became contorted with confusion and unutterable sentences.

"We met in Dagestan and he obtained the proof that Saratov was a traitor,"

"But why didn't you release the photographs? I don't understand,"

"Saratov and Ivanovich discovered our secret and somehow filmed us in bed together. I'm a married woman, Simonsen, they used it against me,"

"But the truth could have brought down Saratov,"

"Don't you think I fucking know that? Saratov and Ivanovich thought they destroyed the only copy of the photos but they didn't succeed,"

"You could have released them at any point, they might not have realised it was you,"

"Do you want me to admit that I'm a coward, is that it? My sense of self-preservation was stronger than my courage. That's a fact and I can't change it,"

Mazepa had a hollow sensation in her chest, she didn't want to admit it but this guilt was manifesting itself through her body. She looked at Simonsen and she expected a reproaching look but he had his head bowed.

"I'm no stronger than you, I've been terrified for years. And the stupidest thing is I don't even know what I'm scared of. It seems like both of us have a second chance to stand up and be counted,"

Mazepa nodded and visited the minibar to pull out two cans of lager, passing one to Simonsen who gratefully took it from her. He began thumbing through more documents while Mazepa stood by the window listening to the sirens across the city, occasionally sipping her beer.

"It's the amount of companies that he owns that I had no idea about. He's like a leech sucking blood out of every industry. Two mobile phone networks that I presumed were competitors are both majority-owned by him," Simonsen said and Mazepa shrugged her shoulders at him.

"And the banks, all these smaller ones that he bought up. It's crazy,"

"He's clever and subtle, his way of structuring companies means he has holdings that no one can work out. He has dozens of front companies based in Malta and Cyprus. What I have uncovered is barely scratching the surface. I wouldn't want to put a figure on his net worth but he has to be the richest man in Europe,"

"And this bank here. This is where my Mariya worked at and it turns out that the main shareholder is Saratov through some fake Cypriot company,"

"That's not a huge surprise, half the banks in Russia are controlled by Saratov directly or indirectly,"

Simonsen was reading and Mazepa felt a shift in the atmosphere. She noticed that Simonsen's face was reddening and his eyes were narrowing.

"Are you OK?" Mazepa said.

"There's a leaked email chain here,"

"Oh, yes. My friends were good at hacking in the nineties, we had so much stuff to wade through,"

Simonsen had his head in his hands and Mazepa was concerned. She picked up the sheets of paper that he had been reading. It was an email sent from Saratov's Sarabank email address to Boris Ivanovich:

Boris - have you read the report that Mariya Melnikova from Global Division has tried leaking to Novaya Gazeta?

She's gone too far this time. I've sent people to warn her about this but she won't listen. She did the same when she tried to raise the Poland issue with the regulator. Now she's sticking her nose into our deal with our Chechen partners. I think it's time to nip this in the bud now.

Can you sort this out?

Sasha

Mazepa turned to the next sheet of paper and the printed response from Ivanovich:

SS. Consider it done. She drinks coffee near the Bolshoi every lunchtime with her policeman boyfriend who was in Makhachkala with Narimanov the Snake. If I can take them both out, it will be a double victory. Boris.

It took a second reading before Mazepa could comprehend the awful truth that was revealed. Her world began to spin and she pulled up a chair from the side of the room and sat down. She kept re-reading the email exchange and the nonchalant way Saratov held a person's life in his hand.

"Did you know?" Simonsen said, his voice muffled as his hands remained covering his face.

"I don't think so, no," Mazepa said, "I may have read it, I can't say for sure,"

"All these years I thought it was me they were trying to kill and it turns out it was Mariya they were targeting, I can't believe it,"

"I'm so sorry, if I had known, I would have done something about it,"

"You did know, isn't that the point? You held on to evidence about who killed my girlfriend in cold blood," Simonsen stood and slammed his hand against the wall, "You and your fucking pride about being the perfect Russian wife,"

"What would you have done? You ran away from Moscow. I may be a coward but so are you, Simonsen,"

Simonsen collapsed to his knees and it was his turn to start sobbing on the floor. Any passerby would think he was praying to Mecca by his body position. Mazepa's phone buzzed and she picked it up so she wouldn't have to handle looking at the distraught man on the floor. It was a message from Oksana Devina.

-    If you want an exclusive interview, Sasha Saratov is at an apartment near Lubyanka tonight. That's straight from the mouth of Maxim! Apartment 13, 3 Milyutinskiy Pereulok, Lubyanka

"Nothing I could have done would have prevented her death," Mazepa said. Simonsen pulled himself off the floor and sat on the bed again with his back to her, shoulders still heaving.

"I should have murdered him at the meal," Simonsen turned to face Mazepa, "He knew who I was, he knew he had ordered Ivanovich to kill Mariya,"

"You would never have made it out of the restaurant, that's if you actually had been able to strike him with his bodyguards nearby,"

"He's capable of anything," Simonsen shook his head, "And he escaped. He'll come out on top again,"

Mazepa was unable to work out if Saratov would come out of this situation stronger even if Bolkonsky wins. But if Bolkonsky won, they could release the dossier this weekend, then perhaps it would be his downfall. The idea that Saratov is an unharmable cockroach loomed over her. He will most likely flee to London and continue running his empire from there, trying to bring down Bolkonsky.

"I know I can't make up for what we've discovered tonight but I might know where Saratov is tonight,"

"What?"

"I've received a text saying he is at a flat in Lubyanka tonight,"

"From who?"

"A government contact, he's panicking and I have a location. We can go and confront him tonight,"

Simonsen rose from the bed and started squeezing the dossier documents into one of the slim binders.

"What are you doing?" Mazepa said

"I'm taking the files. You've left them in a locker for two decades while Saratov grew more and more powerful. I'm going to relieve you of the burden and hold on to the files now,"

Simonsen finished packing the files away and placed them in his rucksack he had brought from his hotel. Mazepa's feet were stuck to the floor, she couldn't resist. She had wanted rid of these infernal documents for years but now they were being taken, it seemed like a part of her life was being stripped away. She looked at the room door and saw Simonsen standing in the doorway. He took one final glance at Mazepa before departing the room.

53

Moscow, Russia
Friday November 18 - 22:57 MST

Bolkonsky's house was buzzing with activity. Scene of crime police officers had cordoned off the property and were investigating the slain corpse of Colonel General Ivan Zakatov. GRU agents were scouring the house, checking for bugs and fruitlessly hoping that the killer of the head of their organisation would emerge from a cupboard.

He had spent two hours being interviewed by various law enforcement flunkies and he now wanted to go to bed. He knew it would be some time before sleep was possible but he needed to be alone so he informed his bodyguards that he was going to remain in his bedroom and was only to be disturbed for a genuine emergency. His message to them was layered with enough menace which meant barring a nuclear war breaking out, he should be left alone.

Bolkonsky laid on his bed like the shape of Christ on the cross. He kicked off his shoes and stared towards the ceiling. He had always wanted to know what it felt like to be at those important moments in history. How did Putin feel when he won the Presidency after being plucked from obscurity by Yeltsin's acolytes? What was going through Trotsky's head at the start of the October revolution?

It was only now that he had an inkling of how it felt. It was both exhilarating and exhausting in huge measures. Every endeavour would tire him out but he also believed every setback was also a personal attack against him. His default reaction in those circumstances was to fight back. Therefore, he couldn't stop fighting and it scared him that he knew he would continue to scrap until every single person who condemned him had been punished, be it one person or a million.

Forget about crossing the Rubicon, he was now Caesar at the gates of Rome facing off against the cowering senate. Bolkonsky could picture himself at Red Square in a couple of days' time putting forth his plan of action to resurrect Russia. A jolt of adrenaline hit his body and the chance of sleeping tonight reduced from slim to an emaciated sliver.

Bolkonsky's mobile phone started to vibrate next to him on the bed. With a long sigh, he answered the phone when he saw who the caller was.

"Oksana," Bolkonsky said.

"Dimitri, I've heard about Zakatov," Devina said, "What's going on over there? Are you OK?"

"Yes, whoever it was killed him and fucked off. She left me alone,"

"It was a woman who did it?"

"Yes. God knows who she is. She must be one of Saratov's assassins, he has them all over the country ready to be activated. It turns out that the bitch somehow managed to lure out and kill his driver. We found him with his throat slit around the corner,"

"What a day this has been," Devina said, "I can't remember a day like this in my whole life. You wouldn't believe the shit that has occurred today,"

"Only one more day and it's all over. That prick Golitsyn is on the verge of conceding,"

"You've spoken to him?"

"Yes, he's been stubborn but I pointed out a few home truths to him,"

"Things have gone too far, I think everyone can agree on that. I've had phone calls all day from regional governors. They want the vote postponed,"

"Bollocks, things would be worse if we delayed. This vote is too important, that is why people are on the street,"

"You will have to govern for everybody, not only for your supporters, Dimitri. Don't forget that,"

"I will govern in the best interests of this country. Starting with arresting Sasha Saratov. Once he surfaces, I will be demanding an arrest warrant and placing him in custody as my first act in power,"

Silence descended on the line and Bolkonsky realised he sounded like he was at one of his rallies or speaking to Zakatov. He had implied that Devina would be his prime minister but she was still someone who had a good relationship with Golitsyn.

"Maxim can't win," Bolkonsky said in a soft voice, "In as many words, he said that to me. We both want to clean up Russian politics, there could even be a ministerial role for him if he makes the right choice and withdraws,"

"Of course. My duty is to ensure this election proceeds without a hitch. But you have to admit, launching an armed assault on the biggest bank in the country is quite a large obstacle you placed in the way of this?"

Bolkonsky grunted, he was not in the mood to take lectures about his behaviour. The murder of Zakatov showed exactly why he had to bring down Saratov as soon as possible.

"The biggest obstacle is Sasha Saratov, let's not be coy, Oksana. Once we capture him, it will be relief to the people,"

"Why don't you let me concentrate on finding Saratov. He's on the run and making mistakes,"

"Do you know where he is? We can bring him in tonight," Bolkonsky said, a rush of joy warming his head.

"Not yet, but I don't think it will be long until we find him. He's a man with many enemies and this is probably the first and only chance they have of taking him down. All I am saying is be patient,"

54

Moscow, Russia
Saturday November 19 - 00:48 MST

The Moscow Metro was still running a full service, which Simonsen thought was a powerful testament to the commitment many Russians displayed in their jobs. Service was virtually normal and he was surprised that the government hadn't suspended the service whilst the mayhem above ground continued.

The train was busy and unlike the manic mood on the surface, the train was subdued with an undertone of tension. Simonsen was travelling to Lubyanka station and at each stop on the way, no-one seemed to be getting off the train. He wondered if people were staying on the Metro to avoid the drama unfolding fifty metres above.

Simonsen was the sole passenger to disembark at Lubyanka. It was a sterile station, unlike some of the beautifully crafted ones that had given the Moscow Metro its fine reputation. There were probably more police on the concourses than normal passengers and the atmosphere remained tense as he made his way out to ground level to Lubyanka Square.

Outside the station, a light mist of snow was falling and through the silvery shimmer. Simonsen's eye was drawn to the FSB headquarters, the Lubyanka building. This location was infamous during the Communist era as the main offices and prison of the secret police and intelligence agency, the KGB. The word 'Lubyanka' itself could bring older Muscovites out in shivers. Thinking about what had occurred inside there over the years caused Simonsen to shudder in solidarity. Its yellow-brick facade was pale amidst the streetlights and snowfall.

Simonsen was aware that Boris Ivanovich was an FSB man, hand-picked by Saratov to act as his consigliere. He probably ordered the hit on Mariya from this very building. Simonsen stomped across the closed road at the base of Lubyanka Square. The FSB had cordoned it off with metal fencing to prevent the chance of more armed attacks.

A ring of troops surrounded the building and Simonsen began to feel nervous and hoped that he wasn't on a list of people they wanted to question. There was no doubt his status as Interpol agent wouldn't be respected when it came down to a rigorous FSB interrogation, especially taking into consideration the documents held in his backpack.

Simonsen veered rightwards to follow a road that spliced away from the Lubyanka building. The streets weren't completely quiet but there was no sign of trouble. He reached the address he was looking for. It was a nondescript, tired teal and white six-storey block. Eighteen numbered buttons were on the apartment's intercom system. Saratov was supposedly in apartment number 13 if the information that Mazepa had received from her source was accurate.

Simonsen glanced around, a few pedestrians were milling about but no cops that he could see. He had no way of entering the flat but his patience was thin and anger bursting out of his body so he started to press the numbers in order commencing with 1.

He waited twenty seconds and received no response so he pressed the button marked 2. There was no response to this one either so he slowly progressed through numbers 3, 4 and 5 until he heard a gravelly voice quickly respond to his press on button number 6.

"Yes?"

"I've lost my key, can you let me in?" Simonsen said.

"What?"

Simonsen repeated what he said twice but there was no response and the door didn't click open.

"Bastard," Simonsen said and pressed the next button. Yet again there was no response, so he carried on with buttons 8 and 9. Number 9 answered with unintelligible words.

"Can you let me in?" Simonsen said.

"No. Fuck off," the voice said. He understood those words with no problem. He pressed number 10 and was thinking about other ways of gaining entry when he heard a voice of an old woman come through on the intercom.

"Good evening, I've lost my key. Please can you let me in?"

"Of course, dear," the woman said and the main door unlocked so he pushed it open and entered. Simonsen heaved a big sigh of relief and wanted to plant a kiss on the mouth of the *babushka* who let him in. A decorator's table took up much of the hallway with half-empty cans, brushes and a tatty, paint-spattered VEF radio strewn across the top of the table.

He climbed the stairs as quietly as he could manage. The smell of fresh paint swamped his senses as he rose the floors, occasionally bumping into the walls and smearing fresh paint on his coat. His chest was beginning to tighten and he wondered what the hell was he doing attempting to confront Saratov? Was he prepared to murder him in cold blood? This was stupid and for a moment, he paused and considered turning around and fleeing but having come this far, he couldn't stop now.

Simonsen stopped outside the door to apartment 13 and listened. The sound of a television could be heard from distant apartments and Simonsen tried attuning his ears to what was on the other side of the door. He heard a creak and turned around on the stairs but saw nothing.

He noticed the door to the apartment was actually open and resting on the latch which he thought was strange. It was times like this that he wished he had a gun. Saratov was likely to be armed. Again, he contemplated leaving and returning to his hotel. The smell of the paint was turning his stomach and he suddenly realised what it reminded him of. Simonsen closed his eyes and wished the thoughts away but they would never be erased from his memory.

Mariya had been in hospital for five months with no change in her circumstances. For one hundred and fifty seven days, Simonsen had attended her bedside. For the first few weeks, he had spent virtually all his time there in between his own hospital appointments to fix his shattered knee.

After returning to work, he would head down to the hospital after the end of each shift and sit by her bed and tell her about his day. Her face which used to have a lovely glow was now a pallid white. He would talk and talk as it was the only thing that kept him from crying in front of her. He refused to cry in her presence and he didn't know why. The best reason that he could think of was that he had failed in his duty as a man to protect his woman and he had to make amends for this failure by maintaining a manly demeanour.

It was bollocks, he knew it but he told himself that was why he wouldn't cry. In his more truthful moments, he would concede that the tears would feel like he was blaming her for being in the wrong place at the wrong time. If only they had visited another café or moved away to another country to escape the crime in Moscow like they had chatted about in bed.

It was the waiting that was eating his insides. Did she hear anything he said? He would stroke her hair and speak to her and for the only time in his adult life, he prayed to God asking Him to bring her back, if only for a minute so he could tell her he loved her.

But neither God, nor the medical staff could wake her from her slumber. Instead she spent every day in the bed in the same position with a collection of tubes removing and inserting all kinds of bodily fluids, medicines and sustenance. Every day when he left her bedside, it was the tubes that affected him the most. They were dehumanising and made him realise that Mariya was no longer there. She was simply the husk of what used to be his beautiful, vivacious companion.

That day in early December was the day the machines and tubes were turned off.

"Mr Simonsen," a voice called from the doorway outside Mariya's private room. Simonsen turned around and saw Dr Petrov who had been responsible for her treatment since she had arrived at hospital. Simonsen walked outside and the smell of fresh paint on the walls crashed into his nostrils.

"Good afternoon doctor,"

"Hello Einar, I started my shift and I noticed you had given your consent to the machines being turned off,"

"I spoke to her father yesterday and we both agreed that it is time,"

"I know how difficult this decision has been but there is no chance of any recovery for Miss Melnikova,"

"I know," Simonsen couldn't maintain eye contact with the doctor whose compassion and directness was a credit to his profession.

"Her parents will be arriving shortly,"

Simonsen nodded and walked back into Mariya's room. He gazed at her face and it made his heart hurt. Simonsen wanted to shout and smash his hands against the wall at the whole fucking situation. He refrained from bellowing his anger and walked up to Mariya's body, caught in stasis as she emitted tiny breaths.

He couldn't face being there at the end and he walked out into the corridor. Out of the corner of his eyes he spotted Mariya's parents. He ignored them as he shuffled down the corridor thinking that this was the end of his life. He caught the glance of a couple of female nurses who smiled in sympathy at him but he could only blankly stare back at them.

He departed the hospital in the middle of a colossal Muscovite snow storm which he hardly noticed. Mariya had died and so had he. Whatever life had filled him then was now extinguished.

Simonsen opened his eyes and looked down at his fists which were tightly clenched. A wave of nihilism surged through his body and he pushed open the apartment door. Luckily, it made no sound. Simonsen stepped into the apartment, awaiting a violent response which didn't arrive.

Simonsen was standing in a filthy hallway, a light was intermittently flashing to his right so he headed in that direction. He walked into a living room which contained an attached kitchen through a large archway. The flickering light was coming out of a fridge so Simonsen moved through the room, passing half-eaten sandwiches and beer cans.

He closed the fridge and then noticed an open container of milk. He smelled the milk which had not gone off and then noticed an electric kettle on the countertop next to it. Simonsen placed his hand on it and it was slightly warm. His instincts kicked in and he could almost taste the adrenaline coating his tongue.

Simonsen tiptoed back into the hallway and opened the first door on his right. It was empty save for a grubby toilet. He carried along the hallway and saw there was another door on his right which was open. He entered the room which contained a bath and sink but was also empty. He left the room and moved to the final room in the house which he assumed was a bedroom.

He paused before entering and thought of Mariya as he tried to summon the courage to proceed. He pushed the door open and stepped into the bedroom and saw nobody there. Simonsen swore and began to check under the bed and inside the wardrobes. There was nobody in the house. He gave the place another search but whoever had been here had vanished. He looked out of the living room window and could see a collection of shops that still had people wandering by at this hour.

Simonsen stood at the window when he heard a loud engine below. A dark Lamborghini passed below the window and sped off past the shops and out of view within seconds. Was it Saratov? He didn't know and it was too late now. He had no way of catching him. The consolation was that he was still on the run. He wasn't far behind and for a police officer, knowing you had your man making decisions on the fly was usually a good sign. People on the run made mistakes and he hoped Saratov would make another one soon.

Simonsen gave the apartment a thorough check for any evidence but there was nothing here except for shabby tat. The actual occupier presumably had been put up in a hotel for a few days on Saratov's expenses. Simonsen left the flat and descended the stairs. As he reached the final flight, he saw a woman standing in the doorway next to the decorator's table.

Simonsen immediately recognised her from CCTV in Oslo as the woman who blew up the Iskender Café. The same woman who shot Peter Kelsey-Moore as he prepared to murder him. Why was she here? She could have killed him in Oslo or London so it meant she was here to murder Saratov. Join the queue, Simonsen thought.

She was of a slight figure and looked almost coquettish. Her face was quite plain which probably helped her blend into crowds and she had mousey medium length brown hair which was most likely to be part of her extensive wig collection. She smiled at Simonsen and his cheeks flustered.

"It's not a game!" Simonsen shouted, "Murder is not a game,"

The woman turned around and walked out of the apartment block. Simonsen tried to move down the stairs quickly but jagged pains shot through his knee and he was forced to take it slow and edge down one step at a time. He reached the outside of the apartment block but couldn't locate the woman. She was like smoke, vanishing away.

Simonsen screamed and a couple of lads on the other

side of the road started laughing but hurried their stride to avoid entangling themselves in a volatile situation with the strange old feller. Simonsen pulled his phone out and dialled up Benny Karlsson.

55

Moscow, Russia
Saturday November 19 - 06:34 MST

"Fucking traitor!" Bolkonsky heard the shouts aimed at him but he was canny enough to avoid the bottles that were also being hurled in his direction. The polling office was relatively quiet but the people that had arrived there in anticipation of Bolkonsky's arrival at this early hour were furious. It needed multiple guards to bundle him into the local government office where the polling station was located.

Bolkonsky was ushered into a booth and he needed a few minutes to calm himself down. The crowd outside were incandescent and for the first time, Bolkonsky bore witness to the real-life consequences of his war with Saratov and Golitsyn. Bolkonsky picked a pencil up and firmly etched his X into the box where his name was. He took a deep breath before exiting the voting booth.

He folded his vote and placed it inside the ballot box and then strode out of the office into the full force of another wave of abuse. Bolkonsky was stunned by the depth of anger but he did not want to be seen to be protected from a few civilians by his GRU bodyguards. However, due to last night's murder of Zakatov, it was vital he wasn't harmed and the guards would ensure that.

However, it was not a good look for a Russian president to be cowering from a few hooligans. The television cameras would already be broadcasting this live and it would be repeated throughout the day. He needed to show strength.

Bolkonsky stepped onto a bench on the street with more and more local people turning up to witness the situation.

He rose up and lifted his arms in the air, more empty beer cans glanced past him and then a full one hit him square in his left breast. It was a shock but it bounced off his broad chest and he glared at the crowd, eyeing potential culprits.

"People, my people," Bolkonsky said, arms still aloft, "We have to peacefully unite today and preform our civic duty,"

"Murderer!" a voice carried across the crowd. Bolkonsky's face hardened.

"I am a man intent on bringing the values of this country back against the forces that have degraded our nation," Bolkonsky was almost screaming the words, spittle flew out of his mouth. The abuse continued and Bolkonsky left and walked towards his car.

Irate protestors attempted to breach the guards and one bulky middle-aged man managed to break through but was easily pushed to the floor by Bolkonsky. He had to hold back all his urges to smash the guy's face through the pavement. Instead, he stepped over him and into the open car door. As soon as it was closed, the car sped off leaving the crowd to fruitlessly follow, hurling objects at the guards who remained stationed at the polling centre. Police sirens could be heard as they drove off and Bolkonsky knew that this morning a few more skulls were about to be cracked.

If the response was this hostile here in a working-class Moscow suburb, what was it like in the rest of the country? The win-by-default that he predicted after the collapse in Golitsyn's support over the last few days wasn't looking half as likely as it did yesterday. The attack on the Sarabank headquarters may not have been the vote-winner he had anticipated. Bolkonsky wondered if perhaps people were content with being exploited by scum like Sasha Saratov so they didn't have to take responsibility for their own failings.

Bolkonsky could not shift his mind away from recalling

watching Zakatov being taken out by an assassin in front of his house. The audacity to murder the head of one of the nation's security services outside the home of a Presidential candidate was something to behold. If only he could sign up the assassin for his own team. She would have slit the throat of that scumbag who jumped out of the crowd to attack him earlier.

Who was she? If she was on Saratov's payroll, wouldn't she have tried to kill him too? Perhaps, the risk of killing the other candidate was too high even for a monster like Saratov to contemplate. He may be evil but he's not stupid, thought Bolkonsky.

Bolkonsky's mobile phone began ringing and he expected it to be Oksana Devina calling to give him another scolding. It was an unknown number which was strange as only a handful of people possessed this number. He contemplated not taking the call but with the day starting so badly, he thought things couldn't get any worse.

"Yes?" Bolkonsky said.

"Bolkonsky, it's Saratov," the voice at the other end of the line said. Bolkonsky couldn't believe it was him but the voice did sound like that of his nemesis.

"You have a fucking nerve calling me," Bolkonsky said.

"Today is a big day for both of us,"

"Do you plan on sending me more flowers?" Bolkonsky said, a pang of guilt passed through him for not thinking about his son's death over the last twenty-four hours.

"Don't be precious, Minister, I know that's not your style,"

"You mean nothing to me, You're a rat. You were born a rat, you've lived your life in the sewers and you'll be exterminated like a rat, squealing in pain,"

"I know it's been a difficult few days for you,"

"You don't know anything about me,"

"I know your staunch ally Ivan Zakatov was murdered by a woman last night. Have your GRU guys stopped providing security now?"

"Have you considered throwing yourself in the river? Because that's what I'll do to you. There will be no trial, just hurling your poisonous corpse into the bottom of the water,"

"You have such a way with words," Saratov said, chuckling away. Bolkonsky whacked the back of the car seat with the palm of his hand.

"By tonight, I will be President and you will remain a rat scurrying around trying to escape Russia,"

"Do you not listen to the radio? People are spoiling their ballots. People might not be voting for Maxim but they are certainly not voting for you,"

"Bullshit," Bolkonsky said, with no force at all.

"You know it's true. Please correct me if my eyes were deceiving me but I was watching the television not ten minutes ago and I am sure I watched a little *gopnik* lob a can of Zhigulevskoye at you. I thought you were popular with the young skinheads?"

"As long I win more votes than your pretty puppet, I win the election,"

"It's not as simple as that, if the spoiled papers tally up to a higher total than your vote, you would be an illegitimate leader,"

Bolkonsky held back from replying. The serpent was right, if his share is not higher than 50%, it would represent a problem and may even instigate a possible new election.

"We are both pragmatists, Dimitri," Saratov continued, "There is a way that we can both come out of this OK,"

"You want to make a deal?" Bolkonsky said.

"I am a practical man, I would like to be able to run my businesses with little interference from the state. If you are the President, I have no issue with you, all I ask is to be left alone to do that. A *quid pro quo*, you stay out of my business and I will stay out of yours. I will send you a location later if you wish to meet,"

Saratov ended the call and Bolkonsky wondered if this was the best idea. If Saratov was offering to meet up face to face, then he was surely on the back foot. The last time he had been in the same room as him was in Makhachkala

Bolkonsky was sick of Dagestan. The cloying humidity, the untrustworthy locals and the even more untrustworthy Muscovite businessmen had almost sent him to the madhouse. Worst of all was that fucking journalist, Anastasiya Mazepa, who earlier that day had told him she didn't have the evidence to bring down Sasha Saratov.

He ended up shouting in her face in the hotel reception. All she did was stare at him like a vacant shop dummy. Then she shrugged and said:

"Everyone thinks of changing the world, but no one thinks of changing himself,"

"What the fuck does that even mean?" Bolkonsky bawled at her and she simply walked out of the hotel pulling her suitcase.

Bolkonsky stomped into the bar and ordered a bottle of vodka which the waiter handed to him with unsurprising haste. He had forty-eight hours before he returned to civilization and he intended to booze his way through it.

Other patrons avoided going near him as he seethed and muttered to himself inside the invisible boundary which surrounded him. After a couple of hours of boozing, Bolkonsky noticed the atmosphere change and people went quiet. Bolkonsky saw the criminal Boris Ivanovich enter the bar and lock eyes with him. People assumed he was the kingpin of Russian crime but Bolkonsky knew he was the bagman for Sasha Saratov, the true spider at the heart of organised crime.

Ivanovich sat at the next table to Bolkonsky barely three metres away. He didn't say a word but maintained his gaze on Bolkonsky. After a couple of minutes of this, Bolkonsky could sense his anger rising in himself.

"What the fuck are you looking at?" Bolkonsky said to Ivanovich who didn't respond but instead averted his eyes toward the entrance to the bar. Bolkonsky flicked his eyes around too and saw Sasha Saratov enter the bar. He walked over to Bolkonsky's table, pulled up a chair and sat down.

"Captain Bolkonsky, pleased to meet you," Saratov said, his eyes empty of emotion.

"It's Major Bolkonsky," Bolkonsky poured himself another vodka, "Why are you here?"

"I'm returning to Moscow this evening and I wanted to see how your investigation into me was going?"

Bolkonsky sat motionless and stared at the man opposite.

"It's not going well, is it?" Saratov smiled and to Bolkonsky, it was the smile of a vampire, "What a shame, Major. Did your pet journalist Anastasiya Mazepa not come up with the goods?"

"I know what you did," Bolkonsky whispered, "You betrayed our country,"

"No I didn't. All you did was listen to a journalist who knows nothing about what I have done for Russia. You are a cuckold, Major. Letting a pretty young journalist give you the runaround. Are you the same with your wife back home too? Does she tell you what to wear and how to behave in public?"

"Shut up!" Bolkonsky shouted and stood up, "Get out of my sight,"

"Sit down Captain, sorry, Major," Saratov waved a hand and Bolkonsky did sit down.

"I paid for this war because the clowns in Moscow have nearly bankrupted us so don't accuse me of being a traitor," Saratov spoke in a low voice and maintained eye contact with Bolkonsky.

"You are a traitor, I know what you did,"

"You don't know anything. All you've heard are rumours from dubious sources. I'm paying for that vodka, I'm paying for the bullets you have fired and I'm paying for the vehicles you have travelled in,"

"It's blood money, the blood of our soldiers,"

"With respect, that's bullshit and I would strongly recommend from refraining from repeating those allegations when you return home,"

Saratov rose to his feet and Ivanovich joined him a few seconds later.

"I will bring you down, Saratov," Bolkonsky said and Saratov gave him a wry smile.

"No you won't, Major. My advice would be to forget about me in the same way I'll forget about you the second I step out of this hotel," Saratov walked out of the hotel and that was the last time Bolkonsky had come face to face with his nemesis.

Saratov had gradually become the most powerful criminal in the country but the situation in Russia was grave for both men. Bolkonsky only had one thought in his mind which he said out loud:

"Can I trust him?"

56

Moscow, Russia
Saturday November 19 - 11:51 MST

Anastastiya Mazepa walked out of the Hotel Ukraina with a sense of liberation. Simonsen's expropriation of the Saratov dossier hadn't disheartened her. He would release the documents and hopefully bring down Sasha Saratov and his cronies. The threat of her affair with Narimanov being exposed no longer bothered her.

For years, she had lived with a sense of dread that Saratov or Ivanovich would leak the story to one of their favourite newspapers. It had compromised her writing and caused her to exile herself away from where she could have made a difference. She had been too scared to speak truth to power but with Ivanovich dead and Saratov on the run, Mazepa was liberated.

She had a giddy sensation that it was inevitable that the tale of her affair was going to come out and it was only upon losing the dossier, that she now had the courage to face up to her weakness. Her relationship with her husband was as similarly detached as her connection to Russia. Ever since meeting Narimanov, she had never been able to speak to Mikhail like she once had. Prior to visiting Dagestan, they would have spent hours in bed talking about Tolstoy and Shakespeare. After Mazepa returned home, nothing in Moscow seemed genuine anymore.

Her husband had assumed it was because of the dark things she had seen in the Caucausian war zone. His empathy and patience only added to her guilt and she could never summon up the guts to tell him the truth. The truth that she had cheated on him with a Dagestani mercenary. What made it worse for her is that she knew Mikhail would have been understanding. He would tell her things would be alright when she knew she deserved all the opprobrium that he could muster.

Mazepa ambled through the park in front of the hotel past the statue of Taras Shevchenko, a poet and liberated serf who was exiled for his anti-Tsarist and pro-Ukrainian independence views. She stared at his austere face staring out over the Moskva River and hoped her courage would hold out for a day or two more.

She carried on through the park to the restaurants hunkered below on the street named after Shevchenko. She saw Oksana Devina waving as she approached a little tavern. Her friend looked radiant despite the current circumstances. A chill wind was hitting them and after embracing, they agreed to go inside to drink coffee.

They were seated in the centre of the ornate restaurant surrounded by a collection of vases inside display cases. A large staircase rose from the ground to a floor above which had an open ring lit up by glowing golden orbs. It was very quiet inside as Moscow reeled from the prior day's turmoil and prepared for election day.

"I'm surprised you could find time today to come and see me," Mazepa said, as a handsome male waiter brought over coffees and placed them down on the table. Devina waited until the waiter was far away from them before continuing the conversation.

"Taking a coffee break when one is running a country can be quite beneficial to your mental state," Devina said, laughing and spilling coffee over the sides of the cup as she lifted it to her face.

"Did you see Bolkonsky this morning with those protestors?"

"Yes. And he still doesn't understand why they are upset with him. He thinks everything can be sorted out with a show of force. I thought he was going to lamp that guy who charged at him,"

"Are the reports about people spoiling their ballots true?"

"It's a mixed picture from what I've heard but if either candidate thinks they are going to win fifty percent of the vote, they are living in a fucking dreamland,"

Mazepa took a sip of her coffee and could only foresee more trouble if there was no clear winner. If neither candidate wins a mandate, the power vacuum at the top of Russian politics could bring the nation to its knees.

"Stop looking so glum, Nastya," Devina said. Mazepa realised she was looking down at the floor, deep in thought, "Things never turn out as bad as you expect them to be,"

"It's looking pretty bad at the moment, I've heard that there are more protests planned for later today,"

"It will keep the winner on their toes. They know now that the people can't be taken for granted, Russians aren't falling for the old tricks anymore,"

"If Bolkonsky wins, he will steamroller them,"

"Maybe so, but I know Dimitri and he does listen to counsel in important matters,"

"He's a psychopath and a killer. He's another authoritarian monster waiting to happen,"

"He was a soldier, and however you may feel about him, he served his country with distinction. Yes, he's probably killed people but he did it in the service of the motherland, he didn't murder random strangers in the backstreets, he did his duty on the battlefield,"

"The battlefield?" Mazepa's head was spinning, how could her friend display such naivety? She may have lost the dossier but she had the videotape. She dug inside her bag and retrieved the tape. She waved it in the air like she was a preacher bashing a bible at an American evangelical church.

"What is that?" Devina said, taking a long slurp of coffee.

"This is the man who could be our next President. This tape shows him massacring Chechen civilians including a young boy in cold blood. Forget your fucking battlefield Oksana, he's in an empty warehouse with his mates killing them one by one,"

"No, that can't be true," Devina said, her cup held frozen in the air by her pale hand.

"Here," Mazepa handed it over, "Take it,"

"Isn't this the exclusive you dreamed about? You could bring down a President,"

"I have sacrificed my soul for this cause and even now, I don't even know why. The tape is yours, Oksana. You are supervising this election. It's in your hands now,"

Mazepa stood up, dropped some roubles on the table and walked out, squeezing a hand on Devina's shoulder as she departed. The dizziness was intensifying now and as she left the café, she had to lean against a wall where she closed her eyes and began to sob.

57

"So, in addition to all your previous madness in London and Oslo, since arriving in Moscow you have been in the middle of a riot, saved a damsel in distress from a burning skyscraper, stole not only some poor guy's taxi but one of Sasha Saratov's expensive cars and also saw your old pal, the guardian angel who saved you from certain death but also happens to be our prime suspect in the café bombing. Have I missed anything off?" Benny Karlsson said, reclining in his chair after a meal they had gobbled down at Sixty, a posh restaurant in the Federation Tower, located close to the Evolution Tower, which was still smouldering after yesterday's rocket attacks.

It was surprisingly busy considering its proximity to the stunning scenes yesterday. A lot of the guests were wandering up to the windows to glimpse the holes in the Sarabank headquarters caused by the rockets. It was already becoming a ghoulish tourist attraction and every time Simonsen cast an eye outside, the smell of burning and the noise of gunfire tripped his senses again.

"It's been an eventful thirty-six hours, that's true," Simonsen said. This was almost the first opportunity he had had to wind down and gather his thoughts. He had reeled off the incidents since he landed at Sheremetyevo and Karlsson had noted down everything, frequently asking him to repeat sections, especially the more unbelievable bits.

Simonsen didn't mind. He was happy to see his friend

and a firm ally in this whole ridiculous situation. He was so worked up last night after finding out about Mariya that he was certain he would have killed Saratov if he had encountered him at the grubby apartment last night. In the cool light of day, he could see what a terrible decision that would have been.

Mariya had tried to bring Saratov to heel in front of the law and she had borne the consequences. However, that was no reason to disregard the law otherwise he would be no better than Saratov. He is an outlaw who believes he is above the laws that govern a healthy society. Saratov is utterly without scruples, with a single-minded vision that placed himself ahead of everyone and everything.

The attack on his headquarters by allies of Dimitri Bolkonsky yesterday may have been the first time that someone had fought him on his own terms. Mazepa said Saratov looked helpless yesterday as he flailed around on the floor with his base under attack.

"You think Saratov sanctioned the bombing of the café?" Karlsson said, his forehead scrunched up.

"The most likely scenario is that he paid the woman to bomb the café. I believe that she was the girl who handed me the note with Bolkonsky's son's address on it at Heathrow airport,"

"Do you think she killed his son?"

"I don't think she would have had the time. I reckon that was Boris Ivanovich's work. But if the rumours are true about Zakatov being killed by a female assassin are correct, then there's a high chance that she killed him,"

"How does that explain her killing Peter Kelsey-Moore? He was in the pay of Saratov which has been confirmed by the dossier and our team back in Norway. It doesn't make sense, Einar. There's too many assumptions for my liking,"

"Perhaps they needed me alive to find the dossier. Ultimately, it's what Saratov wanted," Simonsen said. Now that he had said this out loud he was unnerved at how tenuous some of the links were.

The two men stared out towards the city but their gaze was directed towards the smoking Evolution Tower. The scars of yesterday's armed assault were visible all the way from the top to the bottom of the building. Huge holes full of jagged metal and smashed glass bore testament to the ferocity of the attack.

"I can't believe you went in there, mate," Karlsson said, shaking his head, "Brave. Brave but fucking stupid,"

Simonsen continued staring at the damaged tower wondering how on earth he had found the courage to enter the building amidst gunfire and flying rockets. Simonsen stared down at the documents contained in the dossier. The dossier was the ultimate example of quality of quantity. One sheet of paper contained a list of informers in Russia and the UK. It contained more than a dozen members of the House of Lords, over twenty Members of the European Parliament and fifty-six members of the Russian parliament, the Duma.

"Have you seen this list of his snitches?" Simonsen handed over the paper to Karlsson who put down his coffee mug to read it with both hands.

"This guy is the Polish ambassador to the UN," Karlsson said, pointing at one name, "This one here is the head of Interpol in the Balkans. I don't see how we can bring Saratov to Norway. We can charge him with terrorist offences and we can apply for extradition but the reality is that he's got the Russian state in his pocket,"

"What if Bolkonsky wins the election?"

"He hates him but he would be more likely to charge him with anything he chooses here and then send him to the gulag. What are you going to do with that dossier?"

"I'm not sure. I won't be handing it over to Bolkonsky, even if he wins. The man is a maniac and after the last week, he'll be intent on using it to settle scores with the guy who ordered the hit on his son,"

Karlsson's mobile phone started ringing and he answered it within milliseconds. He mumbled a few words and ended the call.

"We have a tap on Ian Kelsey-Moore's phone," Karlsson said, "Our friends in the Metropolitan Police were happy to oblige once we suggested he may have knowledge about the bombing,"

"The lack of hard evidence didn't bother them?"

"Not after he came out against a pay rise for cops in the newspapers last month. Funny how things like that can bounce back on you. We think he has spoken to Saratov,"

"Today?"

"Yes, a very short call from a Russian mobile stating they would phone back later. Bangoura can't confirm yet. Hold up," Karlsson's phone was ringing again, to which he answered again, "Bangoura?"

Karlsson occasionally grunted affirmations before saying: "What's the address?" and scribbled a note down. He listened and ended the call. Karlsson stared at Simonsen with a serious face.

"Saratov is at the Kelsey-Moore family's Moscow dacha. He wants him out as he's paranoid about his conversations being listened in on, which is ironic because that's exactly what we are doing,"

"Have you got the address?" Simonsen said, already packing away the dossier documents back into folders and into his holdall.

"Bangoura is emailing it over. He has nobody there with him, he wants Kelsey-Moore to organise safe passage out of Russia back to the UK,"

"He's lost the plot, there's no way the British will let him back in,"

"Maybe. He might even claim asylum there and he would be free while that's processed. It's come through now," Karlsson showed the address to Simonsen who didn't recognise it. Simonsen opened the mapping app on his phone and located the address which was in the Millenium Park area of Novorizhskoye, on the outskirts of the capital.

"OK, let's see if Saratov is available for an interview," Simonsen said. He thought about the sacrifices that Anastasiya Mazepa had made holding on to the dossier. He had reacted badly after finding out about Mariya amidst the files. How was Mazepa to know that Mariya was his girlfriend? She was simply one more victim, another part of the Russian body politic infected by a malignant agent.

He pulled out his mobile phone and sent a message to Mazepa:

-        I know where Saratov is now. Would you like to confront him with the dossier?

58

Moscow, Russia
Saturday November 19 - 17:32 MST

Dimitri Bolkonsky stared at the front of the Kelsey-Moore family's dacha in Novorizhskoye and his mind recalled memories of his childhood home. This house was an imposing two-storey modern structure which probably had at least four bedrooms. An occasional retreat for a rich Englishman and his family to use for barely a few weeks a year.

Bolkonsky and his family had lived in a small wooden farmhouse in a tiny village about fifty kilometres north of Kazan. Life was tough on the farm and Bolkonsky worked with his father every day both before and after school for as long as he could remember. It wasn't until 1980 when he moved to Kazan to study at a technical school that he discovered the concept of free time.

Despite his lack of interest in education, his father had drilled into him the importance of learning. So he had studied as much as he could in his spare time even though he found it difficult. He joined the Komsomol, the youth wing of the Communist Party and soon became a supporter of Mikhail Gorbachev who he respected for marrying a strong work ethic with a belief in changing the political system.

Bolkonsky's confidence in what he could achieve once in power was genuine and his heart was hurting with the current situation. Bolkonsky was only hearing negative news about the election. Every time he received a news update notification on his mobile phone, it was bad news. There were peaceful

'Rallies for a Free Russia' taking place in every major city and he was being told about every single one.

The early afternoon exit polls were showing barely believable numbers of people spoiling their ballots. One polling booth in the far east of the country was reporting over 90% of ballots were spoiled with a turnout of over 75%. All of this was going on and he was in the middle of nowhere, meeting his long-time adversary.

He approached the front door and when he was ten metres away, the door swung open and he saw the bespectacled figure of Alexander 'Sasha' Saratov beckoning him into the house. None of Bolkonsky's emotions seemed to be fully engaged. The rage and anger that had propelled him to the brink of victory was sunken deep in his gut, his curiosity about why Saratov wanted to meet was also dimmed. It was as if he was watching a film about his life and he was a disinterested observer.

Saratov walked into the house and Bolkonsky followed him through the sparse but expensively-designed hallway. Saratov entered a nearby room and Bolkonsky headed in the same direction. A hint of inevitability that he was about to be shot in the head creeped into his mind. And he thought, I don't care, I'll see you soon, my son.

Bolkonsky walked into a large study, one wall was filled from floor to ceiling with books and on another wall hung a couple of modern art pieces which to his mind looked absolute shit. No one shot him. Saratov had sat down at a desk parallel to the back wall, flanked by windows with a view of the lake. Directly behind him was a painting of Peter the Great, with the national hero standing up and holding the attention of the admiring courtiers surrounding him.

Saratov was fiddling with a pen and occasionally running his hand over his shaved head. Bolkonsky began to relish the silence as he realised Saratov was at breaking point.

"Maxim Golitsyn has conceded," Saratov said, holding up his hands in the air.

"I haven't seen that," Bolkonsky said, checking his phone, "There's nothing on the news,"

"He's doing it now, a press conference is starting any minute now," Saratov waved a dismissive arm.

"Did he have to check in with his boss first?"

"Something like that," Saratov said, anxiety etched into his face, "Thank you for coming. I thought you would attend with a team of GRU goons. Or are they outside?"

"I came on my own," Bolkonsky said, gesturing to the gun on the table, "I see you came prepared,"

"Self-defence, inasmuch as that is possible in this febrile and ever-changing situation. I have to admit to being grudgingly impressed at your attack on my bank yesterday. That was a pretty bold move. It's a shame that the Russian people weren't so enamoured by it,"

Bolkonsky sneered at the back-handed compliment. He checked his mobile phone again and the news confirmed that Golitsyn had conceded defeat in his bid to become President. He looked up at Saratov who appeared to be grinning at him. He loves to know everything before everyone else, Bolkonsky thought, even in his darkest moments.

"I wasn't sure if I had misjudged your pragmatism. I was fifty-fifty on whether you would kill me the minute you walked in here," Saratov said, his right hand remaining within centimetres of the pistol while his left hand continued to twizzle the pen.

"You might not believe it, but I actually want to make Russia a great country again. I don't want to be the kind of man who murders my enemy's son or blows up a café in a foreign city. I might not get it right every time, but I am trying,"

"I think you're full of shit, Bolkonsky. It is apparent to me that you tell yourself these things but even you don't believe them. We are of the same generation, you know how the power game works,"

"I know how the game works," Bolkonsky said and Saratov chuckled.

"What I find most incomprehensible is that after everything that has happened this week, you still think I am responsible for bombing that shithole kebab shop,"

Bolkonsky was tempted to respond to his lies but something troubled him. Why would Saratov deny being behind the bombing? His cards were being laid out but he still couldn't bring himself to admit that the terror attack was his idea.

"Your denials mean nothing to me. If you were in my shoes, would you believe what you are saying?"

Saratov nodded but didn't say anything else in response. He kept swirling the pen around his fingers and Bolkonsky had the brief thought that Saratov was trying to hypnotise him. He switched his gaze to the lake out of the window. Blue sky had started to break through in the distance past the trees.

"I told you on the phone that I want to make a deal," Saratov said.

Bolkonsky held off from replying, he had assumed this was the most likely reason for him to be summoned to this meeting.

"I know you're cleverer than you appear on television," Saratov said and Bolkonsky laughed at the easy nature of yet another insult, "Pragmatism would suit both parties,"

"I will be President by the time I return to Moscow. Why would I give you anything?"

"You legitimacy as leader is already being questioned, spoiled ballots are higher than your share, the people weren't too impressed by your Rambo antics yesterday,"

"There is nothing you can offer me,"

"My newspapers are the biggest selling in the country. I can pledge their support in return for allowing me to continue running my businesses without government interference,"

"How can I ever trust you?" Bolkonsky said, shaking his head in disbelief at the balls on this guy. He arranged the murder of my son, he thought, and it's like he's already forgotten about it. It takes a certain type of person that can mentally disassociate themselves from that kind of behaviour.

"I may have acquired a certain undeserved reputation as I built up my business empire but my word is my honour and always has been. I can almost taste the cynical vibes that you are emitting so I'll say this once and it is up to you if you believe me," Saratov stopped his twirling his pen at last and rested his elbows on the desk, "I sent Abdulatip Narimanov to Oslo as I had received a document from my Interpol source that there is a dossier about some of my business dealings that I may be interested in obtaining. And I was interested in obtaining it, who wouldn't be? When the café exploded, I presumed it was you that had done it,"

"I was told something similar. That there is a dossier that can bring you down,"

"Do you see what has happened?" Saratov said, sitting back in his chair and staring intently at Bolkonsky who felt stupid as he couldn't read the implication.

"There is no dossier," Bolkonsky said, the only words he could offer.

"Probably not, but simply spreading the rumour has brought down Golitsyn and it is on the verge of ending your campaign too, even with your GRU support,"

"Who would do that?"

"If you can't see that by now, I'm troubled that you may be the person running our country in the morning," Saratov held his hands up, "Ultimately, I can be very helpful to your tenure as President,"

Bolkonsky stood up and glanced at the pistol. He was a soldier and he knew that he could grasp the gun quicker than Saratov. The thought passed as quickly as it appeared and he met the gaze of Saratov.

"I need a response by 8pm, for the early editions," Saratov was spinning the pen around his fingers again, "Can you imagine reading the headlines about the powerful new Russian President, Dimitri Bolkonsky?"

Bolkonsky stared at his rival for a few seconds. Could he make a pact with the most malevolent man in the country? Bolkonsky walked out of the room and out of the dacha towards his car with the decision on whether to accept the deal with his son's killer playing on his mind. Would accepting aid from Saratov be a bridge too far even for the ultimate prize of becoming the President of Russia?

59

Moscow, Russia
Saturday November 19 - 18:19 MST

"I didn't realise this was 'Bring your friend to work day'," Simonsen," Karlsson said in English, pointing with his thumb to the new passenger in the back seat.

"Is this your boss?" Mazepa said, poking her head between the two front seats.

"He is the man leading the investigation, this is Benny Karlsson," Simonsen said and his two companions introduced themselves.

"Can we have a nice quiet day today?" Karlsson said, "If we could avoid the burning skyscraper rescues, that would make my job slightly easier,"

"I can't make any promises," Simonsen said, "Where are we going?"

"It's on this road here," Mazepa said, alternating her gaze between the map on her mobile phone and the surrounding area, "It's that one there,"

Karlsson pulled the car up outside the dacha which Mazepa had indicated. Simonsen noticed that the front gate was open and it all seemed too easy.

"I'm sure that's the Ferrari that Saratov used when he escaped from the Sarabank tower," Simonsen pointed at a yellow sports car which was parked in front of one of the front windows. Scuffs and dents marked the length of the vehicle.

As they approached the front door, Simonsen caught a glimpse of Saratov staring at them from a window. Karlsson rapped the door with a stern policeman's knock and within a few seconds, the door opened and the man who had unnerved him at a London restaurant a few days earlier was standing there, giving off the appearance of a father taking custody of his kids from his ex-wife at the weekend.

"Mr Simonsen," Saratov said in English, opening his arms wide in a faux-welcome, "And Mrs Mazepa herself, was it only yesterday that I had the pleasure of your company?"

"You didn't seem to enjoy it that much, I remember you crawling away from me in a very ungentlemanly fashion," Mazepa said and Saratov's face darkened. Simonsen knew Saratov was not the type of man who accepted being belittled, especially by a woman and even more especially because it was true. He had cowardly abandoned her to her fate in the Sarabank headquarters.

"Mr Saratov," Karlsson stepped forward and flashed his police card, "I am Inspector Karlsson from the Norwegian National Criminal Investigation Service and I am investigating the bombing of the Iskender Café in Oslo on Sunday, thirteenth of November. Are you OK to speak for a few moments to help us with our inquiries?"

"Funnily enough, you're not the first person who wanted to discuss that with me today. Nature teaches beasts to know their friends and I may have made a new friend today. Come in and let's see if I can help you with your inquiries,"

The four people convened in the study and Simonsen opened his rucksack and pulled out a folder which he held in his hand so Saratov could see. Saratov's eyes maintained their gaze on the folder and Simonsen noticed him slightly shake his head.

"Do you know what this is?" Simonsen said, in English.

"I have a suspicion that it may be the mythical, eponymous dossier which has caused all of us so many issues this week," Saratov said, his eyes still fixated on the folder, like an apex predator eyeing its prey.

"What issues?" Karlsson said.

"It seems everybody thinks that I blew up some godforsaken café in a dirty Oslo suburb as part of some dastardly plot to tarnish the reputation of that oaf Bolkonsky,"

"Did you have any involvement at all in the bombing of the café?" Simonsen said.

"I had no involvement in the bombing, except for one thing," Saratov said.

"What is that one thing?"

"I sent my subordinate Mr Narimanov to the meeting," Saratov said and pointed at Mazepa, "Unfortunately, he was a victim of the terrible attack. You remember him, don't you Mrs Mazepa? He was the man you cheated on your husband with,"

"You don't have a hold on me anymore, Saratov. You're back to being a nobody,"

"On the contrary, Mrs Mazepa. I have spoken to the man who is poised to lead our great nation for the next six years and I believe a mutually beneficial agreement is about to come to fruition,"

"With Golitsyn?" Mazepa said, "He's conceded,"

"Oh no, with President Bolkonsky, an accord has been agreed in principle between the two parties,"

"What?" Mazepa said, her face incredulous, "You murdered his son, he'll sanction your death the moment he parks his arse in the Kremlin,"

"If he had a little more legitimacy and credibility, he probably would do that but unfortunately for him, ascending to the Kremlin throne is more difficult than he anticipated. A little sacrifice has to be made by us all. A sacrifice can be as cleansing for the soul as a confession. Which is why I sent a journalist to your husband's residence in St Petersburg earlier today. I thought it would be in Mikhail's interest to let him know about your carnal betrayals with a Dagestani peasant,"

Simonsen stared at this man and attempted to hide his disgust. There was no morality to him whatsoever. Mazepa's face was red and her fists were clenched but she said nothing.

"Why did you send Narimanov to the meeting?"

Simonsen said.

"Information came to me about the dossier and I sent a man I could trust. Bolkonsky did the same and the result is now the chaos engulfing our nation,"

"You don't think Bolkonsky ordered the bombing any more?"

"I know he didn't. Unfortunately by the time I realised who it was, political events had transformed into a runaway train,"

"Does Bolkonsky know who it was?"

"The man is a simpleton, I virtually wrote it down for him and he still has no idea. It must be comforting to inhabit such a safe, two-dimensional world,"

"Who bombed the café?" Karlsson said.

"I don't know who actually planted the bomb but I know who it was ordered by," Saratov said, sitting back in his chair, wallowing in the smug knowledge that he held, "Oh come on, two diligent cops and an award-winning journalist and you haven't worked it out yet?"

Simonsen and Karlsson glanced at each other and neither said a word. Mazepa stood up and walked towards the window staring out at the lake. She turned around to the men and spoke in a clear voice:

"The only person who benefits from both candidates being wiped out and the only one with the means at their disposal would be Oksana Devina,"

"Bingo," a voice from the other side of the room said. The four people in the room had increased to five.

60

Moscow, Russia
Saturday November 19 - 18:47 MST

"Who are you?" Saratov demanded answers from the stranger. Mazepa stared at the small woman who had appeared in the doorway and this strangest of weeks continued to wind on its bizarre path to God-knows-where.

"She bombed the Iskender Café," Simonsen said. She stood barely four metres away, a slight woman with short brown hair that looked like she cut it herself, a plain face with pursed, dry lips, dressed in a baggy grey t-shirt tucked into black jeans. Her age could be anything from twenty to forty. She held a pistol in one hand and a briefcase in the other, which she set down on the floor.

Simonsen's pal Karlsson couldn't take his eyes from her and his face bore a look of extreme incomprehension. His prime suspect had walked directly into the same room as him. Saratov appeared angry that this random girl had wandered into his court, once more a woman had annoyed him and Mazepa was taking great amusement in this.

On the journey over, she had realised that her friend Oksana Devina was behind some of the events of the last week. But she was still shocked that she would sanction a terrorist attack that killed innocent civilians in the hope that she could snatch power from the two candidates, who it must be said were democratically chosen, however unsavoury they seemed to her.

"What's your name?" Simonsen said to her in Russian.

He appeared to be the only one who wasn't surprised to see her.

"You can call me Marcia," the woman replied in broken English.

"Is that your real name?" Karlsson said.

"What do you think?" the woman calling herself Marcia said. Karlsson appeared wounded by the putdown but it was a stupid question to ask a secret assassin, Mazepa thought.

"You bombed the café in Oslo, you murdered Ivan Zakatov yesterday and you also shot Peter Kelsey-Moore," Simonsen said.

The woman said nothing, Saratov was muttering something under his breath and she noticed him reaching for something under the desk. He pulled out a gun and as he did so Marcia moved towards him with her the grace of a panther with her weapon raised and shouted at him in Russian:

"Put down that fucking gun!" Saratov rested the gun on the table and Marcia picked it up and stuffed it into her pocket.

"You work for Oksana?" Mazepa said and the girl looked at her and nodded.

"I need the dossier. Where is it please?" Marcia said to no one in particular as she walked back to the briefcase on the floor and opened it up.

No one said anything. Saratov's demeanour was not far off that of a man whose blood had been siphoned out of his body. He was limp and pitiful and after he had arranged to expose her secret affair to her husband, she was delighted to see him in such a state.

Examining Saratov was the only thing she could do to prevent herself thinking about what Saratov had done by sending a journalist round to break the news of her affair. She was in a state of numbness, trying to avoid allowing the thought of Mikhail's reaction enter her head. As long as she could do this, she wouldn't have to attempt to process it.

Mazepa watched Saratov as he planted his chin on his hands like he was posing for an artist drawing an emoji for glumness. He had been unable to react to Oksana Devina from being one step ahead of him. She had outwitted him time after time and for a man of such high regard for himself, it was devastating. Mazepa was certain that he genuinely thought that a rapprochement with Bolkonsky would save him and that he could inevitably turn this into another parasitic relationship with a politician. The level of self-delusion was not normal and the hubris that was now about to bring him to justice was fully deserved.

"Where is the dossier?" Marcia asked again. The silence in the room hung so heavy that Mazepa stared at the floor. She lifted her eyes and saw that Marcia was holding the gun straight between her own eyes.

"Hand over the dossier or you die," Marcia said and her disinterested, sapphire eyes told Mazepa that this was not an idle threat.

61

Moscow, Russia
Saturday November 19 - 18:54 MST

"Hey," Simonsen said, his heart thumping so hard he assumed everyone in the room could hear it, "There is no need for that,"

He said the words and a wave of futile shame passed over him. He had witnessed this hitwoman at her most unswerving professionalism. This woman had calmly left a bomb in a busy café with no regard for the collateral damage the explosion would cause. He had watched as she murdered his boss with one shot from a sniper rifle.

There was no doubt that she would murder Mazepa if he didn't hand over the file. He turned to Karlsson who was frozen in his chair staring at the assassin, Marcia. Saratov had an almost serene glaze over his face as though he had come to terms with this deeply unpleasant situation.

Mazepa stood by the window with the gun pointed twenty centimetres from her face. She stood upright, like a noblewoman maintaining her dignity during a brazen highway robbery. Marcia was loose and comfortable, no tension in her frame and a portrait of control. A seasoned professional killer, a psychoanalyst's dream patient.

"I will say one more time," Marcia maintained her gaze on Mazepa as the two women faced off, "Hand me the dossier now or I shoot her,"

"Simonsen, don't tell her where it is," Mazepa said and he almost laughed at her courage at this moment.

"Give it to me right now," Marcia said, edging forward

so the gun was only a couple of centimetres from Mazepa's face. Simonsen knew that this was the last chance saloon for Mazepa.

"OK, OK," Simonsen said, knowing that she would pull the trigger if there was any further delay, "I'll give it to you,"

Marcia lowered her weapon and gestured with her spare hand that Mazepa should stand over towards the far wall next to Simonsen. She made a similar gesture to Karlsson so he joined them too. Marcia stood at one end of Saratov's desk and opened her briefcase up.

Simonsen crouched and opened his rucksack where he had slid the folder containing the dossier back into the bag. He pulled out the slim manilla folder and threw it onto Saratov's desk. It was within a half a metre of Saratov but he was stuck in his reverie, barely aware of what was happening.

Marcia kept her eyes on Saratov and grabbed the folder and carefully placed it in the briefcase. She picked a mobile phone out of the briefcase and typed out a message before placing the phone back in the briefcase on top of the Saratov dossier. She closed and sealed the case and looked towards Simonsen.

"Thank you," she said and Simonsen found the words strange from a person who lacked any kind of decency, a woman who spent her days planning and carrying out murder like it's a normal job. Does she receive a performance bonus for everyone she kills?

Marcia lifted her gun up, took one step towards Saratov who finally broke from his dreamlike stake. He turned to face Marcia and a look of confused terror spread over his face as he became aware that the gun was in front of his face.

Marcia shot him and the back of Saratov's head exploded over the portrait of Peter the Great, blood spattering over the depictions of fawning attendants.

The assassin turned, picked up the briefcase and pointed the gun towards Karlsson, Mazepa and Simonsen. She silently walked sideways out of the office and then jogged out of sight.

Mazepa collapsed to her knees and Karlsson placed an arm around her as she began sobbing. Simonsen's heart at last stopped pumping at crisis levels and he sat down in the chair vacated by Karlsson. Simonsen couldn't take his eyes off the murdered man in the chair opposite. Sasha Saratov was dead, his malignancy had been terminated. The man who ordered the killing of his girlfriend was dead and Simonsen felt a glow of relief that he didn't do the deed himself.

62

Moscow, Russia
Saturday November 19 - 19:44 MST

Dimitri Bolkonsky had driven himself to the dacha in Novorizhskoye and instead of driving back into the city centre, he had taken a circuitous route around the suburbs of Moscow. Everywhere he had visited, the people were on the streets protesting.

Unlike the rioting of yesterday, this was mainly peaceful but also passionate. The numbers were huge and they were determined that their voice was to be heard.

"Not in my name!" and "Freedom for the people!" were the chants he was hearing the most, a light snow was falling but there was no wind. A beautiful Moscow night where a little sheen of snow coated everything and everyone. Driving around like this was calming, the streets were empty of traffic as most people it seemed were either taking part in protests or wrapped up warm, hunkering down at home.

Bolkonsky drove into the restricted underground Kremlin car park and listened to the radio as the exit polls predicted that he had nearly double the amount of votes than Maxim Golitsyn. Unfortunately the good news was tempered by the bad. Spoiled papers appeared to total more than double the total of himself and Golitsyn. He forced himself into dealing with the devil.

He parked up and sent a text message to Sasha Saratov:

-    It's a deal.

He waited for ten minutes but there was no response. He couldn't wait much longer as he needed to speak to Oksana Devina and inform her that he expected to be confirmed as the next President. He wasn't sure how to tell her that he had the backing of Sasha Saratov. Hopefully, he thought, between the two of them, they will be able to discover who actually bombed the café. It would be a positive show of collaboration if they could bring the perpetrators to justice.

Bolkonsky breezed through the ornate Kremlin corridors, there was a bustling presence of office workers, guards and journalists who had gained rare access to the inner sanctum for election night. Many of them nodded at him and said "Good evening, Minister," and he was content knowing that by tomorrow they will be addressing him in the proper manner as their duly elected President.

A surge of pride coursed through his body as the realisation that the moment he had longed for was about to come true. Signing a pact with the devil was the price but if it was the only way to enact his reforms, then so be it. Once he had consolidated his power, he could renew his attempts to destroy Saratov and gain at least some measure of revenge against him.

Bolkonsky arrived at the Hall of the Order of St George, the largest state room of the Kremlin Palace. The immense doors opened into the huge anteroom which was filled with even more underlings and big-screen televisions showing the official results coming in from the Far Eastern constituencies. As he entered the room, a hundred faces all turned towards him. Bolkonsky raised a modest hand in response and saw that the first confirmed results from Chukotka were showing Golitsyn on 13%, Bolkonsky on 30% and 57% of people spoiling their ballots.

Bolkonsky's throat tightened and he realised that these figures were worse than his own team's worst-case scenario. Bolkonsky asked a staffer if Devina was in the Presidential office, which was confirmed by them. He walked with his head bowed towards the doors leading to the doors where six soldiers guarded the entrance. One of them spoke quietly into a headset and the doors swung open.

He entered the wood-panelled office and saw Devina sat on the edge of the desk, speaking on the telephone. She flicked a look and wagged an inviting pair of fingers to him so he walked over to her as she carried on her conversation. Four soldiers were lined up at the back of the room and Bolkonsky had a strange feeling of dread, similar to the moments prior to Ivan Zakatov being gunned down outside his house.

After a couple of minutes, Devina finished her telephone call and beamed a smile to Bolkonsky who tried and failed to reciprocate it. The sick feeling in the pit of stomach meant he couldn't fake a smile.

"Dimitri," she said, "I was wondering when you would arrive. We've been trying to contact you all evening,"

"Yes," Bolkonsky replied, "I had urgent business to attend to outside of the city,"

"Oh, I hope you're not planning another missile attack on a Moscow Exchange company, you know how it impacts their share price," Devina cackled and once more Bolkonsky's instincts told him he was the butt of the joke, which would be a dangerous way to behave with the most powerful man in the country. However he certainly didn't feel that powerful at this moment. Why was she in the Kremlin office and not at her own office at the White House?

"No, I was in a meeting, hoping to help place the country on a stable footing after some of the incidents and events of the last few days,"

Devina nodded and refrained from speaking.

"Golitsyn conceded the election, as you're well aware. I'm here now and I see that my vote share greatly out-performs him. It's all looking good,"

"Have you considered conceding too?" Devina said, her voice calm. Bolkonsky thought he had misheard or that she was joking. Her face conveyed that she was not joking. He turned around and saw the soldiers were keeping their eyes firmly on him.

"What the fuck are you on about? Oksana, I've hammered him,"

"If I may speak frankly, the voters have hammered you both. Spoiled ballots could count for sixty per cent of the vote. The projections for the major urban areas in the West are even worse than what are coming in from the East, "

"Fucking hell, it's a minority of people protesting about the manner of the last week of the election,"

"It's not a minority Dimitri, it's actually the definition of a majority. You have no democratic mandate to lead the people,"

"This is crazy," Bolkonsky said, "I won twice the votes of my challenger in a run-off election. And don't lecture me about democracy, I've campaigned in every province of this country in the last six months. Who the hell do you think you are addressing me in such a fucking disrespectful manner?"

"You don't have the support of the people," Devina said, her calmness only made Bolkonsky angrier.

"I have the support of Sasha Saratov," Bolkonsky spat the words, in contempt of both Devina and Saratov.

"What do you mean?"

"I'm not as stupid as I seem to you metropolitan liberals. We held a meeting today and his newspapers will be supporting my legitimate right to be chosen as President,"

"Saratov is dead," Devina said and Bolkonsky thought his stomach was going to drop out of his arse.

"What are you talking about?"

"He was shot in the head about half an hour after your little head-to-head. I'm surprised and a little disappointed that you would agree a relationship with the man who ordered the death of your only child last week,"

Bolkonsky's head started to spin and thoughts cycled around his mind with the intensity and speed of a tornado, causing his balance to falter.

"Take a seat, Dimitri," Devina pointed at the seat behind the desk. Bolkonsky used his hands to drag himself along the desk to where the chair was. He collapsed into the seat and stared up at Devina on the opposite side of the desk.

"You will concede, Dimitri," Devina whispered.

"I can't, I'm the winner," Bolkonsky also spoke in a low voice, shaking his head.

"Open the laptop in front of you," Devina said. Bolkonsky followed the instructions like a robot, flicking open the laptop computer screen. A video file popped up and was ready to play, "Watch the video,"

Bolkonsky watched the screen and was immediately transported back to Dagestan in the nineties and his limbs turned rigid.

A couple of young soldiers were chatting before entering a government supplier's warehouse which was supposed to be helping to feed the army while they were in Dagestan. Obviously, with the government having no money, there was no food located there. He watched the Chechen villagers, kneeling and weeping, in thrall to the power of Russia and to Dimitri Bolkonsky.

Bolkonsky closed his eyes when he saw his younger on-screen image pull out his pistol. He listened to the begging of the prisoners and each shot as he put them down. He opened his eyes and saw the father and young son lying prone on the ground, heads matted with crimson.

He closed the laptop and stared up at Devina. Tears were welling in his eyes and for a moment, he could only think of his own son, Alex.

"No-one needs to see this video, Dimitri," Devina said, "Now you realise that you can't be the President of Russia. Can you imagine the reaction in Washington if this was leaked?"

Bolkonsky nodded, a despairing gesture which took all of his effort to make without bawling his eyes out.

"It has been a tough few days for us all," Devina

said, "That dossier about Sasha Saratov makes for fascinating reading. There is a lot for us to do to clean up in this country,"

Bolkonsky stood up and walked back around the table. He noticed the soldiers moving to attention and ready for action. He waved them down, a gesture meant to suggest he wasn't going to do anything.

"That fucking dossier," Bolkonsky said under his breath. That had been the catalyst for the end of his ambitions and for Sasha Saratov too. And now it was held by Oksana Devina. He turned his gaze towards her as she moved around the table and sat in the chair meant for the President. It was then when he realised the truth that Saratov taunted him with at the dacha, a final irresistible barb.

"You set up the meeting in Oslo," Bolkonsky said, "You set us all up, you fucking bitch,"

Devina flashed a huge grin and Bolkonsky could only look at her and admire her. She had been an acquaintance for at least a decade, perhaps even a friend, a rare occurrence in political circles. He hadn't underestimated her, he had simply not estimated her nous at all.

"You will release a statement at six o'clock in the morning stating that you are withdrawing your candidacy due to a lack of a democratic mandate. You will recommend that I should serve as interim President for twelve months pending new elections in a year's time. If you do that, I will protect you," Devina stood up and Bolkonsky took that to mean that this meeting was over.

"I will write the statement once I arrive home, can you find someone to drive me please?"

63

Moscow, Russia
Sunday November 20 - 06:52 MST

Anastasiya Mazepa drove Karlsson's hire car through the same grey suburbs back towards Sheremetyevo airport. She had travelled through the airport only a matter of days ago but it now seemed so long ago. When she arrived back in Russia, the intensity of the emotions meant she couldn't balance her mind. The dread upon arrival at Sheremetyevo when she saw Ivanovich approach her had transitioned into confusion when he arranged the meeting at the bank.

The shifting tectonic plates that characterise political upheaval can surprise you with their ferocity. Mazepa thought about the Butterfly Effect and how one bomb exploding in a Norwegian café could have such a wide-ranging impact.

Nothing that had happened in the last few days seemed real. She had not gone to bed yet but still wasn't weighed down by even a gram of tiredness. She had tried to process what had happened since she landed in Moscow, especially the attack that Bolkonsky had launched on the Sarabank headquarters.

She had watched video clips of the attack from the perspective of the outside world and that she had escaped without injury astounded her. It was lucky that it occurred on a Friday afternoon and most employees had been sent home due to the impending election. Two Chechen cleaners were amongst the dead and Mazepa noted that Bolkonsky was still responsible for killing Caucasians two decades on from the massacre in the warehouse.

The hours before sunlight she had spent watching the videos of the peaceful protests at the plazas and polling stations across the nation. It gladdened her heart to see the defiance of a people who had been taken for granted by the political class. They realised the people held the power and not the state. Was this to be a turning point for the Russian political system or would it be a false dawn like the early nineties? Mazepa abjured her cynicism for once and hoped that a better future was possible under her old friend Oksana Devina. She deliberately put the appalling way she had grasped power to the back of her mind but she was aware that the topic would start nudging forward if promised reforms are not forthcoming.

Overall, Mazepa was at ease, even the thought of meeting her husband tomorrow wasn't giving her the fear it once would have. The death of Saratov brought her more than comfort, it was bringing her hope too.

"News is leaking that Bolkonsky is going to withdraw," Karlsson said, Mazepa flicked her eyes to the back of the car where his babyish face was lowered looking at his phone.

"Isn't that going to cause more chaos?" Simonsen said, sitting adjacent to Mazepa in the passenger seat.

"I think Oksana will have a plan," Mazepa said.

"Her plan's have worked so far, I'll credit her with that," Simonsen said.

Simonsen's comments started to lure out her own thoughts on Devina's rise to power. Her view on her friend was a mix of awe and disgust. She was amazed at the guts of her friend to formulate such an audacious plan to prevent both Golitsyn and Bolkonsky from becoming president whilst simultaneously destroying Sasha Saratov. But the means that she had used to succeed was revolting. If anyone knew the full story of the trail of destruction that she had set forth, they would be unable to accept that as a legitimate or moral way to gain power. The way Devina had risen to power may one day lead to her downfall.

Was preventing either man being elected worth the carnage? Mazepa could not believe that it was worth the human cost, no matter the faults of the candidates. The violence was cross-continental and on a national scale, the prestige of the country was deeply harmed. Even though it was knowledge held between barely two handfuls of people that Devina orchestrated the bombing of the café, the newspapers around the world had gorged on the idea that it was one of the two Russian presidential candidates who were behind the attack. This kind of thing is not forgotten about and once again, Russia would still be portrayed as a backward, revenge-fueled mafia state.

"What are you going to do about the bombing?" Mazepa said and she could hear Karlsson groan behind her.

"All we can do is keep investigating," Simonsen said, a standard policeman's response to a question from a journalist. Mazepa couldn't resist smiling at him.

"We've got a meeting with the top brass this afternoon in Oslo," Karlsson said, "They're going to lock us up when we tell them what happened here. They'll send me to the Arctic Circle investigating reindeer rustling,"

"I think my retirement might be fast-tracked," Simonsen said.

"Unless your old boss's job is up for grabs," Karlsson said, "That's another thing we need to explain. *Faen ta deg*, Simonsen, my balls are going to be strung up because of you,"

"At least it got me out of the house for a bit," Simonsen replied and Mazepa laughed. She glimpsed in the mirror and saw Karlsson and he was smiling and shaking his head.

Mazepa pulled the car up at the drop off point at the airport and the three of them bundled out of the car. Karlsson pulled his bag out of the boot and dropped it on the pavement before heading into the airport.

"Einar," Karlsson called out, "I'm off to sort out our fast track entry, you'll be grateful you won't have to queue up and have the soldiers trying to arrest you again,"

Simonsen nodded and pulled his luggage out of the car. He felt a hand on his back and turned round to face Mazepa who was smiling at him.

"Simonsen, I wanted to thank you for saving my life," Mazepa said, her eyes maintaining contact with his, "But I also want to apologise for what happened with Mariya. It…" Mazepa tailed off and for once she couldn't find the right words.

"There's no need for apologies. There are thousands of victims of Saratov and Ivanovich. Mariya and I were two more bodies that they trampled on for power. Fuck them," Simonsen grabbed Mazepa by the shoulders and she was surprised by his intensity, "You should feel liberated from the burden you have carried,"

"So should you," Mazepa said and she had to fight to not cry. This man had arrived at her door in a shambling, nervous state but he now had the air of a proud, decent man who had done his duty which was all true.

"Don't worry, I've laid my ghosts to rest this week. I hope everything works out OK," Simonsen kissed Mazepa on the cheek, then as an apparent afterthought he enveloped her in a bear hug. Mazepa finally began to cry, sobbing into his shoulder. By the time Simonsen let her go, Mazepa had regained her composure.

"If you ever come back to Russia, make sure you let you know," Mazepa said, watching Simonsen pick up the luggage for Karlsson and himself. He flicked his head round and nodded to her before walking off to meet Karlsson who stood in the doorway with the automatic door being blocked from closing much to the annoyance of staff who were trying to avoid the biting wind entering the terminal.

Karlsson waved at Mazepa who reciprocated the gesture before she closed the boot, got back in the car and drove back into the city centre.

64

Moscow, Russia
Sunday November 20 - 08:03 MST

"Thank you for coming here today," Dimitri Bolkonsky was sitting at a table inside the Hall of the Order of St. George filled with a huge bouquet of microphones, camera flashes were going off constantly and it forced his eyes down to his page of scripted notes, "This week has been a tumultuous and testing time and that reflects the passion of the Russian people in their democratic system,"

Bolkonsky could feel dribbles of sweat trickling down the ridges on his face, this ritual humiliation was organised by Oksana Devina. She had sent him a message this morning stating she had set up a press conference on his behalf. His idea of emailing his words to her to pass around the media was scuppered. He was compelled to attend and he couldn't think of being anywhere worse right now.

"I have wanted to become President for more than two decades. I am a Russian patriot who has proudly served my country in battle and I ran for elected office to represent my fellow patriots. It has been my dream to craft a better future for the people of our great homeland. I was determined to rein in the power of the oligarchs, to improve the education system and employment prospects for our young people and to restore the pride in our nation that has drifted away over the years,

"I concede that I have fallen short of these standards in my mission to fight the forces that oppose me. I recognise the strong sentiments expressed by the people over the last few days and ultimately, it is the people whom I listen to and that I am ultimately the servant of,

"I officially rescind my candidacy to become the President of Russia. This has been the hardest decision of my life but I make this decision because I want the best for Russia, for today and for the future,"

Bolkonsky noticed another liquid seeping out but it was tears this time. He was crying on live television and there was nothing he could do to stop it. The tears crept out of his eyes like people trapped in a basement for ten years, reluctant yet inevitably moving to the light. He placed his hands over his face and allowed the tears to fall for a few more seconds before picking up a tissue that an aide had artfully placed next to him. He wiped the tears away and noticed that the camera flashes had ceased, as had any background conversation. All eyes were intensely focused on the fallen candidate.

"Based upon the election results, it is my conclusion that I have no legitimate mandate to lead and my heart is breaking. I call on the Security Council who are overseeing the election to help in bringing stability to the nation at this time. I urge the leader of the council, Oksana Devina, to follow the constitution of our electoral process and appoint herself as interim President for a period of 12 months before new elections are called,"

The silence ceased and the questions commenced. Bolkonsky couldn't hear anything. The noises merged to a unnoticeable low hum and the camera lights and flashes morphed into a dull background. Bolkonsky remained seated for twenty seconds before he could rely on his legs to lift him out of his chair.

"Thank you," Bolkonsky whispered. He shook hands with the two officials sitting either side of him, the names of which he could not recall. He walked off into a side room where guards prevented the media from breaching the doorway.

Bolkonsky sat on a chair at a bureau facing a mirror. His craggy face was puffy and red and the capillaries on his nose looked like a road map of Nizhny Novgorod. He rubbed his eyes and wished for the anxiety that was causing his body to shake to abate. In the mirror's reflection, he noticed the appearance of a smartly-dressed woman.

"Oksana," Bolkonsky said. Devina walked up behind him and rested a hand on his shoulder.

"Dimitri," she said, "That speech took incredible courage. I know how difficult that was to go up there and say those things,"

Bolkonsky fixed his eyes on Devina in the reflection. In the distance, armed guards remained in sight. He considered whether he had the time to break her neck with his bare hands before they shot him.

"I want you as part of my team, Dimitri."

"What, after what you have done to me?"

"Dimitri," Devina bent over and whispered in his ear, her alluring voice and scent turning him on at this inopportune time, "I could send you to the Hague. You're a fucking war criminal,"

"Don't take the fucking moral high ground with me. You're a killer too. At least I know who I am. I killed people in the heat of battle, not innocent people drinking coffee," Bolkonsky growled the words at her and Devina stood up straight again and started to walk off before turning around to face Bolkonsky again.

"I want you on my team. Obviously, not as Defence Minister but I would love for you to represent our country as our Ambassador to the United Nations in New York,"

"You want me out of the country?"

"All I want is the best person in the most suitable role. You would be fantastic representing our interests at the UN. The job is yours if you want it. Otherwise, there isn't anything I can do for you,"

Bolkonsky banged his hand on the table and the guards began to raise their weapons until Devina gave them a dismissive wave.

"Dimitri, bury your son and take a holiday. I want you on top form for when you go to New York,"

Bolkonsky watched as the doors to the Presidential office opened and Oksana Devina entered, surrounded by her aides and flanked by armed guards. The doors to power were slammed shut and Bolkonsky thought about his son Alex and pulled out his mobile phone to call his ex-wife.

65

Moscow, Russia
Sunday November 20 - 15:02 MST

Red Square, with the Kremlin adjacent, is the heart of Russian power. Less than forty-eight hours ago, this was the scene of pitched battles between the police and rival gangs, impromptu bonfires and a disaster for the Russian polity. Anastasiya Mazepa stood at the wings of the stage, sneaking glimpses of the crowd.

The atmosphere today was more akin to the Rio carnival than an inauguration. Russian flags and banners flew everywhere, the masses singing songs of joy, in visceral contrast to the last few days. Even to the eyes of a metropolitan cynic, it moved Mazepa almost to tears, although that could also be the air which remained heavy and acrid from the fires that had been burning around the city overnight and only recently extinguished.

On the way back from dropping off Simonsen and Karlsson, she had received a text message from Oksana Devina advising her that she had backstage access for the speech. Mazepa had arrived at the stage which had in the last few days witnessed Bolkonsky's incendiary speech and Golitsyn's terrified and cowardly withdrawal from public life.

The policy wonks and government staff could talk only of Dimitri Bolkonsky's stunning pronouncement. Mazepa listened to the theories being spouted by people nearby: Bolkonsky was a true patriot who had scuttled his own aspirations to protect the good ship Russia; Bolkonsky was going to spend the year solidifying his position at the Defence Ministry before leading a new bid for the Kremlin next year; Bolkonsky was going to enter the Danilov monastery as penance for being responsible for the death of his son.

Very few people put forward the idea that Devina had directed a series of events and relied upon the arrogance, chauvinism and shamelessness of the main actors to move the plot forward to the final destination: the first female to lead the nation since Catherine the Great. Her anti-macho demeanour, the archetype of the bookish diplomat, hid an ambition so grand that nobody, including her own friends, ever suspected she could be capable of what had transpired in recent days.

Mazepa jumped when a hand touched her elbow. Oksana Devina stood next to her, and the two of them looked out at the vast crowd together.

"Good afternoon, Mrs President," Mazepa said.

"Nastya, I don't think you need to call me that,"

"I don't want to end up on your naughty list, Oksana. I know what can happen if you do,"

"Come on, did you want another six years of those same corrupt men fucking up this country even more than it already is?"

"I didn't think you were capable of that,"

"They say that a soldier who doesn't dream of becoming a general is a bad soldier. I'm a politician, Nastya and I'm in a position to make a real difference,"

"I'm not spotting any differences at the moment,"

"Give it time and you will. A new Russia is about to rise. Oh, and I've got an exclusive story if you want?"

Devina started to walk off towards the lectern when she turned round and raised a quizzical eyebrow at Mazepa.

"Well?" Devina said.

"OK, what is it?"

"Let's say that a highly-placed government source has word that Dimitri Bolkonsky will be the next Russian ambassador to the United Nations,"

Mazepa couldn't help but chuckle at her old friend and her brazen opportunism. Mazepa nodded her head and Devina strode out towards the lectern and raised her arms out in a gesture of jubilation to the crowds. The fervour for Devina was real and she displayed no humility about her new position. What kind of leader would she be? As great as Peter or Catherine or one of the many false dawns and disappointments the people had endured over the centuries?

She intended to hold on to the hope that things would turn out for the best. Mazepa turned away from the stage and headed backstage and away from Red Square. She was already thinking about the article she was going to write about Dimitri Bolkonsky's new appointment. Perhaps she may even drop in a line alluding to the deadly truth about why he pulled out of the election race.

66

Oslo, Norway
Monday November 19 - 17:12 CET

After barely a five minute walk from the Kripos office, Einar Simonsen and Benny Karlsson walked into a grubby bar-restaurant with mucky awnings leering over each window. They were greeted with ironic cheers from a group of people sitting across three tables by the window. An unmistakable gathering of cops, thought Simonsen as he grinned at the assorted members.

Karlsson walked to the bar and ordered drinks for everyone which brought forth more cheers from the tables. He plonked himself down between Simonsen and Anita Bangoura as the barman, who looked affronted that he had been called upon to do some work, gradually brought beers around for the team.

"How did it go?" Bangoura said, as curious as ever, always an admirable trait in a cop.

"I'm sure they thought we were pitching a new Nordic Noir TV show," Karlsson said, taking a long swig from his glass, "Luckily, the public nature of a lot of what we were banging on about helped back up our fantastic tales,"

"What about Peter Kelsey-Moore?" Bangoura turned her attention to Simonsen.

"There were a couple of witnesses to back up what happened and a lot of CCTV footage of the hitwoman fleeing the scene. The whole car chase seems to have gone viral so whoever edited and leaked that onto YouTube is probably up for the chop," Simonsen said and one of the cops saw his hair being ruffled by his colleagues.

"What about the investigation?" another cop said, who Simonsen recalled was called Kristiansen.

"The bosses are going to blame Sasha Saratov," Karlsson said, finishing his beer with another long gulp.

"Even though he's innocent?" Bangoura said.

"Innocent of that crime, yes," Simonsen said, "In the dossier there were the names of a couple of Norwegian Members of Parliament on Saratov's payroll so in exchange for the names, the government will keep the name of the real organiser out of the news,"

Murmurings spread around the table. The realpolitik of the situation was hitting home to them. Investigating two members of the *Storting* accused of treachery would be a half-decent return.

"I don't like that we can't provide real justice to the families of the people killed in the bombing," Karlsson said, standing up and raising his empty glass, "But I know how hard you have worked on this investigation and in some cases, like our advisor Simonsen, avoided a grisly fate trying to solve this case. I'm proud of all of you, so take a few days to recharge and then we'll crack on with the next job. Right, I'm off to the bar for more beers," More cheers erupted as Karlsson headed to the bar. Simonsen finished his beer and walked up to join Karlsson at the bar.

"You're not heading home, are you?" Karlsson said.

"No, not today," Simonsen said, putting an arm around Karlsson, "I'm staying out with you guys. Here. I'll give you a hand with the drinks,"

"Good man, we'll head into the centre of Oslo later and let our hair down, or whatever's left of it anyway. We might even find you a wife,"

"You never know, Benny," Simonsen said, lifting the glass of beer to his mouth, "I'm starting to get the taste for adventure,"

Printed in Poland
by Amazon Fulfillment
Poland Sp. z o.o., Wrocław
09 May 2023

de623ae7-308e-4580-91a6-252fb4db9400R01